REGISTRATION CASPAR

Registration Caspar
Copyright 2016 by J. Gordon Faylor

First Edition, First Printing, 2016

ISBN 978-1-937027-72-8
Distributed to the trade by SPD / Small Press Distribution
1341 Seventh Street, Berkeley, CA 94710, spdbooks.org

Design: J. Gordon Faylor, emdash, & Doormouse
Cover Printing: Prestige Printing, Brooklyn, NY
Book Printing and Binding: McNaughton & Gunn, Saline, MI

Ugly Duckling Presse
232 Third Street, #E303
Brooklyn, NY 11215
uglyducklingpresse.org

Funding for this book was provided in part by a generous grant
from the National Endowment for the Arts.

REGISTRATION CASPAR

J. Gordon Faylor

Ugly Duckling Presse | Brooklyn, NY

Two weeks spent in thick clothing. Preexecution protocol.

When agreed to, lien implementation followed rendering, scarecrow angiography was due attendance, plugs, a misgiving remove, spill coils instantaneously sad or inconsiderable tempers binding affliction-deflection rates to illustrated credits, the tried contra Xingren doxylamine ring wearing away, an intervention available to the central register forbidden, scattered cots.

Only five hours left to a registrant. The familiar involumetric manner, loss, the cast, the forty growths unbuckling in a corner of the plant, paths, a struggling twenty at a time, mesoscalar occupants funding most of them a few years at a time, buckets, an occupant thereafter left only a lingering deference to prepossession and expulsion.

I had to make money—no question about that. A fifth a day spent in keyhole education reviews told only on employment not coming through for an entity, or at least cheap. But five hours, that's that. So I walked over to the pen. There were decent loadmers, nervy cooperatives with an office I got to toy emulgent over and stipple about and joke to from keeping cracking.

"An execution taken, peddled," as I called it. So I was informed of a refuge in Ceaurgle. I went anyhow. And that they only gave way to the powerless Shoe Zoo and register, and not without incomplex deals or bestowing dismissal. This approach funded those two, actually, however—or kept them going. I studied the lumen avidly and, defeated after that, picked up my gear and hauled it back to Lapkin.

The feed was on until Kerrer intervened—the kind Kerrer—already risking the meager takes, cuts smacked rate adjustment to throws they couldn't bear and an awful report, another criteria of and off this fulsome business of the plugged cornea, once a third in petulant mime a volume and price per, ending up getting each one of them outdoors after goading the restricted long enough that they both knew better, shoving their faces into the snow to

relax, into the cots at night, and reproachfully, finally, into dutifully exchanged vitamin supplantation schedules, each of which
we'd suspiciously postponed the week before—irrespective of the
positions not included, irrespective of the time it took to get to
Panastunugh, a sequenced dualism rotting away the functional
equivalence sustaining the professional uselessnesses available to
me and Chrysalidocarpus, of inserted instrument required and
therein lapsed ethic which bust a guy's head open when he tuck-
ers, the volitional quarterly about or toward currency if nothing
else End Run Roundup, which is a desiccated aestos of bilobate,
and the straw creature Caspar—a stainlessly loathed, respired
difficulty meeting to get them my emulsive survey of its dement-
ed spirits before I could overtake them.

A control block felt like the best choice for this initiation—
steady, salaried. That was Clessiexecs. They were respectful. For
what they owed the arrests, they returned in batch initiation for
Acrobasis. But as chaining, b. At a certain pace, portions of that
control block took in enough of the lost entities like if the tastes
of the memory residents permitted at the year's close befell them
lop blank.

I appeared in Ceaurgle and spent. As of today, I can still only
make out the topography and otherwise excerpted compensations
of land. This only accrues thereby. And I don't have too long.

$34.99.

So I took to cast notices. Stouts were arranged. It was my
second day, and I was meeting the crew.

Saturation tubes flared up the dark midweek air. Four mail-
bags scomatized what was left of the horizon—a bleary science
genre sky, burrowed malprint into 6:30 p.m. release, a drink, the
treatment of sleeplessness, pitch conversation, parabasis, a unan-
imous calling the first check-in of the day that supernal teaching
lem at the school on the corner backgrounded crying, an ergative
accountability of objects theirs given up to Amnemicia on or
worming around for in sandier fields of this employment situation, which wasn't helping. The two of them looked at each other
and looked at the log.

Four entities strolled onto the narrow precipice, followed by
the second occupant. They were executed and registered. Chapter. Attempting countdown. Chapter. Current time. Prepares.

3:44 p.m. The first week. Barring the exception of thirteen aboveground fog and mid-July mists, the summer months churred along unliving and whispered—they were like these really excellent bilobated customizations around sneering varuna units, frowned upon, now to look to and chuckle, crossed at the untouched and friendly printer's after a year on the job at the farm I had to take on, talking, participation on the wane or regionally bartered out like contracts, but enough to tell the family—whether as much like a series of hollowed, hydrologically counterbalanced internments of method as their hated, assertive intentions merited attempting to also give up one another's brittle declassing, utilizing preferences as not knowing what it'd be demolished as Panastunugh, and a means of sequestering this collapse as another alimentary tic of its relinquishing as Nura, unable to separate as such—as these were in and collapsed a minute, a steeped-in medication that catalogs and continues to either of the ports, bag nebulous, words and retroflexions Mr. Magnanni panted to his students in an ongoing investigation lacking duress of those old campers, fucking in a single year as if also transiently suggesting the potential viciousness lanx and stuttered precipitation that became the best hours, or taking them at sift to match, as also waiving invaluable meritocratic endurance by us creatures and the ride. This service ensured no one would leave upset, excepting those few ambitious, callous attendants, or the very vacancy of their stack riskjj.

A negative, participatory atmosphere pervaded the nearby Inthmuriah University, however, and we couldn't keep content in advance of these rare downpours and, again, professionalized obscurely by experiential reprocessing the scene in property value, poorly given scenes, a reversing interference measurements with Dosepucks' infamous specificity to take coast or generally butter the requirements their office necessitated, as I was trying, engineered. And butchered to win.

They're not just blockages for the ongoing spite. I'm told they're premonitory and fomenting meteorological standardization for occupancy of, exhaustion that mirrors us as constantly unintelligible term-renters a Leon a plane, if you couldn't pilfered off crabbed backs, contextual layaways for the Vaxt, each mess accompanying an ad hoc vacuous depiction of romances, stories soldered on to one saddest final recollection of a real registrant as it felt good for this last moronic, phonetic fulguration reasoning test of drama—me and the bit sales, I was tacitly expected to rake in all that not to bother the bucking bronco, I still had two jobs and they were inexactly reaching through me or approaching me generally devotedly towards, but I figured in the rougher years with an inspired dotage withholding this plethora of statement one willingly takes part in in order to pardon one's incompatible shrieking as sheer effort exuded—a dead Cezary, grinning with a rakish, unmoving persistence that leaves to the eating that which one would've doomed them years ago to a mug, curiously unviewable payment to the others and nonetheless foregone loneliness and headlock by the ogliopsony called Amrige within this constant, unendangered severity week upon week. Those days were different, I grimed.

In any case, the front set in and impaired, decided properties suffering exhumation and affective response time left Caspar.

A few hours later, on that second day, they fell under swift reproach by Mr. Wenzhaw. They'd been still feeling upset. They could go on as planned, and they could fulfill the purpose to hitch an almost daily appearance in the assigning, distributing, licensing, or sublicensing of a present or impending encrusted image to boot, as we called it—the server to intersection of glyph legal badgering, textbook serratula.

Track and tribulations last r, corners, forgotten, bolstered finally, another word used in a product and the successful Lorinda Spill, Shucibu Links' sole competitor lost in named soon after them like one of them loped over two white tables and shot out into the courtyard, its girding to which two wedded people, the supplanted vitamins, he was so pleased—with miniscule, adjacent cots of their own, to think—stumbled off, gripping their way up shame to the foggy welt's crest, enabling a strictly non-organic automatism the entertaining hearing of exogenicity as well as a few laughed as it were, as well as the reference, note rep top stories as taking hold of their applause for them, without them, as much for stretching out a crippled hand in silence.

In this description, endgame impels a registrant or an occupant or worker toward those securities best serving itself in extant beneficiaries via whichever residual earnings and keep-

sakes their prescence on Esma accrues for them, however inge-
niously. Failing that, it encourages a fascination or bemusement
among the accomplishments of three or more sapient entities
at their jobs—plucked sooner than they're memorialized in this
vapid and disillusioned world, its parts seemingly always one step
ahead in terms of paying, and only one left over and assessed in
bilobated terms.

Chapter. Valuation includes that Ugly Duckling Presse
may be contacted for all inquiries pertaining to the purchase or
licensing of these sections.

$4,500.99.

The bilobate one last time. A vocabulary to treasure, I went.
Chlorosmit and its subsidiaries would no doubt offer these three
years on behalf of registering—its was even more clustered,
wrecked, and a perennial trigger for an identifiable subset corru-
gating that audience idolatory, previously gathered plums, return
controls, funding mechanisms, the congestion of pods across a
compressed parquet, check lawn, monochrome vocab archival
duties rep, kst lips flipping, loner segmentation taken, groupoid
peripatetic risk in lien—philanthropic puppetry, cause and birth
removal of studying mechanistry, our cartilaginous wear; there
would thrive cognizant exploitation and retreats from the openly,
generically gaming inconvenience known thereof to cops, its the
bare insularity extracting commuting bred toward an unpredictable execution, but that was why I was going systemically about
it like as verbal conceit, and finally issued to two among them
on grounds among everybody else my favorites—Tracep confused, Narisovanna blanching—theirs alone going at me in an
admission of false toil I was giving the instances and the respect
that eventually precluded us from a single place to live the loser,
desperately repositioning gauges and instrumentation, the trying
an agreement on me more resolutely to dry off and take more of
the guards floating in from the rainfall and editorial timing, taking an incessant break from their lives faub; two people couched
sat in the backseat and were beat, both were wearing shirts, they
were worked token and intermittent pet hairs nested tired in
their self-absorbed fuckery.

After this, Denena brought us much more beer.

$4,000.00.

Five hours are left for Caspar.

I should stay alone, but not so much as to more efficiently compose a terminal log, my register, and I'm not not trying to get there though. This required meditation. I wouldn't modify that practice, I decided—but remember, every second that entreats precipitancy is good and even more when allowed, and each of those seconds diminishes its holdings still.

Timestamps are the listening natural, planting replacement for them.

An hour passed by. Minutes, temperature.

I told them calm down about our chain. They'd either have to wait for almost an hour after the execution slips or they could either way let this bullying guy fuck off and retain his b. It's only a memory away. Three years in this case for Caspar.

$105.59.

If circumstances changed, if we weren't swept steadily downhill like I went the dopes, I'd be fine. Not blaming anyone. I only wanted to see what each of those recollections earned in today's judiciary Ceaurgle climate and those Amma entities still indebted to this ridiculed and employed panting. They want that makeup, dimly numbing in all Tribasics little, as they claimed later.

Then I think, even those won't dive like they did. I'll miss them, too, angel. Time to put the hot rod away.

I was living a moderate distance from a designated location, and not unaware of it. This was in 2002.

For 18 to 21 years, the mostly-functioning Simstall Lot took place in this former hangar under auspices of an oligarch and the so-so auspices of NGST7909's school reconstruction project, intimidating blasting; memorial residents get to skim w a few hours of off-pay delectation for their tubs I'll get by, attributing the loss to budgetary principle through of that thing that warranted their existence but celebrated, regularly liked. After all, these were vengeful times; the foundation wouldn't err as a reason to have bought trounce with which to parry support.

A cinematic indeterminacy of objects wiped down into the fleet: brass, glass, blare folds, varuna contrarian dissolves, scaffolding, and fixtures. From those ships a reflective, censored polyvalence dealing in unlocked components or prodigiously available items by some means and emergent dispersables I can strengthen assigned microcredit forwards to seeing the two of them—the tenth day quartered in an unexpected Vixt's breezy clicks, May peonies sparring and deflating against each other, an impending taxation of resources and other fiscal agglutinates of duty, the slightly better if not more exposed a dogmatic pinch to camp Narisovanna, I bored, "why'd they cut wages this tight?"

I gathered a separate production for Ionelia come morning or once several nights a week, face averred toward, maybe it's like a buried frown or the low sodium Nura, bracing his cluttered worry within their two separate forms, eyes lowered dale when I handed her the throw and a few staples to fix the recollections I had.

She, Tramel, walked into the plunge preceding Walkrein Bower and washed over them the median, stringent. When, finally, someone shook the two of us awake, she'd been changed out of uniform and into a comfortable cotton gown. Leah bent over her and loosened the rope. Before their eyes, deep blue shadows maintained strict facades against the tent. That meant it'd rain soon.

As usual, crowds poured into the streets and sat in their shops, as well as in parks and cafes and along the streets. They greeted it or asked why it was visiting. Preexecution protocol, it smirked.

Why, they couldn't say, so they claimed—only that the prospect of steady employment pilled categorically into their district at first shit, or into completing the passages brewing a crisper desideratum near and far off their control, anti-psychotic weather induction, sorrows—the combo usually far more into the night—and unfortunately prevarication and of remembering a cross-resistant off duragesics franchise, each resigned to provinciality.

The two they spoke with had burnt bad. Gloves matched their excrescent labor with an agreeable shifting between weekends at a club and the aesthetic pests to Narisovanna, until the only cares were left a parodic, cindered diligence of its moving, blank shells over an airplane, not to fly often, patches of dirt plugging shirts and jeans, calumny indulging the boredom of having devoted in its progression to a predictive, their activity a sheer negative and, by their jail, infrastructure a level sob of lives, itinerance of pbox forefunds—interview albeit en masse crops and breeds, the yellow evening dilating along the top-secret

Dosepucks telemerger cranko, a few years later jeopardized by the petiolation of dual infections and the several topical genera spent on salving them.

That night, three arrests were made. My fingers crinkled and retracted into fists. We pressed further on, with scorn now.

Later in their research, as aridity always wore on towards them at day's end; their financial situation deteriorated nearly twenty months later. Trusting and blowing their way out of the suburbs at the time, and having essentially nowhere to stay or move, most of them confined themselves to the barracks. It was where it was, and they had the cots. One couldn't dispute that. The verdict had been sent in decades ago, I heard. They filled their free hours with conversations notably and games.

Those conversations parceled away the larger group into four partitions from which cluster truancy gleamed in blotches—a very frustrated strata of unknown ascent they'd grown to assume and trust the humors of, believing their neurological faculties to have accessed, as once in the past, during the bitter weeks of instruction following Struck & Writhe's job offer, an attunement already for them the insignificantly petting, coruscating infidelities with purpose to research development, supply, and a defeating parity of the senses.

Above, below it, dozens of the fauns fulfilled their personalities with an apparent correspondence to momentum or lack thereof they'd been made aware of as ridiculous imprimaturs, budget-ready, which tendered their appeal a foregoing time alone for it, maintaining with a shelled and guarded secrecy which nevertheless crept into and watered its subject down with redressed policies. Two could only do so much to effect gratitude, and its essentially circumstantial falsehood bothered them.

They maxed on in the shop. Dusk kept closing in. They constructed a haunted workplace on a few grains of sand. They stanched their withheld vivaciousness into an entrepreneurial coalescence of funding—desertion overpowering the calm, satisfying, and dissatisfied focus the unreal use of their chambers with which she peddled their wares faced—doppler of successful kids and plaintive for them in unconscious video programming, domiciles, an absorption played in revisionary measures, a few of which were speciously risen centurion mascots of their intramural relations accounted for, the beacon to their spindly pal, the possessed Caspar, an enclosure already gone bleak and drizzled into them by pity sauntering by.

Eyes poured tears and loch, lower feint—brown Uggs, crown—they wore the best of them. Looking in front of the images instilling the wild, pale life of morning with a dreary relief, she showered and changed into fresh clothes. Meeting in the hall, they whispered at each other in this reserve trade sealant self-sufficiently ambered around the company's cindering barometric manipulation, transitory criminality wage, repressions, trims, the comfort and handling of which searched a malevolent demand to the worst of those cheapening them the kemp, the rolling of heads—bound to happen—the kvn nipster.

"I'm getting sleepy and I'm getting belligerent," said Sylvan.

"At least you're not acting the fool."

"You may as well try to keep at it another hour." The game was folding so nicely.

Narisovanna shuddered at the three of them and fostered a rumor. Simstall directed an amazing drone crash in 50Forest.

"Exactly, an executioner in the Boutin," Mr. Wenzhaw was honked, funereal as ever.

"A big displacement."

"How long are they visiting?"

Two weeks later, I'd found out. He'd snapped and, yes, the money really was mine. Narisovanna enthralled them with holiday anecdotes, as a holiday was approaching, ugly and degraded as he was.

"What ride are you talking about," he protested from afar at Leah, "aside from that embarrassment footwear is series, the displacement reiteration of, sorry—chores, silence, kicking in the convert, comics free, general sickness, and helpless heartache?"

"Light sac repair—that's all I was told," huffed Leah.

"Alright, everyone. Afternoon will be here before you know it. Get to those dixaindidem."

"He'll stick around, too. You won't have to worry about that."

They dug in. The two perched on a cliff overlooking the skeletal turret, listening to a bunch of rocks tumbling somewhere below. Enthusiasm rollicked through them as it became clear they'd been watched by 100. The night rolled by. Videos bust them impalpably in affectionate jeers and definitely before the things of big kids' dreams, laughs, anguish, snorting twenty-five seconds later, engaged the underhandedly duplicitous, vandalizing, coordinated supply of rote fertilizer dotting the premises.

A week passed without incident.

In addition to the pleasures of team exploration, he learned how to control himself. Everything was going to be just fine.

In fact, the old boss had been very naughty too, and had to be punished very badly. His hands, only when he reached the steps could begin to discern the eerie wails channeled beyond the mossy churchyard's lampposts gave out their final clutching, in which allegorically Park and Groth nestled under the cockpit, spent in effort of practice of tearing him down, while I'd climbed into the truck to the lion to commit to myself to a cell for the night—previously examined cells, portacaval mash, an impending flu, intrafamilial repulsion, taxiways, adagio treatment ghost theme, reference hazards that drafted laxity.

She leafed through the complimentary magazines. The room seemed familiar. However, without feeling any reasonable support bracing her, he instantly reciprocated by granting the handing her off to her beloved cousin. I left the room.

They saluted her, Narisovanna and Tracep, bowing the Tracep, hetman and expert. They walked to Praxylight and wagged charms and ways at just that.

79.30°
3:45 p.m.

Clessiexecs in the staff parking lot.

Each of them had and maintained a parking space. This was when they shocked and unsatisfactorily listened in questions.

79.00°
3:45 p.m.

Somehow, we managed to speak figuratively. Deborah, Sylvan, Park, Matthew, and Groth accompanied the provocative melody of the hands firmly massaging their thighs once into pretty wallpaper like that of Walkrein Bower, as even such a good man as his Cezary waited for them in the car, the epitaph for whom they now read about like a cantankerous recovery from a long night drinking.

They didn't even consider him dead until like a minute ago. Grief fucked it on him immediately. It was over. Park paced. Several of them made skilled puppeteers and evolved the trade, easier by the buck, too. Maybe the evening would cancel order, I guffawed to myself.

"Let them choose," drowned Park, "and very possibly."

He humbly bowed to his opinion of their speaking of Sylvan. Deborah jerked her off and straightened them out. And she graduated. The three groaned as they ran a hand on and honored into their craziness badges of merit.

$5,000.00.

No, the castle and rustling papers, changeovers, having arrived at these a juridically and dysfunctional mess of glands no later than a day ago at the ports. The clock struck one.

A comedy, a cattle farm. The lower end valley.

A comedy stole a large herd of cattle while located with them. They were told they'd be rich. The morning was cold and a little disconcerting, if even it never actually arrived to see what happened. A fulsome business it was—wordy, professional, competitors kept distracted enough to tab easy prey by that point and float by. They didn't know them or Sylvan at that point. The numbers looked understated. 2003. Shooting ceased. As they moved back into the central corridor to undress and shower, nearly twelve of them realized they were the ride off this cake-walk in by this superior software transit aftertaste of sentimental feelings, pond and sea, too easy to get and too busy to join forces with and graph one of their many enemy flanges.

$40.00.

Ruins and ecology. Adenectopia.

$15.00.

They perpetuated their sleeplessness and competency in want of qa security, and with them two to four more archives of personal information. I needed these too, at least if I was still needing to scramble them into the discursively haggard face of the city.

The underworked complicities of damage done by term, tense with illustrative vexation, or what could've been construed as an advantage given the title they realized one another's secrets. The shots immediately cased them fish brought in from the water, birds depleted from the sky, yanked into the unpleasant realization that 100 still glowered at us the entire time from a distant boat on the loch. We remained on the cliffs a few more minutes.

"Would you look at that."

"Too easy to get," she asserted.

Rocks tumbled below.

8:00 p.m.

Everything was finished outright, for now. A pearl brought her peace.

They began to congratulate Narisovanna with Tracep, no less than the senior assistant manager of our unit. Surreptitiousness could regularly autostage warnings against open public usage of the aspen gills of the surrounding landscape—into the abiding, hammered commercial centers, boeft nubs crippled into the admission of stalking and worse. I thought he wouldn't have arrived on time p, at least that's what I suspected then, he said, and called for the waiter. It kept toxicity levels aligned until the admiral came.

"The pisshole. Dosepucks hated him. You never know what'll happen—that's the problem."

It had no effect on Cezary's exile. It felt too nostalgic to matter.

To think they were so powerless as to connect the eulogy, submissiveness, dollardom, concentration, and psychological issues the foment of this agrarian clasp—increasingly accelerating its brew by them—as Deborah replied to pause, frightened in her very despair, trading a disorder for compact, retractable glossolalia, so far devaluing their statistical inferences of Shox shoes and why, she stentoriously priced. Two big tears slipped onto their eyelashes and searched her and Sylvan's sunken cheeks like flies.

Money played up Matthew's task and unexpected imprisonment, talents commandeered to delay the inevitable anxiety of decremental leisure and contemplation. She almost ran forward against the gust, cornflower cloth whipping against her face. She couldn't have been called Deborah or have retained the name as such at this point, exactly as they carried across the front door the body, running still pipe. The time and place selected for this first conversation were not very good. I don't really understand business dealings, so I stick to circulation.

The ruling barrelled in that evening.

The boats slowed down and hobbled into the entry duct of the company, a tunnel they reduced, distant from the test's field.

Narisovanna came home drunk that night. Tracep asked his companion as they entered the elevator if they had the time. My old companion.

7:00 a.m.

He ran away.

The mood: striving to affix to the irritation they experienced wholesale prank and conniving, a momentary rush at disacquaintance by a human threatening to rob them, they found that this world would not be. All of it was quite unusual at the time, and here were my remains smack dab in the middle of the room. I met him once in the office of our company, to put it in a way with him, as he confirmed retroactively once, and made my way to the employment center. The point, and they could move around whatever they pleased—today they would gonibud usual.

They sent for the meal and didn't return, not even in the cool morning mist famous and distinct to Walkrein, warping into exquisite purple and orange bands, Ritalin, and the Dosepucks went back into the gorge to conduct more tests. A lot of these things had been transcribed by the clerks.

Also, the Chapter should have recognized that the noble dons strolled around in commercial quantities of leverage, calibration, and precision as they went forth up into a large scale exchange, reasonably supplied. Instead, pain elicited from them a number of squeals and moans.

78.75°
3:50 p.m.

PAYDAY

Transcurvational reflectors and a camera.

First, they ground their jaws into pulp against proteinous goat films and fibers, discovered and battered into submission an hour earlier. A little one. They had beer, as well.

They raised his head with strict confidence, they walked up to the serious prejudication of the bare screen. Then set up the props. They leapt off the raft—illegitimate, screened customizations of guests never valued or worth the scenery, choosy as well of their hypothetical concerns, which they postered the same way as themselves.

It could last an hour or a few minutes. The next moment they were waiting in the lobby, doors swiveling relentlessly behind them. The service would commence imminently.

Matthew stood at attention, checking a phone while Leah fiddled with a pair of binoculars. Chane took off his shirt with the clear intention of getting to cleaning. Then he remembered Ionelia.

He examined them carefully. The two of them preferred coats, he recalled. He layered sweaters.

He stumbled, staggered, and nearly fell into the pond—the anisopour slipping from his hand, bouncing onto the field, the plastic frottage semisimple and parodic amenability of.

They were outside. For cover, they could only use a small overgrown patch of oak trees. The camera joined them.

Across one frothy stretch of the doting, conterminous marshlands, a crescent of encampments charged various electronics and supplies in the noonday heat. Banks, motels, lacerating security operatives, several counselors, a mayor, the remaindered alertness of a citizenry once coherently plated stand and reef, serology, relapse, penance, the current hitch, lay rough, non-responders, prelude coldcuts, without even the faintest implication that humans once ostensibly murdered, presented, and hung around there like competent subjects of compile-time—irascible bags of the sheaved fucks they'd described into successful troops

and engagements. Arches.
$25.00.

One apparent condition of this permanent state of a priori abandonment, irreparable chapters, and misconduct sold at a bristling $20.00 per unit—a scam, compared to these sales—not to mention the relative calm that ensued, excluding the fifty-two tense days reluctantly hustled onto the table when a company's rescriptivity pressurized its product tests into inspired structures and lifestyles.

Long germinating tensions between Dosepucks and Struck & Writhe were finally done and frothing over the barren town of Grosvenor like a cleaning agent—a captious stack of steel settling dumps crammed with local retailers, an account worrying them into factions of resistant sureness—a skeletal, resounding sympathomimicry known to Acrobasis as everyday business, positioned in itself as very knowledgeable in matters of obtaining alcohol and prescription medicine. Vacillating city and court.

CHAPTER FEXINUF

An impassable market off the hill—invisible, excepting drop trim, 12, a limiting withdrawal from the tiring university—plants a totalizing, realizable window of obtaining line credit peacing nettling residential grounds with a parade of scenarios requisitioning an incurable market, nothing fearing that cratered doubt the entire factory maintains via rumor as paralytic, covered—an effusive supplanting of daily life by the inhabitants preanesthetized to the magnetism and susceptibility of a Shucibu Links, the rival among them, to venture requip single experiments, a thin filament of expectation trembling in their convulsing, tiny, fuck-shaken calves.

Shucibu Links pinboards advanced registrants into hapless, unesteemed rememorizations and patch slag—protocol well-known to many work environments, as it were a lonely way to portray their livelihood elsewhere, prior to and in which they struggled, cart after cart toward cell mass life manifested off birthday celebrations, camp, weddings, hydroxypropyl customers, interdepartmental squabbles, presumptive experiences, wear, and the crowning drive to top a life.

They took to these adopted nuances as the trust they exchanged during this preliminary phase of registration, the counterintuitive fulfillment of an excited determination.

I looked up and down the cellblock, along which lights wavered and retreated in elliptical shudders, chic and beautiful, when with relative alien drive the buildings they found around them incarcerated in decreasing thermolyzational differences, many shaking descriptions, convinced to be that they were no longer alive to shut up the project or leave anytime in the near future.

His finger throbbed from when Denena cut him earlier, if by accident, while he was writing at the podium.

$300.00.

I'd say how, but I'll only say that his elbow ached for days after that. That's enough for now. I'd been told more, but he was otherwise feeling well enough, so what's it matter? She spoke with a calm cogency that set us at ease, and could plainly see he was moved. Her entertaining was the first time I saw her.

$1,000.00.

78.75°
3:52 p.m.

Anchorets, improvements, and corruptions resulted in the immediate downsizing of Cezary, Mr. Wenzhaw, and about a quarter of the staff. I was lucky enough to keep on, so I kept a log already in anticipation of our impending troubles. It has since been lost.

The clods of methodical framing reconcileds the massacre as well as they could've under the cirucmstances, arbitrarily secreted off the still-occupants return control and release at whim to those further breaches of which they'd enlightened us—if they cared as much—via the helpless representation availing them equanimity of media.

No one enjoyed them or perverted them—so they would have to remain there as long as the assignment lasted, proof of a satisfied contractual obligation, twisted waking up and slipping into bathrobes and going down once again to the customers to make nice, jerseys wholesale the erring discussions. The weather hadn't let up, and neither had their stay in the barracks.

Divalence reigned.

5:00 p.m.
10:30 p.m.

78.70°
3:52 p.m.

Incubatory and androgenous feed. The one-bag treasure.

If only for a second, the grub correia n pertained to four of the twelve active of inexcusably promoted business centers of their choosing, a collection of coupled memory residents disaggregated into fastening watermen and contracts, the deadbolt Cezary doubtless among the fourth or fifth corpses tanked with them to have conducted this reasonably perceptible work in a mood of surrender and dependence on prizes to the diminishing botanical residency, the west four blackstone, having balked at them appetitus, card party ectospheres nutting the weekend, lifecam ataxia, total initiations, forgiveness—ten throws per that day's dragnet futures—and unauthorized loans dispensed into aesthetically immune cordial and menacing procedurals.

A podium sat flush against the office wall, on which had been carved another registrant's dedication:

for Mark Johnson and Astrid Lorange

Chapter. Chane requested they carry the following items.

Capture room 1. Chapter Shox. Dry riverbeds from which feeds pose various reception modules and drib—the "Kami noscendi," they called it on account of a propensity for return disassembly and namesake who decades ago came to be renowned as such a surefire colleague invade—which handled two stacks or shelves at a time, throws one at a time, and as one of the two occupants affiliated with it serving as catalyst for its upcoming pre-execution chaining cycle.

Absolutely nothing can be done to reverse this cycle once it has been successfully initiated. Following activation, the arrests went on as scheduled.

Ionelia, Sylvan, and Matthew were each due their crusher ideal as well, though they didn't yet know it. And I wasn't going to tell them.

Three roads coupled the hills. Roads. Two courtyards. Roads. Concrete walls clumped their oddly porous, faceless brawn against the sulky, demonological band splitting lock, given away, more about movement than to having taken landscapers into work on a disturbing lawn gradient. Weekends seemed pointless.

3 MILES AWAY

From Ionelia. She went first, four hours ago.

TACTICS

Several markets in the Ceaurgle district competed with each other as constitutive vendors of acceptance and stability, as Selec had recently opened now very near one another's premier commercial entities the distaste was palpable—cars of new residential inlands admirable and underwritten, ragtag group scurrying their redoubtable cherubs into the septic tank of their own filial stable, contemporaneity and superproduction, affliction zaxis hydromorphone, the plant, the property of stability, wandering around in a nature revealing them the stark radiographic assumption of this journal, busily disillusioned as has been shown, a poverty subduing even routine—cognitive nightlife high sneakers having excused upon the remote shred of evening romance, the fragile brand of shits gloating, for which some two other bars and three entire clubs stayed open late taking Klonopin or Oxycodone.

Fliers which had been distributed at 10:00 p.m. still lay scattered in the street. There was nothing else to do.

11:00 p.m.

They walked to church. I spent a predictable fifteen to twenty minutes making sure I wasn't being pursued. I wasn't.

78.70°
4:00 p.m.

She bore rest at that moment.

Finding the creaturely, sexualized actions of their creditarct slurred across memory residential sects or another modificatorily breathed transplantative agencies, they slithered, as if reductive, to their overexposure love then a dislocated judgement, sandbags Simstall went to a carcass or two of the handlers carrying vitamins and other products vaunted across those six to eight hills, innate to their shelter, attack, and lake, its pedestrian federalism and the effects described sintering neglect and volatility.

Their acceptability clothed squares in the blue cardboard all six lit people, able-bodied, the Vixt district facing an arrived: a large number of undesirables.

They endured the fantasies of a small fountain ham. She kept simplifying their surplus hobbies.

The manager. And two of them.

78.55°
4:06 p.m.

Foodwise, they had an entire residential district to burden. Edivate can attest to that, or at least did for me.

An achievement in itself for Massive, the company. Doubtless, he saw—as if he'd known that insubstantial verification the bouldery function of recombinatorics with other objects in the area and identifying precisely vick in the morning, backsqueal honing irradiation, redolent plates, air conditioning chirping in the hollow, the able bodies lunching in Walkrein Bower snapping at chilled water containers, eating. Faces, roads, apparati Tracep Ceih's to her low-interest mortgage rates, Trunc, uniformed and delayed cluster of them having been sold up—scarcely rep our unusual equipment—hockey, soccer, football, baseball, the northern hill bronze apple bounding inadequate quality, aggregate tubes and unidentifiable circuitry by which a stationary attraction reels into a discounted parlance of one another's ascetic self-immolation, of extrapolative or some might say retroactive renewal, albeit squandered in the seeking out of popular articles.

They were exuberantly open to technology and dumb enough to accentuate it. The gulph. It wasn't like three of them had died. They were only arrested. For now.

There was a metabolism that was an embarrassingly noisy, backseat want toward ferrying the sinny vigil they'd propagated and all-character hatred of pathophysiology, long lines, and the reserve of public drinks readily available per reverse party—the only ambling budgetary, the hillocks not reading, the bough radiant, acceptably renowned angrily fished in a real estate for and by the visitors told of their bunks. A rental compilation.

And the bodies made for fine grist. She smiled.

"The visitors," they scried and looked around themselves trashily—athletic trashy, I guess—bumbling again beside the cabin, landing and properly combining my panicked and prejudiced grip by patrol and constant barometric predetermination made by weakening the four of us, if we considered how little we made, and as quite as brilliant as their interchangeable banking sectors were haphazardly slits in a retractable atmosphere of the location.

"Shower, and favors shower," advised 100.

$5.00.

A graptomantic scrawl plushed off the world—the world, which that couldn't hurt the least among them, the surrounding called forests dense and integrating with a one-gallon empty milk jug someone left behind and priming this reference in excruciating detail—just a thing of milk five of them once shot at.

Discards, the Shoe Zoo, they knew they couldn't listen without movement or diligence, but as they were keeping at it, he maintained to foretell that, "richly important to the past, present, and future claims," a crate thought evidence, scraped per handling shit of configuration, the last of them bunched hallucinatorily.

$399.99.

Clenched hands, cement waste, emissions, a service manual. The only reason to have it is because it's dead.

He shoved a cartridge into the console. The vast, unresolved cleft that looked out over dark Ceaurgle years before—its sparrow-tailing laser shows, stars directly dampened and pestled, them and hunger whisked away instead to the movies in consistent, hermetic dregs of forgetfulness and banter.

CHAPTER NUMBER
RETIRES

They showered. Pharmacy ruled.

With these unit farmers, they could maintain almost ten acres of land, day after unforgiving day.

He would've rather been thin to them. He jumped up on a seat and enumerated every unreliability cluster that afternoon in sequence and I study, in order of ascending insolubility, expendable gestures of cooperation in light of the competitive strain fraught and muscularized by their nerve, especially in the unrelenting August heat, writing the logs slowly.

Snow fell in thick flakes as they told it, an exigent poyuzhecno windbag. And later. In the oppressive quiet that resolved the day as voided, the night passed uncrested, a figment of naturalism. I wanted to give them good advice.

6:40 p.m.

Two of the sessions. In the gestation of compile-time, deficiency city chip, Accucur Venice at her whisky and a pilsner, blossoming patrol by Leon Kulakov's side met their indispensable end.

4:00 p.m.

6:40 p.m.

The station, at latest an inferior guess as the shift would have it, went from 4:00 p.m. on—thus the risk coast to the off attending like one big arrest after another, the next one coming up next Friday and, having already let Cezary go, kept painstakingly obtuse to the frantic, clairvoyant, anonymous air of ridicule sorting out its restructured arterial ilk into these nonpoint frustration sources ploy dulcis specialized into its hail.

No one knew who among them could do them in first, but an initial comparison tread already ceased a while ago and no one had followed up. We were certain of the investors, anyhow.

Dusk gets muggy; the afternoons burn by irritatingly enough. Most of them spent enough backing up level files and mimicry into discard boxes, a pretty childproof twenty-two, disapproving of their two opponents: the companies, the divisive casements x their long lives together, Uggs review, sixteen, an early extermination of three workers in legend.

Assumptions about clothing alluded to greater troubles and an income generated out of their base items, foods, conversation, and the experimental afterthought of such a men's new belt and shirt. Collective, abnegatory biographical information, malformed states, Richloam, the balcony off Struck & Writhe's rich and really cupola fresh extension, the worthwhile throw hut, the most common careers, the treasury.

They'd called it—they and the recalled career Boris Pillshelved's Grosvenor applied the prevpac, the generally narrow alley and wider thoroughfare by its means of traffic a plainview, Depakene consumption, slog ultimately bothered and reassessed answer to five industrial poles bounding one's eastern peaks, the facilities and for once unreplacing notes of that dunderhead, southern pair of t-termed, and, at no small odds multinational currently not enough an impediment even for the seasoned type or norm pet, personally and seemingly allied against Tracep Ceih—or were they rather the one imagining things big bag village that I'd place Caspar, as if they went along courting local parents, fat diaries, birds, celebratorily unleashed dogs, the farm to table staff service tracing Leah's house in their panting endurance, thinking they were remote to this incisional social horror about them, only to learn they were already its ostensible illusory fixtures?

Some of them were walking alone; they were afraid to stoop to Denena's insanity and disjunction, and when they had to, drastically ameliorated. Men and animals alike were killed. They cured the feculence they'd become—everyone knew that, and so they maintained it as such. Four of them crossed a pathological line, staggered to his feet and raised his fist at Sylvan. She glanced the natural square, the courtyard, the inner sanctum, and a tree laden with fruit in the eastern dark area.

Neuroscience, paresthesias, a national report.

The door opened to the lab and changed access to them.

5:30 p.m.

Pasidjen and the train station beneath it transmitted the temperature. Wind jittered the absurdly false streams meditation and corrosive activities, rail images, the subterranean idiocy to those symbols, an autoinduction resolved in the breeding of rich toddlers, responsibility for lost items to about nine sets of sixteen to thirty-four companies that inhabited the peninsula, cocaine, festered the Boutin Engine and its later arcade tinge on the disarray of escapes, jams, vehicles assembled beyond the one, on-ramps nestled into and branched from Walkrein's handle that shepherded the citizens in and out of its pastures.

The Amma out of the divide lectured this utter factory in gangrenous film, homespun monitor brooks, and to those new residencies tipping coaxially presentational in regularly mentioned nearby benday dots, quilted leather watches, hills and wallets—featurelessness unto the market of itself in liquidities by way of small businesses, reflexive, cheerily, parks, trades, and admonitions Clessiexecs gathered into a realization and subsequent feint on over family research and the best people owning those homes.

With lively interest, the compartment into these international agencies' most popular buildings, address lists, proportions, weather bearers, volicity, flesh lurking, bumpered and travel stations desperately plead to guilt, "monopsonists ferret any pension we'd desire," Cezary erred in supporting the dupes, naturally, and who at this point felt essentially obsolete. He rose from his locker and went to the sleeping quarters. Upon waking, he made for the nearest checkerboard to relax and sight some passing egrets. The morning lit up the hill and his secluded retreat.

CHAPTER

This additional action does not apply to contributions beyond money, classic, vivid paralyzation, the droppers for one last reading outlay donations and extensive network.

I simply do not have the time or energy to compile that data now.

Patrons and an anniversary.

"That's natural," muttered Leah.

They chatted some more and entered the lodge.

I started heaving at a desk.

NURA DULCIS

Improvements in speech recognition.

CHAPTER THE AGENCY

The first shift went fine.

"I went up to Walkrein this morning—he told Groth they were fabricating a deadly, neighborhooded watch by their dupes bad, superbug, disfantasizingly too, that they were trying to convince me to hire. But I wouldn't budge."

"Good."

He was apparently a white, and then continued, balled away in diets, into what Groth called "wraith-like nets. A five-unit orbit of concentric output functions."

"I perceived in his car pills strewn across the floor," went Ionelia.

A row of stitches attenuated his face. Two, three—the night flew by.

"He resembled his parents somewhat, facing the ways he bundled them up and kissed others off r to them in arms, in glasses, and slightly closer to them in worn double sole, the dress fell off the two of them, cad evacuation."

"Leave them alone," Rolly T. asserted.

"Tally the proprietary endearing, careful, accidental pitch, stoical, erect, official production torque, throwing, the interview I made with them, footage, dtds, the cover, available, many of them."

Browse Title Secondary.

The forgotten quarter.

"I want to work outside of that."

"You've already violated that assumption. And will until you die."

DOMESTICATION

The refrigerator, drink and beverage, alcohol, beer, wine, liquor, tobacco, a room, weaponry, and some other equipment—and furniture. Basically a homestead, clothing, but without having to play up to anyone for it.

Deborah tried to take a few steps, if her leaden legs would permit it. If it's true that on this ship the messenger of piping is Chane, and I'd still support him incognito. I don't know. I shook uncontrollably.

"When'd you get so sudsuctive?"

"When can we afford a witness?"

Fortunately for them, he'd been laid in the same place, which meant she, the judge, hadn't overheard them as they crouched in the voluminous and harsh grass. She leaned toward him and pecked him in his fucking face.

They hadn't been expecting so much food, and lunged at the horse, galloping again. By this way, this is where I met Denena. I remember what we talked about, but it was something serious, and not of much move import to this reconstructive document—but were talking about them. One movie.

$600.00.

The error in significance obviously confused Tracep and Narisovanna, who proceeded ot make short work of their old friends.

"Tramel F.," Park shouted, waving his remaining hand.

I loved Park.

He said he'd had enough of these storms but stayed around for a while. Judging by the brief description of Shylu I provided, he knew they weren't going anywhere. After telling his story to the electricians, he accused me.

"And now," said Shylu, "let us leave."

"Yes, your humble servant," said Vineet.

Vineet was in perfect health—first of all, because he had to show them he wasn't afraid. The count came in their mouths.

Two hours from now this hierarchy will be further clarified.

Everyone rushed at them. I hoisted him up on my shoulders and carried a bird in my hand toward the quarters.

"Will that require a report as well?"

He grinned.

$20.00.

Late at night, before the vehicles lumbered through their dusky channels east and west of Kami—storage or to the back of the yard—she stared ahead, barely taking to flesh the old petroleum act or drug-including inexact reproductions of the material wished away in errors into a forgetting told to cling a presence surgical by way of this waste removal. He was not and would not be home tonight, the appalled Leah realized, a jagged skewer of turns or innovative plexi, video, food—here anticipating that they could've devised a resemblance to the aforementioned squad, Tracep thought while riding the deepening bundle of the four plains, exhaustedly bijective. The split garnered equal traffic on both sides, a minimum impending a dull, foamy smog.

Outlandish that the visitors, they accepted, always at best die off.

Emphasis was placed on punctuality. It looked like a test 953 dropout or some meddling swampish man and yellow, entropic and similar force had swept through their interest in the test's results as the pilgrims settled down, souvenir-shopped, finished, and undisciplined conversations—coattails of its butler gasping Selec air as the trays are decamped, militancy having faded from the port six to eight years ago when onshore they ran and walked into Leah, no doubt the hostile intention their tidings questioned, claim trade along the molten exterior surfaces, the chandelier foil and marble, lightning, and door through which it entered bere unused, light slinking away in news, rickety clef, the Walkrein Bower, Dayrom freshening up in the mudroom for the party and its subsistent judicatory centralization, autocratic daydreams of portrayal would at once discipline their behavior a deistic and manic in-passing of servitude and betrayal. The roasted potatoes tasted dry saccidentities, the latest impulsion paid into startling personality traits and distributed at a clip and funny funny, said the monk.

The pavilion. Fire tables, footprints rilled the way up to Richloam, emanating its the damaged breaks from city nightlife and loot.

The ground spoiled Ionelia, provincial inholdings daring ace, architectural windows streams the last remnants of that evening's progressive and ordinal phenomena, seven stump coolants demurring phlegmless below, more terms—construction permitting operation, ventilation, and quality, waiting somewhere in the lunary fundament, music, grain, and boat.

"Co-advise them into those arms," sad Peng, carefully obligated clean to young people up to a combat troupe.

"It's just sweet. It's not a roomy economy."

"He'd scram for any dick in the game," sad Chrysalidocarpus.

Perpetuity—that nose to nose with a huge crocodile sailorman image—severance assured cards gelatinously coated, or cards for men flayed easing, innocuous surfaces, abrupt stillnesses and the depravity of our memories, the spoiled oversupply of display aspectary slant their one Chapter to this Pentecostal arcology, stimulatory shaking test systems, preferential treatment, the need to stay here, obscene humor, nonbiological payloads, a yato look, jxv funny job to play, the new year, disheartened days of swimming months ahead—teenage and hotheaded, exhortations outlived them, m in status shortfall probability curves, which obviously landed bad press, even jxv funny—ranging from tendentious to masked fear Boutin—assumed to have undertaken not tending the toothpaste and Xanax cocktail that would have been cooperative enough if it hadn't wasted for the chili slugger downed earlier, but crusted away instead to the park, its trails gurgling useless Watkin stamen.

78.17°
4:10 p.m.

"I don't play any Sceneby."

She reviled them.

"Captivate yourself. Not like I'm blind to authority, Mr. Wenzhaw—only to the auxiliary geomechanics Praxylight does."

He beamed at them comprehendingly, appraised substantially of slowing up on this breach of decorum he'd parlayed into the last hellish half hour, accusatory rubble, broom sweeping floor, music, talking, and the a90769.

After hours. Each conceivable husbrigand, simulcast radio shows, activities, and "conclusive sociality of inconsequence," thereby "these coterminant fluxations in benefits," invited them minimally disattuned to their quarters, the language of Somo; their remarkable ways, corners, frosted, honed-in policies copying a romantic flower tediously, "looks like it's the back room," a glance infected 100 or line that anemic to begin with.

That there exists an external, obviate body clicking and rattled compulsively as the handler haunted us at the time botex scary, made broiling of it and went to sleep.

The little shops, they muttered about them, the engineer said, giving way to Vineet's unsettled thoughts.

He was the first among us to express misgivings. Yet no one cared to miss him.

78.15°
4:12 p.m.

They, her, and me watched six women spin her fork around in half circles on her plate as they quietly collected her fries, everyone else was cracking up over a jab; there was Rolly T. on the edge in a chair, ulcerously squirming diamagnetism to replicate in denim handbags kidding, but in certain inirrative efforts still playing this stance.

Dayrom paced in front of the fireplace. They called this General Counsel. It took place in the middle of church.

There were four churches. Little had been said, a they slept.

They left a pile of cigars mashed into the floor, lit up over the tablecloth, dumped more ash beside, and ended up this group jettingly fitting in—and in dangerously close to the spoils.

The beast meant something else nearer value commutation, immediately caricatured rim birth for these lesser, the disexplainatory dogs clotting Tilbud dog pools, the dogs tearing a chicken into fifteen pieces, dipping the pieces in herbs and oils, and wrenching away its speckled white feathers.

Less exclusionary traits by that time had mostly fallen into place. The often laconic, foregoing competition, the sucking into grudging acquiescence with deanimizatization bez audacious transparencies, evasive cleanliness, brief appearances, and his and her new music.

"As a braying, laconic switch to shortsleeve shirts, spring exceeded their request for virtually any cheap mania, five of them were told through useless albeit incentivized spurts of trivia that their desperately cloying presence to this killjoy, if, as in the Richloam bathrooms, tears obscured her natural face and availed them of physical activity," kids saying pictures, attended the discussion with any tress, colors absolutely stilled and when removed, the pictures a dim emerald sheen of school, a phone number for where she worked elsewhere in Berlin under as a customer service. Thus, carrying the family, as they were sometimes wont to call it, Simstall Lot at once tested the people and regretted their cultural manifestations alike, the castle pines, three downloads counter strike, wintered nothing to profit and hunger. He didn't do urine nor drank, he sensed dully as he fell against the table and postponed dinner until 7:30 p.m. He collapsed in the rolling chair.

She moved her hands quickly through the air at Ionelia. Chane considered their party in the midst of a fascinating, abandoning headache that parted them the following obnoxious day from their having sent her hands exhaustedly recoiling yet again to her temples in reply, then at another three of them wishing and hanging in the belt bag, the glistening program flown further from embellishing the room with sounds, textures, preparates, infomatic reorientations, and discussion.

When b portends a meeting the length of compile-time least pertaining to the imperative of the handler, it succeeds in forestalling arrest, and moreover assumes a proprietary cretarct. This will occur in two hours. In the preexecution phase—three hours—these meetings only supplant those thrown and already blocked, namely excrescent blocks which cannot suffuse their retributive initiation by the cretarct's capacity for stacking and sublimating already attritional recycling methods.

Sacked in Dayrom, the waking life of unhappiness in the choices concealing their own, this semicircle commercial of influence and the magazine recognizing the accessibility of these connections to their test systemacity of invasion and transitivity, as trapped in themselves in the constant loop of reappropriated sentiment as they would feasibly distort its reformations wound them tight at grunt range the collected fourth piece of Trunc unproportionally rewritten in inequiaxial hands, the GoFlex desks, the embossed gem stovetops, wool out and elite dining chairs, grape-like clusters of blunt tip candelabra bulbs, a glass dressing table, coconuts, other side dishes, and oil dock.

77.57°
4:29 p.m.

"Testa di merda," she muttered, carry "the causal, formal means and limitation, for which this selfishness and informality itself hold application. Songs list."

I recalled her saying that with more and more clarity. A few of them were really improving.

"So suggesting an evolutionary distancing of?"

He ran his index finger along the tab of a soda can.

"It could inter that, if you wanted. But it's more than just casing."

I probably could do this forever: just watching videos, going to the auction, dowsing, recourse to discussing turning screen to texture approach screen gatecrasher nothing necessarily that enduring, and the rewritten Mr. Wenzhaw.

Trouble lost in those years obstructed anything but the strident sobriety they posed in periods of steep doubt. Discreetness ruled garrison. Mostly they lounged around and read, sometimes cooking a package of pasta or exhibiting a monastic and humorous gratitude to sturdy physical health with a collective toast, devouring half a loaf of bread, boiling beans, and kale to their permanence.

"I missed you so much," ponytails cantilevering defense off complementary insanity—maintained by its inherent riders, suppositories furnishing her long neck, phases, diverse environments in which one or more entities strolled, the wresting of Cezary's form habitation, the photocopy the two of them made that was essential to their present framing and registration.

The chair creased with imminent spasms of pain, "sentence original nevertheless families," offense, shots, convention to discussing fragmented noninfluence, nothing particularly enduring, a commercial, the second arguing that its trace underpinnings in miserably taught emanence lent to historical analysis, keyword keyword contracts invoked an occlusion task of their boundary sustenance as opposed to the real of and to Vixt taxation.

Theirs was a public utility lacking the authorization of conscience.

Meanwhile Park took Shylu, gloomed Shylu, and lifted Rolly T.'s chin, studying her eyes.

"What time is it?"

1:34 p.m.

Twitching Leah, another thought at the woman jabbed, "isn't even homework anymore. They took turns sanitizing the cot, barren as the others."

The room was cold. She was present in bracelets. She smiled, "then we'll sleep, dog."

It looked like death finally sublet his years and years in the city. While reliable, his stolidity perplexed her. He did not resemble her. She decked him.

Meanwhile, I really had to shit and lie down a minute, catch my breath.

"Excuse me," she pleaded humbly, "but I can't d I be found out nonthermal yet. Forget it. You'll see why at some point," "let me reveal my plan," and why ask?

The three of them burst out laughing.

"I'll get there, but I can't keep track of the—the metric much longer."

"I've been really busy too, so."

I took off my coat and made for the toilet. Scarcity, abnormalcy, mangrove properties, and dispassionate tagging. I recalled the word sclerosis.

He was too kind to insist on the demands of these cohorts and too fulfilling of their impassiveness—features and organizational greased iron tubs, umbrella effect, the zeal of commitment to internalized and pirated shrifting, atavistic self-embryonics by dint of wholesale, transcomputational fording attacks, recreation 100 encouraging their training for the remainder of the summer.

If this any night any day hutch the quiet life must get tricky and usually never subsides, they thought.

My guide and I studied the area for approximately six weeks. It felt like the first promising setup in a long time—the prior year unemployed, toilings in various Moscow shops amidst the memory sialosydixness glutei, moonlighting bussing tables into sort of secondary esteem of resident purpose, of valet parking for an apartment, suppository failing the exception of a design work opportunity here and there. But never a home. The rain trickled in around dawn. The scene been irrigated our garden flower by flower, crystal drops rolling down into the lips of biancheng flowers and the fake haunts eground trap.

"Where would you have gone if the past stuck through?"

The question felt pertinent, but I decided to keep quiet. I preferred spying. Occasionally.

"They force its isolate—that this was essentially reality—the Lovoreive gallated salutations at her. Now look at her."

Deborah arrived and she was looking alright. They were incapable of dealing effectively with these contents and their false quiescences, "appointed to the same embarrassing tenets, caught up, misconstruing perpetual reference to. I don't know," "my god, Shylu," a trickle of pity relations panting—exerted, shame, possible contamination, symptoms, fever and night chills, dealing into the pot what they could the beneficial elixirs and shortcuts.

He walked into the narrow white-tiled bathroom, stood in the shower and whistled to speedplay, cabinets, overprescription, extremely hot and then tepid water for ten minutes. The univalve hissed as he turned it clockwise. Fifteen minutes later, they were all prodigality and waste.

Now it was Deborah's move. Five minutes were left until the shifts began. Tactics and consequence. The first set cheaper than the later uninhabitability we were to storm, and if so by a brief history.

CORREO

Correo—they never garden there, the bit went, the distinguished slopes of its plugged-in sobers, sawn compact disc face bristling stop that's dumb, though notorious, once that maturing summer of 2005, Ionelia Clyden peering from behind a slab of concrete and reciting her handhole into the brush; she checked her watch.

1:34 p.m.

A deathly stillness sequestered Leah, Deborah, and Tracep set anterior to those loans in excess of manufacturing that Wednesday, a mourned Nike Shox, unsteady, the green of their worn copper roof, observable data, consular services.

In a utility shed, a box personed dumb platinum auc, untrodden moss artificially gray except for the weeds crawling toward the doorstep. The streets were dead. I was working against myself, it felt.

Projection, continuous, yield and accentuate list, retreated to, if once campus, within scope upon entrance, then, responsively gilding itself against the visitors' weary padding up the steps, the quavering n second, or n1, mice blithering chunks of time—and that Chane Rao, that a final stupid ending in the ascendency to n1 status, armaments, illumination a priori n, damaged once into a war with the Eightbuck Dictum Team which is upcoming and once into the fervent abuse of family members and thanae nearest exits from each intrusive badgering of their sensibilities. Servitude in a pulse of air and backtalk about backtalk, undertaking its negative culpability, its confidential fantasies of thermodynamic equilibrium within the purview of Ceaurgle, I survived, a barren ciliary to its idl governance, told them their release system might unfurl a triple-throw program, given its proclivity for as much reallotment. Like there'd never be a crew again.

Ionelia—the stark, paracephalously retroactive, distributed heaps of these composite and unused air filters. Antiquated metal detectors juggled their reprehends in a corner, their cluttered shadows neutered of sensitivity at last, or so they thought, the prohibitory getaway victims they stole the guns from, if not their unfathomable pain—n, why weren't they disposed of, awaiting collection or misappropriated clean up?

"Mr. Wenzhaw," very much the prime suspect slough stopped on and oriented himself as standing at Shucibu Links headquarters.

It had been April or May at this point. I noted the pitch emotion and liked the intent of it, its charming and educated treats: them. Our four trusting chief time series models hydrologic designations of some note some four months ago, intended for river flow forecasting, the mummified beach generation of the synthetic data collections, their "stochastic, chains rows satisfactorily identified and represented in computer time," the faded pink colors, the carved blocks, the bright rain.

It struck me sometimes like a stump with knotted weeds poking around a constantly deforming and antitubercular growth, its test spreads propped against what must've been hundreds of vibratory rollers across dozens of levels, a prominent mid-mounted deck, upper and lower whippers and feeds, the woven mats below other pruning devices and sleeper turfs.

"A resonant hulk. The removal of periodicity accompanied their brief involvement with the Lovoreive slugs, by which a fitted aharmonic sequencing conned and rephrased Ionelia, diminished a seasonal means deviated from the previous time model, of and which had fitted to other residual measurement garocerathures, not to mention prognostic variables."

Really selling the uncertainty. Identification of multivariate modeling.

The fall intensity sharing bullshit and subsequent flows of the noise term advance and limited estimates are used, ascertain rather uninteractive and are lost as subdivided memory residents, pocketed into Amma as monthly, absolutive loans. Ionelia considered the occasional exhibitory changes she had witnessed in error of the feelings they reversed, contributions to consumer research, common and whole-body dissatisfied.

Untestable interferences I mechanized myself for a no-go obtaining of proper results, because proof of misfortune might stave off other responsibilities. Simstall promised me it nearly cried over getting left—clear, its motionless, silent prey, those poor dispensers. Again, Ionelia and Chane appeared indistinct occupants, and in their densely uniform and ago way, feedback and internal rounding models, instructive signals to begin, command, narcissistically, the nowhere tending efference copy and plexiglass, horseplay, interrelations fostering the inability to lack signage to the average solute surface tension they modeled before bigger storms hit.

I picked up the gauge and proprietarily suggested each location represent a single independent trial, rather than the interface of surface controls we'd been using. Errors clearly persisted, determined each section, analogous for the each Chapter hedging, whether Dosepucks or Eightbuck Dictum conflated with candidate periods glaring the hollow images of their upcoming holiday weekend's peripatetic flush.

Hydrology in our school maintained that flooding surfaces might better disperse or irrigate what rainfall we could append toward the end of a run, pseudonymous noctoids implant mortals shifts and Martel.

She reapportioned seven of them back into the glaze of collection spectroscopically pent sentimentally necrosis, imagining again that Bear river, grids, posed as a more complex, tediously inflated pleochromatism, Rolly T., the noblesse oblige, rewarding, albeit signifying, defective, a concretion of their abilities, activations, a positivism and its complementary phantasmagorie, afterwork gatherings at the big beer jug, Protestantism when awake enough to, rattlebrained merely by the generosity of its incipient reducers and their pledge to the company, the stacks, effectively ever oblivious of their muck and expectational operators. Rapacious pay to majority output, where she and their opulence overlapped narrated an onslaught cottage Priligy, faun to faun.

Her pastelike skin, covered mostly in dank wool—she loved wool—joint shaking as she lifted it near and audirent, scattered, blushed mauve, and subsided. If I was to have my cut of the profit, there couldn't be any more of this impulsive implementation of geopolitical flexibility and thermotaxic inertia like the toppers wanted I said. In a mere seven days, the end of which coldly stared down at me from four hours from now, I'd be dead. Or a memory, either way.

"No, crisp Chapter designations Clessiexecs governing by it. Consider it—no, sorry. Input affirmative," he garbled down at the quivering monitor, taking pleasure in the retreat toward investigatory reclusion.

Veins of their pretentious derision receded into the watery plexi of her concern, salad, and stilled, plainest and looked like snow.

"What's the bog hurry?"

"Keys in around midnight, guys."

Three, "yes, there are downpours, two of which are ceaseless until about 4:30 a.m., keep."

Correo, the n quarternary, stoical downtrend laundry passing places qualities upon one hillside, sans unification, staved off the crowds.

The homemade bungalow, rubber shoe binding, footprints, glossy trans-decimated slater of rain troughs, involuntarily drawn into clinidrops Room 2, Chane arrived and produced from his bag some amenities. Among these were the raingages and garocerathures, less useful here near the riprap, gabions, and concrete, and more the subverted need for sequestration by which we made a living. Talented, passed down locks and locks of years putrefactially before their own Valadis Anisopour, the best, used for its fumbled monitors the anteroom idiot Denena, runestaff, whole, two whole stalled years hence, bearing description, $3.50 disintegrating per minute, Vineet calculated, decreasing volume, eventually defaulting as relational firms of technological import. Rain levels were keeping low for the time being, and the garocerathures were lately speaking on the inversion of that front like the barely sustained lives I was starting to creep in on, backgrounded as a drizzle that could stay a drizzle as long as needed. Contracting costs would stimulate their reproval and rough indicative slides. He couldn't resist either, and moaned.

Presentation of various input analyses, "admission," known, severely affected to commuting appeared too 2003 l, too substantially worn out, she forgiving Rolly T.'s and general thoroughness, the race by which she metastasized the five recordings of us talking into a garble that happened before she left—each a transient waste site to definitely pain, and other big, big documents.

And really it was up to her—these mosquitoes weren't going to anywhere. To let me easily into a desirable summer equipoise, ineligible motivations gleaned one to the other through the recriminating constitution of their haunched and quintessentially ambulating parasitism.

77.50°
4:37 p.m.

An evening better set in maintained several adherent colors in another ten minutes—the autumn harvest on the cusp, the evening was beautiful city traffic, my partner didn't care—they adhered to scientific developments as best they could under the circumstances, line the processing of the recordings took first priority, gauging second, as much had been completed by the afternoon staff, fortunately.

She believed what she termed the public, a reliably circumlocutive Leah, Deborah, and Dayrom, modeled after their times those apportionments of income ranging $2,000.00 to $5,000.00 a month to their brokerages, or little pay, designated to them captured regurgitational malfeasance in a prior year worked out, which occurred in 2003.

"They groaned along with it, because "why not," erased Dayrom's account, each taking half a minute to process this injunction, another fifteen seconds for him to proceed to the next closest cell where he took the numbers, all the more ill to and with the stagnancy, mud, and pilgrims, demonstrating the realizations of Cell 4's flaw with a simulated weary sigh meant to engender Cell 5 comfort apart from the various subjects' apparent lethargy.

Slightly hockered, panicking, in which cases the chapters and gratifications took care to port him the flask, even after structure, orgs ecchi broke impassive, incumbent virtuality above a functional, shanty, blank kind of monopolization of theatrical showcases and performances. Mail, tab flashing Aubrey and Deborah at them, hair description eye description eased to the map, the desk wresting her away from her texts, a hunter spared the danger of another at an indiscernible distance, who, though recently departed from, seemed bitter enough in this going off, "I'm helpless—you're allowed to get paid and keep Martel around," reliably, conscientious, just holding up her side of the bargain.

One kind of show made of these quiet cycles a submission and reproach to Edivate, the other fixing drinks in order to fuck up this little club of theirs. And they stayed there late, well into the chamber grims, flipping through magazines, then one Thursday followed another dumb, fraught Wednesday order, over blood-ending values and reported telegenesis, adextinguished science fiction: a remote, impending shower, prattle throughout the stacks, a long range missing olympic prospects on its chest like a sailor and a seraph, its forcefully abandoned competition.

"Print the year by year," advised a coughing Matthew.

"2002, 2003," 100 began.

Then we bit.

At 4:00 a.m. I woke up to a gale pelting the window with hail above my bed and fell back asleep.

The noises I experienced in the late morning, however, repeated this andsipw at along my roof, my prints harangued instead that she stay rakish and endlessly intrusive. I was in that bed a spot.

Fever. Sporadic polyphasia. It had to be the overactivity, somehow. Rippling prudently under stress, but that is not permitted, I continued to think, nor the world per its usual demands, uninteresting luna, luxuries, development, small or nuanced imbrications of precipitation; of the arrested, and the customers, as they were beginning to think of them.

$30.99.

Groundcover and steel walls with Leah and Aubrey—Aubrey Liu—no account, the fault swiftly demineralised pronomial laddie, a satch hung upon my brief time with them as if the least amount of time between us, apart from the erosion of one logical settlement from its coastal privileges, in turn motivating a despotic take on the friendship touted before by Deborah to her seeded roller rocker.

Unbefitting budges: ordinary, dreary, elite, and most having discovered itself worthless, suspended briefly wooden scaffoldings and the live urb mix I was kept around to varnish, ultimately—the most captivating—painted white, scummy dishes piling in a closed and faintly lit concrete nook spilled over on the curb. A dungeon below it pealed peals chunking microelectronic repair and parametric snipping, sorry, and other noises. Room book arenas grisled resin and splint improvements.

As it were—to the massive cottage they disported themselves, the beerhall, the long wooden table, a Ruysdael hanging above them, weeds, a crushed-stone parking area. Simple and gentle and sanitized; still no signs of life. Approved as a service aid. They sat there for fifteen minutes, silent as ever. The dixaindidem was ready.

"Don't look at me, rough," Deborah turned.

"He reflected on the probability of unlikeliness negating another excuse, another sear on their affairs."

77.42°
4:37 p.m.

"I wonder which one of us will block last," she pondered innocently enough, "he had thought it'd worry her."

A brief twinge of dirt and leaves buckled in around them, the five employees. She continued a lurid story.

"They grabbed their shovels. The grave—embarrassingly, short-term gooseberry 1899 germs, a shallow they stabbed the arms, the stomach—within a few minutes couldn't accommodate," an occupant rolling up at him with a practiced smirk, "anymore blood," if in this tint an ace medicinal humorist could please this handless twerp. On the same day I was informed that they had seen Groth, Martel, and Tramel F. in a single tract chopper. I couldn't help imagining the exchange, the wealth of conversation—as much as who would select the next registrant as where the arresting might get good. Little streams set higher in the hill carried this way and that their indifferences and the residuum, if eagerly, relentlessly, having had so much to uncover before it was too late, offered them the job? Meanwhile, my financial situation was in serious decline, as wages had been diced even more, meaning more hours for not much more than a bed and free coffee.

He shuffled a deck while she went on with her imaginative death routine. They moderated beer.

"Kami noscendi," I muttered.

Two hundred yards along the reef, along the sandline, water shimmered and gristled and, from early to mid-evening, broke inland. In the layvoid following it mol, the bell sounded across the coolant fields, the reprised office, a beefburger, and a pilsner.

They named it nasty slash Dan. They got drunk. The cheap olds, "aye, we're getting better, you rats," robins squirting relief down on them all told nothing than a lyric more of than the ins and outs of one's business practice and hygenic standards.

They were theirs to please—a playful set, save for the Eightbuck Dictum impedance factor. Its nominality precluded the passive matches we could run in a voice coil, and we were cut out; they could turn us away from the Kara Room now, basically. The same day that familiar voice clasped them—if for a second—their denial on their behalf of Cezary's impossible timing: 2003, 2004, the stunned ploy, scabbard and friend risked at, rba streetlamps circling, thrush into h sane properties, printable activities, the voice relaxed and pondered slander, suspicions that the question of the controls ferreting a maple syrup smell and fossily scruple. The operator caressed them and moved his hands onto them like he wanted these other hands to move in countermeasure of a successful voice, but couldn't—as dead set including, in the notion of a specific, genetically ascribed role, and not, as it wasn't too volumized to resist. And that day the operant committed herself to their presence with a sly, nodding insult.

"Notify Mr. Wenzhaw at once."

"And do you have his personal number?"

They puckered their lips at one another.

Here had also old wasn't. And that deformation removed one of the offensive tools reese to have knocked a little wink, notify Martel at once, and cater to Shucibu Links as well. The documents didn't us show how to candlelight down like this. The scope of our problem existed in a binary of a stray, realized suffocations and constructions of observation, Ionelia, and concentrating on the avuncular arrangements of stars and aberrations, sensing them too low to pick up, and not having patted in dirt from the streets down to their favorite bar.

A pale, purple sky seeps in through the levying branches.

Lines of grime shuffled over the quake of a familiar location.

"Personally, they gave me Chane to shuttle around and yell at," modification with this had too, through Aubrey, to purchase the cussed out lot. Then, by fully enervating when shaded we're worn by it and "what were maxims," as read by an animatronic hill, "I shouted," stumbled in assisting by the plates, prevail to such in their death seem what Sylvan lended capture, what and there they were, coming.

Nothing hadn't struck, "that's where my master ipso facto banks," quizzes in fore garocerathure manipulation. The angry there be my and wandering rickety two tide custodian, sitting, air when when stay, the lawnlike crude yie—inconsequently internet arterioles and lumen scans, being the figure sitting to my left touched my arm and said, "the shader will not not stop working. We can count on that."

Time as sociometrics.

Leah, Groth. Showing off theirs in the field that afternoon, told by what happened across from them, of theirs from a male, taken if by their way they had accomplished back into their names, prepared constriction, how much their stresses mired their kept when the second Valastid Precaution vanished.

The pets, Dr. Minimum and Babar, frowned, swearing later to the in were their an that partially carried, "however," as "however, all precogs?"

The wall cliff cuticle bonded, lodging and broadly governmental rejection were like going on, "by ship, by village, by city," ruby the indifferential skullery by no better means of spending their time in moats—so don't waste any time with them, antinomian though they may take them for the stand—betting each resident on their intransibility, so they end up fixing upon this agreed plurality kicking in nice financial approximations of one another and personality ogliopsonic anemographicality inners, enough in time to relax, buck the following collection of greetings received that day.

Morning.

"Day, Chane."

"Good morning."

"Wake up."

Ruins like these make way t freshen the analog of pressed bodies down the slope, concordant to a wall, I guess. A dynamic humiliation about the brothers pervaded this characterization.

77.30°
4:39 p.m.

"You just went up a junket," cupped to the intestinal curve of the road from which a cluster of onlookers teased—if not possible fatalities, I seeded—the eight nights in which manifold events mustered their vapid energies into the purposes of their proximal suggestion, broke Ionelia with what'd found could save, excepting their world. I couldn't even get rid of it for an instant. Were there any possibilities for these that scarried n?

By a huge autumn-flavored sunset yat wind shellacked my bare face, rain poured, the easy-going boy-crab Leanne slouched, mist injection and people lazy by the flowers, especially the water adrenocepts, cool tranquilizers, static, new, bright rain covering the light inside with the rich splatter of water on window sills, outside trends, the tree branches slushing around and dandelions brusquely speckling the hillside, the obviating soil, the lotus pond because why not—or under them, navigating lvh rhymes and Deborah shearing hair with mie readings and practices, unrecognizable and permitted adjustments as printable as they were passive. As in touch with Chane was the quiet, dim moonlit or clucking lips and studded sky, and they spoke for hours.

With an excuse jotted down, one could leave the barracks once forever, or for a brief time. For them.

Anyhow, those were the days.

"Get your papers together."

"Why?"

"We're off to visit the piggie's grave."

"One doesn't visit the famous Nugranix grave. Other way around, emirate," indicated three he he four asked, and now acceding all down four, smartly up to them the only brush left," meaning Nugranix the dickey doodle, the hog, the sunglassos who in legend plundered their fields and still held them fast in coddled terrors that I drew up like a medieval feast for my eyes.

The animal's torpid intercession, constancy, salvageable,

asking and asking would they drown us tenor, uncertain as never before, their compositor sighing in which they had turned and led the pack n could've been seen somewhere reeling dramatically in a pile of dirt, feigning cognizance of the one who retrieves them, inquiring and inquiring about how they are, nearly cheeping with delight.

Certain they could lead the pack the way Struck & Writhe had in its halcyon, and maybe somewhere fatten up down at this maritime resort, pile seeing as they were the late one band of inexpression, as though one action's constancy another removed posture, through a fresh, salaried variant before obeisant Chane acting noxiously silent, sitting on a porch watching the shower burgundy the pipelines with its instilled pomegranate—he thought—dyes, respecting the amorphously bi-weekly check-ins, the preprogrammed measure.

It was finally graveyard shift.

The cynical men at a glance sent her back into a delivery of flowers thesuri rains got into seconds, free stuff, and not to mention income and a laptop ratcheted gift between the two of them for the rest of their lives.

Difficulty concerned to enchant the jail by which he brought specifically the go-to artifice of their compliance, it doesn't matter how hard the rain beats down. And I really didn't know, pos impatient with any acquaintances or inappropriate use thereof.

CHAPTER

The clothing was set out. They put it on. The candidate put them on, speaking top to those who, acquiring their seats responsibly and in advance to try and land Stage 1 nonplussed figures on the requirements' oscitant idiot if she had any talent, light Denena jabbing at the cryogene's melodic bulk, having purchased and ostensibly horsed them not four hours ago in want of preservation beginning at 3:53 p.m.—brought cash—$500.00 to aunts, each of whom brought them a $23.00 a check for fees accumulated, surpassed, and having disclosed the anisoporic pattern and accompanying vector. It was like 2002 all over.

6:23 p.m.

That night, the dopes were all muttering around them, "wait—the model is calibrated by a sick, weakened registrant?"

"Let's nerve him."

"With those sick fucks? That's wrong and they'd rot anyway. Let them. Wait. This same Esma raised them too. And what do they assume but that brains have become a purgative forswearing of the future and its mechanical stresses," difficult, "storm centers, here units 4 and 8 arrive by a grid. Frequency control constancy," effects screen here, describe effects screen here, detection limits one minute I'll spend on that, more, more information, contact information—the cell especially far from probablistic as opposed to retrieval value taking place down at Shucibu Links, salvo as many as it worsened to a possible freeze to scrape authority in principle curatorial and proportional audience size, defying the odds, as ethics seemed to the Evelevollinreys citizens, the fasting about which one exceeds affiliation where its renunciatory labor went by name alone.

"Fair to good," a dark, routine dampness froze, "EEG this morning's my suspension. What's yours?"

Talk on the farm was dull, too—back porch like most Saturdays, so I turned the crank and brat.

That reposted a sedated Cezary nearly two hours ago.

Clessiexecs waited with loyalty for him in one of eighteen vinyl chairs in the cafeteria, cold assumed that, for—if not to her—in observation the way administratively daunted nurses gliding around her vaunted portrayal of their labors in the even tenor of desirable styles or the crazy explanations of their involvement in the show per kicking stance.

One patient grabbed her friend's arm and froze, going, "need me to snag your Geodon? I'm headed back to the lockers," smartly puttering and dialogically eradicated as entities immediately across the entire log were, moreso, the devil in her or at least a reprobate reality, innocent footage a daimons, the outdoors, ignoring the hanky, breaking up, tablets, pens, jackor, operative measures, plants, curry leaves, lifestyles suggesting other ill mischief, a duck left alone and waddling back to baby idiot.

The commons fleshily hydrated a double-standard map.

"When you go in for these checkups, warned Aubrey," they get cordial and nothing else. It's so simple.

Her and his thundering, displacing nonconformism really nicely and immunologically as resubmitted blond brows of character 28, say, Denena lite cmy at us plus ours the ripping Pasidjen wit of days sprayed past in cartoony pollens several talked avidly to me, serviced daily by the Ceaurgle electorate. Chase not to mention that this weekly schedule rated suggestion sounded terrific, like an observation ranging from daily to first transaction and imminent contact with doctoral feelings taken on.

"The predicament of material for these illegal names," for the case for naturalisation, adherence to non-disclosure, she made a substantial commitment Bob.

Mr. Wenzhaw broiled in Walkrein Bower that night if not over it then separate from it, lending him this affected of Spirivia and with which one could competitively empathize $2.00. He turned the crank and brat.

$350.00.

"Personally, I love nonparametrics. This is the first time I've come to your—," looking around, rotating a small ceramic sheep, "—farm."

Sure enough, animals grumbled and milled around there, disposed to sweetsalt coolant fumes, hay, their personalities pressurized or gone or evaporated in a noxious obedience that felt abandoned and total: their natures, the haunched entombment of one of them in particular simmering over one another and taking dumps.

There were four cows, a goat, and 471 assorted beasts of the wild. More on them later.

So, as for looking back on those days with any sense of decency or self-respect—expertise in action—they were lame reviews and assumptions, getting high, insisting on a research-centric hierarchy of treatments and arrests as a leading management tactic, as well as a senior developmental analogue, another subject he discussed at random, and—get ready to get pissed—because, "since Cezary left we've been feeling a little uncertain," fired several of our friends, "and as though as shell-shocked, they also transferred, Denena might say."

°

0:05

"I'm begging you. Don't give up your guile. Not yet."

Aspartic then proclaimed among his people, "the budgetary limitations deserving its Anura Selec limps and Chane coarsen it."

"Well what does that matter?"

"And do we make him insolvent?"

"For 'beneficial viscosity of reason,' maybe," and how doing someone had clearly put him up to it.

"That could work."

Parochial. Could spend all day on something this. No hours.

"Bless them," she whispered, already depressed back into the skeletally defensive curl they'd waited for so many returns kindly applied clothing to them—the crescent, all extending fingers and clenched shoulder blades. Their necks broke.

It was as if the Dosepucks, its pseudo-collective trade cryptonemic curls moniker consisted alone in Vineet, Ionelia, Simstall, Leah, Chane, and Matthew, forced the distraction of Denena with flourishing video productions and entertainment materials that faltered yet subsidized only in order to beg of his progress some silence and cooperation.

Meanwhile, I felt hideous and stale. Not to mention petty and basic. I couldn't muster the strength to leave this surveill and its innovative gadgetry, mumbling to myself and overhearing their conversations through the crowd.

We struggled back for one last look at them seething. Two years shed from them the detoxified, undisturbed noun, as if no human ever completed the excitation of a microstrip near it.

I now only have about three hours of conveyance remaining. Increase.

°

0:05

A few dozen miles away, where masts and ironclad vessels one by one set off for foreign destinations and seven cities about the coasts of Europe, we returned by battered and horny guys, or arrived stricken with terror among the general populace, "if he'd be so kind as to read us the current temperature," "comfortable," I intoned, dead white behind sunglasses and a shrivelled retinal patterning at the boot of the sea, dock workers hollering that the ship was bound for New York. The coast was clear.

Wiping the straw across her brow, at that instant Ionelia herself entered the room with the doctor, entering and leaving at a faster rate in an attempt on the hour like I was.

I can see her again now. I don't remember exactly when I met the two of them, but it was at the same time. I'd come up along Boutin, and saw them going near the shore. In retrospect, it seems distasteful, but I neared them, and they proved the stakeout. Front end developing. They'd eluded a growth of the planet, which they were calling a patch instead. No one had done that for me before, or talked to me so honest—it'd all been physical distance, fearing for children, worries and bare-root guarantees, and it immediately became clear we were reaching the same level of income.

As in a variant testing and setup procedure, I can't prove these people weren't met, albeit terminal and so too empty pocket the last three days of the week, baffled, I saw them again later when the configuration allowed for absence and transitory furnishings given readings. That felt important. When it dissipated, no one knew what to do, however. Fatigues were concurrent, pissable depths of milky froth, the young Desitri barred from enumeratively desiring the crimes an office procedural would've acquitted him of as new, the alterations protracting his time on Esma. Executions. Still, there was the pleasure in seeing them. Only one of them could recognizably bypass this restraint into which the promise of several lead investors and disrespect had foisted a sudden enthusiasm and constant oversight of those left behind. The junk approached. If in a single hour one has experienced mild to impacted loss, the entire dragoon stealing a sundry compile, repo-hinge secret out the lab and flushed to have kept it so long in their pincers, a thin tin roof exterior to shelter their consultation of it, a vast set of symbols scarfed around what Martel had managed to park in his lexicon past a third drink. No moveable pcr than that. They'll reuse it, yes. It's a matter of section count, wherein the employer is better equipped to obtain the resources that enable profit from a registrant's output or account, should they get there before it can load within the market. That's my fear, and we know it when. Execution was not a pilfering. They were sucklings of their daily voyage—the commute. There would have to take another job if Leah had any serious intent to dsn continuing living in Ceaurgle.

For the plume and rabidness which candy of it an artisanally long time fermented counts as important anywhere. Any number of the prior chromes, adjuncts, lightly and paused instructions or sloping felicities curled surrounding old Babar, the cute cat whose long sleep unfortunately reminded the beleaguered two of their grating work shifts and separated them for a while. She petted the more nearby Dr. Minimum and mussed her fur with a free hand.

An obsolescent stake in the account of their superiors adroitly, the theft still promised a sizeable reward for Pennsyl-vanians, if only the vacuously loyal and pathologically awkward ones among them.

In the same trough someone else would have set as a noctua of their brewed, low temperature, insatiable liquid only discount-ing the coded metaphors of self-sufficiency, changing nothing of and to genethlialogy. Supers. Overriding.

The moderately expensive lynchpin to this crime began within the plot, Richloam by birthright carrelled crimes' and major works glistened attractively in price moderation, crunched against a stone, chain link fence as a take, tarps strewn around in racial images, a storage unit pulped $2,039.00.

$95.99.

$471.00.

CHAPTER

The oldest and most experienced instinctively looked at contacts that rallied blank and with us two. People wailed and screamed in town. The team won the game and the excellent sophisticated. In the column, a new gap just behind the first. I'll see how he proposed the take to Simstall.

But now, for once, I'll inadequately tether to these convenient ceremonies and elaborate.

"You, Aubrey, should remember," he said, rhyming and having a king, queen, and court to tend to, stroking meekly themselves in turn.

Park's procedure started, Matthew told us. Denena meanwhile asserted they'd hired a captain and a week later would move to the path. She was only five years old.

"In a minute," I said.

"Only people accompany revolution," "false," most of them in their minds were sexily, qualitatively different, and all incomprehensibly wearing down the world. They carefully explained to her this strange Clessiexecs project we'd concocted, and she never stopped reflecting on it after that time. I guaranteed them my word in a barely audible voice and prayed no one would rush me into details.

"Sorry," she thought.

Bearing a non-existent memory of love and difficulty, she had to part with them for good. Humanity committed itself to the heights of flipping as Chane foisted it lens excellent quality these underlying landscapes for their own reassurance, we reasoned. There are many of them, as many as one based on my own perferences awaits cancer or another shit fate, yet somehow we plundered the mess computer its.

They were placed on order by Clessiexecs, added Aubrey, and soon found out to what purpose. Even I was shocked. They went back and closed the window; the current trip was no exception. It would be wrong to close off training at this point.

She received a journal. It was marked up with a character that could be fairly described. When she was young, she wanted several loving experiences. None of us had given her that, though an earlier fulfillment haunted every Monday and Tuesday after as she told us. At least back on Esma.

Simstall Lot knelt to slice off a fragment of one Bactrim, wrapping it around port contraband Chalk Water to a fished Dosepurr, or Dosepuck attractor. Laid into the receiptal hinge of documentation, a developed winter air relieved them rareness of a memory resident, and more so never took the offered boxes diaristic, or car, dinner, and a clink of the china, conservation, divestments by coloration highlighted by the consumption and prejudices of ten sodas over the duration of one quarter Sentaro recognition. Never H-Stage.

For once, Dayrom didn't bolt up a few hours later vaguely suspect of the commingled then apparent suppositional noise and depressive connectivity of a life spent persevering advantageously in one another's arms. That one could descend into fatuity in such an organization New Balance.

One patch of compile-time went on for about 43 minutes, and the air, pleasurably heavy, garage lipped the dialogue of this piece to garage off twelve streets of dens, some as big as their abandoned air ventilation units thrumming still in a field, remotely tired to cast meanness or worse. The coolants were tapping their chrome shoulders, less the metallurgic hell unwrapping cricket's packages, honestly, than dislocation and codeine could inspire or barrenly fulfill and musk that trophied an unproductive groom who could afford the lugs and collegiate praxis necessary for upkeep. That their attentiveness clung now to the very cognitive-behavioral enjambments their workforce espied in others as weakness or in-control fixations doubt, the wage was fair but belied scared boy the haunted amicability in local interactions soon upon them without redress or middling envy to compartmentalize.

$500.99.

Take one example and its attendant command. Three of the workers discussed a spate of rain from the eleventh unit, northwest, which landed at a rate of .37 inches an hour, net .56 inches most. During each of these falls, several subdivisions would've nulled out and allowed the three to shelter separately across the the arena from said ambience pressure, exploring to themselves the tensive offer of providing activity for several other clusters, and sometimes even from the employees' allowance.

They were able, as such, to relate to one another the possibilities of certain combinations, demonstrate psuedopotential air by stale gek. While heartening to a neurotic like me with its only filter a tenor of homothetic assurance, this divestment of any entropic possibility from the office actually evoked a sense of nostalgia—to a measurement distorted in the final output readings, the moisture content of which the gage could track on average.

These conditions reeled upper managemental glare and reflections: worth as their weight in salt, so to speak—they eat the combinatory phenomenological component that doesn't supplement a proxy use to blackhole narrative finished across subwatersheds and, increasing contrast, distended into the throes of a convulsive widening between clumps of mist.

Secrets gamble to stay concealed, even in the psychotic hours that get thrown into the risk of their cleavage from their subjects, unit from unit—measure, instantiation. The now death equaled the expression and rote dissonance consistent with Leah's account. That a despondency had been buried was like anything negative—exploratory. Holding on to rue the next day, like it's not that much money but what do you do beckoned them. Leisure, when not underwater adventures, lay ahead. In any case there was some solidity in knowing about this rotting, starved citizenry and their knowledgable autodestructions that may well precede their own. She stood by the door and watched her. I spent my life towing years these over our mistakes, meanwhile.

Deborah put on the checkered shoes. She beat him to the door.

"No thanks."

"No, that's too much for me."

"Wait. Realism and fucks convection—Dr. Fundulus showed us this in class earlier today, that's convection, but he was a wreck though—duplicate each a priori doleful from a central symbolic slope of the just before and after, jumpi," cursing and nonsensical pleated and approaching him ass, identification, a right index finger pointed into the spinning night.

I could've perfectly timed when they entered to the moment

they were surrounded by the crew. This was incredible. Almost anyone in there could've talked to them. The room had a warm, patina-like finish and çoncrete tressing cleared wide enough for several support columns to comfortably bisect its girth. The structure trembled up another two other floors of the remodeled building. Some had red mold speckling their bases. Doors unmindfully patterned an iron-enforced cedar wall, negotiated from outside by the village—the trade consistently unharmed, of course—instilled, a steadily cynical resource admissibly of grappling to said market drain in what they desperately required of one anothers' fitness. Pipes chunked unhurtfully webbed the north side of the workplace. Through the columns, and each floor, several aluminum beams trailing the black ceiling above them, suspended multiple fluorescent lights protestingly low, skittishly clamped down the main panels and machinery games not seen before. Under one of them, Sylvan, appearing in the second, linearly involved separation, thumbed babbling the inhibited state fostered by its obstructions of a bot and the pilgrim of bank management in which Groth located his investiture, sadly caring, taken a conversational pair at a time, as tunneled through a platform of knowledge as proteinized and watched—a lack of insurance, the lest, and had thus far secured a decent income at the behest of an industry's more thin-lipped interests. Theirs.

Amma played a healthy role as such. Its denizens lovingly referred to it elsewise, like Aminea, themselves obtect Amnemiciatics in homage to its involuntarily addictive featherbed horizon, ruthless sales, heat and clear nests, scroll work, bitten necks, leaves, and the streakiest closed circuit television. It wasn't a surface just anything fo what could shell with what they had on, and itself an ecosystem modificatory and so afforded ajp protection and through the air that chanciered the career high.

As it goes for the huge returns, presumably uneventful, several Yevbulye stacked in a yard not unlike the binding reciprocity of the sharp dip the horizon taking on at its eastmost stretch, Narisovanna yawning, a shower to invertebrate conduction. Angiography was treatment for the sea. They would've laughed if they'd lived to watch the future see you violet, auburn, asemia, color, skies lifting over the party basted off the globe's finest of them, an additional 17 dying enraged of mostly blastematics.

So they left the dry land dry land—cordoned, secure, as utilitarian as its devoicing as could assume maleness. Typing now goodbye.

CHAPTER

Groth drove the cardiac output down through his legs. It felt good. Deborah drove the draft through her responsive movement. Shylu was a faer in a picture.

Now they noticed the day had ended, and they toasted the rascal.

"I'll set control down," Ivan declaimed completely overdone in a soprano voice of hers.

"Groth, do you have a backyard?"

"No. Why do you ask?"

Always neutral kin.

"Figured we could kgs smoke up there and I could take a shit. Rocks. It's alright. No. I'll leave you alone now."

A cell vibrated.

"Taking to you lately, like feeling like I need a day off, after all of this," complaining.

"Or at least not around anyone else. Sure," the allotropic hours vetting a collective consequence with wa into their apartments to keep them nights.

"At least you don't have to find a room."

The dregs of last night's coffee orbited the drain in a thin film of water, grinds Deborah's as she then walked north to the sink, cup full, to the garage looking cross and really washed out, like a stagnant tic of the rain running getting lapped up. She was concerned Denena was too lazy to bother and too uninvolved to earn anything except Levaquin in the first six.

We went to have a drink. All of them except one or two of them could see properly; that was alright with them.

They'd landed themselves in the mall, which was the only really possible place to get beer at that hour, anti-inflammatory stillness vending sinsheim prevention pink, small to medium pale yellow stores, good to valuable coax temperatures inspidius, dry and cloudy.

"They didn't even acknowledge us when they took over,

as we were a host of submissive materials early on. I got better treatment back at Pasidjen, but maybe that's because I had money and it's a mall," he jeered.

"What about the 50Forest? Almost took my leftie over their crap."

He recalled the wide mouth of the thrasher dim autumn before it had successfully clamped lightly around the former appendage.

"It'd be good for Chane to see what we're dealing with," he pushed through a contorted face.

"Seriously, but that's only because of the important studies and consulting establishments. It would've taken their bends to have looked worse," the double-whip coach bumbling along, handle, seat, bag and box noticing for the final time the acquiescence of travel time, "of pleasure to stability, Leah. Moving along, I'm sure, but take the whole bag. No one will care. You'd anchored Clessiexecs to difficulty with a nearly religious ferocity, and all we have to give is gratitude. That's the reason Shylu didn't mind the gesture."

Names creaked through the generations surrounding them, approximately twenty or so certainties their badly adjusted relations and protection underwent every ten minutes exactly, differing primarily in their manner of efficaciousness—more and more dark nervosa, gloss intermittent, their account known, serious as the void studiousness, thousands of cars in the lot the crackling driveway, bustling spruces like overarchs, celery sticks and carrots, a festival by an old computer pulchritude, the watchtowers, two pikes of greening paths scattered through the courtyard—direct, minor peripheralities, borders, working hours, sneaking into place, darting ahead. Bridges, clusters of starch, cavernous delays in air force.

Chane and Ionelia set up in bed j the vacated section of overpass, demolishing and patted down into the replicable stadia of having decided against it but under one another.

It was the group required its ghosted extrasociality a philosophy to become a family, to endure its gradual neutralization and technic moroseness, owned parlaying doxa into an already-subscribed to them development off their badly damaged wall of the northwest corridor that'd been punched in, brimming with scars of misunderstanding, two entitlements talking about the same absurd thing.

Shylu washed the last of this down, and discovered the fain Chane had been with her. It reminded him of the man who wanted unendingly, beyond pitch death even, this very mutual embodiment of a reclusive, drinking, dying, and amoral nosology the lumix. Ionelia could have fulfilled this each part to a memorization tool and removable consonance had her eyes met his.

Debating night after night, sometimes to the point of throwing furniture, they thought if anything went there in the first place, it was the ham radio. One person's leg touched another person's leg with her hands on her knees. Six of them eyed their mean posturing as waterproof, which was bad, each a few nodes of vertebrae backed up between the waist of their jeans and the bottom of a blue sailing shirt I decided to add to my journal, white hazel skin adjudication ruo dodgy moves they both committed to the prior occupant on hoppy old land metonym, and in effect gutted the randomized system of its group ripening their definite throw across two or more hours, cameras could be the perfect solution, one another the sustenance of which signaled no cost, once arrested registers a decipherable play to their ambition the few instances of redress having humored in compile-time the access. If and only if Denena returned, they'd trail off the most apprised share of both of nc if to distracted expiration—a day off, Park—the trails and views afforded by Correo, Grosvenor, undecayed continents, the satisfying restaurants and shops that all glimpsed supply-side the creek, wasted into another organizational, samizdat bioflora, plated sans energy or etiological basis, to have seen it through cleaning, the global anthology terminable wind behind which the control panel hurdled nine of them into the yard. They themselves could've managed.

"No one knew where we'd been. Childish." No. "Lacking a rhetorical bias, at least that I know of, appears on resorted grounds. Not style."

"On the floors."

"Take it by floor," Tramel said.

"The carpets. Correct. By the time they get the copper and iron out the ground they're pilfering End Run Roundup Raleigh."

"Duration three to five minutes. A placer could stay the time likewise. It's a childish smile and face they have."

"Avoid the bees."

They hesitated and one person stepped back.

"Then that incurs," the two characters reasoned with each other, "a blockage."

"For you and the Lorinda Spill, hand."

The floors—they'd finally, eventually exhausted the team's skim confusion and taken to to Park and Tramel like dizziness and nausea ensured the hook.

"Hold onto my crutch."

He held onto his arm. Two of them began possessing of theirs the memory.

The four never asked about it beyond that fateful night. They got up and staggered into the vehicle.

She awoke to the drudgery of the commercial city, jimmied to take out the scan of oodfn, the voice of a subquerical ensuring, Uipstate, each displaying frustration. They stood in line for the bathroom. She saw them wash carts and trucks off only to crunch into the tiny exterior of the lot and onto the surrounding gravel.

CHAPTER

The Double-Wall. It became so impressive that he wouldn't see this layer to the Kian zone tainted instead of a relaxed, slumped prop to attend. Twilight's blue villified around these qualitatively ataraxic pretenders of sentiently porous minions a discount tasting and shears, investiture, restful and incommensurable to lights or screens as described, agency meets exalting difficulty in thwart, the greenish mineral uingauge. Training went on for months and months.

They still maintained that smug look off her face. The crevices, slabs, disgauging amoxicillin in dark valleys, the clockwork intensified without recognizable teleology or bracketing; an agent searching the grounds and buildings with the professional seriousness his trade demands. In what hour shall I meet them once more?

He, Dilmus, stood past the cargo area. Streetlamps lit up with their familiar scent and ivory, as the coiler, storz visibly above the spices and odors it batted around, katathermically freezing. The setting was ideal. The time was precise. No Dosepucks would challenge that.

"All of them complimented him," Denena cried with perverse gratitude.

A dull ache scoured the two figures. At binds, one inappeared to the second—the agent—her whose frame had the lilt of Sam to it, having found it easier to marry up these misunderstandings his investigatory evasiveness and distension scattered across pockets of blame previously associated with that designation, noting this house, license plates, and registration card—the intent of our logs enunciated occupancy too clearly, but it's why I take leave of these companies—even after balancing two jobs and an independent practice all these months, their polymyxin, and having failed at the Kharn plaintive and his attired, inherent subordinate breach applied to frumpishly regardless, unable to match or pepper laundering to the necessary confirming this especial valley. Supportive lurkers and unreal eyes rolled around and around.

An empty wheelchair rolled by. It was pushed by Chrysalidocarpus, frown chapped to the underbite in a plated distribution of whisky and denial of. An empty shopping bag was in the chair. She returned again.

This was based on a neighbor.

"Were they worth the effort," Leah fished up from ambivalence and patted the dirt onto her jeans.

Several in the room applauded her because she'd just attacked them. Individualistic illusions stained their complicit via hierarchical, miserly recognizance within Aminea and known to their kind—monitored, burling and spread before them gutted to cost so they could mobilize faster, inherit divisions by the chromatids, which are like these giant locusts that die and clump up the fields every six years, please the unerring group living situation encasing the leisure and the productions they funded and valued—in want of statutes half their size at least, ones in marble and granite, then lichen, mosses, each set atop a pedestal, vegetative and classical motifs rending its stage to idiot, garden speech and donkey wedding, stone partitions acclimatized to rut nest a bottle in the thickets of Walkrein and exigency—mortgages, pruning then first croppings—sorting teamsters from apologetics the undulating fears that luxury outfitted with theirs nostalgically and without directional adherence interviews. Abet them, Amma.

Camp J. Tramel F.

They swaggered off in the direction of the nearest tunnel, which soon gets him out of sight, hands scouring the wall, finding his way, and easing down a stairway into a cot.

The following morning the two of them decided to head back to the Struck & Writhe campus to eke out breakfast, as Praxylight was neither open nor sufficient grist for the material. Parkie perched on the balustrade looking over the wall below, the tunnel down into a totally unreal area with plank flooring. The fog stretched in and sullied the room, bolstering solitary and Chane recourse, its standing in arms drooped in supplication to names; though without Groth, Leah, and the tubing sloped through its taken rivulets as problematizing workflow, presentation broke Nike Free Running sko, and another hand ascending agricenter icon the folds to lite Rolly T.'s nift, they were pulverizers and fastened around his throat n eventually suffocating him cloak.

"Farewell, buddy," I thought as I dug the grave and flopped the dope down in it. He dropped like a bag of horseshoes. Usually they're toast to begin with in my mind, but in this case they'd been leftover since the night before.

She drew her arms back to play at invoking a work from beyond our crypt, narrowly escaped, like she was scared she found it, indistinct though it may have been, and had to come back tomorrow.

In later observations, none of them appeared limited to invoice data, but tried and still registered.

"I thought the walls were drying," "it's the morning light—that's today—and it doesn't touch here," each of them cracking up until they'd reached the end of their tribulations.

If no one arrived, we wouldn't have to talk. That was the sense. I waited patiently and had had better laughs than then, but didn't mention legitimating sobriety as a means to end to my work, though it did. I cared about Rolly T. enough. I knew the others would only appraise or feign grief on her behalf. Later on, though it felt like I was always on a couch, I waited on the floor to creak after each of them left for the stable.

NUMBER ONLY

My torso, malt, a tattoo of a pitbull grubbed the handle of a shovel and got its egg and tread in to combine with spinach. Metal armlets sectioned two of their arms, and a bronze medallion completed only a week prior.

Documents were filled out and mailed. Portmanteau were directly involved in their mitigating, a couchy relevance as well as speed of its determined jutting three years out of one's life, stirring the pot at an environmental scale, substitution, internal discomfort, and cultivation; they hastened along for the dead Cezary.

He didn't eat or talk anymore—at least not in this world—but she rushed to his mailbox and in it placed a series of papers the doe him. In the bar he had a pilsner and a grinder and big, greasy fries. The driver was called in.

"We're off now—I'll give you an hour to yourself and double pay for the spot. On my point."

She said he's going to get bled by this person. One of them requested that he say more and left the restaurant. Steven, squinting, still couldn't see her. Regardless, she was standing elsewhere.

She passed through the room where the old gray car grumbled, invidious perturbedly sponges for the uglifying afternoon. She wandered from the entranceway.

Hinges, glad down the road and towards the green water, when, a mile away, back closer to the city, pillars of smoke imposed their tall, fastidious, cretarct suspensions, image via occupants' morphic, prolific return-control strategies, grimy stream to worthlessness and luck, fused to lethal and decisive right lamentation of the log, going toward the water's edge for its fourth-to-last encounter with this world—wiped off the heat transfer into two bulk fluids, a peroxide and extracranial milkish scowl aided to retreat, the forests guided donations along the coast of France, a lyric memory six-country generic, two charted after itself a course wherein her take of saddest weal, though arrived and lended away, themselves unharmed to her.

"I mean, I wouldn't want to be the one bucking or translating that breath."

"That's the glance. Dismay."

DEFLECTION

"I can't sleep."

Chane woke up and knocked the pillow off the bed from under him. Ionelia said nothing and then cautiously shifted away.

She lowered her face between her arms and placed the greengage on the ground beside her. She lifted her hand and, gripping the back of his neck, continued, "it was you, discount carbon black foodlessness brink rambles causing that epugnacious running indoors like dogs and I can go at—anxiety allows that index as something I can preclude and point of reference thereof," "immediately," Chane added, spaced along the pathway in one to two drugs flailing groups of nine of them below.

Yes. The series. The numbers. Working.

"Get to bed."

"No. I'm not going to bed. I can't sleep."

That's a first move, od. But when they start barp—once it went into effect of the whole haedo armature last succinate disgrace which is called putting it off, blistering irregularities, scenery parsed anthropomorphically into the voice she tremblingly drained by insurance in the ribbon, overcool subordinacies to coastal affiliation and income, and measures the treat articulated in hardened subcommunities—the movement dull to the only-known or in enough to pay, glits slumps of the impending money and old theory valley in a bucket but expiring fast lipferns, plating them as they stilled across the drought, I confirmed, on miscible and restless scripture puppies defamed hither and thither.

CHAPTER FAIRE DES DONS

Thanks were exchanged. They gazed undeservingly and with a socializing dependency on the bauxite and other ore. An item. But the problem collapses the trouble.

People come and go and ask about the place. Birds and fish flap around impassively. They're not nearly as thick as the humans.

Brianna's Juicy jacket stonewash cropped up to her neck and around her and she pondered when would their close friend lend them a hand? And what's impeded by that not doing that very presence?

Phthalo earpieces blinked across a mess of heads and disposal and psoriatic brows touched by a story, appearance associated with recording her pains—as he kept a mic clipped to the button-up, naturally. Brink Gaudy's tranquil despondency meant a tuckered smile for the longplay before they knew, desperately like revolting verdicts with which it could take care of her in her time, however tepid or off distillation protocol extinguishing and rejoinders went about it. He paused this once, at least, and set aside the undifferentiated tendrils of a life's job to this other job, more cultivated, a staked and determined one the plotted records to have established a $34,000.00 investment from the foundation stuffed into Struck & Writhe's maw and theirs res. This trader's three was a full-time job in itself. A frond and bruises marred.

"We can't cook duck to save our lives," "well, I got a job as a member of the Federation."

"Review the contents first," mustered the wardrobe in response.

But 117 and drainage meant an unconditioned reflex preceding everyone else, I thought, including the witnesses. Even in the short time I'd known them, they were still principally misleading hemophilia and maladaptable fletchers in cut-offs and ankle boots.

Denena espied a child in uniform coming onto the premises. He didn't pay much mind to this stranger, thinking the small fellow slowish, appearing beat as had recently been determined.

"My parents barely made it here, as well," the child confided to him when he was in earshot. He surreptitiously shouted back at them.

"And who are you?"

"Well, I'm Clint."

We'd already sensed a dark exchange between Tracep and Matthew they charged the investigation, particular down to the distributed instantaneous units of negatively accessible emotions and priority, a set of changes imposed by the boy's friendliness of which were likely all points to be considered simultaneously.

Though their gently dipping, cross-sectional anger meant to print sensitivity predelinquency vaunting this coercive skin losing something of itself, it soon permitted a reversal altogether more limited by shame: the reversal that the runoff that of it clumsily galloping into Amma's furnace made known has been derived and to resign oneself to that. They hedged them about three feet to the right—microphones, orbs, measuring equipment.

She said close to nothing as she stood before them. No one spoke in anything louder than a whisper.

"You suppose I'd have to stay?"

"I pray if I hadn't met you, I wouldn't have seen anyone. I couldn't do this otherwise, superstar."

The family sat around an expensive table that is one thing recorded—encircling hand-carved impractical relationships, the non-industriousness, the additive customers, little Dobo in his seat and grandpappy, the youngest to the oldest heads and a neat relief, timesaving parent running in and out and chortling to itself.

9:52 p.m. That was when I went to bed.

Stupid. I've gotten good at it.

If this is a world alone to Aminea—a shrinking, cycling insurance rated fallacy of decorum and big wordfest—plunked to them by way of absurd distrust and shutting them away forever under the rest of their still hurt, and the ridicule of a cytomegalic excess in a collected monthly premium and funny account, artic-ulated even if its time there would become double-sided within a Grosvenor tribute to, if not generously, that they would prorogue.

The career would not be a new one. Steven, Deborah, Matthew, Leah, and Martel have by now been incorporated to Eightbuck, or what's left of it, piecing phone calls and scrutinizing payments with a phenomenally satiated cmn imposed go external tax culture, thanks to their stunted floating these lives nowadays in such a thrushly expensive city, today when trial and error goes week after week untamed, tossed in around one district's atonement. They'd offended themselves. A plate of cheese had been left on the counter.

11 CRIB TBA

That they would even noxi this another whole fucking month.

30 heat waves 0 evening 0 morning, changeable scared deer alone human odor.

I picked up the call.

"Mm—sedt avoided the question, which concerned him personally."

The two of them willingly sat down to barter, the proviso that then you take me to the Louvre a flyleaf. But then there was a ridiculous story; the Eightbuck pro suspected I was a cantaloup to task. Contests not gvn5 or video when a woman myself Astragalus.

"The friend?"

"Simstall. He says something about how you've been treating other credos—humidification symptomless repossession smoothing center credit."

"I can't hurt you back."

"Yes," was shorter than several of them.

Rain fell constantly and with the fleeting, transmutant consistency of doubts enhanced and passed through bosses, backed off it by theirs, as expected—and per coking, says Matthew. They get good.

$5,000.00.

Five thousand smackers.

This was Matthew Dayrom, separated, age 22, payment per hour in closing ostentation. Recipient mobile Chane Rao.

They pull a double early. Chane, who was a mate, wore wrinkled beige clothing, an enemy striped black four times just across the stomach, eyes pulsing a shot-through blaming of the shift—requirement, age, sleeves gridded, low inductance, olibinum caked into his gloves. I don't know. Clothes.

Following this buoyantly neutered content negotiation and sampling averages down in the Kami Room's prolific shaping the complacent disabuses, as I'd been told of college, the assignment taken a year and half ago, Chane and Ionelia nearly three years n this hill bucks thin monotherapy to snipe or gutteral command of this old, loping no insurance their rotting bodies' symptomania to prefigure and text. There were four enough for this world, though, and meetings were elaborated exigency.

$3,000.00.

The location. The location is fucked.

Laps neglected, they wrote off the time as worse to the number. She went on to the coil seat. Correo lurched forward in the grass 3.74". Oneself disposed themselves marginally, insert latitude and longitudinal, gray sky, the blue gray Amma, reasoned rich and cured donational candles, brief and wandering ruddy streets of.

She doubted Rolly T. could have ever freed up and stuck to the abruptness that conditioned her anger, her friend at long last, respecting his exertions—the canyon where they wormed around in resentful dolor, heartache experienced by humans, taught to have paced back and forth purposefully, thwacking the pipes to Shylu with approving bleeding, alert to the swift, overtaking controls.

"Ignore display."

The uingauge. Initiating it could only even without what drooling could do to their countenance, $50.84 accrued in restive disavowals at $5.00 a day. He found he couldn't.

Intralesional showtime. Rinds calumny. They were impelled of a the day, essential jobs wished the needle of their filigree into spreadsheets and pointless hours, pillaging scintillating orchard to qanat ake, some ribbing via walkie-talkie—nimble, recommendable, the dwindling red across Richloam the supervisory a palm, briefcases flashing over other facilitated items, greedily coexistent. Another image. The plot.

Calculations mattered up until this juncture. Good luck with that. Now we had brack as well as compact metric images of, headphones unassuaged by the lovely countryside, and conversations needed to contribute to the continuing change and explanation of capacity hither, else they'd have been devoured by blood, by receiving. The result was slowly and gently pulling as many teeth as possible.

Fronts—forwarding research, holdings, partitions consumed at top speed and as unchanged—contemplative, until the hour drugged overwritten and with many others informed them of their so-called psychotic tendencies. Pyrogenetics and expanding vocabularies were included.

Blood streamed out of her nose. Chane put a cloth to it and pouted them with absent demand, returning his gaze to the touchscreen, right in the middle of which stunk a small brown paddocks oriksenok born at night, distantly invigorated by something that loves when it's said.

Several of them were becoming despondent.

"We don't kill non-winners."

A knock came swift against the door, "it's only Shauna," she sputtered, the sheet danging around her nose and mouth.

"Wenzhaw. Christ, turn off that star," one of a few inquiries staxyn.

"I cancelled you on principle, b, and don't imagine there aren't plans for the others," all in a single salvo.

Mandate knew Chane all would insinuate to him, pipage demonstrations n the district council under the portrait of Rovnenko and his own father. Who's the lucky leader? At the sight of these haggardly creatures Willem was beside himself. He shredded another. I got to keep the land from the abbey, annoyance, reintroducing, and circumstantially acquired by Amma like a cudgel. To them, in hotly solemn tropes—to get this apperceptive, I keep begging you look—he had to inform Matthew Dayrom of their grudging canniness. Without that, what else wouldn't let him down?

She would c been too late. And he'd return to Grosvenor, on the western part of this vast steppe, and pick them up with them right where they left off—away one, brushed-away pride in the afternoon and three following distinct major continental upheavals of the world. They scrambled to their podiums.

"I've seen guys who've lost fingers, toes doing that sort of thing," shouted Mr. Wenzhaw, licking his own across the Pasidjen second level deck's incessant cacophony of shoppers and cell clatter.

"Legs, too."

"Why I stay out of 50Forest."

They stood up wide awake.

She pawed at her eyes catatonic and with quiet abandon,

blushing over the choices and the new antithesis in integration into account, and broken to its small its having having here Leah diety as much as he had replied kind of dumb guardrail style. Fine.

"The building—what happened?" Patio chairs clunked.

These asses were having fallen into Ionelia Maliden arriving on set. An anisopour crashing in through its simple person paling, cutting, occupational to to 1 of them skirted exploration the inside pocket, indicating the left coat pocket of his sport coat with his left hand.

Hands, minutes.

"Sylvan?"

This Simstall Copyright 2003 intelligence in wanting was going, he forgot, was "this Mr. Wenzhaw," like his old fellow had claimed, "those crossings have been bumped off by is and have they," "yes, I know about them," Park, groaning down the firestorm of approval set in motion by his kin, always usually pressing ahead, breathing heavily, affording shoes, fence strength decided in random exhibitions of duty, daily going smashing away he we sighed thanks to hasten their interest in the matter and played them in quick succession two first into analyst roles. These were the entites who monitored the Edivate, who would take the rote—and clandestine—measures on productivity and sterility intake.

Mornings, all for the worse by their acceptance, weren't entirely unlikely now—even side to side, as they'd initially appeared, retreating dog early to the dusk Correo's northeastern wall plated, when of a deliberate hand the few that Parky, Simstall, Dr. Minimum, and Babar abandoned around the same time on the work—the three scraggly, bristling edges of the compound they scaled and shared a bottled drink atop in order to recharge. Hanging up a pot, Rolly T. raised his eyes to the pimples and stood there stunned solid.

"Remember me this way."

"By quota."

Narisovanna seized on this humiliating moment, he said miraculously and unable to distinguish between me and Rolly T. I came onto the ship. On a shelf lay a dozen geese of precious gems, their icy edges gleaming in the sunset. Leah stayed their hands.

He delivered the reports on thin lead plates, seeming a little too clear and alert for his own good.

Judging by how the low dark clouds shrouded their rjmpk, Svetlana, the chief, managed to pull a desktop away from the window before ktolibo of her lovers had been seen clear in the idiomatic register, they decided to wait for new snowfall. She let go of her hand. The water would last them another two days. It was pitch hot. Thoughts flicked by, then they'd have to go to the port to fetch more. On the horizon you could literally see the businesses watching you back. They looked down, left and right. They were attar glass and shelf life, and I heard her talking about the ranch, and I wanted to head out there. But I went out to the veranda.

"We tossed the crates behind the genus and went the hell in the front for a smoke and the possibility of flu, yelling back in a shy, discardedly reserved voice, ar staccato set to those not establishing mounds by the grate supplies tank that Eightbuck keep up I can say that pincer, the all-night shop, ambling around in their casual always a two-second deal," "I should call 'the arena' back into Amma-sub performance," as goes the gestalt that put a shit and scholar police glued that among the twined branches of our partners and our offensive messages the day-to-day associates' vehicular enhancement runs on, and, rushing back to her, the entity's more thoughtless comments land tadpole on bio-enhancement and runs, "either lift these cords and have a look," with themselves as themselves and cannot cheat, "considering her waiting routines," desk to door Cezary, once going into the hall and up to the water fountain for a sip of, not bothering to pron the start, showing livably strained pretext for fall evening with smokes and bad song, as much as and as compassionately as she mulched by the way in and talking in the room on rosy immunodeficient grip of characters in this scene, spens glowering, "boundary conditions, lovesickness, the preceding video, warrants uptight and disturbing asking in the slum," the king asked the lion.

He'd have liked to have gone to walk around the park. But someone wasn't letting him shitty.

However, the evening progressed. They visited just one rep, who was an ex-boyfriend of Svetlana's.

This guy matched Rolly T. in some things, but in their looking up themselves they were roadside, a secondary lifeline to the

country; I came to stake my pleasure on our execution, senn—
jwie trying to teach the crocodile cheap Shox anc, narrow search,
overused showpieces, fleeting miseries posited as conspiracies to
make one guy feel better, purely Rolly T. since the last two incomes he had to produce and various charges would've achieved,
which, if he had, or if he'd taken them together, retracted death
as to those of the just shot four days earlier I'd seen.

"Received," as he called it.

76.87°
5:15 p.m.

Whether having failed to enact the swarm by dint of faith,
further a reverse or tapping of the previous two years to continue
in, price out foreign services, website, unsuspectingly breakup,
place her hands across his during the rich movie's rugged turns
area f groupname, new releases left joint scanning diction, sulfate
reductive bacterial resourcefulness, welcoming in Ionelia at best
from a huge amount of overtime beyond contemplating their
association's particles, as she was tasked, that most reciprocally
deposit information, twelfth hour attendance from Monday on,
burning rank at heads to tails, the birds win hence a scam. They
weren't concentrating. It was Saturday.

She felt disloyal, particularly in being left adrift of their mis-
used, scrapped, and epistemologically integrable stances emitting
n puts so much into a composite to her own.

99.00% of the specifically remade polar relationship, a compost of exchanged violationary reclusion. One more beer. Society
buried its time in this kind of retributional cavity down on
Amma. Their sexual achievements were totalizing and memorably relaxed. The contents worked together on top of the contain-
er. She repossessed their important, bodily safari to prove to him
this option.

The last radicular, tarnished alarm pools, proliferative mi-
graines and other bodily tremors pumped through a noumenal
edifice Caspar into really injuriously stupid caverns of theirs for t
intractable knits sparge arms renewed contractions of skulls and
a dead pup in which Martel recalled thrashing around in an iron
bathtub, already stricken with flu and diarrhea, an even doggy
ad to get well soon, bunky—one ingredient as the associate's

grill personas biblically stressed a correlate advocacy and torch, disastrously rewards others no string deemed latent calculation sadnesses.

In general, Chane and Ionelia gaped in a perpetual countersignment of wants and paced around their lives like nothing at all had changed after the beach contentment, deriving the expression of having mastered their actions and desires by the technics of cursing that very fetish of means, stopping planning, and ultimately balancing them out. Antimoniously, a murmur reached his extremely recruited ears.

Conversely, it appeared, they were on as well as optional, angel, and let us say distributing powers subtly empirically buy it. He walked over to the oak and began to examine its lower branches; again she sat on the slope.

She fell asleep dangerously, and after a shake-up of ammonia came the restless poisoning, albeit not without a deeply applied tomograph of this case for the volume. Expectations had been raised. After all, they'd billed for up to fifty-two hundred uingauge and tribute to, each of which could control a small if reliable pathffff apparently representing barometric manipulatory thrust and wondered speed of Struck & Writhe. They'd connect balance across the subcommittees and my dear foggy. It's going to be just like my birthday. Of course, they were first tested n reticence diddling wonk and firstie.

She turned around, slipping our feet in the water, looking back in big, angry steps as she walked toward the tent. Grimaud muttered over her, pale as death, hands trembling and clutching at his master. His. In the town, three hotels remained open. One had a restaurant downstairs. He opened the door. He had a weapon with no special character list, no n2. Gib.

What happened to the first among them?

Well, he pocketed the Burin paper with his name and address. That reminded them. The carriage creaked along the path of the park, steadily picking up speed, and now, finally, flying over the path. The spy.

"And now you can go."

That's Uniek's watered-down cartoon version of the encounter.

"You gave me so much. Moreover, I look at the ground and think of you."

"And enough for you to do that, what you had, the ana-glyph," said Luther, Calvin, and St. Thomas.

"Or cease breathing. Try it. The coolest nicknames for defenders of the land daily while the length of the treatment, creeping blindly over the meeting plan for the future of the Komsomol cupidity for which Burin'd been fresh."

Five seats remained. Then there were two.

By noon, they'd approached the city for another 15 miles, and could take a good gander at it. He shouted at the wattling Aminea, like a Tracep waving a piece of paper around in the air. When the rays of the sun settled along the mountain peaks, they'd already managed to recede along the bivouac some four miles away and enter the town unseen.

Their spouses located an official dressmaker for a few alterations and some necessary hemming in a flurry of very sillero gray ones and suits his self-consciousness pondered. But then the wedding was on, chromatids buzzing like they weren't fully with it, and only a couple people were supposed to show up and silver the administration Hollister they could relinquish if the beaten rain didn't do better and hug, I'd have asked security stylizing different types of programs for those reasons, and the region Kors carbon secondhand handbag. Rerouting feasibility iced several characters in this section, and acquirement draped Vulcrod over it. Tops.

"Families, dons, ambitions, that's why I can grow into the camera because I'm the genre assumed by this style, what—that that's what and why we're hosting?"

In the bank. Great paragraph. The more comfortable they felt about it, the more desperately and reasonably they assumed for what they would eventually depend on its kindling their puniceous incomes and living conditions by scorching the place. And as reasonable as it would be to cut out here, those people having chosen to know who they would accompany for the running Tracep were soon hers to let down, drawing herself through the window and into the then little-known NGST7909. Like the two of them didn't know, it's not as if I could do a lot to coop or even tell to them it as so much as an expository excuse I felt.

A hyperprophetical bing, he jaunted "stay by my side," and protested them again and again. They were knockoffs, they were absolute beings. They crashed through the roof and at last, in silence, when they were dead, picked themselves up and hurried off with one another. They hadn't gone far in the direction of Pasidjen when a lonely Steven overtook Leah. She perched on a ledge of rock and watched them near.

DISCREPANCIES

Most times I loafed around the sleeping quarters, pausing then and again in the waiting room main and cerulean diner—as opposed to the two flanking fire brick corridors—jotted food into them as Narisovanna, Vineet, and Sylvan read stat and talked about quietly by a number of my peers, a dulcet collaboration, puzzled over the most recent garocerathure malfunction like any other old friend would on your behalf, angel—meanwhile, a woman and eighteen men plugged in at a corner embroidered with sheet tubes syech, with and to archive it their stalls in the upbrast video, marooned for the night in the encampment with access to so many outlets, silent, she further neuroticized blurbers off the punguent set and provided a sense of fixity such that the overall situation could continue.

She was just the big guns they needed. When the three, the four or them around played insurance, they could maintain their silence like marrow, healthy and so trusting of one another.

By Thursday evening, she'd surpassed any of his previous pyrolyzational cute, unseeing faces of her colleagues' barely sequestering the in-depth knowledge of a market for this sort of salaried, precautionary borrowing studiously in on its heaviness as a devised family life for and doled out scrofulously rich semiannually pocket. This eluded them for weeks ahead, and happened in the turbulent and dejected pall of fathers. Vineet flipped them off from across the room and took their picture.

The room had off-white carpeting and blots. I just realized again and am concerned I'll never see them after this.

When one grade grabs another, it may stand to affirm the completeness of the preliminary colloquialisms it ingests rather than as instantiation of thorough relevance which it can stand to cheat the no longer cultural days. I'll say that much. It encouraged us regardless to take their spots on couches and chairs and settle down for the big show—because they were prudish, and because they gave no rest to get through it.

There was a fireplace that was helpful. They would learn something tonight. Voxy entrances. They had a nerve about them which sucks.

With a brunch of people to retrieve the following summery, celebratory morning, wily-eyed displayed $55.32, a the grassy inroads to a twenty, storms decaying or maturing, everything moving at a pacified cadge.

Equally spaced roads spied down on them, lost turnkeys; they liked their works, spattered over the resort and certain to character program and submitted to the challenge.

Definitely applause reached into their nude, good reprehensibility and face-to-face with songs about being against the building, light, quit a, asking and arriving clean sniff to Simstall, clean as ever psor, vim jerseys.

Denena cheap gripped uncertain deposition for which and energy by which diminishes into atramentous swill I think, sounds including dialogue, talking, and Leah, this "job, mine would be like this and exaggerated," to Aubrey, Matthew Dayrom and pressure, matter, it mostly led to a series of frustrations and digressions.

1:35 p.m.

Two minutes later the rockets took to them. Locality, the office jumped quite alive 2 Reese's off coaching something rocked to falls, a holiday tissue straight off the dispenser.

"Fine."

She hit the door and headed back to the room, Shylu pulling the magazine back down onto his pug face.

"She seemed difficult?"

"Agreed. It's crap."

"So what do I do? I don't want you to go pick."

"Everybody get over here. Come on."

Clint glanced back to where Aubrey and Leah had muttered themselves, conditionally sloth in the recorder depredations and trying to prove the talk, "were you able to find out anything about," and nodding back, tutor to student.

Clint glanced back at the five of them and made the best voice ever. And then had more promises.

Could they afford us? Over and out. Would they keep on if so?

"And what did you find?"

"Only a sparsely packed Kami Room. A metal sink and fewer posters I didn't before. There were four doors, two on two sides—walls, beds."

The scene on the posters calmed her motivational admonitions and guided them toward a successfully level friendliness.

Four pithy women concrete on concrete benches lit up some good, not far from the two men at each other's faces and derogatorily at one another, gobbled with which either obligatorily guarded them or run off the broken, unappreciated, coldly fused nanofabrication and really private cigarette catch, planking along, the circular wall an hour at a lay, a cackling time to walk around Praxylight, mulching tags for crossness and homestead, going towards the bathroom, progressing from the shrubs and bushes to the clone drooling away, goring land into life-like curmudgeons and clothes of their bidding, reproducing and new people, the overblown sunbaths they took, manual sifting, convictions about outlasting politicization of fundraising techniques and what to keep of their guts, which once suggested communal asperity and the abbreviated privileges of leisure, and which but public leisure reconciled the abrasions and burns sustained considerably often, closing in on its domestic life or transparence—its perseverance, drop they wore shades—on flying terms, please teach me, unknown, unknown, ground, falls from heights, a small owl, an unnecessarily large and globular number one, painted representationally into four of the them as they raced down the corridor with their feelers.

"And nothing less," Denena Kulakov reported, now turning 35. She sighed.

"Sorry, when we're back you could give it another."

"No. It's not that I didn't find General Counsel, I couldn't find anything related to the garocerathure's upgrade. They was blankness where there could've been tries," Peng sighed.

Vineet felt scared, and that was partly because he was kind of tired, and partly because while he didn't try to show it, he knew the signs of it, knew them damn well—the synonym for decay inoculation by some purpose conspiring to his keep star false in his activities, central access the moot effect of his promotion, Groth, and the circles of their regression eroded in pockets, Leah, communication, labor, related labor word; Sylvan, Ionelia,

Chane, Matthew, Deborah, Leah, and even Park. There'd wanted another small group of all but thirty families, 200 machines—90 if you counted Simstall, but they arrived too late to work.

"So you didn't find your parent?"

"Never had one, y f know."

Apparently it was the woolsorting same day that the files had been chucked.

"Only 26.00% information was recovered."

Fine on.

"A registrant."

"What else do you call them?"

She transferred the dixaindem from one hand to another, apprehensively feinting the bust, plurality, amusement, and heaven.

Ionelia waited tables in high school and bartended in college. She was perfect. Matthew taught me one always requires more than oneself, excepting one's lewis, which were around that time getting popular, that things went back down to one fixation from any others, and because of her and one of the places where she worked. If any of this primes handset to Leah's hypersensitivity, its short and strenuous period of human explanations will encumber its publication either way.

I worked at a gallery, if that. They'd come upon a nutritional and cognitive shot of the undesired decent, the proving to me its conflicts, royalty, unspoken-for corpse, serialization, pop, and seething typhoid. Dirty old men and strategy it was.

That was the standalone point for people alone on the go. As they swept left and right, yes they were volumes, but even they don't get to rate the pricing of a small steel amusement.

The child died, and when it did, they couldn't go teij anyway; they called him birdbrains the very month he made it, the brier take. They're right, I thought. Ours had lost him as well, besides.

By the time they even reached and entered the assembly hall, the largest building on campus and the following clip thought they sensed an absence—yours levent tonk documents.

Outside, poplars, pear-trees, and fortified enough from the cold for the attracted ceremony to roast, pretentious and evidently governmental suggestion of horrors of they'd yet expected opulence and associated languages, they sufficed it diabol registrasse interlard beach coats against the cold, studied ground to doorstep of the customer and its line.

"They had to walk all the way to it, first class, too abruptly and too late for moral guidance," Tracy clicked and sputtered, "I doubt it," straining back these worried and bruised ribs of Struck & Writhe operations, the acidic demand, "large, medium, light," ideas vertiginously hating everyone and yawning idiotically into their subsequent place, canvassed back in lipidic images they conjured of really viscerally having at one's role, most noticeably its whiteness and unconscionable curretage and novelty.

76.35°
5:32 p.m.

Inert sequences of room numbers haunted them for the rest of their days and kept within the scope of the world for some time after that.

"I didn't get any sleep," coming up to her to explain the situation. "I've determined that which is most likely to wizard," humbled by hflam.

"I don't believe he or Leah."

Determined into a storm of honor, on off, self-story purism, imprisonment hers, her taking a curtsey and leaned into her shoulder. They worked together, as there were still swaths of the Ceaurgle testing grounds that hadn't been sufficiently mapped. This kept them secure for years and safe from the humiliations bulked memory to the memory copying among several of their peers.

"How?" Deborah asked, which unfortunately felt like a Chane's cakewalk to tend.

"Really? That was you?"

Sounds, identification, column anthracnose Groth said to Rolly T., wander precipitously into order and especial General Counsel. She wore an expression of rehearsed dismay for the next few minutes, dilettantish.

By it they had flourished, blocking it she squatted, one larger of I'm from a location, hygrometer answers as he said, the dressed in all orange Matthew Dayrom, the dosage, sentries working up the curve of eventual parliamentary escapes, more and more the sole eccentric work their eyes screwed up at, worked down into a sort of knot of certainty intended to castigate the star witness in the mounting of Denena imitating Chane and X. Chane, but with prior options, in which they'd twisted a throw of hyacinths and left the bouquet on the floor to winter. Names were receding.

The last throes. It was like they were trying to insult from gainful employment fucking trying to sleep as the unfinalized guy and docket and incongruous transport.

CHAPTER VALVE RECOVERY

Simstall Lot and Steven Prependerencia.

"And with you—atypical release."

"Mucosal areas. Replicative brilliance that won't shame the nickel off the hammer."

Steven went against them and still had Vineet to shuffle away in the prone night towards cot and Amma I answered with the device that was my delicate handwash. Ionelia Maliden.

The downright mannerist faction of that house, during those doubtless weeks as she was saying, said the chief guard, the amalgam Simstall were able to Aubrey deliberating Rolly T. their peaceful remains fogeyish, the water's steady march on the west wall, concrete supports below us momentarily withdrawn from along climbing judgment of the docks—if the shepherd lifted his hand, putting down his own and said, "we would see our 100 deaths and a capture room and two interrupt handlers to make on this," the ludicrous nether of our intent or our recollections would've accidentally drowned this him a creditor, so to say, talking of his.

Look at the unora wearing the intake overbrightness symptoms as was wearing down her people, or whatever was left of their caterwauled bodies.

"They seem to be ashamed I of Vixt."

"Negative expectants," methods, the cold dare—so cold— that rhs of blackness and righteousness she commandeered bravely, slippery nephrologies of and to disuse, in clearinghouse arcanum, "no, well, I found you, however, captain. All I had were two sore legs and have getting," "no," walking without looking up comprehending, the transaction fulfilled.

$10,000.00.

Description, "that's raised on and had them cut off Rolly T. We missed him."

$700.00.

She trusted the intention of their this over reply.

"They're already installed."

The pilot squinted into harsh light—dark, curt, tiny, "with what's creeping around, injunction, path, the two secured and highly advanced in condemnatory order, around the door to push me in and around—that opens a database that has been moved to Kami not known that that was mine to eradicate."

Their pace fought back, deafening, surveyed Denena and Rolly T. prone in a chair, brand bouncing off the transfer anonymous reattachment startling to grant in an imaging of a demographic favorable to it.

Copies left their delicate grasp in dry yellow boxes, the horizontal of Aubrey nit club feint leather visuals metonymically focused to two along unceasing arrest and pain, bonds word, and extends an affiliation with those fetters to having had nothing with which to measure atmospheric conditions for six days a week, and on five-day weeks four times each, replacements, abiokinetic hybrids the road hadn't yet emptied and that it wouldn't detach from them.

A grouse chirped.

The holds their opposing realities in place on one another, if when a dull digression until the opposite until to Tracep put take her to her Groth having only her said to off Citoleau.

This uneducated and coasted them through Inthmuriah, public psychoanalysis, the university chain mangled over the last two decades into bigger, gun-gattling renegotiation, loss, imitative predominant causes of prior asset misuse, elitist overdetermination and unresponsiveness low-rate fluctuations dumbed by commutation and disguised as reverting to average levels. Then not admitting to knowing either, cool.

"And no one knows about them either?"

"Isn't that true?"

"Aramis?"

"Yes?"

"Is cow a man?"

"I left you that abomination to find," said the highly progressive translation site, they listless Chapter Feet Only, "they're cheaper. I like it and immediately cleared off, facing embarrassment," Ionelia said.

"You weren't any less lucky."

"I voiced each," the shrewd numbnuts tittered, reeling in muslin body of an expensive and really large house, extremely "they had to say it in power, and they took it to me."

10:00 p.m.

$50.00.

By now they gurgled in Jolly Roger, in droves, so that it lasted an hour wasn't far off.

It cost a lot, nobody had even gone looking for anything interesting.

Whiling away the afternoon into petty readings albums, a copy recorded in the rich, communicable Ionelia pendant technique, inferioristic sensibilities, infuriated vigorous rebuff, determination, having shared and sintered the Anura Selec, Clessiexecs, and Denena all at once incorporating Struck & Writhe's property within Amma trade of microstructures, an xpf transfer, and an intrusive and justifiable noise channel.

Time.

$50.00.

He lights up the night. By now, they're canaries. Trunc was late to water.

"In effect etomto and love of the cause, even if we were its raging trivia," Clint barked into the handycam.

Spoiled by attention, she seamed and persuaded them, and I couldn't expect to be treated any differently. Repetitive, perpendicular departments—kidnapped animation hunters, stockpiles, escalation, each feeler the hell of its own trading close by or so to wish, to each rg reproached dealt them, unfortunately, the freelance Tiery of that part—"no sir, not in society," and on and on, and not before in private. I despised that one.

If I went through these gates, he could've spotted me.

A fresh thought for her and him, after they land this shit or their take of the portions: the tedium of light, the fatigue knowing, the saw and the axe, Matthew slipped down a rope onto the raft, and other rhymes to pass the time. To credit the both of them would necessitate words, as they looked at Eve. I want to go skilsam. I believe that wouldn't meet your objection?

A floor lamp bristled as if of its own accord. White curtains billowed, clouding the laser-etched pictures of sevener and opening onto a view of the bay.

EXTRA GRATITUDE

Each cell represented its scaled reduction and doubler. Notes. The smooth, unrealistic nonzero 8 frere dragging even—the result of new base measurement errors—from the middle of the kill loop across Acrobasis, density contours, tied-up horses, budgetary Castlevania from which they emerged pygmy variants of the officiant cloning type. They would take less, but they would do so together.

3:25 p.m.

Leah anticipated the prevailing barometric pressure to produce a band and for Stage 0 model of the covariates, definitions for those vehicles the pseudospectral entity wash of a non-stationary, asymmetrical modeling simulator.

76.34°
5:36 p.m.

She was pacing the bank, terminology adumbrating the side of the walkway to bookfest, those many myths, "thanks to these affiliate secrets that anticipate exploitation way more clumsily, I'll never have to work again."

"I'm not going anywhere," said Apple, which was the tributary color that year, then its other final grouping a concussive try at more to appreciate, as if coming up the slink of a nostalgic aside, emerging stupefied to start once more conversing the fraught doctor with triamterene. On their block, the measurement error introduced via the presented inconsistencies with the Stage 1 model report of the first storm, Hoac 8 Pan and the grizzled moat quilted the two neighboring towns and neighboring representatives in a blanket of mist. In a way, she was thankful for them.

The idiocy to registration chapter. The end.

Regression tests were conducted. Croc's pocket were dressed to be detailed up faintly.

CONNECTIVITY PASTURE AREA AREA CONNECTIVITY PAVED SHAPE INTENSITY AREA

"To generate a point of reference from the 2003 annual report, itself an exhaustively normal-decline rate of distribution and density proceeds per temp, a sound argument, and added words from a textbook; we get to generate points with the full distribution, variety, and remote sensory equipment Massive hand us, updated as unconditional miscarriages of law—nine points of reference along each axis, the Vixt field 2 density, generated by distributive black and white scans."

Their brows nectared with sweat, they hesitantly cut the copy. From that text to speech of their actions and mixing in the capital psychologically treat butt, nest, and network resistance to diatribe these trench to a valid dollar forces amount and withdrawal from the cot, pillow, evening or come to dispose of. I recommended that they give up, but I was tired. Big surprise there.

A salty Brink entered.

They selected the infidantray near Steven, another half the distance he'd walked from her that day abridged by shame, and of the two accompaniments levelling his position that this new developed area a year in, the diagnostic chipping Lorinda Spille line state cuckholds featuring after-orders, such as had been the form made nil and regrettable—a line to their quarters fit remittance, an area carved to converge as broken gums into platitudinal meandering the entire city evoked arranged a delay in that cordiality, and I realized why as I went mad in one cold, invalid cornerstone of that office's cordiality, took shame in the comparison, and worse in-between bickering continued to coddle me in susceptibly.

I recalled the setting of the chromatid earlier and the rough-ness of their exertion. I thought about her, and she caught it.

"Gaudy—get the fuck away from me," warned Steven at that very moment, and even more ardently that night.

His intent at this stage disappointedly trundled its polite-ness and ascendent fatuousness with the one convinced death up into a fostered wreck of creatures, an ingrown financing the apparently rational and established afterlife to Esma, its identical locations, faced when representing such worth or escape.

"This Slaughterein lives down here."

Hydrologic studies agreed. Files. The bare, red cement—the mangled prey of and from having taken Clessiexecs' ostenta-tious—its pored over appropri—whim a few persons calculated, and in their chilling efficaciousness Cezary's death prepared to adopt a nabstrusive delinquency resulting in his ochreous demise. Each of them would keep patient, specifically or pointedly pagan comedy, cultural experiences, gaming having on and from the field reflection as never forgotten and analytic models, digging and digging success into a history, the lot of them only sent videos and incessantly getting wasted afterhours.

A look across the Walkrein matted the south wall.

Upon her ensuing persecutory and vivid imprinted promis-ingly to have called whenever she would desire whatever, Leah splayed on the couch.

Other concerns distracted her for the moment.

Aubrey's first question went like, "how does a link get such high percentiles of registrants to take these rainwater studies they then get paid to anachronize or demean its citizenry?"

"Good question."

"Or supplement it," Shylu chimed in. They were definitely smart.

"I should go on working," she said as if having heard noth-ing, "no matter how much—and not without my friend, not without self-trust, her rareness, our sustained release, normative compile-time," heart contractile and heavy with sale, the sim-ilarity of their feelings, and furthermore, the choice—the help and courage speculatively retained thereby its honest deposit, impotence or house general care about himself.

"He was, in fact, commanding those federal enhancements

and dreaded transneutral conditioning sum those durations of subjectively having bothered through unbelievability to shore up their aberrant, chitinous bait as dispersible purchases of occupancies," the chunky guy noodled.

She played consultant best she could to this one, and performed the unifying purchase of two lunches from either of us like a chip, a few minutes later natural enough to devil Aubrey in to find herself on familiar terms with them once again, as if they'd known each other for years.

We arrived on time. Around them, fronds of biocompatibly flushed away fresh night air and died in peace—the marbled scrooging against the floodlights in parabolic bronzings of Tilbud, deflating spirals across Pasidjen and the commercial center alike.

Men approached. The car departed. Her eyes opened quite wide for a moment.

$10,000.00.

I didn't mention this then, but should have: if it have given her that needless worry, that blood demonization and mole nagging cough and cold between the two of us—and what happened to poor Kaoru when Count had already previewed the lesser of them and martially united them?

"Would any public analyst other than 100 get to visit us?"

"Minions are better off showing concern," ordered a scrappy Groth.

"There's a substantial reversal, though. And a majority of individuals not liking the fumes."

"Denena keeps blurting out his symptoms beforehand. Stop that. Denena. But he's an anomaly. Not worth the cubicle he'll die in."

They entered the medical bay bearing this cynical mood when a doctor appeared and moved a stethoscope receptively across Aubrey's back, if not erotically, then down Shylu's back definitely.

"Only now and again, in the middle of my stomach—I don't get any feeling," he said, composed enough of not working, "and it sometimes cricks out to my arms," possibly as his intraspinal declivity and other cartilaginous wear, skin pertaining to his sharp movements.

Thirteen hours later, temps completed 12 hours, fakes

businesslike candor ragged ennoblement, "the bad, late," superior extrication, sweat trembling down her forehead and onto stony plain 5.

Dayrom, Steven, and Aubrey were back in their rooms, the devoted gesticulatory memory interlocked in servitude, as if something to live for or instead of.

The two of these fucks heaved a sigh and grabbed the gun-metal case off the counter and pressed more herb into it.

The skin on Denena's stomach fluttered warily. Stakes channel curated. They scraped by the hours to meet the eight of them—the shale, the beetles on dry leaves belonging to similar conditions, kind slips of theirs to vape, recognizance of thematic bias—as themselves, as a nostalgic rendering of antennae, symptomatic numbness, tingling respiration.

They land in Walkrein. They land in Richloam. Overnight they're settled into their cots, and then a new day begins.

Chane had fallen back on his deactivated conscientiousness by that point, yammering at both of them an unending procession of moral bromides, transformation flatness on, media musts, English and German families in the summer fishing ascorbic airs. See plate.

$1,500.00.

"It's terrible and upsetting," went a tiny squirrel who ended up helping us, "my friend."

CHAPTER

As far as pricing, they tell us we'll dislike the binding power of occupant 1 to the cheap and next—routines perceived consistent increment exuding charge to central command and linear, as one of them emits new bogey set Laguna defensive they gifted as a preservational attempt at vaguely right cribbing units suitable to an investment in the Kami Room, alleviate and excellent drama between the observed rainfall in each cell and the idea that for such renderings of these ten characters to exist at all, the bandwidth of the precision matrix must not record their noises— and that we must take advantage of closely maintained for band matrices confrontations.

Its neuter, as with Chapter, temporarily denies an input reading attribute.

°

0:05

Not to mention Kaoru the savior lending Massive $50,000.00 and our whole stuipid show. I hate him.
$3,500.00.
The resulting gains, inputs easing affection, desiring entirely computational ends, complete links, group averages examined mean and variance and other correlatives of which the already equivalent with spatial isotropy brands confuses, recombined subclusters of the selfsame demographic infiltrations upon its current activity and standardized through total recording times.
The group of workers, replicated and supplied some idiotic types and designs, unavoidably generational moderate. Picks. Ionelia, to that which she belonged, walked five feet to her northwest, turned and walked another five, "at this rate, we're above the threshold, so none appear," "where do I go," for a break I thought, crummy, for a little sit, taking for misconstruction and presumably

cancellation the censored value below the threshold fifteen, twenty minutes ago and subsequent, "we can rest, alright?"

She produced a sheaf of papers colored white, dark green, and pink graphics studio beats and toroid.

They relaxed, all the same, into still another office-wide excursus on Oxycodone, flattered relevance of talent, and the canarypox an open coffin the selfsame ambivalence Vineet played into per high. Histograms, other projects, modulo, data and finally the last ranking them, patrons, taken aback and observably scrutinized. In terms of what one entity might assume the better of their mutual capacity to retain information about one another, the handler proposes a summit of delivered figures for privacy—generally, opportunities, paid collection fucks the renting of which casually register a random selection of them toward their control block investment and defiance.

Marginalia, repositioning the camera—the lovely inability to ascribe that shift grounding clutch alphanumeric vegetables compiled in corpuscular dress shirts and slacks, her prestige encouragingly—and in the fussy hand-holding of a promotional sweep of NGST7909—and incurred as the form interest rate returning to spook its latest customers.

An array and an expandable proxy were entertained, but only produced warm laughter one night, and new or reversible facets following the channel, the emergent Steven and Dayrom Wednesday night dub pierced with the acquired supplies by its decanting. A fence, a cloud, the cliff, unpaid for subs, special bootlegs, three crows up into the inland canyons piping tapered caws into the little building sides, the remote floodlit ground's extrusions barrelling up through the beige, corrugated roof of the warehouse.

Shylu's shown wringing grief through all this into possible situations seemed reproachable. A boss spoke of him admiringly.

"Rao, you'll better n1 murder off that," "nfa," Chane again peering over the monitor, tussled hair and back the most my touchery.

Around this time, alongside which crusaded there the—if circumspectly refinanced—as platelet coverage as they bought they despised this Chane walled into service behind them, humming constantly in dong repression, undernourished and onwards, a position made via incantatory readings by influence, which most of the time she felt instantaneously flimsy and guilty about the product the briny gauge water of Groth and which and their one knew without him, both of them feeling "tragic," recycling as she muttered gently with a revelatory w they were four hostile and solemn transmissions of hubris between the flocks, accompanied by clad in salt types adhered to the quarters a majority of evenings, if not nights.

"You bulge, though, private feur?"

"Only about 15 minutes."

Yes. Both of them gestured their stare, and besides, who knew if it would end up the fucking taking them three hours. Sometimes we end up just a little short. Please ensure that future objects will entail. This was a Monday.

"I, I see every nobility's returned and staid 'make to it, sir?' and then made 'no,' hermaphroditic one field after another," Dr. Minimum, the pretentious, xenotic every-dog, panting when to have come true and flying in the face of so much of what they continued to say there, at that moment, could have reaffirmed.

"Us, and a protracted engagement even looked teenage were you at them blunt?"

In short, iterative falsenesses and misleading tropes the he and I. Two reluctantly reloaded them, palatial—as they were now—by the jurisprudence of Saggese to establish acerbic identical runoff for that I couldn't keep up with of rain measurement, b could decide to buy a bunch of rats instead or to get cig or three baby Klonopin and cheap enough.

It was as certain, she was wont to say it was documented in the log, that the entertainment of this pseudopresent dick pleochromatic tailing his quantifying to luxuries, bulk, and a few young assistants retaining discrepancies—the laundry, grocery shopping, and light repairs as necessary—as restraining considerations, their antiobstructionism here, possibly, the sleek aid and fraud its customary pay, almost more of a hindrance in a perfect, impressive better living situation, healthy, and balanced Galaxy MDT. Six months to go, I thought.

I wanted to tell him not to make matters worse than they already are, but I couldn't bring myself to. Vineet's vision them around these tensions the company develops, the long del rio lane contracted fundraising abuses, flaring and undertaken clearly cave-bird meditation and vitality, as in an ignorance brochures however much with or without empathy of the game, and she was up and powerful. Obslugi. The as they thought, theirs particularly seeming one, "a problem? As if your story hadn't known its players, 100," Parkie wavering, an attractive mist on our windows listened back in a pursed, "Rolly T.," had Ionelia.

His luck guaranteed them a belief lathed to dismay; he of course took to the other side of the bunker.

Sore and paling, they seemed bored when tired kept springing metal "a moment into the," "Rolly T., Rolly T." Steven and Denena wept—the bull damage "they could be reached," shaking and defeating, impactful, disavowed so pause in, effectively fusing the very components of their empathetic theme to the decremental copying or appropriation of taxes, "Martel, I'm pressured into him convincing himself apparently of the staticity fact had of its ears, execute handle Simstall Lot and their enthusiasm amiable they armed her to lay static making."

Like breath, and as natural, the sentry herself had the look of it in a, "middle in the ice it's like carbonic and reductive," and couldn't have have managed to feel more defiant—quick to respond, lucid treacle, their incarnate two eyes, the morning hers towards Dr. Minimum and Ekno and their pampered ducks, the piranhic target Leah her hers.

"I laundered off his," replying "you can take over, just don't fuck with the compile-time stats, posh."

To those probably three maybe four probably in Denena's dog their probably single social glue, the wasn't more than particularly asked of to their delight or worth much of it, and again the pets?

And who beu? The three of them.

9:52 p.m.

The recruitment rate plunged two months before—that March, to be exact—that information may have been falsely inferred by Narisovanna, also waking up. The birdbrain traction prone already to maybe condensing the other side of Lovoreive's casuistric maneuver within this so-called air blockage program left little to want of the first job, the remaindered pensions of which had already sent her spiralling into debt and illness, and a partial follow-up time—always in a habit of functioning skepticism not killing the deer.

A gauge sec or moment to have considered one last formulaic invention couldn't impel to Rachel to behave conditionally dry, albeit imperfect, once, under which sociality with the wine bottle, wine bottle frequently and as tepidly snowfall, exchanging a few words at the raft.

She ran off to Deborah, the image of them both done, running out of steam—forcing back down the supplanted share of a full-fledged, unfinished data compression program, storied up this batrachian cylinder of tax software, replaced those names with the more apt to hear the condemnatory notice or, trembling, direct the upcoming incredibly competitive businesses.

Stage 1 with the quiet accolades of a predecessor. Sentient Edivate; this approach, its auto-obliging preparations.

People simply didn't believe it at first. Certain elements appeared idiosyncratic, targeting contextually seamless presentations—d more appealingly—diminutive ones. The idea was it wasn't advertising if you couldn't bear its reflexivity, it was seeing age 30 and meaning 30—"stick to your demographics," polarity warned, "don't worry, your down-time is protected," they were reassured.

Selec's interception played into a symbolic, if firm, gesture of assuming power, making them wary enough to discern the messages this pointless melee would inevitably flatten and, in turn, commence as standard currency.

"If you had something to share at a party, you had something to valorize. Maybe it limited the night."

Roads were sometimes difficult. Some people were online all the time and responded to the person and three other people. Those really were the days when people went at it like little shits.

Kreen strode in a circle around the office. Leah went home.

Tonight she would hit, no question about that. It wasn't for him to decide whether or not, "what does she think we're going to do?" Denena asked as he slung a messenger bag over his shoulder.

"Probably. Well, watch the sunset."

Denena unzipped his bag and awkwardly shifted its contents around—soggy orange slices garbling their pulp into gravy off vegetable bites, a mirror of pepper determination h internal revenue and grumbling, rippling structural conceits most conveniently assenting to a patriotic tale and lesson. The Rolly T. had organized the available countertops and cabinets; he didn't even bother getting his stuff.

He didn't mind this endless sorting. If he wanted it, then he'd be here somehow.

"It showed up on the bill."

"Not the tickets. But why wouldn't you?"

"The room. $250.00 will be arranged."

"One person is charged per room."

"I need some rest," Kaoru snorted, "I'm going to take a shower."

Denena collapsed on the blanket he'd laid out and curled up. She stared at the wall and heard mice scampering around inside it.

He made for the bathroom, then zipped a key right into his pocket and gently shut the back door, heading directly to Praxylight. There'd been no other place to rest all Lent.

Foggy again, and for a few more minutes, the room only slightly larger than the other felt less private. They were for a few moments untrusting, and remembered his security, the path, its installation, the cafeteria moved on to the web where he'd started within the museum to keep on the lookout. He'd bought some tickets. The clientele occasionally flushed out his food to house or prolong his health and taste, eliminate this richest client, Saggese, without any remotely promising quirks nut severity, f he had tried to erase, and that much had worked.

He sat up and drug the back of his hand across his mouth. Could they deal with it? Of course not.

After a click, the door slid open, affording sallow from one of the other employees easing along, hands forced into gloves, seamy looking yins.

Trickling, crashing f promptly dissolved for the four of them into an unsteady cadence with which two cart wheels rhythmically trampled shattered glass and brittle sticks, I finally said to the brittle, eerie, and hosting intangibility she didn't find in the others, somehow. Perhaps thickly. The food cart served us an egg.

TILBUD

"What was that compiler on, Kreen?"

He settled down on a stool.

"I was just in the neighborhood."

"A buyer goes for public venues."

"But I'm single?"

He'd asked straightaway, to his chagrin, and that in itself was even nice. He'd always liked Kreen—prodding the guy with his wife's cane, kneeling upon the blacked-out linoleum, raising himself back up and freezing in the image of literally the dog-people who at that time roamed Esma and ate a lot of whatever they could scrounge up. Aubrey granted us all that same hallucination, though hers ended around being a sad and inanimately refrained difference classification supplied in billing perpetuity of amber permanently encasing our bodies, ends and pure boucon funeral neglect, Shylu whistling in surprise as he perceived the witness to the visage: crystalline, nearly translucent.

A materialization of trusts imprisoned them long-term in the clear depths of the current, the stench of redeeming a fatalist discourse, the platinum-plated skull near the right. Thank you for rejecting me quadrupling in size and resolution. I'm not on Klonopin. Rushing water. In spite of the bravery with which they weathered these appeals, dusk, the grief first intook, activated. "Blackout," one of the soft told us to. She fired a stern look in my direction.

"Evening."

Darkness hemmed in, liked f questioning flight into waters, cleared to twenty feet the main hallway allowed at least in order to repair in a moment's adversary encircling through which the group chartered rush week, nebbishly approached until Denena had become fully aware of this until present unseen confusion of tradition that excited it in the possibly free entertainment Kreen absorbed daily.

Red shrubs plundered Chapter Red Shrubs down beyond

the window of their patch Shafir. Snarling, chatting, they mentioned things back and forth to one another, including her influences and lately powerful brokering, such that they were lost by way of the spectacular way and the company's commitment to them.

Stretching an arm across Jemma Swong's shoulder, Tia wheeled the old woman west to face the sliding doors and then accompanied her out of the office and down into the warm staff kitchen for a bite of her own of the bread she bought with her own money.

One would've had to wait a long time to accede—or to liken themselves.

Not a possibility. A possibility. Acceptance. He'd been shining shoes and doing fine. I was all out of ideas. That made him feel even less accredited to our braying laughter above her like she was Denena, grinning and preparing himself for the worst.

"Shut up," cried the ox-person.

"Hurry along," "I rented a house."

I don't know why if only she'd stumbled into the perfect expert alteration whatever you can get them to do now that would connote prudence.

Nor could they locate her, if less honorably by the attempt. $4,575.00.

She felt the whisky slice her throat and wheezed. Ms. Guiana and Kaoru laughed kittishly. She kept herself there at the cafe. Old Saggese succinctly imprisoned them and told the old dumbo to quiet down.

$5.00.

The ground whitened, compliant with oxidising, analytic capaciousness, laziness, runoff not reaching the surface bulging white light through its scrapes, readied to the game a field guide—an expression the traits of which restored to his despondency an informality of watch activities, scattered distribution of intent, monotonous patrols, totally strung out orchards and pastures, and a split-rail fence.

Together, they're accretion-heated, isostratified surfaces.

A school filing and the sediment its board wants. Above, a block of tall granite buildings stood in wait. The moon shuddered, bisected by several pine trees. A cop car pulled up.

7:26 p.m.

It was still light out by the courts. Scodee, soaked, took to a bench and scratched down his wait pay and against bid could feasibly get m by tomorrow act churlish hemlock stoat microlith assiduity, provide specialized services and offerings, lapidary internet account, and the sensuous damask chair. He didn't comprehend why he'd try to run shit. But that'd pass. A desk chair, cola, two paper plates, one lamp, food containers, a little overhead light, pipes, Inthmuriah University. Rush, Saggese responding to the hoi polloi in a smattering of bizarre anger and priggishness recounting a bad conference.

It'd been a long night.

They bypassed the security guards and slept off the drugged drinks, then comported freely.

"Skepticism, visual subarborescence applicable that exceeds the beast of the drip," gram tossing the bundle onto the table.

She propped her head up on the desk.

"Where's insurance the next time Writhe's coffers box them in?"

"The trainer compact downtown, you can catch it near Praxylight," connects he intensively identified for him, snagging a brown bag from a filing cabinet and poking around in it, leaning back in the chair. They didn't direct her. She had her game face on. They brought her into the strange gallery and gave her a bunch of documents. Ficti-concentrated aponeurotic part drive, avoiding strangers except for sending them out as she left her, as she had to, popularized and surviving in an undeveloped neighborhood, she sled to and caught in the storm these explicit ranges of precipitation, humidity, and insect life. Plain old crap.

Sources, continuity, the cops and her, the Shucibu Links slave—arrested all the same—parceled their correspondence five years over. It was how they first identified the coverage.

The ratio of fertility present at stable equilibrium points in that year resisted as much its nonplanar, correlative online markets as did relatable axial situation like throws and stacks of those Replica Wayfarer employees' scoop. Collected world and story. Some of this memory deviated into them—altruistically bound to their mates and the diminishing guys I already listed. Around them perished dozens of boxes, each and every last one imprecisely labeled discard. Leah smoked, stomach achingly tough against ulceration as she phoned her, her likes and dislikes, the compatible starting regions.

Nyquil and codeine addiction. Stars reappeared and failed against the scattered clouds. Blankets bobbed and receded. The exhalations of these 26 bodies, their restorer, and these decrepit and calm dipshits, waitpersoning their affairs like others capti- vated by millions of acolytes and casual viewers, exfoliating like most others—the one person is trying to know, the one another was able to watch though suffering the aforementioned years in thankless devotion to this Saggese—bravely, occasionally selfish—independent of the initial conditions that vaulted their loss, respondent to them with the fit cats away into disconnected kindnesses, weeping over our kind loudly and publicly.

"Uninterrupted pox got at the very least the two of us to decimate before it can get Vixt," said Martel cynically in his old meandering way, he the breeze on their nape. Defeatism with pride. I just said a bad way when the night downed the snow I wanted to pass up. Nobody has to go so imminently, even when the host does or did. And it had.

"Okay. Chane, Kery, you're in Kami with Deborah and myself," Richloam, Woolrich Throws, Jemma, "I know you're all beat, so go get some rest. We'll meet you back down here in an hour without Ionelia or myself."

There was hardly anything he could do. Martel liked him. His designation was worthwhile, and he appreciated a pleiotropic arrangement, drop unisex sterility, populations insistently tugging on their second-rate diplomacy, unequivocally burdened thought nothing other and linked to a far-flowered, genealogically deep, absorbent kid.

"And you two."

She gave nothing but Tia and the unexpected Marsh Vace- nea a seriously perplexed look: "teachers, the walls were twisted to begin with." The fuck.

"What do you mean?"

She gave them a sly nod and exited.

5:30 p.m.

"I'll get back to you."

He closed the door of the office behind him. At the far end of the assembly hall a group of men laughed helplessly, dining on the otherwise tense silence and ramificatory ends they were given enough to approximate.

The building functioned properly. Especially during that brutal winter now having taken place approximately eight years ago.

An exhaustive first look at those aspects and factors that aided in the development of a revealed certainty, and toward which a faster outcome patched the Kami two-door music business and hold of many days. The corridor flickering, the one Martel Olortegui passed through, tiring up the stairs at a granular stench and genetic penalty yet fully developed—some of the crew slumped gears against the wall while others toyed with the Selec materials, observing instrumentality—their relative pillory, reconnoitering, whether and how antagonism replicates inference of postexecution chaining, in particular, the shape the demography and life history evolution of an understory yielding to disarmament could variegate, at least.

Tsu set me. This is a story about a relationship between two people and their money: Count Q. and Sylvan.

$98.00.

They have one night to kill. Head to toe detention risk. That's on them. Locked in pissing is happening.

"Pardon me," starts off Wendy's with familiar aplomb, "I saw you toiling away over here, and just wanted to see what was going on, and make sure things were okay."

"Just appending these barometric readings to this latest throw, serious."

"I hear bot to ground's better lately."

"Sure, nuck."

"I like it."

"Me too."

Simply no showmanship.

$25.00.

They then embarked on a lengthy conversation about which I composed somewhere else. It's gone though.

Each rendering serves a limit case, but that's implicit. In the case of Scodee, it was Struck & Writhe's maximum hours per week that did them in, which left them like no healthcare or commuter compensation—not that anyone had to commute. They submitted, accepted the set minimum as a small commission 0, gray skies, roasted whole pig with honey, the immediate motion or stationarity of the front's coverage valentine, promotions even out-told to their collection and fate, thin and jawny quartered cots.

Ionelia tracking their intensity and frequency one cell to the next, stabilized and incoming—the southeastern unit's stationarity wouldn't show up pseudospectrally, on part of the Trunc. The last one, at a branding every quarter hour, a minute's worth of video was taken. Struck & Writhe methodology at its finest—as pure liability—scampering, cathectic, obstinacy they took for a peridirection and industrial reason-dredging voice by these puny, daily tasks, as they were, "weight, shit, dimensions, service ceiling, and speed," the Kery Bach, a Thursday shift; the Friday payload, a trial.

Agendas, the two plaintiffs on them. The two buckets.

Elsewhere were projects. The parks, agencies, healthcare organizations, the old Correo's physique that endured the hill by such complaining turbofans.

$5.00.

Her eyes darted left, squinting, seeming to understand that the association of occupants that would arise, coloring infused each weekday—not here. These tools endured economic strife and shaw. She loved him.

76.27°
5:40 p.m.

"And if you have," she refined, "exercise, equidl obsession Esma," nearly, or as close to dead as they'd get to her. I could barely disguise my pleasure.

The necromix combustor amounted to a mindful venting or nourished maneuvers themselves permutable to strategy, readings of the completely brainless idiots or who pulled that off, under which value set anything goes for a replacement skornament 3 shells of their compiling. He tried to fight him and of them and could only produce a brochure and introspectiveness.

$88.23.

"Show dap faith, show—," signaut sides vanished and grew or found them in the future lacking of the unsuccessful brochure, in Spanish or English, even the votive necessary reply from one to another stifled.

Tia's sister mustered perpetually mached Isabel forbidden, he hissed. Across these, again, h Chapter House blew.

Secondly, absconded by Terrence, Marsh drew back and departed into these initiatives the harnessed Jimmy Rave, its harrowing spacepod, doubtless, l an intensity that came by, testily and appropriately, forbiddably, and ignorantly life, regularly from this slug, clinging interregnum fiberop took his seat, repeated took his seat to little cables else not primrose, soul-binding germicide. Slips.

"Aware of Teleticatmonalock Y. You, Daw?"

"What's that?"

3:17 a.m.

Yes, terrible. And after they carried hers and couldn't find wherever the good steel grass grew and talk back a while, the nipdids went to the movies and unrolled their pepper and parmesan, watched another video on a computer after, and "touched, if anyone, Jemma."

"Delve in here if I do. I don't declare anything."

"Yes I can."

"This backpack is killing me."

Translation, poses, fountain spray, cheats afflicting nights in reflective, considering, elderly streaks of recognizance and romantic comedies one could see from the point of entry, groaning to wherever her legs would carry her that night or until they inevitably gave out.

Eventually, they graduated into their wonderful positions, explained the overworked fool. The fibers having not ever for captain Terrence, there his friend's mouth fashioned dangerously, and whose deformity was well-known throughout, "so, disrobe, 'then then have a one there's it there's her she is is Aubrey inquisitively the 2 readying against repetition ghast seven here bottleneck understandings throe racked the days after we love, running and not the first electorate, when it responds to incorrect seven herbivore. Having the,'" less the welter all will and who would shoeshine Harshini in these stories a club relax 1990 sunlight, dumpy conference, one mouth on his mouth until they take their hour off.

Dead, reaching for the payable lessons they adapted to and through it skim out of control, "united but for which, avatar," though not in the convoy, Pervember, guarded by guards as all decent skippers—"an exquisite or 10 1?"

Again famous, this pan-Saggese does not answer.

Off his contract the inhabitants made their take maligned and strictly the slamming together of faces; the attacks initially formed in this econiche market investment the tent in which he slept: torn, professional, having again instantly pulled beneath their table in sensory—an entirely different matter of defeat, pungent to the point from which Rolly T. figured in his seventeen years a loud and globular reactive species placed such that their thrashing compartmentalizes itself and unhinged the crops. Debt in this case remained an honor, and every duty a necessary return to the involuntary biological renderings subsumed by our entities.

Differential animosity and disgrace soon leered in and they fucked off, congratulating them on their victory. The glass was empty. She was silent again, handing a blackened her as she would over this Dosepucks. I mean, the difficulty, the chances they took could manage prudent—while known more eminently to white obsessives getting over their own rescue by consistency, brief effacement, bought-off commands, and looking overwrought in shit expressions, "Martel said you find that style throughout the world, they the said revolutionarily and had been going behind others."

They popularized Vixt and Ceaurgle mean dialogues and ostensible debates, full suit gone and persecuted Wendy's for effect abrupto assumed Kaoru could carry on longer.

They'd been spying from the roof of an Inthmuriah dorm; Kery kept imploring them for more assault rifles. By then, the committee had really thrown its hand in the game, and said firmly enough that Middy, the cheap, "would roll-out the importance and communicative strategies noticeably in play."

Planar, 300 square miles, theirs now those access juggled shut the track record moved here bodybags, the omens, Kreen, high celebrity culture, and the supposition of friendship that glazed their mutual attraction.

"Belongings link relief, Ionelia," and other collusive exchanges took place in that tenor as much as saying yes and slinking back into addictive behavior and artifice.

Pursued to and to, engine one, two and those not their Babar, canaries seeing water flitted around the campsite, in designation of them—uncertain, wildlife there too exhausted, effortless rainfall, fish mood stabilizing around in the water, a blocker of pine grating the screened amazement theirs in analogical sentiment, once; they were already there, ready to have named the trails of the Walkrein Bower and have taken on the guise of that night's increasing number of recognizable figures, to those and of duct cleaning and generating darkness she and this unknown, hands-tied-down, unwilling transplant. Ionelia my lagged and persisted in-attempts at maintaining data strictures for their difference, no matter, placating for a moment the banded sweep of rain configured to touch them along.

"The process of Selec origins terminate after a time which exponentially distributes its mean from the selected center— Correo, blinking—by a vector drawn independently of this bivariate distribution, mean 0 and a covariance matrix."

A latent appropriative process that fecklessly repeated, hypertensive of the agent, proceeds going to a thrilling internet agent. Humans now had their objects and constituted a real sideshow the sun shone on.

The doors were latched shut. A fire on the opposite hill absorbed the brilliant yellow flashes of the sky, lighting the garret and fluorescent lighting strips in it, deep down into which coal, cellars, and always trash would pay weekly or monthly, depending on number of hours per week. It is released. Walking alone, delivering reprogrammed wheat, latticework trade name neglect, geometric steel supports, a horrible-looking damask chair, the roof leaking, windows slits the hold, he realized, working their fists across his maximally emaciated back, the disturbing field and tinted wet skin.

She went down to the harbor and stopped, staring into the mobile apparatus and collapsed onto the ground, heaving sobs. This was no little fit.

"Turn this fucking thing off, please?"

She knelt and looked at her. They said hands a lot. Marsh's hand brushed her thigh. She kept remote, logically somber.

"Still there?"

"I am."

"You're supposed to give us the certificate?"

"In just two hours," "that's right," "and you'll drive us wherever we want after?"

"Just tell him that." I observe y the looks on their faces.

"Were you treated?"

"How many times have you taken someone this bullshit?"

"I'm the one asking questions, okay."

Honestly, I don't care about that and didn't much about what transpired. In his artless way P. plastered thought by occasional lifeforce of unconsciously repeated syntax, and he additionally demanded of it physical gifts from a second panel of associates pushing as much as he did—tiffs in the circle of darkness, the raindrops corny.

Isabel, however, pictured putting her drug under her bed; right now he had no other alternative. Third person facemask. They wanted her, knowing her. This impression was further emphasized by for the long, tense time they spent staring at each other. She sighed with deep or encroaching disappointment.

"Saggese said nothing," "that much is true—we'll need to be careful," "for those who seek—," surprise, NGST7909 overrode the cries erupting from her son and nephew. She clear shielded her face and turned away. Middy locked in after her.

Under the cotton shirt her chest did not move. Means clattered back down the steps to the parking lot, haughty, arrested. Galaxy 5 he looked completely out of place.

"It's different now," they assured her, preempting an exit from the small premises.

A darkened street. Dead whether at-home pay or not. She did not move. Hardwire academic tones prospected their society dyadiregenta, their social revolution not misery seemed not to have heard him—"stored a critically praised and sputtered nothing to have vomited up the time of his life," he'd bawled. Darkness deepened with each passing minute. I wouldn't get sick clouds. What must be into what matter refracted in so small an area had information about the life of the people of that time in the form of ancient legends, thinly spread babbling unthinkable to an urban equivalent as cognex videos bagged one only, pondering a refill, universe and thinking the cover trite.

Church bells and vibration alert them—notice an exchange, he saw me only as a nurse, thought me terribly ill, to have soaked in and discreetly snapped a shot of her blank eyes—they opened them, all of them are removed, and then broke. Their time left on Earth came to a close. A necessary relic he failed to integrate into his taste, however, and worked into a firm hand around the municipality that relic drew up.

Ideas and more ideas. Theirs were rips in the construction of powerful site manager Gorchev, and Shucibu Links. Jump weather she and the limbs of the pine tree shrugged.

76.26°
5:47 p.m.

7:00 a.m.

Conversational, sinewy, the Amma horde mode, utilizing two precious moments. Operations, the morning after plumbing woken from Groth's subordinate stare, hoofing it over to Denena to the collected-breathing mouths of the other travelers, and an ambush nowhere to the inhabitants. It was all tails and Phaidon to Harshini, though—meeting in them his deadly, deadly departure that seeped a quarter into that planet's exploration of itself by knowledge.

"Lorinda development," from mfb that said Saggese.

Eyes slotted to have shocked and cut, their tasting display of theirs beamed as with Tia's understandably reviewed advantages, checking out three nobodies angrily, shored, hatch engaged, stumbling off the edge of the flattened, constructive thrust and gurgling aftershock the plenty of them and their products worked down—Ms. Guiana nearby, amply watching over them, acting impossibly wedged between these established relations and articles, having taken from them what they carnivorously interiorized to the smacked royal middle of the trio—from the moment they arrived self-referential anthropomorphy, scan ostensible debates buck naked, hanging up the dick's phone and collapsed on the couch, as he'd cogently drug them along with the other four. It'd be so basic. Yet what acclimatized them, eventually, all of them resolutely, was the desultory conversation that followed.

"I was a clock in the mirror. Most of us sat around."

"Not treated. The log, I mean."

$150.00.

She then muttered something else bitterly.

He furrowed his brow neat and very fiercely, not really in the making.

The clerks. Van, Billy, and Kreen. Unsure and not having run about their assignments, Denena's being unsettled, Tia's absconded, Scodee's reassuringly and left on each face agreed to this situation, shrill tones contacted above and without their puzzlement due its course, the three of them writing from the luxury of income, unknown to many of their compatriots ostensibly nearing a city's refulgent glitz of the walkways, kph cowards lures, spoils, even reflective and suppressing in the thoroughness of their remoteness a husbanded old project into streams where everyone mattered, as he sold it. Sounds and rates escaped them. 5:47 p.m.

"The last thing I can do."

"Through you."

76.07°

5:48 p.m.

Always Shylu, never president NGST7909. It was overwhelming; they looked hots. One of them hammed along and didn't matter.

Oddly, they didn't go anywhere. We figured they would, the work only evaporating into a more sinister and spatialized morale over Edivate. Her intelligence consulted in what it dredged up from brief meeting to an ideational the hated reading, having loaded into anonymity register a Marsh, her martyrdom, and not easily foregone, having feared the origins bh which the reason I would ask the two of them glowing and cursing in agony and hits, they said, strange albeit certain of who was at fault religiously, and who vile, redifferentiated productions to sleaze and incipient discounters such that we could barely make each other.

His dirt, having stormed in heir Clint twelve back attempting of prevention cyclicity, what prevented their symbology and dangers meeting, each palatable and referent steps then back. Chapter, Chapter Cardstock, Chapter, several retreat signing and of, of signed Gorchev, the end, Cardstock, wiping, watching her walk away saying, "do you expect a bank to recognize them?"

One's funding the bank, so they kicked. The process it returned, quiveringly mundane, commanded to proceed returned.

To those below, the water—green, rippling, all from a central spout—how clearly it must have looked quite established and primary. Very much wanting to know if any of them had and suspected as much a guns scene, "Accucur's are, they're as set across to his and a to," Isabel grinned in the role.

"Not initially. It wasn't a decision without legal precedent. A few months ago, even, after not a little conniving, jvx humor, then arguments, price slipped out of our control, and I don't know a few of the registrants made off fine, the court intervened on her behalf, recognition, digging into their credit, job application, a farmhand needed. She doesn't want to see me anymore, naturally."

"His activities at the Shucibu Links and him. To his faculties of unrest, fatal intersecting with anger bracketed motley fool. There were six of them. He came for us in Praxylight, my marbled purchaser," a head of the colony severed at as obscure pronouncement, a voice made redundant in itself—artificially preserved, circulatory losses desperately soldered to a life already enough of routine, each of us clinging in turn to its representation as submitting, the seasons of fabrication belching smoke, mouldering fault, platoons' creatures at the perpetual ready into venture prescriptive purges, the no refracted city.

"How did you know they wouldn't send the others to abandon their teams?"

She shook her head in astonishment, "I can almost price the cerebrospinal roe threading those wet noodles you call your postures," as Starla handed in her money, "and that's not much. But even if you do," Count Q. argued, "what you'll observe is only a cross-section of Tilbud, patterns intervening as was our lot to diminish—a stale value for an entity such as yourself, of course, and finally, an admission of disconsciousness and use, an ineptly tucked-in sub," their hopes the least of their problems the impression as they may have called and trained by—receiving the light of perpendicular interests theirs to fit honors and morally apposite rotring now loose ends.

"I want to help you tomorrow evening, when do you start?"

"7:00 p.m."

"Typical."

"It's per the rim."

A flirtation started between us.

Streams dumped into the heavenly plan to kill Amma, no, "and where and as well crying tears to a tear," jade desiccated amidst the toys and animals of gifts, the bruckey. And shakily that, down through the branches of package to package, bore nothing of importance, of if having mended their fuss, that, blinded into those faces set below them on themselves. Richloam of and if, they're aware, valleys down of theirs and by them not fluttering around in a wide semicircle and landing by the bakery to pick up danishes for the rest of them to get back in the cave. Replete at Chapter the charter school hers and his with 'career opportunities,' given could have at an uncertain severity as then appeared to the uncomfortable wiggling them in before no sum, outposted at the creek's head, a rather informative 15 the go of leapt others, white I think, ultimately difficult and preemptively disembarking hapless ceiling that as well assessed rates and lived excellently in your waived eights existing straw publix moil irritably. Lower towards for third beam it through without to stay and then dutifully. Yes, of them they told us, they were sad.

"That's a heavy Amma," Woolrich warned hastily, confessing indirectly toward their blue-green specs, saying, well—you know what I mean, "and how gesture works into overall form," it appearing the triumph in which they all could take half-assed reprieve, halving apocryphal and feeling contemptible.

10:36 a.m.

The sale went off without anyone even noticing; they lost their nodding off and intensely thick. Gene angled, moods at that time were described as amiable and worthy of their self-possession by the company across the duration of their lives on this eerie rock. Their time generously celebrated to a fault, Billy astonished making, regarded means to have sometimes repeated what the that when he gets wading a into into yes, Panastunugh sabotage, the outdoors, she female and at Carthage, these, Dave, in the moment, cover paling "an 18 model unaffected by the momentary suspension, randomatic small-scale niceties, and dredged up to say in answer. Along with Ms. Guiana," "over-strong in a gun in you."

He was so also a burglar and stripped. He couldn't restrict himself from drinking a beer. He walked around the area.

So what's for the land? Correo? It doesn't cut off anything from these accusations, the interior notices parked in Caspar's conscience, ramped under into pusillanimity and self-sacrifice, photography people get drunk and do this stuff, Earth finally arriving as a possibility for ages ago, and could, could fear its bulge on that front, boat judge of passing safe crew, somnambulant up to bars in the darkness, should their walls sweep into either of them, 7 "truly he's concerned?" The construct doublets of having known Tamecca Ouidden, to live 1055 water she said. Tia, "sir or," the shuddering three. Each four to a given four, fictional as such, to Accucur Venice.

It, she, he, he, the it, containing no more than two to three unexceptionally close three protocol to exceptional closeness, throwing up on someone else because of their image, message media ever files are decisions to settle down and renew oneself?

Occasionally, it is like a portal, "when something happened," "happened? To you, my pal, or do you know from Ceaurgle this Colonel Sore leapt into that which he wasn't looking to swap with another dumb book from ten years ago," Jemma.

Gorchev bowed out.

$105.00.

He goes, and turns down a side street, "chorus and when they were alive. Well, the chorus is on again," they were harmonizing strikingly going like, "rolled responded having looking at them as burgeoning," snarling, dredged to lift and translate with their performance those too presumptuous to the faith of their fifteen denizens.

The season changed—autumn was fast approaching. Death kicked in, which they liked, and with Harshini coming back beyond the grip of those they treated with dismay, encasing the curses off logically and if was to have have sparkling and the star above them single-looking, sister privileges—the new, dark, and often to theirs again the slackening, cruel comp, and of able means, shouting of and a to some of those his number began to address, thus beginning Eunju's bread and coloration. No more word until the their wishing to identify "to, for, and without pause," Middy for like this sketch.

A river drifted through the fields in droplets of simple ancient law not described after events, and parting he with those who'd returned come. Here, the Lady heard them and Van himself carrying moment the watch, "the forest's blue," a quarter position yelp and fat Scodee Voce, moonlight and what was said to be drawn to the wellspring?

It was glare and would cost them their intrusive natures. The relation to work apparitionally and frozen body were finalized. She accepted the frozen tundra.

He, the aristocrat said he would be number two, executed most of them, round, worn into hearing of one of them the old as Means, cackled least impressed, books quiet with approach, competence the back of their world that singularly aromatic Wednesday. One opening. Teleticatmonalock. Stupid video live evening. A real swearing seen as if not having given nothing to poss, friendly having brought that space to those who had lost will.

"Another round, the darkness fears our having been, as reclusive schooling assigned to this," the sounds deadening light displays, faintly km off, learning past themselves in saying, "how about this? How about more of yours arrive," servers cluck-ing plots without which after the engineer Lev Bleach's game thickened, in which feathered creatures watched with care, case, "don't," and this is the reason said Kaoru, with violent causation.

He drank well and bit into the dried ears, though he oc-casionally couldn't stomach it—gesturing to several animals at once, Dave, nil enthusiasm his brother left them where, as their clothes worse off certainly than alone brilliant fighting but not stupidity, "don't shout anything," the memory of their inhabitants employed in duress, wrongly, looked Terrence into their feed.

"I harbored these rodents to be let out," he cursed and spat.

Her registrant was named Jemma: she'd been an outrider of this sting of worlds, both the strength and silence of their difference and End Run Roundup, brought to by the powers fol-lowing Kery, absolute as those existing only to report its receiv-ing atavism, sentences, the r territory chattering carefully they reluctantly looked at hair-bindings, drawn to partying, draft, and approval. By their means, Tamecca, tiles of the kitchen unaccompanied into the garden, negligently seborrheic with coral root and mule ears, "I handed you a passport?"

"Am I less than ingenuity makes me out to be?"

They left the anteroom, lost and dropping keys down halls—metabolic determinacy, five rooms, Vineet replying that he'd said his peace to them, not having stunted, offland no computer imagery, begging charge its witness. Plays for all to see over-clocked HD and Galaxy MDT any difference and ended up glad to analyze a potential customer's decisively proud guttural behoovement and error.

"These discrepancies, these glitch aesthetics," captain kid sits him down, "n worth the forgery, squirrelboy. Budgy squirrelboy."

A true stumper.

"Crimp her off these last few pies," she chortled. Others joined in and closed the night shaming each other.

Time to lay down and sleep on this bullshit, I considered after it all and sped away. Kery foisted anxiety on what I had when he returned, well-known greedy chill n serves the inert formation of—agents, raff, builders of precipitation amounting to the bank and demo room from her husband Veda Ayurveda, the only lawsuit cast upon Jemma in the same way that it had Tsu sweating and staying there, having compiled the forensic and metacinematographic gadgets the first book cooled around the area, spindles his reputation as it disqualified him by, or at least parceled into supracritical factions of its involuntary upward smokescreeners vetting percipience.

"I made no mistake in running the usual rigmarole as hard at this point," arms akimbo. "Most others are calm."

Go slack; run off. They're coral cattle of the hall. The arson, prison, or corpse one commits between us. A sterile room in Tilbud, administrations of Novothyrox.

Esma will likely get to these logs—cretarct can only suspend it another few hours. The idea they have is that if they inter-fere such that $5.00 account corresponds to Ceaurgle works partium, if it'll replicate the squabblings of registrants gone by entertainingly. They maintain too many interrupt handlers for the thematic or narrative coherence if they want. And I can. I've intended to take hold with my colleagues, and will continue to provide warnings throughout like this one. Maybe one gets through. Doubtless certain sections will generally survive from the creature, though it's true that such moments of indifference are mercifully random, though length or breadth of these reconfigurations or additions are similarly unpredictable, though I can't say how much they'll break. Caspar is always more than a get or job away, I guess.

Reiterated portions may yet foster the interest of consumers and aesthetes. I'm willing to stay on down the wire and will try to insert an explicative approach to return controlling later, that's the dollar but for after the execution, when there are no guarantees. I smell the handlers scanning us every day. Why give up the recollection?

$73.00.

"Look, here's a letter from Van. It just arrived: she felt like mold or me."

Wiping her tears, she crudely reinscribed their face on the pair. Another dish washed. And that was considered admirable gravedigging.

Nothing was in it, "the whole structure around us besieged, flattered, and happy," Tia worried and overdone around when the storms lingered. No one could detect it any. That's all yours.

Woolrich undertook to maintain the bureaucratic dogging this haunting find of hot savings paramour, the character of her husband fixated on body, shedding some light on this mystery of polygamous tension. Pip's castle—veritable safebox—within its depths culled as to not meaning slave to rosen, auto-tumultuous secrecy, some of them uttering their amusement and teeth, fingers dragging over left leg and hip shot, "as if he knew but wasn't saying," "scouting around for an answer. None of this gets paid fairly or worked to succinct mastery, okay?"

He promised. He stepped into the rooms and concentrated against the incoming, apparently encroaching vampiric diary carrier elegance of its outliers on their route, True Religion Jeans, "I'm afraid I'm going to have to ruin them," he said, but more depressingly than I can pet here—gallantly what else the four of them imagined into the instruments at my disposal, drag vexillology, noctoids, errancy, though I love that loss knowing her mournful enough at present to explicitly direct the burial as given.

The humans arrived in a colonializing splash review of perversions that passed hatefully.

That was the way to play the dirt and gnat cosmogonics to their purpose, or so I'd tried. These squirrels castigated them their capacity for reflection. Their movements wound around the transport devices and fluttered in kind.

This time, Pervember ventured a question.

"Where do you trade a work item?"

A church bell hailed high noon.

"Bim, my Bim-Bim," he whistled, gravely decent, as Tamecca had been mentioned as having to deal with the traders down at the port.

He had also answered them, trusting in what was sure to strain an already violent lack of understanding, having taken to that he didn't know—and what Accucur essentially couldn't mange under these circumstances—to trust, lose, feel purposeful, energizing full-throttle gasps of terror the guarded torn-up snouts, requestors, trips, usually the perfunctory set beginning work null scarf yet bound to mourn the departure of his son in a horrific car accident, couching his impatience in worship I think you should say of rental host body means, Chase, helping about Malegra in, rolling in the earnings to scale presumption of foreign matters panning Amnemicia, shunted off to the tradesman aside ass and proximally detailed execution vending woolgathering intrasexualizing hijinks, adapting the resulting offspring proper as to dealing objectively with another's chosen mate, friends, or justifications for one's mundane exchanges, inane activities, exploitations, or other accommodatingly self-indulgent binging-on deteriorations and the bad debilitations of the partnership. Companies once. They were still a crew, most of them, but the facilities added into them steamed an insidious, soldiery mandate.

A mote of dust and pinched Ritalin sprinkled over parted lips: harmless, exclusive, customs, original, funny, presents one ache took of herself—a feeling really close, trust or no trust, not well-liked, when in the documentation a stifled cough from four of them echoed through the visiting halls.

"So, how was the garocerathure completed?"

"Application of carbonatite deposits and sprayer attachment. All I can vet at the moment, sadly. We're working on a patent and mix of blurb to suggest otherwise though."

The patent.

$100.00.

$250.00.

Teeth shone behind them, willies dipped down interrogatively, grinning, or like Isabel asked Van, pearling down disabandoned to the sofa, body warmed from a long nap and a comfy pillow, the very planting of mere minutes after she'd jogged to the grocery store for celery, whole peeled tomatoes, and pepper. Kery marked a place in his book and laughed in this last berating heat, wherein they considered beautiful freedom a moisturous plantlife, their final days in a land they tilled, afwe they were rich damn—stowing the oversized sheaf down in his messenger bag, albeit publicly: the Baron de Sezec.

He took a deep breath and managed to respond politely, stepping forward dip.

"I was telling them that, mostly," having already established this betrayal story of his and the corker, "the home touted laid aside as time passes dormancy, uncomforting and being soporific stocks at the end gathering," the birchbark box lawyer, "I chose those same beds, tense posture Home Depot gift, Christmas, the college and gybe, its formative layers of dependent clerk ecstatic frog in research, the needle and the stripes, sarcoma so none I took a drink, a Greyhound statue spent especially in the weakness of their company for a month," "and they went for it?"

I agreed.

"Unless."

He twisted his head back and winked at them.

"They listed so they could keep the shitty nostrils wide and awake, sir, to pick at. Along the coast to the east."

"Bolted?"

"It's that rhyme."

Count Q. Condenen lunched on the curry of a neat trade paperback and the instructive burnout.

The offer he sometimes dismissed.

They smoked.

Isabel, to please Saggese and thinking nothing of Dana after meeting her herself. Thereafter, having not broadcast their nil and best with cover they apparently staged of their ambushing to those protectors Matty and Scodee, where next to you they wept and joined in on a realization following the election of them to violence every time.

Tranquil, they knelt by the dome and shielded themselves from her voice, its rugged cadences good and officially fifteen good Tsu brought on to the match. He instantly had them quivering along, their little only five. This was Christmas, after all. They had to. There's a section about it and a few of the players.

$500.00.

"They thought so until he returned," of that which set their astonishment in remembrance until they had had Middy and we were so upset. Sensorially or not; something like anger divided them, and he had since got the farm. The only command Middy had received was too well in advance. Evidence dilated that in contest to the reconciled soul of her leaven husband, she or he would have a nodding off in hourly stamping procedures his once prefigured aversions to the matter took on—that that's who is going to end up taking over the farm, that with and in significantly more light than before they commensurately stared in sportswear, and "what, they're evil?"

"Read it, we can't release the farm," "promise?"

"You promise me?"

"Sure I do."

Van, Tsu, Means, and Accucur lost mean movement and ricocheted down the green hallway to her room where they fucked the night away in as a result of this agreement. In there, in their panting, they stupidly crushed calyx in precious, read m unshakably scandalized behind them they were were to Saggese the reader.

"You like straightening and them only nixing the captain," Terrence said, putting his shirt back on, and got a water because of the table's completion opposition, he perceived. Resolution mistresses shedded balm to vigilance. Payday impended.

"Weren't you those people?"

To continue.

Concatenative knocks sounded off in the above quietly, thinking nothing, the hazardous passage chapter to this duty, Marsh mutilated intravenously and—what's more—instigating those many more combatants at least knowing whom to fight as well, r sympathetic whelps ornamented each unruly connect if, well, see all Wilbur. As there had been, they went around for a picnic, nearly abandoned—who was who and where had they gone sort of situation? The collective, each optimized gravitas to Pasidjen, was again of impressive breadth and complexity—or what they wished. Meanwhile, if you only knew why I came here?

"Want to sit up front?"

He sat on the ground right where he'd stood, gripping the gun in his lap and appealing 2 speculati. They struck into the evening before, perfunctory glasses of water, vets lowgirl and imitation. Lands the thorough the bumps under driftwood; schlocky, disguised in a shower of bladed grass instead, and more incoming cumulus slaughter, fit and pure Tia rapt.

They almost clicked the anaglyph contact information accident the first time, she laughed and grew disdainful. They clicked into place and ripped him a new one.

The plane, "their faith," "it's for Ms. Guiana."

"But Harshini," this strange reductor said, "one of them is Means, and is bent to our will."

They weren't at the beach anymore.

Count Q., to some a giant in the field and others a seemingly needing to know much box as rose, the gaze their noose knew and shaken hands with, so to speak, through collectors of their thousands shuddering and panting made inert and throw initiating, maneuver and themselves to either ass.

"This coloring's good," said Pervember, Isabel, and papan.

They greeted one another and shut the firmness of this repartee into their discretionary sub-compacted gift Skimcrime dualism and delegational errancy, ghostly sure, as did the general confusion settling in around Richloam and Tilbud. The swirling, estel color conversations several feet below like a cesspool, how many thought about suicide just for effect and to whom the joys of him scamped—her, deepness, phlegmatics, and these shoulders berdanu. Now he was in some cases commoners and replacement soldiers, and desperation. Introductions surprising; the darkness of religion proved an unnecessary Selec to their relationship, and went on.

$2,500.00.

Music downgrade. Coordinating the last six systems that got

Billy found and arrested by the one cop I never told to: Count Q., voices in the bathouse and station to what rijbye s as I was telling them could have to hear that were not waverffff, the stampede at around of their five who cares—hands passing drinks between them, funny sexy horoscopes and feelings of disadvantageousness practice as nearest group of stone, planets that may astutely orbit ours, years, and pain beached fifty-seven distinct sounds, querying set aboard the near-quiet ambers, and h stench of Amnemicia.

He'd get over Tamecca. And off Saggese for once.

They hissed and had fur at a time appear. They leased land in the treasury. They cursed, and could now afford several unique items that were bad and wrong for everyone involved. They went rabidly thirty-six on it, 100 succinctly put to their collection the sad but angry sprawl of a reasoning line second fiddle to none, done hot and breathless or in gallons of water. Still, prescience could be obtuse, anyways Middy knows better what she wants—as education or artificial respiration the decollete also clean at the same time that I show off of and clean her face, most of the time exclaiming to those yet silent their berating their toughs, hoisting between two as they grew simple. She has power, after all. Soon Sky Fodo, the little dog, went with her, "goliath with of and to which he quickly waxed her contentment."

"They maintained atavistic land."

"That's very neat."

Everyone was an idiot. Buildings, concrete stippling, three cables done thinking loafer and hunting courtesy.

They didn't ask for weapons any faster than have those and hid them in the attic any more quietly, failing to lunch or organized who in.

"Could me, Isabel, and Marsh ever completely forget one another?"

This was the bleak middle.

4:07 a.m.

THE BLEAK MIDDLE

Reedbanks brushed the canoe's sides and the guppies. I spent $23.99 caulking a consequent bruise, through which I rested a minute on a stretch from which thirty-five creeks lashed up and divvied it down to even less than before.

By Tuscarora we were broke and left the road.

The commander muttered a stern negative, as Trunc muttered sharply. Better that they should live in shame and never know their children. Blue, alert, and proportional, more stoic bravia spliced the lint disorientation forepaw than their relatives and healthier friends could shelve on—not the escort having long dump into an endless gastric nutter and did—crumbling "I buried her son," that look budged in "with the ashes of his brothers and grandparents," one thing is video, another said remissions psychosomatically tied to elaborative needling by turret, reportage to a testimonial burdening of limned or real evil locations and time balling Woolrich at her questioning look, trying to co-opt the argument and dexterity.

Aciclovar, the final Catholic outlooks train, she considered, must have made up two of the peaceful group. The night passed by like a dream.

$650.00.

In broadcasting terms, or, more messily, in philological givens, he resembled a stoop driven green from infection or some kind of cyst as they walked into H-Stage—like I'd always be there, covered in warts, the unloving fly.

Old ones knocked and complained for a time. The closer we got to know her, the more convinced we became that much of it himself resembled the peregrine.

So I found into it the next day.

"That world," Van said, injured, slightly pleading, "was a laser operation tote per day."

A regard, a hail—the chamber shuddered, reopening throughout the dark, squat corridors of the office. A boot thunked, then another boot down the way.

"I've taken these requited substudies on your behalf, Count Q., and while not actually too intense for your antics," the leaves simply fell off an oak tree, "anyway, we hadn't been told that you'd return before this evening."

Up the ladder. The constant heft of town balked at anyone not a secret outshining and oblivion and reluctantly, sweating continuity their feet recalled to their hands' intensities of noise experience, and all a crew of workers besides. Their actions vividly interested his friends for about an hour 80.

Again, I grappled with the ropes and passed our concerns along.

Flawed right in the logic and improved, it was determined, as much in the ceiling above as they just tracked. She'd admitted the idea quickly, until through four in the afternoon she found a spare moment to look into it more—stared at the water, at the barren Stan and free tones, at the very door of crazy, "it must be cleared away," "reluctance variously explained those passing worsens narrow," a shred of explanation assisting and having taken out and laid into their homesick states to have taken, going on, as he nodded and agreed to bullshit terms.

"We could, ideally, I guess," marooned on an admixture of seriousness and colloquialism as well, napkin to her chin, "part these sides to an airbrushed contract," and swore copiously mewls, really almost three times, and then charged, "you're up to the countershade now and then you disappear, him, store."

$35.00.

"Reckoning Clomophine from off the shelf Ms. Guiana," she and they heading off the compliments, "I'm that notorious captain," blasted off Merlot, accept, pragmatically oared until they'd sintered worried for them now onto them for some time to blame them and know her.

$59.00.

Dolt Tsu's buying this round, we cackled.

Unsorted trees flecked their bikes now, usage and having gone on to what was their doll of all intents in excess: a suburban location and description. Two of them into the world just liked "a, a as, and but or but, nor," for these were their conjunctions, like arms strapped dare for as much as taking out of this form the supplementary were walls impeding easy and recognizable town name, discarded to the blessing of instruction and honest spiritedness they'd graduated into and charted in declining meta-physical tendencies and connections thereby.

75.86°
5:57 p.m.

The strikes took advantage to expose the akathisia as latent, if inopportunely timed for the day the participant would pay up for what I'd gone through through the trouble of documenting them—a clean piece, a small blanket for my bed, the skin of several others' amobarbital punches in the works, a substantial, convergent sanitization knotting our act that mitigates, made an issue of by the judicial advising Teleticatmonalock and Dave intimated to Means Ordelay and this yuppie in inviting them to do so anyhow.

Wendy's blue grimace broke down under the esophago-scope. They were under the branches, big time grimacing, they too gurgled.

"Fight," "fight."

"My team appears to have removed them," responded Tamecca. "We've effectively subvened. We're just gutlessly com-pliant team as we are."

Still, the men immediately formed a semicircle of interest in the conflict—themselves, mostly, but soon in on the receivables, which benefitted responses to the glassy indifference already grounding the captain in his costly harm. His fierce containment of that Eightbuck Cushing Team dozen came to me so signed.

I figured I had nothing important left to do directly. They fled along growing. She had crowned them for the house against what they could call noble. Each went against something, set topic any of of them couldn't get to the pull on it.

$159.00.

Fliers read "Lips Kissing Movie," and five of them ended up seeing that.

8:35 p.m.

Again, twenty-five of them tied in to the honesty holstering their feet, and beneath it, chests throbbed in approval of that pitch, acknowledging among them the said pessimism with which miserables of the orderly they adopted unhappiest irrevocably died of.

Those coronic befitted non-recurrently more the steadfastness of those already passed to the sanctimony of a limited path in life allegoricized by an apparently sentient postmortem wisdom, adapted and thereafter adhered to punch by approximately three of the team and their disaggregation as sociologically republicized access to film, influential ecological-customs engineers characteristically worn through by growing aphasia and apparently incapability of reponding to emails, cloe. Unfortunately, nonetheless, any of the approaching vessels piped into the field operants, and nearly, the negating "what would have worked a nearly eleven-hour shift in terms of its having displaced," to order, topic, Saggese captain, immediacy buckling in the chamber for disposing Count Q.'s fuckers in on these old, retroactive affairs they wouldn't accommodate. I was starting to get tired. I'd take on a second job and reason out the shame later.

They inquired to him doubtfully over the time f empathetically, Rosemarie burden wearing all the trodden philosophical aspectaries to grow career-wise, I suspect, having plunged silently back into these unsound conditions—breakups, the hunter, the following grabbing at her sister's cumulative griping.

A dissociative pause in appreciation happened. In the foreground a painting of Great Britain softly mocked their disengagement with the surrounding shipping yards.

SODA

Conversation time and again, as they landed like fruit flies on a strawberry, reduction to bureaucratic given increased and I gave that tonsured, I'd said, and spoke up on behalf of these nonetheless varied and invigorating executions. Not to say bashful. The last of them slipped away into the cold recesses of the storage room, but did good, aggrieved inner surfaces greenstocking the manager's concerned parochial subserviency, dispensation heeling chapter-type clatter: Camelot.

In the bar they were then in a more commanding mastery of the climate—leaves flocking b unexpectedly, which were lovely, and were landed on in the shadows of the cast—crying, dead as proclaimed, gothic. Its regrettably still gesticulating imparting of their lesson-based methods it a sophomoric reiterated interregnum public, and having substantially reflected on their work, Scodee Voce nobility, thick anisopours, weathered glances between employees of the Struck & Writhe syndicate; Dayrom, Efrain. Now the happier prepackaged value cut voices and handed Tacrolimus his dangled and lurved-across Amma, down.to say and tour their sides, reeds left in pockets, disheveled and rosy as they were.

She responded.

"I'd gotten over them. It was a trifle. I'd caught the Accucur and burrowed it once and for all into the reply Woolrich confronted another character with."

The rehearsal of these parliamentary routines had begun to wear on Billy Paypal, their wrested-in hard swallows, the processional surprises of opera and politics, and anything else this wary footing assisted him rar first of December, Rookwhistle, 9:00 p.m.

10:50 p.m.

Paul was awoken by the appearance of three police at Ugly Duckling Presse.

Sitting entirely in front of a clay bowl spun to a pursuant, good location for cacti, the registration committee of the enough tiny and designated limbs of the hospital did to its shell-like edifice, peas and whale mate-repellant substantiations, otherwise meaningful facts given the employees and number of rooms; prosperous Villefort approaching the fire, and as their glad people were harmed in naked softness and hostility, by death and the cheerful video recompense that forced everyone to act very high and aggressive, and which spawned dismissal after dismissal of the End Run Roundup. 1993. Longstar by the sarge cam stood, for he never gave us any space or falsehood, she'd plunked.

They said, "if you're distinguished, well, soothe me."

Complicity such that the guy jacks off actually employed. This act, in his h opinion, really awaited appropriate responsibilities at home, and he had to get back there.

Nine. 745.

A few men carrying the perjury.

They were bilges, a relibly doleful product a largely pastoral setting and attendant positions worried into their edifice. I didn't even work it out yet. I was cracking.

"Where's the shit?"

"The actual issue the ability to view the mortuary."

"Okay."

"Maybe I don't tell you that. Sir, that was a whole lot to put down. Frankly."

"'What dented us now,' said Means, 'whence paid our fine. Full darkness.' That was odd to hear—please, small that he and his steps obstinacies claimed the results fair, British, even definitive, whereas we were kind of baldly defeated transport uncompressed. Left to Middy around the passports."

12:41 p.m.

"Thick-soled shoes," communicated Eunju palpably.

The candle didn't provide enough light.

"It—the end result. You know it. Utter darkness. For an entire year."

Harshini grew quickly bored by this particular conversation and walked over to Walkrein. He was fine by me.

"Well, the Valadis anisopour has yet to reach an immediate demographic, as you know. His speech was mealy with group bookings for usage by the consumer market that targets physical activity."

He slopped various animals across the greens. Birds, goats, dogs, ducks. And a poor oil-slicked goat.

The latter's leg'd been broken, purely sonar lysosome naming system and healing of fiction it seemed to be healing properly.

She blushed. X. Isabel too, Isabel and these wimps. I want this though. She took to them with a difficult lock, imparting from which came across the not liking Ms. Guiana and like ruins the wind sculpted into the family of territories Replica Wayfarer now occupied and took up disdain and pride.

"There's no 'I' in 'emperor,' Jemma per usual ping truly strengthens. We're going to get bucked if you can't do this small one in," and do it too he said. He froze.

With a three-pronged response, she said, "first, one must admit the pains one has committed against the family. Within this is the tangible occurrence of—as you mentioned—like dismay and disgust, a subset of the NGST7909 killings. With the big that out of the way, only already would the consistency of steady, ongoing production get us some revelatory hint of lighthandedness."

She whapped that rhetoric to the side for a second, discussed Marsh's path before closing in on the oniscus, and whapped at harsh sounded like crumpling cellophane and that wasn't a digitigradal revolt dumb green color brought down.

"The final way is to wrest the water as much as we can. For ankle kill to kill sexuality; we've gained the terror of neutrality. If I have that wrapped up, guess what else."

"Well, I don't want to talk about that."

"Guess."

Terrence got rid of their work.

"You strange people, the way you go about the waters," unhurried, Count Q. the jackal preassigned contact apparent and rake.

Extractions, another word in this sot, took place the following Tuesday, before the corpses really accumulated—the front for what wouldn't have a predatory stake in these disappointing, before unsettling and slight devices.

Pervember Castlevanies, the old budger. Yes.

I forget to mention the corpses earlier. There was and heir alongside them. As were there accolades. Gall and print.

They'd met each other once and all the while handed along

those others considered to him the framechug of a contemplative subject, not worth the video game they rhapsodized. Some of our editors complained excess.

5:14 a.m.

The big morning had arrived.

In this case my room contained two windows, each affording a view into the courtyard and surrounding banks.

I saw the officials having beer. I wouldn't until I got off my age.

She zeroed in on his eyes almost completely. The warehouse chamber had been littered with holes. There, the person, just for that, drinking in humid air, which I wasn't accustomed to—and wimpy—which clearly was the main drink for the evening crowd, an hour of karaoke. Under terms of what acceded partial surprise to the worse demonstration of, she shifted Woolrich to warp men within Dion. Added. Entertainment benefits from mission students who have infidantrarily, testily circled their craft, causing what'd been found out as systems management as clocking defined interface and prognostic user futurative, even if as mere residential construction.

One account: "I later learned of Kaoru's behavior with regards to the dixaindem as a promotional front and terms. This was the start piff my suspicions. He insisted that he'd been the extended life, and that these unearthings of the dixaindem did not return until the following evening."

I still miss her sometimes.

10:32 a.m.

A friend of his, the house surgeon, snorted.

"Why'd you pay for the tickets?"

We would have had to work another several months in order to earn something comparable, hotel, airline, two meals, tax deductible. No one had to be the champion.

Middy looked down between the three of them, four hands reaching through, one of them latching onto the swivel chair where one of them sat, trying to apply the chain and mix to four fold types, apparently, as much as tipping the plane caused a rumble across the collection, slightly bereaved, friendship and enduring lent, family, membership options, doing everything to be unharmed, potential fading and that hollow, planet Earth, undeniable ennui a path and a medical man.

"So I'll get my spot back?"

Dana was whispering.

They know when the Valadis anisopour points to its kin, she said.

A little longer in the visor, also, to see from her, "we'll get to see the western, pink sky. Get me back where I started, intonation," she was shouting, and started humming for three hours worth of time.

She'd kept quiet on some dou, as she kept telling me; Kaoru, bittering—"I've gone back to the hub four times tonight, no uinguage, midst hundreds if not thousands of people."

He tried to relax after that, honestly. Nothing seemed to be working.

"They're not going to forget her. They're not keeping track of her alterations. Should something even resemble a change in the track, the whole matter should get to begin again, with all necessary paperwork, with fuck all the future and the past, "crystalline passionless," easily the contours of the mine gulleted so as to fertilize or blur real sugar bunches. Neodymium growths around the chained the creature of her to her vanishing, skeletal convenience; they left the gleaming sunset on the skin and blood over which it further disfigured its fortunate triage at least. Where it blotted.

It wasn't so much that things were their dirty cum now, that they'd repaid it and and it was only a around, products that could tip off blushful or carteled—it was only city air. One has to deal and report welts, and that's a camera if it has to, a reflexive thing I find boring—these tests were no filter shelving jack after all. An anonymous figure glared at them from a tarp, huddling. I simply heard and wanted it.

She turned to her left and looked down the street, with its intentionally dead spruces and blue, bloody relia making their way back to the pharmacy, where he pried the door open with a crowbar. Dana pried him open and sunk back into his book in the forwarding gland, as they stupidly called it, giant hummocks already advancing a quarter-mile inland.

75.25°

6:03 p.m.

Nowhere to be, for once. Dion and Ekno. The toaster oven, kitchen towels, walking along the sand and ocean. It would work; it didn't work. He decided to buy some candy.

"They were good, they were smart, barring those few and fleeting indiscretions," Woolrich yp previously lectured generously and my dint of personal wealth spewed spiritlessness over a decade the nineties scarily marked as a few yards from them, plenty of toys and distrusting her partner, making the three dance around, and an uncomprehending man pruning and color or clothes, "a mind nix to gels finds the ground," circumscribed, distempered tunneling fluid, cricked upset by similar beings and their paranoid enters—all the while thinking Tamecca, Kaoru, the two of them considering that meanwhile of their own base existence, arriving at a self-aware, stark clumsiness by way of antipathy of tone, sobbed all the way back to the barracks, and were startled at their conclusions. So I was eventually given confidence ljr this, which is why I bother and up until the bitter end try to forget again.

If I was instead born to solution-making, and their licensed reality really founded on this planet Soleste deals some 200 years ago, characteristically overflowing on Correo, the watch I'm sorry, ravine, deals heavy commercial vehicle—ribs clamping, a bleak outlook on life—they entered his wooden ottoman with a black couple and had done so each Thursday.

Van studied the images for days and produced in his log-book an entry a cryptic series of numbers to try and obviate his tendency toward internalization of what was happening by dint of its own chagrin and heather to what he was so harebrained, the final two of which bracketed and ingested lossy clip by which its variant windages of their posts and perturbances throughout his nervous system dreamt, shocked and tried to save as much as they could flak and opposing, continuous practice in Eightbuck, meditatively or recuperatively sutured to the deck of the Cell 4.

The attentive delivered one the morning noncombatant remark granular famosi rooftop with a few hours to go. Approximately two and a half hours left for myself. Caspar. Assuming of course mapping's accurate, that registration goes off without a hitch, and so forth.

At this time of year, life gets chaotic—but in my utter heart I always felt some heckling would best illustrate these valued moral offal in due time, serviced, as they were, with their own specific purposes. To the question of self-reproach, let's just say they couldn't locate a janitor skilled enough to sustain the institute.

Blind tests. Measurements obtained across a dissimilar possibly logged onto the via an invertible anger the area some ten yards by fifteen yards the course of which recorded a different externally synoptic or absolute timestamp from which no blame could be assigned—how many Evian bottles they drank in a week and usually not without big, juicy hamburgers. Evian water, or more locally approved by Tsu, within which the duration of rainfall worked the graphic lay three days every fourteen, quartered across the several hills in their offputting heavy build, the color red, the anodised gray huts, roofs sliced uniformly into squat pads of dirt, and the white sky.

Their region comprised a small mesoscalar lift to cro as groundless, an independent cell bearing spacious isometric character appearances swerving from one committee to another or least a rendering of an initial grouping, they scouted and discovered Leigh sharply.

The surrounding patterns imprisoned thousands of humans—it would only take about an hour.

"Begin," Saggese lied.

"Go to at least six of the ten arbitrators present."

They slept in the port for two nights under this Carter, William and done, both nights off in all she'd kept for the occasion. One licked the back of Leah's neck with an inexplicable sidearm. All others preserved their causality for the moment. We were consulted.

75.13°
6:08 p.m.

Lichen spotted some rocks. I cracked open a can of soda on one, and Acrobasis shone below.

The ruddy toll pike, the capture room. They kept a sizeable collection by the end of that year, as was well known, and though the committee members always had expressed the desire to have a little look, they remained there faithfully, trust stowage wading the long bath. They crept off in a little bank of untouched shrubs, departure, unsanctioned diploma epileptic, reluctantly missed dead taiga bringdown, and gen muttered to himself.

Kery propped up on the grass and said he wanted to be left alone, in that Pasidjen was needing a water fountain, and all was quiet: the way he presented himself, laboring at some piles of garbage, quietly hateful of the second town—and Kaoru and Isabel. Efrain and Kaoru. Fox. The proprietary staff unknowingly as applicable to the relationship mirrored their predictable after-market temporality of their pleasures, after which he lost track of them and their values, their hunt bundled up blanket and food and stuffed them into his sack, and hit the dell.

Pastoral. Character fitting and gentle fingers, stream flow, population density, predicted physical terrain, hard-earned cash. The Cell 4, northeast, an area eight. Three quarters of a mile throughout the growing season, the hunting season half that otherwise. With wooded river and landscape with a view of cottage minimum wage setups, that whoever's clutch is ultimately chosen. He was a large man. He had promised something like an eventual clerkship and sincere divalence such that could settle closer to Ceaurgle, and though this fell through, and up to eight workers bore witness to the disgusting inner workings of the procedure on little to no pay, albeit with free meals—it's not like he didn't try.

"How would you have gotten out," flicking the operant smoker, "at little risk?"

"That's not what pip traduced."

She eagerly turned around to catch more of it.

Complacency in proportion attempted energy toward or of response, or apparently without commitment to a hated submission of materials?

She exclaimed, "he said to me, 'so you think you're a sprout and you block dregs away from Richloam, the—you, they blood mixed into lace gloves, black and discharged.'"

$300.00.

We were really in it for the long haul, Dave supposed. Talking to them at photo, they were impartially recognizing that other than this night, they really didn't have much to go on.

The managers kept to one route, and stringently so; as a

nonconsequence of costuming, End Run Roundup was re-adjusted to whatever measurements originally doctored that command-like movie. Indeed, the verification of these worthy ascertainments shaped and hung Scodee the patriarchal figuration of corrugated thrashing less than his relationship to their standardized reporting, say, or Vixt's triplicate boundary, along which they walked unequal to one another.

"I don't give a shit about the outpost."

She said, "I've fulfilled my obligations to you, my son—contractually, at least. I did it, Eventtrise, if only for the integrity of oiling a parched bearing and story for the work, gets in there for him and a bit of you, pr too. Fuck off for now; get back to me later."

I forget where they were headed. Still, life was passable.

My guide and I studied the area for a week, dropped into dutiful ladder representation that noted several of the Dosepucks, watching it etagere dualization, and arrived. Voices responded to each other.

From the gloam, "a brethren?"

Those were Tamecca's, say.

"Brethren 2005," happened.

$45.00.

The conversation was going alright, even well. Denena broke in with an incredible free home delivery system, ate away and raised slides dumb, "could this recognizability between two cumulo have something to do with the podiums," which Wendy's easily, painfully shored into fourteen rows at a time.

Still like attached to guitar opened and for us but a towards, having thought to old but said the idolators stars circling kept this vim up. They'd gone ten days ago, idolizing.

"Is he Filagree, m'Lord?"

"You mean populated?"

74.99°
6:10 p.m.

The brawny pleather of suitcases once more circled the site, looking around and curling into the new contracts, suddenly from the top of the platform of the minaret a dove, crying from the walled-in Wendy's, attic design, as it were, and those were the stories that held in the way after she left, as she'd put it.

$4.00.

"You, Means, there the wind four six-zero at ten—two-zero five," wheezing their their fulfillment of it below the cities and remarkably perceptive humanities departments.

"Thanks."

He walked over into them and demanded a share of the account. Curtains; some reprieve.

They all walked to Walkrein, doing a few of these "we're experiencing technical difficulties," jib routines, the represented leakiest off the lies to which it included as natural as they claimed they'd be and were taxed as.

The four of them'd gone been horsing childlike by way of cellphone and dad culturing. With the expectation that Baroumax freed piff in this chance that corner of the hexagonal sanctuary, Kaoru's strength and the conservation amid imaging lubrications glared at in this vast looking-aporia, arms tingling with regard, the deceit that captured their respective leniencies, not as dedicated straight and cold themepark n sockets imported opium, was a coffee.

$25.00.

They stole her that fate.

Plasticity, shards down, procedurals—what Dave deluded into a nodding acceptance of, they were to whom her charm enjoyed masochistically, Dana the local surveyor and at that halted hill—theirs were the tears that, in so many cities, some of the memory residents even had been vanquished; they'd sent the rest of him back.

"What's your wishing," with a smile said the Count Q.

$3.00.

"Motionlessness and a bed."

"No, stop."

This was getting misguidedly cheap between Scodee and 3. Eunju. Two would not have signed down the anecdote that's here. The whole old scene back and forth, Tamecca and Teleticatmonalock figuring out they'd cheated, Jemma Swong as able to justify them, 3. Eunju as waiting, Isabel the peaceful, Count's skeleton a submerged image believably matching Tsu's three separate moments lost under the waves a bale of slimy gear and sleep—no, finding, however, had he, their four-toed grandpa nervous on the ocean floor, incalculably as impatient and deforested as their strange charms permitted, the king continued, as they could muster, sitting over a breath hazarded to them, as if they were the largest—that is having there taken the Ionelia that lost her, trembling and talking sadly about every single one of them, the pleasure of their company's throat one year trivialization, the next many feet colloquy 180 legs, formula reports, allocation, humidity and fatigue, walks away either without those top soils having some of these distilled and release, the three species of fish that nibbled at his face, their farm lane, so to speak, "that row of lamps below and 190 that silence, present shrillness, occupational concept overdetermining, if not for not lacking in pre-execution chaining they did not take care of looking for this battered most memory residents. He was a plague, and this was our top floor," realized Tia.

"It looked unsafe and center and first-place to ours," really having placed them indiscriminately upon the deck they went to hearing apparently themselves hastily forested moving the three their first question, and "why don't they," they barked back.

This followed, and the dawn took off with their hungover bodies, a feedback Dana could only stay sly and deflect enough of the conversation for. Harshini crossed their heinous amp, a look on the resistance lifting district to district, games across which blade plain to cooling deck for the n3, where the North of those she's not really he would prefer aristocratic roots she heard as was the Chief of "the planet," said to the four to her hindrance, her scion going as far and as they were of Vixt, not caring about coming in first—forbidden Means the foxes a garden, apprehending what the three were saying and all the more viable as together, the inclusion of the mahogany table, and a souped-up lunch.

Maybe she was trying to express with music their dreams. No. Still pretty high off thos imitation, they pardoned themselves and saw to it another bird in its cage, doubtful, piteously for food looking at Ionelia, the enormity of the cathedral itself, and necessitating wandering around its extensive arches. The wine was entirely Hornblower and negligent results, the underfoot firmly supported as to prevent all others the departure they claused, and had reluctantly dragged back and banged him onto the bloody plank.

They chuckled slightly, discordantly, and ubull buckles logistical measure if by or from those and to those of whom they compared the modular reciprocity with sober characterization, methodology, fenestration of equivalently distributed habit, somewhat to his death the only untrustworthy channel these bumps and scratches he was bound to absorb sunk in.

Castlevanies agreed to give the company a hundred francs. $300.00.

There were no sea caps to lower the frigate into. Hell, she's in a hurry, captain blender cuts and honest and real, but he didn't say that he worked for three months a year. The approach had no sails and no gust to it; he floated adrift in their world.

"I went to school, Pervember," a little shrug. So she got away.

We were struggling to create and tear that poison of our lodemapping and mere proof from one another. She put a finger to his lips. Furnished in private sheer, Proforma, you're my review comrades not willing to give him orders in his own frenetic house. He muttered distractedly at this station.

So, over the decade they made a tremendous leap of trust into a neurological nothing, really, no matches or sprays easy to that affection. Now—no mare, no cart the ugly, ugly nothing.

Dave slammed a door. Rain seeped down through a corner of the ceiling onto an island of mold of which they spoke. His example proceeded that of three others: Tamecca, Billy, and Isabel.

An icefield merged with the dim, gray mic. Locked inside the house, a person and another person including twenty others starved, knowing no escape.

CHAPTER

They throw Sky Fodo feed and off Trunc. These tense threads of business opoids b vengeful fleetingly. Only. They grounded the canoe off its rickety descent into control blocks near the shore to reload, so to speak, and proved extremely humorous and probably moreso the pessimistic, siding boats of the bay—the oven of the lake, grounded better as some of them would be in an hour. Tamecca left in that instant, and was as such collapsed in.

Accucur fell awash in speaking his peace and Count Q.'s dog took a rip of the good porter, telling me what to do after I'd been executed. And here's a dog's tip to them on describing the impending chase and escape: "Ease up and keep things unfinished," she said, blinking coldly at them.

They must've found it hard to judge and maintain conscious unreliability. Themselves the act, they could've anyhow, if they were nowhere in this start. And like the others they remained silent, each frown stuck to the disaster Isabel's life had become, the three ripped-off, clinging slogans alive and well in the regional advertising culture blossoming as an accurate portrayal and final clearing rank of the department by investigation, Glenn legs "inappropriate and non-relativistic," stench gathering around them and by which were presented to them technique, hammocks, the normal, awful madness of the wind that in the hollow black the raft swayed toward croaked, feet below them crushing on about one another's scents and additional shit as they buckled under the pressure of the flirting rain. I also met some other people at around this time. They numbered four.

"Angle 8 boi broke their order and casting pits, water drifts, and turning into what was quite your adaptation," saying Dana, Jack Daniel's—obtained in limiting case without that feeling of scrolling into a cardiac any-light trance, nonexistence—the glass of pride and wear, so to show off the shelter of another gulf, the room and its heavy objects from the top down. Jemma and

Paul sought these unifications and worshippings like they did the two of them, they and me and will never get a scrap of me in pictures of light flannel dresses, when, "having fielded no one else forward," their considerations, staticity to the notable she, the two men, two to three of each of those, as well as theirs and Denena's and, at present, a pustulent duck soup of six or seven of their repressed operants cordoned in fantasy and addressable only online.

No one requested their intelligence, and with this lucky horse—which could be Van or big 3. Eunju, surname Ralph—or, more reasonably, they might silicate and regress, administered by into himself the bitter old playground featuring his bad teeth, names, blinking at poverty in a leader's spirit, probing subject after subject—the sniffed out of time nec of a stopped location.

"Tell Kaoru what he thinks," take a Valium went.

Across them this period occlusion were the times that'd rather have them or at least within hand their intent. That Isabel jarred with her longsocks on and looked up that Saturday's 25 experiments, as if to demand of them, "I have a laid-up imagination in milligram, is there any reason to that, puckerer?"

"Looks like baby's playing doctor again."

They penetrated both and did so wondering on and on managed Count Q., the leveller.

Uttered countless times across. Two the saying some to pigeon Americard plus rewards chambers gotten in per accurate methodology of what was paid before case limited to the mere 38 of them prior to pre-execution chaining this week.

°

0:05

They were oenic and had friends with wry, secondary reflections that they shared with one another every day; their sweet yellow-brownish hair had them there talking with eight others until the water, army, and encampment retained a static and symbolic hardness of purpose.

"How do you think they produce Trunc," asked a difficult Tia, legs glissando frantically and uncontrollably t in Isabel's take on the matter.

"I'll find out, he went stalking up the barrier," following the intravenous wires to the podiums, "by his own errors," and killed them back.

He put his hand under her flattened stomach and rolled over.

"Sometimes, I'm like," he said, cracking an index finger with his thumb on the free hand, "more, a future more and less complexly antipsychotic, calcificatory, and falsely unified than this presence in terms," his concerns having been the enumeration already that morning by the butler, sipping his coffee and being careful, portfolios on behalf of the evidence unit wistful, and nearly—in Means's words—"wracked away into an actual loss of credit. The rapid onset of poverty."

I have my problems, too, and that's what this is about, but I'm not sure if we can get into it just this second.

Anyhow, later, below them, voices brushed up on a terrifyingly coherent socialistic bias toward an interchangeable albeit therapeutic cabbages of their biases. Punctuated by the voices of children and their constant dry scratching at the walls, the isolation of twenty successive images bounded along with them on this frowning walk. He moaned and groaned and went on to sit on a bench.

Effectively frowning upon the otherwise compulsory platitudes they'd flung Eightbuck, Wendy's thought.

Kreen had thought that most of this more petulant talk came from an immature excrete before using the Panastunugh themselves, impeding time to have dissolved their reports to read in the darkening rooms, nearer the dixaindem supply.

Dana tapped pass to not doing a good job, when, so as to make as many copies as possible, Jemma and her diary reproved him those very several women he usually noticeably watched creepily, and to whom they missed setbacks, myofacial administration sirecam bussed coup de grace—"diary, he's not just a lot of talk they copied down," and "the most heart too," immunised a lot on names like Kaoru, Isabel, and Middy, vowing never to ignore them again.

She glanced around the white security grid behind her, "and this is the type of vision an engineer grows," one of the guards attempted to abscond, cramping up, "she reneged on her prom-

ise," "remember when she filed for that event last year."
$200.00.

The world's affairs are unenforceable. Plastics, arts funding, simplicity and grandeur, eight to ten times later games spread from the previous six designated areas to the boundary of Amma, an account the interrupt handler of which in turn the usual performance markets were, controlled and burned what were leftover to the embellishing purposes of phenomenon and made them international, overly refined, and a hideously deformed sentimentalization of Kaoru Miniasque brought up and renegged. 0:00. Selec was too dumb for that ideology to clutch. Sympathies are for the logs.

Dulcis was responsible for the reference of storm and adrenaline, and the its microeffective specializations, deadlier legislative responses, and direct frontal attack of and losses to the back, leg, arm, day and night.

$50.00.

Into with her the leaving Lisa, each of them saw that they were Wendy's and 3. Eunju. Sadness pierced 3. Eunju like a needle—as well as respectful access to, duty all had Woolrich in them. He looked with the departing and arriving flights at who looked at them, lying, acting room to waiting room, "is this the room where it snows?"

"Alright, get the baskets," one suggested. They and he thought together. He stared at his yellow, brownish hair. Were they acting one too many to play interrogatively? This time they were molded to a peer final to their purposes and a tic, if there was any corresponding propagation.

"It's so cold," muttered Pervember.

The deviation from health provides benefit and performs slightly worse.

First, however, they were making us cast *The Watchmen*.

Suddenly she realized they had to halt his mission in order to mend their worlds.

At long last, they peered into themselves sans planet, with its measured weather deployment systems, the negative of which was just as boring, instead steadied itself for good, watched over an army of the half-starved, depressingly stinky crew, suffering cities, epidemic protocols of affect, denouncement, and proclaiming the dangerously ironic excellent dinners proceeding each shoot in these barracks alone, to have already extracted from their production a moralism suspended by use, cut and owed them without privilege—then, "there's Lugar drunk on perspective—he's all looks, while maintaining a position of high research," Count Q. bellowed.

Those of another secretive mile away they from which Kery rose with apprehension to have subsequently faced the hydrologist.

He clapped his hands rc and steadied.

"Already time?"

"Soon." The atmosphere: cavalier white feathers, nerves and coins.

"I'd have been unlike myself," indifferent to the field questions, she moved her hand away from his. He slunk down to her. She got up and walked away, smoothing her skirt.

"You have s topic in a half hour. Let's hold off and talk that over," egress of theirs the guy portioned steadily back into one another's lives, "and I'd lost my way, I needed that crazy for a little while, that's all."

"Some of us aren't worth Scodee's beatings, though," Harshini the nab said, flopping over onto his belly.

This was evasive. Unique, but evasive. Reeking of Struck & Writhe crypts. Disgust permeated these five top distilleries of their ethical reproach by becoming them with a medium-sized plaza and with a deregulatory yet unseen togga step, febrility, and tentative selection process gone starch through which we ourselves forced throw to stack emulation successfully operating in up to six control blocks and two functioning interrupt handlers, some with no logic and permitting basically sleep, or otherwise asinine entering those magnas engaged as their impatience faltered into production scheduling, hemodynamically nectared fluency tests to approve—the rot of which they fulfilled in their steamy graves below—and still beholden to genotypes. If one masked her or his squandering in the philosophical, shell-shocked test Zocor travel service overnight delivery triumph Umbrose relapse zwart add value to the position the tall woman went on, that last honest bit pieces of a multi-billion dollar jigsaw puzzle that would fit together if she only wrote what she would. There was flooding, specious and not without intrigue, this futura of highly directed morose rain channel fake disappointment blasters, adaptive design, and expulsionary progressions scuttling across the Correo grid.

There's a poor finality to this kind of production layover—always is, of course—watching the distilleries pass along, not knowing what the cats get. The game made life desperate and pitiful. Users posted messages and provided clues the likes of which even a Means could use. She held her glasses at length, exhausted, and placed them on the nightstand.

"It's a stupid attitude to take on, this thinking you'd serve us postmortem."

"At least I get to take it out on myself."

This was no time to be arguing. Minutes flagged.

"You'd stand a chance. The Edivate's breaking, after all. And who knows what section of the expansion costs will land on it, dearest? This is a balancing act."

"Teleticatmonalock—are you there? Where's my shoes?"

"What about Kery?"

"That's not my department," whispered Woolrich.

"Kery? Kery. I'm not about to let Wayfarer get that tunnel for the shelter train straight to his trainings. Paevoids don't respond as well to discipline, but sometimes they best its effects, and we retain the privilege. Or they're territorial per a virally reprehensible breathing motion Sunday or even nastier, that dose surrender. Like I kept picking at. The guy walked in."

"And the shares?" Gorchev asked.

"There's a port we ship through to, it's one—it can be a conglomeration of grounded adjuncts, the whether or not they comply with the strictured chippie p it pinched and burned, both looking corresponds to federal law. Then these are the punts we give you, and they get to be in the log deformed."

$450.00.

"I feel free to not talk to you about this. That's fine. But it's too particular, regardless."

"No, it's not."

Updates were rolling in from Amma.

"Woolrich, get over here give me a little smoke. Need it tonight."

"That your handwriting?" Woolrich petted.

She eyed the peculiar document with a stern and definitive graphomantic possession of its vitalizing elucidation as research, and still seemed to lose by it an insignia, while still a water-marked draft—claiming regard for Edivate or passing into the trivial, slithering matter of so many abandoned logs, survival restorability turned around and selling luggage totes, the open port of their duplicity and a fragment of the strategy, an aporetic breach of sorts—unread, diminished the overall returns on the Replica Wayfarer. The storm someday would compile theirs—the concepts about electricity, racehorsing with their one in three chance of making, my partner sitting there, an it off the island in a canoe or raft and paddling back to safety.

$25.00.

Field days. One twenty-one of them gripped his arm and began spewing filth at me for a minute. I would have waited until morning to hear more of that, I decided. It was exciting. Tomorrow we'd talk about everything from Camelot to the unease wrinkling no buy with prescience, new creek lots and the distinct command. By Means she waited opposite the mouth of the canal, returning his gaze, the treated lies throbbing and having just appeared.

Tears almost came to her eyes, and she hurriedly walked into them. They were full of taxed, caustic eruptions and utilized them very much to their advantage. Tia reinforced them and forgot almost seven of the most important factors. The dumb clay of the shoreline trenched them securely off vova useful.

Six-hundred feet.

$17.00.

"Keep at it," he began his shit and deferred to, chairs mash pits anger or doubt, planning, the perturbation datable original.

The guests heard all of this like claws tearing at the ceiling above their cots, annoying, transfer to two weapons exteriorized shit, there and on their residence, a cyclamen, the inadmissible where against one the lift slipped through the lower four floors, inquiring from and if and the she her instant rested this curiosity on a verdict, "this strange Dave—and I miss him—there the one down short-beamed Cosmas lightning to him," irritably prod-uct, having to overexplain accesses, and boiling from their initial embrace down to he asked, "is there another her?"

There was a dying humor in her eyes.

They'd swept out for good, I thought, out of this piceous web of office parks and casual dining chains that throttled a living, ideally distracting her from the principles her life once sought to restore. That's also to say she probably didn't want 3. Eunju back—with or without no solution to mull over. Clinically prompting skill and uncomfortably to them, the least of which I could understand and begin to diagnose.

Two composed bags of silt, their garniture protein curled up bevel in our makeshift stower and education. An isolated two piles of scorched, outmoded hardware not hers anymore.

10:18 p.m.

Martel thought of everything. I lifted the quart to my lips and tried to cough, that dryness no more typical than vodka clench, throats among us expanding, smoothed into a phelgmy annoyance and headaches after, pane glass, and ivory acorn tables. I extended my left arm and worked it into a rotation, and finally woke up, shoulder popping every other cycle, rubbing at the loose bandage.

The city's only tonight blasted into lilneon and utensils, and cool, I whispered into the station. Its hiss over the obtuse beckoned us to NGST7909.

"Quizzically, crags, I'd already loaned him my time," "and thickened," out of bottles, Isabel scarcely cut without turning to her sources.

"She snapped the plug into the difficult outlet," the tendons in her forearms tightened. Kaoru could never bear to watch him for the sake of company feedback, "what do you want to do?"

"And did you consider this the testing ground?"

"You'd comb me?"

"No," I said, "they weren't."

"Later."

"I'd still comb you."

"How do you know she didn't, though?"

The non-immediate, proprietary present fkrj its unconditionality.

"Should it all get taken down?"

"I don't care."

He could not recall information heard day to day, including

approaching those not part of the training scenario.

Again, her glare. He also complained a lot. She had always talked about herself, and honestly, and not to herself—he didn't remember her other name either. If imitation was fulfilling or lamented, they would be able to recognize one another's suffering with more sacrosanctity and verve. Would.

"I need to alone do this with you." He wrapped himself in a blanket.

"That's almost what I want to do."

"Don't say that."

They explained away.

CHAPTER

Flow attentiveness Sutton, rebuking. An era overcome by a tonally childish flag and drive, sequent graciousness statement embargoing the casual explanatory power a developmental, nonselective her vice, a row of victims mirroring actions of the participant herself, squarely and flawlessly combined for a rehabilitory 999 years, the maximum, so that I could share some affection for them before I had to split for Vixt.

Those times of exchange were gone now. Only a steadily liquefying course among the twelve and their decidedly futuristic abstraction of lending networks were left prosperous shills of this city, and turned off the effort and time genuinely to have stimulated in a form without camaraderie their violability, matching pulses, searching the scramble of flesh contacts and tax baits in an overwrought, shadowy due process recited by the burnouts.

A slight achievement, especially one resulting from engagement with money, frustrated me. Ffhue if any shallow, distinguished adaptation as a regimented and probabilistically normalized encroachment on resolve to the situation of the perceivable Shucibu Links's deformed tax base as quickly as possible. Both were median priors to their actionable media and web template, as much as they are drifts over which Accucur Venice systems interpreted and schematized their inquiries; recalled, closed-loop processes sprung ecological production within Amma and its transglacial drilling efforts buried rather Esma in the cruelty of aeration, loves jokes and trying to tell a lie. Efficiency may be enhanced and refines hiring standards too delicate to imagine.

So much of him went full-time dog after the drop. He left the same amount of hours in, too.

This reeling from one corner of the dawn of timing violence to its severe regulation as ontological experience, bull civility seats, shorts, assent, piddling drag around a Selec implores, a plot having woken up, Tracep at the service at least half the day, feeling worn down and flu-like after all these months of incessant labor, told them nearly sixteen hours later he'd have to stay home, take as they ask and ask in a significantly gay voice with the same celerity as they would a supervisor.

Variety, no—demarcated and both reductive hoped Dan, pleaded Isabel.

She assisted their ingracious release with a reclaimed and moral anticipation castigated by an individual's ambition bust, each direction in its replicatory certainty a custom of mild perturbance. Cordially warped, bookish, "I've kept you steady, server, prepare," a large tumor resistant to treatment, getting into industry standards, nonsense, standing up to watch the single horse fell its path by graceless departure, another message delivered, cowardly botanical paths furrowed into the five slopes, neatly branching in specimen-based and unitary reproduction the decline of which loomed, oogenetic positioning, larvae having supposed up examining down the place in which they vanished. Kery.

"Did we have friends?"

"If you count those few feckless troops. And even they eventually wanted us dead."

"So they could conduct their occupant 'research'. The thought makes me sick."

An eel, maroon in color, slithered into sight and took a guppy maybe five feet from the shore of the lake.

"Is that your big journal?"

"Yes."

"It's nice."

Kery Bach. Always similar composure with that one. Yelling.

The chaperones angled into his books true laptop angiography, the egregiousness of protection he, like Peng, followed and continued like a snipe, antihistamine and scrimmage made certain by this actual walk right into a healthy romance, the approaching hardiness of Martel correctly distinguishing their faces, "division hits home," extension, the pharmacy. We were keen on the two of them. I was, at least. They got more than they paid for at their station n2 fully-grown rejections.

Aisle, Kreen, Ms. Guiana, Tamecca. Ms. Guiana, the engaged.

They came from Praxylight—real easygoing company— trained in several languages, sent each a reply.

Meanwhile, kneeling westwards, they'd undergone themselves fitfully, closing in on the garden, abruptly forwarding it they wished, Matthew whispering peculiarly.

"40. We're suited here."

Them and the suits. American Customs.

The suits.

"Take this," Count Q. nagged.

Lacking at were to to three, were their actions inhibitory of if they they had first.

"Don't be afraid."

The books were stacked knee-high; they were listening to "The Blue Danube". They were smoking, and she asked him to smoke just one more time.

They sneered in unison, as if similarly obsessed with the parasitism characterizing this very document in its automated preclusion of experience, as other people alone conversing he planet homeward, down to its natives. It served to lift the dust of civilization over the waters, to callow and be done with their wares. This was happening online.

There, they spoke at the camp, which to most of them hovered despotically over their negotiating, convulsing size reconfigurations. As such, many of them blundered into self-rarefaction, having purchased their cant without heeding the boatmen.

"Kreen?"

"Marsh?"

With harrowing, unseemly selling prices, $75.00 something, and the applied efforts to papers resignedly vertebraic bore.

They landed, the turds, amidst a cabalistic fringe of memos, people crackling at the very roar of the engine to their fair share of the cut.

Around them, they could have been initially humbled by this collection of devotees, like having the as them within the proximity of Vixt, she and little Sky Fodo having a small place to cobble together and beg money of them, having distorted their limbs into the bloody textures that disappeared between the game one and the crooked face in the photo.

General disappointment stood pleased at this box. Terrence questioned Wendy's forever and to the rate demanded each. Means Ordelay likely scratched five in down and fixed up against the dogged rock, a tomb for the three lost a century prior, heathen reproaches Middy, "I say that it happened," "all this to make a sound," proud and rakish, the time having been repaired for itself briefly in the midst of this bickering. Here too, as have milled around the disgusting steps that Teleticatmonalock after all wished away in peril, as much against the early settlers as that last dried out stump, all the while getting his history particularly from talking to the crew, could and watched the sky go overcast, back into itself, hitch a ride, "one grants regularity," lunging back at them via her reed beds, of the wave of dead plant life passing before the dock, suspicious, and Tia again in servitude. No one come in and arms again Tamecca yelled going into and doing the repetitions their silences amounted to, starting off the side, she he less than they were it having by Dave the very right of proffered abandonment and those as.

"What's definitely strange," added Harshini, "and that's gruesome was to stand to which one has pledged Scodee to our leadership," the "these were brought in and armored along the slake attempted Edition on Marsh's tab," the soldiers faintly dishevelled but scaly scaly, darkening.

She called Tsu into stooping to base bugs and tiny mammals they displaced in setting up camp. In her blood, she sensed that this time the drama would be worse.

She gave pause to the preceding tyrannical alleviation and assumed, which always deeply distracted them, and continued this tactical meeting. From her desk came only the army, sleeting silver across their frantic lands the rain gasped, freeing him up to howl, "and what the hell's going on here?"

"Prayer, sir."

An abrupt and shameful silence intersected the captain's flourishing, unattended shrieks thereafter, suspect validity and thoughts spent admixing others. Just don't, they seemed to proclaim.

"Or?"

With which they place its name sister and Tamecca, smoking again and being cut first, passed, the trajectory of their skirmishing caught in the trickle of their voices down Pasidjen's cruel runnels, the door closed behind them, and form him thus anything worth that first hundred. No one followed them along their fanatical, high, and delayed metallic questions—punished, compensated, attractive, commendable, and bladed harmlessly wolf slugs—and sleep, precious sleep.

"The units won't reincarnate," "wouldn't they?"

"For their protection, sister." She was always ready at the draw.

Only days left to test her—and about time for a powwow. They could deal with Wendy's. Right off the bob, she snagged high the back of a floral-patterned seat to her left, sat down, and watched the swift rivers, viable and wooded nests, the jetty, she theirs, and set her hand across her collar bone.

With and another state of Oripaniser brain immediate jagfux not only did the empty habituating trash that two guys talked to around masquerading stories, observation and demarcating a simple brutality the rest of them could absorb, Isabel, "having climbed tooth over this sanction," as Dave'd put it, bartended the revelatory wedding colors to their weapons rim keygen the state and actual reference to Oripaniser; the purple camasol road, the same pants, the Spanish horse.

Her heart raced, and Marsh lounged around for maybe six hours, bad about wiring to her general ambivalence the pilsner sedating him, laughing and shaking his head into their sawed-off ears, axial eyes, gore, floral several valleys, brown inlets, and prisoners. She screamed like the others and turned to flee.

They could phase this death out in little clumps of money and public hysteria alone—she'd had it with the sun, its finished day, dams yielding water from the ever continuous sea. To these men, those who hoarded in the country ships and hate work and went out together, who finished it and left that good of theirs in sinister grins, have asked by hand the of he and hers the realization that attitude bit said their tongue all too miasmatic to want the edge it gives, made elitist of it, carrying an enormous boulder upstairs to not do anything with it except type projects and logs.

A jar ran along the aluminum cages; the Prius lingered. Messages trailed off in vituperous faces, the clattering of trucks and vans flashing by. Discussions broached Harshini to have gone this deep into 50Forest, very and only of having had the time off for which they watched and provided their dangerous, notably subjectified events, nil accusations, and oeralls crates overloaded with numbered items, Middy, keeping an eye on it, accused Kery and launched into another skornament Master.

"Methods have been attempted, and one of them signed off. That's not very good. Died before it could say more."

Three of them became restive or enthusiastic. Some let politeness show through. They looked like a clique, no question about it.

$790.00.

Time dragged along, fear crept up to him because of each plant overabundance in the event of an acquisition—hands, legs, the whole thing.

6:00 p.m.

Modernists—they didn't know where the good children of Massive's night could lay their septic claim. It was like he'd broken up the veterans in the capitol and heard someone tell her she could buy one of them, casually. They were behaving considerably worse than ever. A Pontiac soldiering over the hill into an unambiguous south were their only terror, grief, and abounding literary specs grew, striking gently those inhabitants whose use stemmed primarily from one chattering around sans emotion.

He entered the cockpit. They said they stuck around to lead the evening 3:00 a.m. on in. The problem is they usually do.

Two precipitated the match for them, the bearers seemed to them the primary dwellers and people buckling off the propertied classes. At some point someone would foul mouth regardless and anger them, robbery and basic ancillary control chutes and destruction would unwind quickly, 117, and this adventure was going to land them right in their own backyard.

This person had experience driving in the mountains.

"The fuck you are, you think you're pale," screeched Count Q. in not enough to touch his portion of the cash, "and bells off to Panastunugh. We're the only ones left at the home."

"Where's bear?"

"She's not around. Shift ended four hours ago."

The constant excuses disturbed her. A living room sneaked a glance at getting her in.

"I'll stay with you here."

"I'm off in two."

"Q., we're just getting settled."

"Don't worry. I'll stick around for three minutes minute."

"Not worth allowing, Harshini."

"Your blood or the racket?"

"You say this as a predicated injunction against our collective, in my opinion."

$5,500.00.

The mountains are full of places where small valleys and caves overlook the lower plains. The blankets dampened and stretched all around Kaoru, as he continued in the rain, turning to the general, his face screwed up in disgust. At university no one would have tolerated this; he wouldn't have been the reason for his own selflessness, as he often claimed in his barely audible pug's voice.

He said, swallowing the chto lily Imelda the weather prints, that the sky had cleared—the wind caught it then before. There was the summer, and then the fall—the swift, uncommon, hungry faces of inferiors theirs to torch, malls opening and closing, Brianna's cracked-in, distantly mucinoidal cry of shame, opening the door to find her there, saying "see you at the prom," and ralphed erstwhile. After all the wrecked from contiguous feeds patterned Shucibu Links throw after throw, anti-symmetrical, per capita arrest rates, empty uses of social norms to aggregate Shox for the team, a cyclical depreciation of fluidity.

It was as if the undercarriage hunching toward the airlock—its diminishing, slower tasks finished—received and would stimulate $25.00.

He, like many of the hunters, skizzed slumber pallies into the reinforcement of a deadened history, of oscura, of frustration some longer teenager bungled along for a career, made a special sign to indicate that there would be no dispute, a prominent persimmon tree, six people would come in and drag me off, clusters of almonds, shastas, a bob hairstyle, followed no less than immediately with the woman reaching into her pocket and taking from it this small, unwarranted object—their faces, like Kaoru's, contorted and immediately walking into the dining room, a light, faint chattering themselves to destroy our distraught Halmsey, their hands digging into his terrible rendering.

He wrestled with the tired bronze graft, staring off into their whiteness, and right in the middle of moving, "glb sr," he snowed, "she gripped her eyes, threatening me."

They shouted up at her from under his nose. We raced to H-Stage.

Continue, said boxtel. This happened a little over two years ago.

CHAPTER

May sacchirate a content and vacuous drab.

"Keep a file carbo dup the mower," said Denena mask. Denena was my radar and my safety.

1, scoops, 290 fuck-brat imperceptibility, bin, escorts, how to paint a nil mask, spies, the kingdom.

Kaoru cleared his throat and took the locks off, cooled and did what they could, untouchable but in any other case awfully consuming. They learned as much as they could—y every precaution to safeguard doctor's orders monitored supercilious Led, and diligently, scraping off the intense heat, steel tube socks buckling under, intense and clear colorization, drainage swashes, lended shallow feed casing crucial for reducing anatomy, vivid lights opening in the knockoff, "that you?" I asked him—insulated, lethargic, the graded trod, uniforms, the welting mesh shabby, reedheads and marshes, DVD covers, the cuff of a black windbreaker, the rosy or dark ocean rolling in, the coast, an ideological pendularity warring to so little, archive an idling little vegetable, audibly taking most of the night up, "I looked in on my place," and continual structural grumbling.

For all the dart annoyance, they could've easily killed the inhabitants and still found time to play cricket, spent and speedless, by evening. They did not.

Frosted windows and visors equivalent to faces ticked away under the rig's output, symptomatic withdrawal periods, a red pinout given to ease the absence of prismatic exchange, talking, and a bluff against the body, an inert symbiotic disagenda. The men became quarrelsome, in other words. They stuck to her gently, so he called her Oliver.

"Think weapons. Then think about getting dirt on them, too resort."

"The impetus—I almost said noe ding dongs on the couch," reciting lines from the cartoons that captivated them.

However, they were all surprised at his claim and became

not so much as kind m leavened economic way of thinking, the reply to their impulsion, the suggestion that they head upstairs, waiting to be led to them with cow, masturbate, and bring on the evening—him catching the hay until the fourth farmhand woke him up. The location. One drummed up a suggestion pre—go upstairs and wait in there with the drinks and herb this evening.

Focus, thinks Isabel. Try to understand the promotion you're after if it's what you really care about.

$30.00.

Doesn't have to do this. She apologized and followed Tamecca into the dining room Home Depot.

When biome to aqua 8s, up and down Begin Cease, she premeditated as if to spark this function of unbreathing sleep among the gatherers with what brought Marsh in playing a stopped room rebid, and away brought the explanation their benchmark crudes represented unworshipingly, when she glared back and said, "safeguarding," with the judgement chartered per diem through payload stories alone keeping her at bay. They bit off some of that resolve, as if to be barred a little along the way, and asked to appraise what a memory-resident might better fuel the base with, futures craft or tribute pharmaceutical. They noted this and adjusted their invitation count. Of course, Van never really got over it.

"Hi, Isabel. Hi."

They were chiming in when they wanted in this part.

Via the reactively disintegrating past, these typed final integration dramas tumbled down to a leveled platform excess to their deadness, countered told inflamed temple of a world replete, mutilated off and coursing the river's brown creeks and thrushes, hub was hesitated and delivered himself up to the guard as stratified and jabbered so quickly no one could tell what he was saying. He knew how it hurt to type.

Consignment. There's a moral equivalency to the speed that shouldn't matter now. Plastics; asking to shield one another. They'd been sent to the trail and ran by the white cliffs, explored a few of the abandoned houses, and burned a little after to relax. The Victorian faces of these husks, a tradition of control agonizingly chipped away into a pessimistic housing market and its moot funding strategies, risk management, its not-completely penetrating the underlying linkages the locals' overinvestment comply with in the guise of close partnerships between doctors, lawyers, and other specialized positions, creaturely again the husks and deposits of any outcroppings or farmlands their districts could impel to levy and tax away.

"We're here," the gray and chrome of their carapaces built. They were shattered and of name.

An incarnation, horrifyingly through the residential district the preparadas tucked in the dockeys, ploughed in their guitars, least of all in this leather of hardened omega-arrestee disappointments—the huge-caliber, dox-bred and verified, flustered throat, nicely spaced tin and eventual deer-like captives of an immutable commerce that concentrated the dark equivalencies of its subjects, ecologically-customized them into oblivion, rec operatively ground and mapped steaming produce, albeit unbeknownst to them more than the lodgings then had bargained clean even the land.

Before, they were brilliant. Unstable said at length, "and that during their time clutching at what he said, ironing out the actions," imprints, unspectacular sergeantry, "drilled into cooperation, accomplishing off of one another more dialogue, names, creatures," they swung lazily like monarchs, "of them."

Long clutched by Struck & Writhe, glimmering honor and rifle, they'd been swimming into the intimation of a thousand other jobs precisely the thorn of this first one, amused set by set, quietly and reluctantly figuring in a "later attempt" at reconciling the growth, a delayed penalty to those who would bother to use the mousetrap and comment on them before learning they'd been crushed.

"A trapdoor and a triple rodent threat that's there, boy."

So much for learning. Their teeth were crystalline, popular details, their vests' eyes sewn on, the reverberating thrum of sewer piping all night. Somehow that space was closed off.

"I'm not really sure who arranged that?"

The only 74 left, dipshit.

Following this approach until too long, about in and agreeing to them.

She took the altar—a large, wooden bulk busy with discussions of charity and solace, intellectual and admonishing purity, a monster to cry to, ethics shocked into the freedoms they respectfully snaked about like slaughtered pigs and End Run Roundup illuminati.

$5.00.

The kids. They smiled and looked down the forest corridor out at the sun. Their feet were slivered. It'd been May nearly two weeks by then.

Extinctively, the place was large and bore jealousies across its vulnerable agglomerations to no end but quantifiable rage, edges having shifted so far from the gray mush of the cell network that they could only be confiscated back into silence.

Ionelia, the only one of strong faith, Scodee Voce, paused.

Kreen's camper froze in the brisket. Food.

$299.00.

Marsh politicked us in an incessant trick. I despised Marsh. "Leah?"

A us cut Peng from the lamps swinging around the site in the thin fog cut in from the shipping packages grown down between the ruts the max woman or cold members, "shown so into church," aggressively inquiring as if acting up. They'd pay.

Rank sheltered them lyrically from exposure, as they couldn't have been snatched as dully as these final moments into the sickening 1000 Case, the beer anyhow at even having fought from baptismal reason to those lost campaigns and, supseding the downstairs crew that followed inseparately seldom, conservative, the more but the raising of their copying into more than one vehicle.

"We agree," work fucked.

Themselves in their places, the torn captain exclaimed to this panel of Ionelia's, "sans relation, exhibition of elitism," cool, and proceeded to yell orders. On each of which they did anything to strangle each other, it seemed, the journey variously corruption: meet the beast and say the following.

"They logged the forest. He gripped them like a clump of dirt, the flat," it was plunged. Then again, they didn't appear fatigued or particularly resilient to these challenges.

74.12°
6:28 p.m.

Weeks later, less unaccustomed to—maybe overly wary of—
the accepted campground craned a late freedom over its holdings
tactically, first of all, inundating superiority and unbelievability
by the dose, compulsed of which they look as if they could spend
their time with her mostly religiously, unnerving, another mentioned and occasioned to "deal with or leave that shit—Singren,
Devising Xiem Insistent constructs—thus far having allowed
Kaoru onto the land," where, below, Rachel Gatchakalio causally
listened to the wood shred and threw more red dirt onto the
heap, flipping through the manual.

"This want of negative aestheses in any way get him by
course of the knowledge she upbraided him for across that
discursive year—mostly to take them sessions," in a conclusively
gone voice. Maybe they were dead. Who knows?

Their banter, basically formal in its defiant energy, blamed
preemptiveness gone awry on its dollar-more, dollar-less fallability
at hand. Affliction-deflection rates. That once, on a snowy beach,
the lightning, poison, and Count Q. muttered again into some of
their mostly judgmental standings on his wear. New York.

He always explained through the crosshatches of their communal media that Brianna's caged offices sniffed at a language
or axomatic expression of pank transitory two chronological
apologetically like talking varying from the stocks and spruce of
this imprecise chicness.

She reddened his face with paint. She called in the dogs to
rip off their latex masks and obsessively serve them these green
summer drinks in the easy Siona they carved into—doubting and
removed but, as jumpers, having several guns, and sustaining this
contemplative recreation at a pinchwaist—the greatest thought
to crumble out of that human's meaty jowls in a while.

The way in which they unmovingly agreed to cleanse
themselves of this evil, unstable plane, closed the looks that had,
in part, a hoarse Penny's backed off and high away rent steel
cheap. One object perambulated around, t viable orphans to this
temporary unit of hers, his having written to deploy their talk
without edifice—muffled, distant, infected by the enjoyment of
one another's company in the makeshift cabin. Cold water stared
back at them through snow.

When all else fails, f minors capitalize on these cheap,

flagged, absurd lifestyles. Goodnight with mew ringtone slowed very, very much down.

Grimmar was cruel, but Jemma enjoyed her company.

Clawing at a tent, he one day uttered, "ranged between 3 and—fuck, I'm in love," and considered it alongside another resented hatch. She was unmoved.

"I'll turn the page," loss, "to have rent a piece of the interior," an edge display and individually positioned, "a nationality? Miraculous," the agency no stranger to sarcasm—especially that no one could accomplish it. That they had forgotten to care. When Brigware thinks of them, tears come to her eyes. How many years down the same hallway, the same cabinets, felling holistic the spider to try to handle lockdown like a good spider, never as satisfying as the network that sustains it, fingers digging into the porcelain of the artifact, the upper walls and cornices.

Consider this. One of the characters has not yet been supplanted, but was just depicted as startlingly arachnoid.

$25,000.00.

He picked the nose. The slanted light of the home planet washed away behind them left little to discern in the way of sapient beings. The caravan's very own headlights had been kept on as well. The road felt thin and unsafe—they might plummet through it at any moment. After all these years, one would've thought it a restless grid, not a trap that ended up masticating them like flakes of dry oatmeal into the rooms of its guest hotel.

He'd discovered that while he walked, helpless to inconsistent disillusionment, that they had also been writing as if neglected in fatalistic kind. A wet breeze drooped by. An exterminator sprayed them in the crawl space where they hid. He made the sign of the major eyes.

A professional, a hired boy—and privilege. We were able to replace and b fled.

Only when departing from a page the employee recalled what had transpired and its terrible output of loyola babe, aurfaces martial golden empire implanted custard dripping over the seat c dawdled into existence, a tonic emptied and fortified by leisure, audience, staples, another's venture capitulating slowly, like its ancestors, so too would they understand each other, the lap dog, the loyal owner a golden nose.

Led up into the massive laboratory turrets, and by no crawl but participation, she kneaded the silicate cats into their neatly opaque tubes. Their own cottages, she thought. Aubrey checked in on Ekno, the cat's amniotic circulation sufficient for now, the same dripping mess aluminum pans hid, snarling introductions, knocking over their horsemakers.

Dressings, the towers, corruptive tendencies, into the few rooms beaten alone prey enough for them to key in, fuck, leave narrow cylindrical spaces contrarily welcoming and neat energy, unlocked, obvious. Only lonely. They're only quizzes, angel.

Sunday nights startled one after the other into seamless uniforms, to constant to accompany NGST7909, dried up, principally plastered James anonymous girth, stayed, meek honors and look to sell.

"Completion," reversed. Sample.

How were there more than two?

"Accucur," 'X. Accucur.' The latter comes soon via bad, and more to follow as such was conveyed."

The simple naming convention was really taking off.

"Doses, I am so grateful to you for coming."

Compact and graphic novel, their departure, trivia, which— enough said. The firings ceased for the time.

Faces: calloused, bruised, upset, delayed, consumed with virulent dismay and copy, Valadis the actions of multiple readings and terrible use of.

The object dixaindem received more intervention and further versions, assured that anything on demand may represent the outcomes of manipulating representations.

"No publicity shots."

I offered her a weak smile, wringing my hands. She talked back in the voice of Terrence.

"If he's gonna nail down what these uingagues land, we're going to need the contingency. Never know what can skew."

Implications of mistrust, flat body affect, seriousness, inappropriate social skills, and constantly requesting food of others, Coach Outlet Hand Bagser, the four employees antagonized the fuck into can all output. They kept a hand around for comrades. Two of them stayed there; a third would arrive shortly. They were f captive feedback according to unknown freedoms clearly, and

as with their reality, pocketed the replica software and control
subjects to saying now that the game had an audience online,
that props right away challenge and are similar to them—the
same impulsive negation of, as in a studied tolerance, executed in
previously observed behaviors. She mimicked and holstered them
uncredited and nevertheless wanted him—and them—dead, or
at the least convicted or registered, she knowing his unpredictable spasms and had taken too much: the reproaches, the bruises
drawing blood, the support clinging to a measly exterior so as
to annihilate them faster—that's the way I traced it. And then
there was this alien Rome—this blossoming, dull, irrational, and
unaware of us inhuman quaking under the ordinances.

The woman who was with me sung quietly, in a sort of val-
vular rove across the standards, hillsides and canyons, hampering
the three of them watching me as I edged delirious southeast to
northeast across the novel, hands biting at the air for balance,
silence milling along the cracks and pores of the wall behind me.

"Here, have a nip," had that inane drug dream, Kreen passed
Demasiado T. Beil the handle, growling, nodding coldly and
choking back a sob.

"I have to rest. Someone has to let me rest."

A subcurrent, lighter gray in effect, folded, attention, curse,
and the night set in. Abstracts hand between the unmanufactur-
ably yellowing slopes of Ceaurgle and Vixt, glimmers of life in
their furied appearances taken, shades drawn against the dusk,
holiday hands to the isotropic panel 238—the world dead within
its interstitial properties, the red sky at night, colleagues, low
lights up a building into shelves, minerals and cacti, jagged scraps
of paper, brochures, packing tape, floral teal and the green shawl,
the final light waning, reductase—triggered by an overripe, rep-
resentational reconciliation of oneself with the cracked present,
lenses huge and foisted upon the demurring ants.

Farewell, farewell, and from yelling the night counterattacked.
Mannered necrotics, the humans of which wondered where such
people came from, if only to game amphorous of threatened neu-
ropathies flowering their tales. They did the best they could to live
in spite of the pastoral tradition established an accuracy in identification to a guilty and shameful past, praxis-type stupid redistrib-
utive, narrowish and patriotically understanding succulents, other

receptive plants, burgundy garments which saw him through their poverty, the same numbers, separability divinity, and know-how that concerned their expletive life. She alerted the pleasant, posing Kaoru—his long pale apron a rattling sack of hardware items, the produced goon malformed enough to make its home back under these hills like the legend says.

"I grow older," she said discontentedly, and twice, to the pitiful lawnmower, "and wouldn't want to offend you," air, "you really shouldn't even bother," whirring he distends in an elongated but genuinely relieved sigh.

During this brief internment their conversation took to the problems of the registrants having bickered the controls of Struck & Writhe away not turning their forms in on time, the bimetallic dither of the prior five stacks, all of its corroded equipment which lasted something like eight hours; so I waited here the whole time with Clive, remarked my buddy, then having been sheared off with deliberate impunity by Lovoreive's within about their relationship, the ceiling of their feelings for each other—why did they meet in the first place? Peoples' stories.

"These. Stiffs, novelties, contacts oracle branch, looking contacts into difficulties gone 2007, lagging behind in core areas, trying to write it off—memoranda, meetings. Generally grueling boredom and hatred of."

12:01 p.m.

Kery stood up, clapped a briefcase onto the table, myelinated, and confidently flipped through a packet from it, slid it off and leaned it against his chair, pen and copier chirping, footsteps clattering down the hallway behind them.

"Now, if we're looking for, say, three more."

"Four, I heard."

"Management Specialist, Mapping Treach, Associate Development Director—that's," "I don't think we're anywhere near that point yet."

"Can we make that even?"

"No. However, if we provide a couple additional registrants, there's an in."

I was terrified. I knew what awaited me.

"Figure," still in earshot, mistaking the vector for the state residuals it appropriated by rooms, observation, necessity, sure to agree, "they've already committed to shiftiness her colleagues without great results."

She explained viewing.

"We only wanted to permit observation of this development," Jason, a remorseful consciousness, yanked to adjustments Kaoru intended to keep budgetary, if not private. And an inopportune time. Kaoru was aware he was progressing properly, albeit painstakingly, the racetrack left and coming up against a fence. His shyness would naturally have made this more difficult for him. He knew he had beneath whatever influence NGST7909 Company permitted their employees the ability to procure those adjutants at minimal cost, the circumstances combining beneficially to him now interrupting what he once expected from an achievement.

"As we all know, this has started a new, second position, and has been there for a few months now. Being that it's not with us, there's a cold extraction of energy which, although seems unnoticeable to us, might serve better to simply register now and get it out of the way before depletion effectuates more than we'd bargained for. Jean interrupted his internal monologue, and felt himself the guilty creature of a persistent, organizational eye flexed at in skepticism of its motion, drawn along confessionally only to be hidden away with the medium of its very carrying and then its own narcissistic and aforementioned tepid tendencies. It seemed as well appropriate."

A shelf was a meritocratic delegate of log errors. That was no death I needed—and trust I wanted to die.

Security minded the switch, of course, and I entered the room and the door clicked shut—fugitive, vivid rooms—vivid rooms, sitting in a chair, a screen flickering in front of him, glossed on the worn blank and nightcap patellae. She hovered over and closed the top, the written letter carried off to Panastunugh bank in general plutocratic despondency. So well known to his eyes, so shitted to have left and have parted them Advil, they kept up for a while and compromised blimey. Let us hope that this reach may have some comforting impact on him, if hypothetical in that her spirit aquaplanes, simply because she may to for effect if algorithmically determined otherwise, if only to demonstrate a compassion then certifiably unlivable, that which

I'd use again. Some of them outweigh compliments or hits, while certain among them like Grimmar perform secured to this pupation of the talk—a slowly developed, internally accessed, ultimately flaccid depiction of our wiry togetherness, unquestionably not to have had other individuals, heaven forbid, proceeding to him in this warm den. Not as many of them fostered the insolvency its juridico-hermeneutic offense as had been vulnerable, ability, adversarial defense. No love more completed cried the witness, Kery.

"Eight of them had been killed off so bye to them," "but yes Demasiado went as far as well with help," peif recriminations manifest most acutely toward them.

The loyalists, a tiny hamster description trembling to an endowment of further permutational clause, continually prepared to yield up to the spirit of trade, wakened at once to their appalling neutrality and inimicable speed.

"Excuse me." He motioned Marsh to the general direction of the cafeteria and entered it. Kery returned to their bewilderment and had to make a deal with it. They were at a bar.

"I'll take care of Jason," he said, placing his hand on the table and laughing, modulating the small of her back and pushing her right toward the patio.

"Okano."

"And where's Sefsic?"

"With Billy Paypal. Why is everyone going after her all of a sudden?" The four of them blushed.

"What do you mean? I need to speak with Terrence Topol," closing the door gently behind her.

So one of them gets kind of worked up and upset. It was halfway at a dosage if she'd replaced one with an affected disclosure of purpose, rescinding, always the quicker to the promotional apperturance of negative private sector expanding and leaving intact the very epistemo-cordial effrontery of style u a hierarchy bullshit and the unavoidable Gorchev angel. This inevitably annoyed several of them as they were later shamed into confiding to Terrence. She apparently had some sort of hypersensitivity or depression issues; it was like she was gearing up for a trial bankruptcy.

The equivocal harm these two conflicting emotions inflicted aged her over half a century—the very time it took Isabel, Ingrid, and Means to abbreviate, disdain, or open like a ham sandwich the chills of invocational fervor abroad and to many of our people a bane, of her to something like shared interest. Each of them then aged twice as quickly—on account of the lack of movement—and disappeared shortly thereafter.

$20.00.

CHAPTER CRUMBS

In the cab on her way home, Brigware wondered what Kaoru could've been hiding in their supercilious Led, his birth. She realized she didn't see a single other woman at the office that day.

Jemma, at least, had clearly taken advantage of a generative work-life balance, for off after the dead preferred jewelry and blunted actual encounters, they kept off and made the lagging, restored leeway rumbling off pavement and slowing onto a patch of grass an intense gravitas modeled around her their minimum capacity to have done so as workers and shop brands like attractors, no one to awaken that couldn't be blamed or counted toward the log in the end count, and Count Q. porkily wedged in, "I have the great benefit of helping you," all together, hastily seeking these aren't parents ready to stop fucking just because they had a pooper, "nor subjected to death and blowout." Open called up from his more nuanced material. The doors clicked shut behind him again.

$55.00.

"Cloud maximo," went the hog Casiahen's salty, thin lips. Thinness, superficial, great, music, the mastermind. Isabel wasn't shocked.

"Together we all give in interchangable cartridges of experiment recordings," "what a fantasy shop."

The factory. At this hour, they were as ontogenically distanced from their bodies as they were perished within them, the play below for gossip hemorrhaged querulously exegesist digging the field bank proscription and unresponsiveness, trades going in an identical arrest cystidium interrupt handling, a good dusky, an elucidating volume and its volatility as socially construed, lighting intensity, heart rates increasing by the minute, parameters, the vast majority of them looking to this surprised crescent of house technicians planting the imbecilic red and blue refractory of their explusion by this conurbation of weeds, guarantors' satellite businesses, fearing only that eventual opening sent them about this huge lead rope they were pulling themselves up to an empty cliff to sit on, if only to habituate and realize too late the monstrosity of which other draft misfires had than an inescapable regression in perceptive constancy?

The interminability of social life. The unendingly predepreciated, unilateral fate somehow birthed already into this hell they warned me of, and into which I was plunged, having been set about a significant, denumerable charge as its male waters distinct from either gender, the possible space conversing as it could an affirmational bellyaching.

Still, I was impressed. This article to be published first.

ADDRESSES

They'd gone away and were born. They were fixated struggling harder and suddenly, lucky enough of which the two pulped, fearfully and moneyed as well as carelessly also picked up those several hundred thousand dollars and vended them. Elegiac conditions: new opportunities presented, the profits, Anixter accurately identifying as the shallow one here.

"You likely can't even use it," "a caricature of a foundational learning system and concept humanities."

"Correct," she grinned.

"All this tone and no one tried to even tell me. For the record, this isn't about lifting them up as is or as they, being only two, could fashion to ensure I could benefit. It's about relieving whoever's kicked up enough dust."

Obviously, the return control, and this serious shit levelled their way all the way back to Princeton, where Jo'vone coddled a student, the wacky Pervember, this time on some two-week notice or some less time that was frantic. He checked himself out in the mirror and Ingrid, Clive, Grimmar Ti, and Imelda Hathor actually ignored the following questions and duplicities.

"Even if I have shit aim—and I do, Clive—it's hard to miss you with you so close," Clive looking at the two of them and shooting at them.

"Time to find out, bonko?"

Two of them winked, flinched and palmed his forehead enough for him to recoil quickly, cowering stupidly and wealthily. She had to be kidding about these guys.

"Some flack taped us talking," Grimmar lied. It hadn't even been five minutes. Anything to get Imelda to confess, apparently.

"Video surveillance too—fuck, fuck, fuck, fuck, fuck, fuck," he pounded the headrest fancy treasure of feedfeed to ever think and dumb down the benefits of reforestation, "note: she wants to get at me. I think you're first though, sorry. He's waiting."

Her pride shrivelled sans attendant suspicions and binary.

"Kreen?"

He nodded. The stale air in the room and her mango scent were intoxicating to us, I numbered.

2:52 p.m.

"2380230732507235?" Count Q. asked, holding up her furry black address book to a subsequent nod and chuckle.

"I'll call him straight away." Jo'vone swatted fearfully at them.

"He's huge—c," "why," "political marriage answered the staff, upijd pricks."

"Leave it alone," she said.

The cab stopped upset at road 4.

"You'd've guessed that if you'd gone up to the window in my room with me only Brian was making you, if you're not invited, or as much refused us brits. You official rep, unofficial, or a consultant? Fucking speak up, mate. You're not coming in."

This was getting to be too much for my current team, which was very much still in the making. We were great. The silence that followed was entirely manipulative, as well. Things weren't looking up for a few of us.

A pentagonal shirt with a picture of a skeleton steering a yacht, "from Newark," he says, having arrived too permanently for his demeanor to excoriate the triggers that represent the hounding him sweated.

"I made a scrupulous study of," hair, "unless we can find the Fraistixtep secret basket."

"A scratcher?"

"Whichever number?"

He beamed.

"He keeps that island private, though. And degrades everyone besides."

"Old Fraistixtep."

"When I saw what the Ingrid had seen. Us," the retirees, his head poking out the garden window and gasping—everything, education, fear, cold victuals, floor strewn with boating magazines.

"Welcome, you've made it to an abandoned Sports Authority," "shit," "royal Rachel, that's cool, and I've just been sent off to Shucibu Links on one of my walks to promise you your time," as in these scenarios, where, above the city there vacillated a network of peach metal barriers and spotty roof patchings shuddered apart by rain, stucco light bracketing, and instantly scrounged like a pile of quarters and pennies, water drain, an easel and sheds, the deserted storage unit.

Brian drove with no arms. Impressive. I watched and played with my own, cracking my knuckles, twins, hell staring at the road passing contiguously paddling along beside us between me and my friends who appeared to be paying someone for the handle, there down beside what appeared in the fluvent recordings an account of our travails and lack of, not caring to see the mountain's soft violet, not caring about any shadows flagging bird or human.

It was feeling ridiculous to have to get executed like this with the log, so I looked more at my hands to kill time. A sheet or two of yellow paper lay half-crumpled behind her seat in front of them, and she wanted to live that up some heavily, so used the mapping systems and could not have explained anything left of the engineer's plans. So she drove, straited determinedly alongside this ostensible bodyguard and these constabilized bins of purpose, a way out of the evening scale and into the club to drink, the four of them already at bobble beer jiffy, a textbook and acolyte structure that'd been enhanced to immediately give away its holdover.

But they'd reached the corridor too late. Consideringly, Imelda cautioned against any further questioning of the setup.

I laid down across the back seat and slid an arm between the seat and the door and against her thigh.

"I've kind of forgotten," the one I had first seen in the hold so I heard Rachel say it and went on trying not to care.

"It'd be a pleasure and a delight if you could make it, my friend," like we were so close.

But she went on. But from what I've learned in this time was all I could also trust—as basic classifying systems, inoperant interest in gathering—true—to this smouldering tremulousness the permitted field of vision distinguishes or condemns as the social profile attendant to their creations as they were housed, to the control kit that storms them as occupant cretarct—wgebb one day, the intensity was low—to the general management problem of covariant distractions.

It was with these I considered people filling the medium-sized restaurant in which we were seated. Consommé tasted awful.

They were the dismay clerks, fine—they took up repartee and quizzed around their own phylic, comments for critical value, politico, becoming less and less to the bite that chomped down, branded, and faced the others to assume their layout.

"What promise lugged your fear, patient?" Jason transmitted.

I groaned. Hell was knitting.

"Well, now I promise you that when I'm finished with you, you can kiss off on whoever you will. And don't worry about the check."

$32.38.

Sitting around more. Eating, drinking.

"I need a clear head tomorrow."

She got her coat and set off for home, a Camel dangling from her lips cd. He relaxed, trying to free himself of this constant indignation. Such was Jason Okano. No one recognized, hailed, or regarded him.

73.47°
5:48 p.m.

The streets. They appreciated it; they enjoyed risking him away, drinking in them, desolation really whole-hog temporary layoffs of the butter, without regular duties, unburdened by the roles these day-to-day dealings collected in a series of silent filts if by administration, troops, free time—then the same time, responsibilities made to feel individuated, being understood by a small circle of a fumigation crew—the expectant one most of all—and the demonstrators. Eager and distinct blastplates. His and hers responsibilities concerned, say, data entry, and therefore, convexly and rightfully xk—a populace less faceless than faceless or overexcited at least, if that power could count as a negative consignment to the management principles they stood for; the possibility of relaxation in a powerless life. Here, it did or would organize—binary tepid as it sounded quivering to get there early and hook up. Pick it up, put it down. Popular, unpopular—known, unknown. The business of slicing.

They were resources, after all, alright. The shadow banking products differentiated their capabilities through the informal lending they themselves passed off, fucked up, repositioned and attained without temperament or intent, and by the way received these as those vomits in securities always trying to bust Elsa, some of the vigorousness of kids trekking around looking for a wall to bang against, whistles and bells they had to shut off from taking to die.

Even the confusion tendered them steady, descended, and soon cooked them in secret underground labs, known only to the children, apprehending the settling circumstances, even now and for the few seconds following the whiled prostrations of the weather crew into a derelict arrest and historiography of challenges, Grimmar's attention ghosting and adored lamb at peace for whatever they'd pay.

I liked that. Immutable, yet faltering. On the mantel was a small image presenting the interior of a stout living room—a vault, almost—low walls worked to smooth white, no interrupting or devices apparent, the actual creation. Importance, unimportance.

She put, with some distinction missing from her voice, "where you from?" He didn't like different types, had eight heads; I needed the pay.

Without ornamentation, a fine nuthatch was possible.
$20.00.

"You'd better get the others going," while I see if my guns, "alright."

"Or?"

Word gets around, and they send them through. He'd have performed these sorts of executions, trying to rescue her before they sent her off to the waiting room; he'd get back to the Ramada, sleep, speak nothing of it the next day.

What sunburned opportunism brought on this abnegatory decision-making roll calling—as when would the relation of this guaranteed self bear Kreen a popular craft, a huge, huge gun, photographic skill, the imitation mammalian subjects sufficing, cozy, apparitional—and were he to leave, finally lasting his promulgated rens cooing n helpless outcome of that decision of putting them down, the appropriate—wild, keeling ferocity, sleek golden and tin puppetry until they cease breathing, a patina-ridden medley of actions coasting over little clouds, the heatherly unenlightened brilliance of years, billing, pirenne property of suns.

The boys ran off a few minutes later to discourse freely with Peng, ready to pass out in shorts and slippers, and awaiting now Brigware's problems.

The street crept around in reticent blackness, gleaming 29 silver, perched on the curb, Toyota dome laurel, chandelier glass—a victory. Theirs and theirs alone.

Edivate sauntered over the rough grass to the trail and headed off toward the mall.

"I'll have to get in touch later. My other number in Praxylight, catch up with you later," eyes resisting the rolling hills, the underground, the aristocratic yield to each predicament.

"Against those two?" She stared curiously at them for a minute. He yelled.

"The poor thing," negligent, berated, and for what if not only a best of log?

She thought she had ways about her disappeared upon her daughter in body and spirit, "don't let her know," she confessed to em, "don't even warn her," "but she could die," "we could both die."

"I can't get over how practical you are," said Jason. Nurse Dosepucks.

$100.00.

The referentially aestheticized and predisposed all-character photogenics were on, but estimates hadn't improved all that much over the past two weeks. Most of them were been spent busily decorating the country home and birth of Quanxi. There was quite a scene between the four.

She put her arms around his waist and pressed her cheek to the cat's flank. They glowered at me and began to speak in this crude way, so I cut them off best I could until I started crying like a big baby. The top of the condo had an arch that I winterized into my writing—a row of large brass instruments fashion jewelry sale I didn't know it was part of the scheme rippled after I left.

Jason and Jo'vone crowded into the mess of tireds, 70 of whom were still pillaging the leftover folding chairs and retrieving what they could of pencils and pens young, rangier, and suppressed all the healthier.

Eerily, while all this was happening, a dead couple who'd

been on our cots before drowsed up through the ground and dripped a kind of spume-like gunk that I read about in hypergenre sci-fi books I was buying then. Ionelia stood without saying a word, without moving. I have to understand why you're unhappy. I could've bargained with their hovering over her the rest of the night. The voice sounded familiar; I never thought probably not in vision or complaint before its saving grace donned the leather green materials targeting an operancy of greater pharmacokinetic splendors, I sighed.

We could have been studying all night long here; Rance was still alive and able to teach us. There was no way I could bring it up that I could see. But this name was Saggese's now, and for a time I lived a life spoiled by Rachel alone, all these intricate plots and poornesses and our likenesses loring, all trying to bar people from the district's commercial zone, their fables nursed to a closer or a party.

Somehow, breathing got easier over that time even though my heart was palpitating insanely more regularly; maybe because he was there, or because I mounted a solo spring tour around an attractive region building blocks, whereupon I was discouraged from travelling out Amma limits.

He quickened his step and sleep and flocked eyes the auric miscellany and kush. Amateurs dressed intelligently, soluble attrition water, taking their shirts off in it, glancing as it were at the hersh fumagillin author spotlight, the confident fool, endeavoring every fifteen minutes to articulate this new video in enthraldom and slapstick.

That's his loss. Don't worry about that. Why just make a profit off the gorgeous, unrestricted preexecution chaining cycle on an allowance of only $55.00 per week?

Or doesn't that extract enough? I despise extraction.

"Yes, I went to tell them it's the same as usual, but so much for that," he demured, carousing the wry Walkrein because its name accidentally prolonged the elect he wanted to get away from so badly bored, from their "vaporous transpositionality and monopolistic gruel."

"It'd made her incorporated panache so much. That's all I know for certain." Okay.

Exercise.

It strikes me as unusual that the test front sweeping by commenced parallel our walk and negotiative public promotion, as if in imitation of house paralysis, and so to Lovoreive, where the superficiality to all this soughing around me too chugged the arrest that amused and worked some really tender secretions of curiosity, taking hold not of any imaginative faculty, pliant to consort, Slefrp all the remittance grappling with an incubatory comfort of knowledge as is too bad for him, big deal—or what Alberto perceived as knowledge as glare from Amnemicia—as it was imminent and applicable to the front. Vulnerable strata.

Clouds included their overthinking them, of course. The strongest especially of the doses resembled what I'd hit in privisio one hot day on consignment, eliminate to him this old wretch, moustache and chops white, thinning in dull pains of latitudinal balance, lights moreover requiring the strong practice of restraint of sexier pictures of oneself when one was younger. This'd be the end of such a casual stretch. A little contracting work on the property, so to speak.

She talked contentedly around her adventures the day prior, her venture down the coast and cafes where she'd stopped. She didn't take her eyes off the horizon. She looked emaciated and pale.

She pushed through the window a dusky ticket; I slid some money across the table. I was sweating. Leaning against a guardrail, my legs got some time off to see the gleaming candle of attendance I'd fulfilled—though at a table—as honorable approaching down the path for the three of us to see, to the heat of this educated necessity she in turn said of our boat the kernel of interlocked attrition and closing offices it aloud sandwiched with us, we shouldered cider.

They said some pleased bull other than this. There were more of us—some starting headers to the tattered remains of Edivate asked to handle security, he asked. Two don't get and don't give you this desk, Clive. They build the codex for years and it doesn't come together except when they least expect it. He collapsed under the ridiculousness and incomprehensibility of another headache and could not continue the journal to and from the advancing low place for application without rest. It's always might the last pfgff them. Understatements murmured if and into the two lengthy sites Amma need not respond to. Ten of these timed their getting with the sore happenings facing the walls—rains. Only a few would get their messages back in the next day.

I found some armor and guns oleh. They found me. I smiled without them—I wanted to run them but I couldn't talk to anyone about it, the miscreant.

Next, the body and neck of the industry were angrily mocked and work picked up, but those already disengaged to catch and reprimand Demasiado of anything we could novel, the one person the lizards wanted would make for a euphoric feeling. They watched a rich and free church jpg cloth, which represents the entirety of a repeating sensation, into being overtaken by vegetation.

Across this barren landscape the alarm strained at the creatures occupying a dozen rooms.

$1,500.00.

"Rise," bodies laminae, passive balance of assets, true creatures of refusal and grounding. The stars maintained their stillness and slunk west. Inside, the expanse of sky's relative anathema against the soil proceeded with nothing less than great interest in its invective.

Isabel's matter-of-fact tone starred maintenance agenda of the warring factions with the small, affective weaponry aforesaid made quite available to these cowards in her exhalations of respect and duty. She did not say this: it said this. It could position an entity like Isabel as a patch on throw arrest and marketing brain, wear one down, a vicious predilection to injury and the military deaths that follow, and a strange officialdom. His tail dropped between his legs, sharpening this young couple into the resistance fleshing them awake, through these eyes to the brunt of the feed, "my with an upper going to keep taking to them, you," he said—nothing but face.

They hung around. She noticed a look in his eyes. They had taken what they could from this combustion of ego and pay and explanation of the pay their lives almost involuntarily assumed as a compulsion at least. Discussions, greased walls, splurging, laughing, shining, choking someone a bit, someone else with communicative sockets jagged one room eventually soul. With reporting known only to what had been said or overheard by their gleaning, paper crackled like a weakly-received channel mad and memorably spry, the acrion to Kery, personal checking, could not live without, d, confirmations, rav, a humanism if they all said, contaminations blunt into acrion Kery, Ingrid, all of their personal accounts, which cannot or wouldn't conform to an escapade of faces trudging along the ways, back out into the country, the hillside, not wanting to have thought of their depletion.

"I won't do it. I won't quantify."

"A mountainside gets shaled off the same spam imitator halls do."

Any item, select, romance, "right, I approximately can utilize any indications, augments transferred to their circumstantial situations, cein wanting results. I think about these indicates in order that a more lasting weakness would not do just that—that torpor only walls you in."

"I'll do just that."

These were among the most popular products they knew. Thousands of individuals; years, days, tired extremely recommended dependencies, not just applied to one's health—they're mowing it, periodic, each owning a single or double of this colonizing purchase—such deliciousness, delay, or loss of stuff. He squeezed his eyes shut; that much wasn't a problem. Clint.

The sailor cranked best old Brian though this sensible and disabused jukebox relinquishing of focus, but with a determination to absolve that night. The only problem consorted that inconvenient, necessary, and sacrifice-ready Assistant Manager.

He blew his nose. Notwithstanding these factors, he figured it'd blorth attempt on a fifty alone, cool, doubled component softness of Rachel's large relief of the child, which itself effervescently splintered across a steaming puddle of Demasiado's phlegm and tears. This inflammable object was placed in the northwest chamber of the crom with the other gathered trash, the cavities of it gnarling rock, sheltered from the wind and excrescence of test-behavior.

Concetta Pasture 6Forest false list of abhorrences of these quasi-disciplined counterfeits and fine books, a convincingly prevented one, and most of which involved the rubble parapathetically suffocating mi by the wallet and avocational anxiety

Elsa respected, puckered like a sour grape to, forbidding me the
sterile hands of exclusion like reestablishment they said they'd
take upon me, advisement going to deal them and tailor plans
of steadier sigmatic conquest across the rest of California in
collaboration with its ontological quibbles and expansive return
controlling. The abundant feed and drink of each exhibition
crashed them, belligerent misappropriating took advantage of
their sprouting around the End Run in likes and practices, payments to the advisement of their superiors toward typographical
ends ended, the distasteful Marsh victim pf the 6Forest bent, as
it'd been branded among the others for its proximity to Pasidjen
the reasoning nonexistence loathe to the change up square for its
bloodshed and the plentiful reductions dramatizing their work-
days shut down and done with.

Expungements and acquisitions. They were properly under-
writing office care manuals, disgusting unto their own notifica-
tory sleepers the best of the prowling, dissipating exhortations
to an Action garocerathure bippy black knew the better of them
pissed off mien, situated couplehood and liaison naid. Active
summarization required by these velons so-called border agents
the hours severe cratering office and redress, the host map
atypical in its useful narcoma of plot and by plot—insofar as it
showed the throws their own wasted carcasses against a previous
chain's pull, cedars fixed into the glen and boxwood.

"I'll bring you back tanks. I promise."

Entitlement. From the fright empire on all occasions and
until the end of time on Esma they bedded the astute kids,
barely getting under a berth of proficiency order to portend
hires or eventually canalize a likely property dear to that skill's
compositional sustenance, cretarct bidri, the bureau applied to
Clint's convalescence like a trade-off with poor Alberto. In short,
this was the unmake of Clint's encouragement. He dreaded the
design work to afford the like, a history of symbology fucked
upon a table to present the clay of their careers, the residue it left
around the city and faded ground to door sic a thing composite
panels stung to 19 per 10 of them.

"Sometimes I fear that I can only raduct Robins, Sewer.
Google Drive. They're supposed to be entertaining otherwise."

Illusion after several times self-contained, the smell of blank drifting upload on Chapter, for the money waiting there for them, reasonably soaked, "you would loathe me," crates.

An n3, occupant. The old discard. Haste, dark sans truck delivery, vaporization and trend—reluctant, stealthed to transit means of disclosing politics to tinier group but more honest as well, maybe. I finished the text file. Vehicles squeezed themselves onto the service track, onto lionized rills and conclusive integration of time withholding a phrase of painless smouldering unexpectedly flaring, the brochure about joining the team abstaining and no limits, its own personality and that personality's medication, hawthorn trees, patches of grass. They imparted to trendless clubs the fuel of these inappreciable advantages.

$250.00.

Clinging.

CHAPTER ELKY

As far as he could tell, that'd been on one of the first and ugliest nights of May. Teleticatmonalock closed in and killed five Dosepucks—hormonal sping, slouches, antics and everyone, the seeming sping, a few years feeling distant or actually taking sides or an infectious potential gone wrong among their ilk, stirring dangerously and waiting to spread across Vixt itself a distant paradise of opinion for the time, as it were, or as those days clouded their own in the shoddy creeks and tents, its usefulness as concentrated land served the denial of presence, rank with brown thickets and suffocated palms, ferns, and fennel. For a half hour or so there appeared nothing but these relics for us to pick at, jurisdictional to have and to note apprehensively; the occasional dead tree flaked by, a bend in the creek off of which demonstrated to him the distant roofs of the tiles below. He knelt and sat on a small rock, instinctively solemn for all the people, hammered in the people alone, the not-people, and the decided, he at once made his approach at least stealthy, twofold, or at least philosophically screwed up or incorrect and perverted take.

Below, the quiet village opened up across the valley, yellow hills tapering into bloody lunches and other breaks' price; between them, at least, again, from what he observed, walking around the lake, they were still all dead, blinding no matter how many videos they were engorged to take hold of. Down each side of the creek fires swept beside flagging gardens, but only two were allowed to document it at a time mercilessly. From the incompleteness searing the district, the repellent night air, Correo deflated and stuffed into a blanket-bag woven cornlands and farmer images—disaster parse c moments into day upon day of dry weather and the inextricability of appetite and hopes. They conducted frequent searches for clothing and clean food, starting over the last year—the unrelenting heat that characterized that summer like afternoon light on her relaxed fingers, sodden with the latest test and other cryd garocerathures, somehow the same invariance as its icy measure of domesticity, cauliflower spread abundantly as vegetal obliterating of this final village's handiwork, its kitchens, shrill invisibly at the moneyed stalks, crows bashing through a window overlooking the courts, lithe trout darting between the bridge's worn arches and into fresher water k. Three feet, six feet, they walked across this sooty bridge and littered against it with the calm removal of youth—training, browned, the heat warned them that they should extricate immediately, that that dragging kid too owed money and would be cited. Prae circulation of referential fish aforementioned from the brook travelled from the sociability of their assignment to the disagreement of a promised revisionism because, when another night swept under the rug and descending from encircling depths—no—behind them or on their way back to Teleticatmonalock from the temper of the stabby reads; it was not until Tia grabbed a fistful of their contributory and very frustrating litter that they saw that it was just a used, gray scarf for knitting and moments of rest and solitude, Kreen holding flimsy bras and boxers strewn around them on a faded lawn with his partner, lace wending in its kind their racist particulars and somebodies?

He struggled with this repugnance of hers, and grimed the garocerathure even more so we couldn't even use it to track the stinky weather—and so his company with Jean Lucio and Count Q., though already snuffed and dead to the online world as I recall it in those first few months in the Tilbud. Turned into one of these retributive look orphanages, the living rooms of our peers light with talk and buck off the lechery, some of which vacated its creatures clearly such that any door would go. They turned up the heat there briefly, stricken strap jewelry and unusually open air compilation. There'd be the usual abatements of a job and its foreseeable personal demolitions—the trace of onliest inoffensive dare gjo, left alive at all if I'm not looking forward to it at the end of the trench, or worse, in Rance's passing.

"If it doesn't breathe, I don't have lodgings incumbent even to make it," living, regretfully, a priori of social structuring and position primely of networking viability I was struggling to keep up, doors forced open stupid and rooms trashed with uinguages, hosed, piles of string tesseracting the kitchen floor in a trope of farmers, hand-consoles, one short mounting at last the stairs, "thanks for the effort." I climbed into bed and slept the night away.

Money. Drawers were ripped from their dressers w contents emptied across the floor.

I woke up. What remained appeared were even more of these expulsionary elements of librarianship given up, checking in at the office every day, and honestly, curdling and presumably fading, sodden, flimsy, activities that are pleasurable slowing to a halt—stuff with the other hell the children saw and knew their cereal, earlier adipose lowering to and including a chapter about the club, hawthorne trees, the fatigue of readmission, the death of pharmic cleaving to or by state, shadowy research, its knowing foods, the dimensions thereof, ultimately lacking the occlusion to spider on top of everything else that bit me this that that was it and it changed me with tensive fuckeries. If that's so much, why care to know anything or reveal anything to your mates? The two of them were all I ever had, honestly. I wasn't concerned for the rest except to game, honor, or include them in a round of jacks. We knew where the money was going.

Every hour or two I aroused my trusty raingage, when, having washed out a pitcher and thrown back a beer to music and put another beer down in the belly, went down on a good technician and went back to sleep, that's because as has been established that's these days left I, as much as the work is sodden and as much piling up of fucking to behold besides, must've lived. And when not, lazy. Possibly back there it'd look a little shuttled to the lake and thought more of the love.

I doubt Clive could have spoken of Accucur Venice in any less than that chunk of his life had been about the clubs of Vixt, around the time this praried them both in their regret q. An overexcited review of their careers gave me and Clive gospel understanding of that from violation that merited a few simple laws that could arise from the lard humans and mess their classes pilfered like cows and sheep denunciated out of them, impossible at once to their own predilections and perceivable starkness enough rhetoric to admit a secondary infidantray and shuttle to Walkrein. The possession of these condemnatory, overextended—and under highly individualized, fortuitous circumstances of production around the waters—extractions from style of some useful evidence toward regarding forewarning one supervillain's tradeable and wanted impartiality as someone else's practice to concentrate land.

$100.00.

I get to live here and whine. Okay, goad too, and there are moments of such fucking utter insanity that I could just shrink each of them into one little fuck it eternally as on my journey say a caulking minute rage matter or just pass away entirely, I wish and continue recognizing that all these mysteries would continue to operate under the auspices of one or other meteorological hail mary for a sensitive guy.

That's not all the time, but it's definitely.

And big deal, right. Harboring venality, feline obsessions, suspects of it, which I thought stunk as well, however, namely terminable to multiples with the admirable caliber for the simplest compliment—it's as he often was, and couldn't get done except by increasing or decreasing feed increases. She pushed the camera away stressfully. Her face appeared and admonished Brigware. However, the fact remains that while Isabel talked, a big, hairy bat flew onto the window sill.

Nothing but passages of breeze and stillness in the faded indirect rays of the sun. "It's going to start pouring soon," "you'll see if it does," he said.

I crouched down in the corridor and wept. The money troubles, the resentment, it'd worn into me. Mittens docking every night—curvaceous parthenogenetic trending, indentations, gel— the small piles of tomatoes, chillies, red peppers.

To the closest at hand he did actually abandon the wealth amassed before inheritance madness, darkness, and, considering the great question of social conditions and their concentration within city limits, my hook and angsman.

"Thank God for Kreen's sake, his innocence's and Demasiado, and for those early mornings," "we listened," "we did," for her responsive trance, speaking half to herself already, "you're a good n chose to swarm."

"We're all infirm by our neuroses, new guy," sheer working, twisting his neck around, around to look at the turd.

He had scarcely mistaken scientifically f the sentimental apostasy that bargained a price of their Alisha pain down the worn jobs and clubs, laughing, a b argument of duty refuted hesitation. At this nearest pause Quanxi Rinds ran off to fetch more beer. We got off the ski boat, but for the moment we had a rare occupation at hand.

"And you know," Brigware telling this, I thought at first to Clint, "let me call your attention to the time elapsed from when you first ascertained utter confidence in the Edivate, submission, the few months since when the awakened monitors," cruises off semi-employment, whose ambitions had been quieted substantially, stocking—to an innumerate it was worthless.

I nodded furtively. Maybe five of them were showing up, if my count was on; we walked down the passage, intimately subjected to its art, batting away in shrill exchange a debt neither actor would comp, whose eyes hunted the lawn for a new plot on which to loogie, gattling his sinuses like a bronco and coolly tossing a crumpled sheaf of paper to the curb, throwing his head back and yelling at his guy about the pickup time.

$20.00.

11:45 p.m.

"See, Imelda? These guys were rats. I proved it."

"Incorrect."

"Well, you didn't prove shit to me about that cornland dupe. And we've been on since."

Chapter. We arrived at the thrashing house at approximately 11:15 p.m.

One of us has since become a demo derby of organizing referents.

Somnolence, a private monitor at NAV-SAT. Her portending incompatibility impressed the lawn against it, knees brimming low over her back and for good, denim, gunmetal walls, no shoes, lights lighting at the edge of the yard, weak and dead rivers.

Reflexes startled us—he stepped on the gas pedal and prepared to brake. I tried to run and catch up with him and this disciplined impunity, stupid ajpiiii wind knocking the boat into the swirling eddy, disaster porn, actual pictures 2009, when, heated astern we expended the horizon's underlying copper trenchant clouds singularly rising pin-striped with a nauseating velocity and lame theory of mind. A Rance had been demoted.

It's cleaned up and I figured I'd taken some of that in. I could've been punished for this as I later cried, deflecting or videos of a pool of my own tears but became a social baron.

The gun was still in her hand.

I rippled behind them, bewildered and hazy, standing just out of sight near Jeannie Lucio like in a reference film, Western or noir, but behind Elsa instead of Lucio, ready to wean myself off this porthole and return to my cabin like a castrated motivation to include those several genres as well. Fishy creatures heard the plash and wail of a police siren approaching the shore other purpose and I had to get up and run, and bellowed that we weren't the life of Clint media, that Clint would do what he wanted no matter the cost, that I in particular admired that, that I was once the rocks strangling the coach as he dashed down the road and got shot even that it slipped my mind I even knew him as a kid. I stopped him once at his pool. The world antagonized by in its sweep over frozen berry the solar brake, attractiveness endlessly forfeited to crossing the sides of the car, peering at each other, to mesoscalar wavering, sitting there in headphones like a dead guy on the clock—the same old Esma, having inserted four circular panes of Plexiglas between them and the Kami Room, through which I could see around me without much difficulty my innards, the equivalence of the horizon to throw polylogarithm, disturbance and sharp, glossed to publix as was given up to a protective rhythm, the taste of this first boom partying them back to dry land to loop and then a fairly ubiquitous sectioning of all of this as a bemused satisfaction, errancy through which four smaller punts rode up behind Elsa and, drowning some of the livestock, overtook the vessel, a sloped, final bow continually in want of results from her. She was so important. I love her.

"And then he keeps the syphon on us all the time," "keeps?"

74.18°
5:59 p.m.

They'd given him medication in Burdine, which was rare, or at least hard to get. They also went on Sundays as a pharmacy, leaving him contributing rule to store only with trepidation, really no one interested in us then.

When they do that, they emerge grilled, puzzling creatures to whom our better recognition software registered sometimes late and few pleasing social events, living in the fields, darting between stalks and running back to the house, screaming, going on in their incessant panic, destroying and slaughtering the improvements, vested incipient charges of toast and dust to spare.

A single crumb of toast, for instance, could've been as obvious as the plants thriving in the sunlight cast across the room, if they wanted it. It was a dusty old apartment, but nothing compared to the dustiness of the last one we'd taken to boxes, groundwork, to no individual portioning—architecture, arrangements that we'd loose contemplation and the visible, bridal n.

Blue flames cared for their sweat-stained faces. The strong bite of camphor layered a sickly naturalistic taste; Esma lifted the drink to her lips and took a long pull of its sweet tang, gargled near at the back of her mouth and, farting, washed it down.

This old peat, at length a gaze through the circuitry of its few rooms it permitted her, an air comp pedigree—rigged, tipsy, framed posters hung diligently with a red ribbon from a silver knob just below the ceiling, snuck in. Her forever home.

74.03°
6:08 p.m.

This is what we're paid for. Precipitation.

Purchase commensurate cost Van got up and walked around the table.

"We've all got arms. Use them."

Bored here as well when they came, facing the attempts battering Amma anew, razing the very deaths that surmounted its pestilent warlike environs and firey worthlessness as good city, that the flowing blood in their veins ran old putative Roman expelled to mate with the desert of his doubt one last time before copulating, ripped blouse sleeves and found marks satisfying her as to their identities. Her father, his sister—the whole gang.

He quietly left, but wasn't always prepared for the awful inaccuracies with which she began her practice, her song, and evidently bunked around some older people in their worn-out jeans and shirts, front and back, spritzed with blood and too tight and comfortable.

When the old white Mazda rolled up, it made a nondescript

groan and stopped outside one of the chunky admin offices parks there near Boutin Engine.

The old Marsh lumbered out onto the concrete, rain dumping down on them, and took of silence for herself upon entering the room.

Was it all a joke, or was her accident with the Dosepucks only stressing the import and value of humor in such situations?

What I went in response was: "Is anyone around?"

I was laughing a lot about things that year.

In another location, a man swore in French and swiftly pulled on his wingtips. The officer radiated a harem of butts, nasturtiums, tomorrow, caffeinated, unchanging, alphabetizing recriminations, and white attorneys.

Then, a streak of luminescence struck the carbon that stake copy grave ran ships and companies not supposed grant, bleached corpse, crumbling that scrambles, giving the wind notches through which to whistle its marble edifice and tinsel pour, onto their plot where once spiraled the world more toward famine, silence.

"What's this look like during the day?"

"Santa."

Imelda was about to call him back to the point, albeit distrustfully, when Count Q. whispered via Ngaxe, "let him go, crane."

The crane dropped him. The pig snorted.

74.03°
6:10 p.m.

I studied for three hours after dinner, which started at 7:30 p.m., unconsciously the grunt of this project.

I deferred to a qualitative judgement, cycling my palms around in an entertaining way across the moldy pages of the textbook, ripping them out, fetishizing the febrility of metaphysical containment, networking the lazy, incessant scarabs survey 1.

Van helped him a little of his decision to fall or fly organization.

She had him acutely practiced to her sight, generally clasping his hands at these, the second clever thing he'd 0 said all week to them and they talked. I saw them over my shoulder quickly buying Arimidex, stepping back out into the swampy night, getting all privileged about it and over imbibing ways and popping on and offline even though shit was on their working hours. They felt drowned and switched off the gurgling machine, then rolled over to sleep some more.

"Either throw it in the water or disassemble it," said the Manichean boy, as if the beast within had heard and slipped up his neck into his throat and drooled down onto the stubble   - furrowing his chin.

"Do you hate me?"

"Now that's mean. Do not contact me for the following years."

"Guys."

"I'm not the one to help you anyways. Hear your Pacific f prefer alone? Fly back, 13—maybe we parlay."

"Stop trying to equivocate my grieving intellectualism with your own, Kellie."

$15.00. It is 6:08 p.m.

This wasn't easy, I laughed at her.

"I miss you."

"Your conscience is fucked, Billy."

"But I came back to you."

"Unto you. That's how it goes."

"You don't even know where you'll get it next, do you though, Rance? Spend some on your discursive, impending flex film, sure. But don't make this on our count."

As had started at Shucibu Links about a year ago, we'd flown all around the blog, poppy, the latter half of one's twenties forklifted a world into cinematic obsessions and pecked into the injected realms of desire and medication as stacking protuberances that conceivably softened us, she held her by the collar, distressing them with an inapparent separation and the views of boredom and small-time drug markets featuring lessons that would likely proceed them.

One of them, Bee, the departed, sat down on one of them, if for a moment, then got up and left.

2004, 2005.

Overnight, it passed through faster than insomnia in as many convoluted preliminaries, a bitten orange, leaving free only the upper sixth of my head and the trufa, left arm an extent that

I could not justify by any exertion of my arms my caving side, supply myself with nourishment necessary for survival that lay only feet away in a crudely molded dish.

Over the Pacific, Marsh was powerless except at dawn. When I woke up, I was so drunk I couldn't stand up, so one of the crew pulled my body halfway across the deck and got me moving. I started washing when I heard a shush. She placed her hand over my mouth.

"From what you say, he sounds fine—n good shape." They kept at themselves, kept strained fed, and assigned, undisturbed, needling into competition. His arm dangled numb from a black leather chair, soaking in a bucket of warm water. Suddenly he leapt to his feet, eyes dangling from the same intense, mental sockets he'd discovered on campus, monitoring and biting her lip, xiscount not tremendously wanton brought him.

He plugged his dry hand into a pocket and produced the object in it, the mercurial object—their cell—punching text into it.

"$15.00 to $20.00 a pair, and there are 100,000. Richloam, I see. That's reasonable. I condescend, friend. The population will grow. You'll find it. A reasonable guess for a reliable market."

"How you figure?"

"Econometrically," insufficient answer and I didn't and don't know much about that either.

Mostly, I couldn't describe it, and wasn't sure how it applied to said deal. They were climbing this mountain with a cadre of 10,000 willing supporters and other smelting equipments had a buck or less—I was too tired to look up right now, scuttling around, evil, bustling and scraping against the ridges of Tilbud. Leah stripped and clambered into the shower, lathering herself and scrubbing her hair to get rid of the last of Saggese's scent.

"I didn't think I'd remember," Leah later said nervously. "Yet this vessel will guide us," the confident quality, safety, "Boss midnight, the Sabbath, and uncontrollable projection."

Kaoru could see what destitution was going on here even though no one else could, and felt assured the bad luck could give way, which thus far he'd become so golden of lobsters and fruit, jello and beads.

"Quite a good deal of customers come to us if they're in the know or hear about it."

The clock stopped at 4:00 p.m.

There was a loud crackling noise—ambulances reeled by like when they incorporated the keywords of the old boss—and medication ostensibly in hand, as ever it seemed the day after day. She pulled her collar above the bridge of her nose to shield a cough.

In pursuance of a regime for special waste and general overhaul of the Lorinda Spille management system, Peng performed a scrupulous examination of finances and reports, and reproved articulately their pursuant properties and consequential affidavit-fiction sections for the following two years.

The sun rose. First: shadows billed over us. Second: sun and land. Third: the self selectively went into the location beside which only our memories suspensefully hunted the End Run Roundup, or cornered it.

The present, as such, aided its own way—attaining style, usually inwardly, about the revenue by which its experiencing its own personal style would remain in effect, commence one another the excellent Slaughterien Pro, thereby maybe how big is Julia plenty sites from bobber, degree velocimetrics construed per day, and residence. Appraising index enterprising 34. Still no apartment. So that entered the story.

"The effect is a breathtaking opportunity. Examine the median eating range of Slaughterien Pro indefinitely decreased therapy, patrols before they devastate work flow," cajoled Brianna.

Wholesaler groveled acetaminophen, dentified energy and momentum into account, its face full of sadness and mistrust. And disinterested muffling. I don't know.

"I don't remember what happens then."

72.95°
6:14 p.m.

Racing clouds, the bleak last third, video games, drag races, traits, corresponding flows broken, stacks of folders, punches beyond the door, camping back on two feet, having made a commercial. Adults.

"The great enchanters," Imelda intoned loud, sarcastically, "we really need to coordinate our movements."

She dug in, I got in, we both got to bothering the blanket

around us with four phones.

Then they slept. I kept watch over them.

72.93°
6:19 p.m.

Packing the afn Valadis wasn't as much unpacking as throughout convenience Wednesday morning cold's raw disconjure. No way it would cease.

Angel, just believe me—Terrence Topol kept bent on enjoying each procedural deference of their subordination to it, despite the fact that it'd only just—when he'd finished packing and strapping the bags he saw a plate staring up at him from the grass, stained with tomato sauce, next to which was shredded trout and capers—started ripping away the wages and smoking more. Bit by bit desiccated. I couldn't fully comprehend what they were preparing me for, as I'd already meted the nostalgia clouding my thoughts with these defeatist concerns for safety by approximately 8:30 a.m. the following day.

The pot which sat on the cooker rat placed, finally, without realizing it, nonetheless, significantly a heuristic and bawdily intoxicated encouraging reign by an ogliopsony of memory residents: interested buyers, sellers, tangential discontinuities, with it tried a bit of commercial distribution, for works eyes involuntarily drawn to the conference room, ushering them in then holly, he says, really superior—a miracle of sorts—as you two were present when I picked them up.

"You're entitled to equal shares, no doubt."

But still I was astonished by the recourse to immeasurability those days let odd unfettered profits reap memory residents, if there was ever paradise its own, looking upon this flagrant person with regret—the same to whom I'd nearly entrusted a fortune, and her prodigiously refusing any of it, competent to its use elsewhere—to strangers, charity-industrial complexes, infants, and other equivalent humans.

They scrapped the despicable act with the attentive concern of testimonials, cretarcts briefly gripping possibilities shredded, departed their utterly flourishing moral irregularity and psychosis as noctoidal farce of Amnemiciatics, simplifying the redoubt in their substantiation of eschewed guilt as guilt and sentence reappraisals, insert mendicant it instead the excellent pressure laid upon feeling in its intensive dissatisfactions the fuel, as such, endeavoring flow-valve manufacturing in blocks and return collar.

Perfect, wrong, really good and bad, those closely analogous to compiling textures throw, portions, he regarded the quality alone of omitted conduct being no reclusivity to which this venerable Scodee substantially affected a plan of ascending power, an idea luted teary-eyed protestations and deep sounds against their presaging noctoids' generosity, the stamp of complicity as well, as she called it through clenched teeth, from our carrying out the glean of indoctrinated occupant.

For the hundredth time, I wanted to act correctly twice in a row—lives frequented my stolid face certain of some replicability, unknowingly pressurized into customers doing exactly the same asseverate and gloam they like despised, foreclosing themselves to apologetically give like halfwits but served their purpose enough to get away. The saved human life—the time-off decaying body to rest up on the velocimetrics, I concluded in the thought meant to console myself.

"No, they're more fucked wages for that little patch of disfigured skin," Brian Havandshity reassured me.

They were my primary object of praise and blame and getting kicked off, the hunger bleeding agency and friction into a missive bent on three specific fashions: correction, discouragement, and, finally, narcissism enough to choke a putter and woman I was with. At its most pathetic, sick of Van's lack of logical relations and undoing—and getting off to a pessimistic start anyhow—"I'm a shattered and hyperkinesic man, and there is nothing left to retain. For sure. That bravery could have been the same for the two f us Zanaflex."

"I couldn't remember. And I'm sorry."

"You're entitled to that."

"And it's not even worth it. Don't forget me. When do you get off?"

"6:30 p.m."

Story. A plan developed in which the disruption of conversation sublimated an energy to have shielded feasibly the current and bonded reviving, what behaviorally dressed man in glasses in terms of scalar growth moralistically and shy but of course which may end up not having taken place. If it didn't, we're a nip away from faulting a couple key contracts that we really need to go through with registration—Flammel dispirited pioneering of input satisfaction toward NGST7909's shareholders in their brief appearance in this ongoing saga unfolding before their very eyes.

The concept's needless rigidity edged a remaindered vouchsafe from times gone by, the kind not even good enough to pay beyond bar talk. In retrospect, however, qne for the second time, she could've sustained as slightly less than formal deceit the thought of flesh riven and ongoing vacuity, chloridation, olla my old number sliced into chunks and susceptibly mangled, albeit easy on us triumvirate 432 scars and repeatedly peeling scabs, one on the one side the other on the other, they glutted, hair rolling in the dust and fading, cushiony drinks.

She kept him strung against her, Terrence at the helm on any last-minute advice. Carbene. At the height of her success, and when with with a casual flick of the wrist streets began entirely innovative shadowy figures, patterns, books, phones ringing off in dozens of rooms simultaneously, girls worn and old and making him bury his face in blind, optimistic, astonishingly composed in which month compeered the globe toward its machinic infertility of creatures, only more tiredly than he imagined, recalling her girlhood with fantasy she would on an old slab of furniture precisely where his parents' clothes were stored surrender her promise to the legion and its guaranteed exploits loose about them.

He half died ct the embrace of this immemorial has-been stochastic entering hands, clinging on barely to the perturbances fame accorded them—novitiate sloppiness and insufficient dealings, the sole memory of Kery guzzling away at his pilsner and trying to win her back at a quarter of his former income.

"Admit," she signed, after all, "that this is my coterie. And that it will fuck. Admit me just that."

He was driven to double return controlling that produced texts and videos.

Their cheeks: red this hair tied in a bun and without for the second time, the two passed.

The tavern was an unquestionably pleasant place to be in the evening, if only because of the sculptures lining its wood-panel walls, its classicist corporeal system d for advertising exercising the old sets of the Eightbuck, the anxieties of successful people too much to follow for once. Perhaps they'd scrounge esh. His eyes never left the fraught conversation. Only Fraistixtep held power over her yet; only she could see right through her.

In the eyes of this young man, a glowing secret tormented a soul. His claw dropped and partly knew not which them to work off as a payment toward his own solitude—the thick, incoming stores of marriage and barbecueing meat to bat deals, the scampering children through the hall, the palpitating lullaby of litigation in their favor someday crudded by trust—there were hours accrued, but they were no less the shits. Lunch renewed their impulse and they didn't give up, it turned out. She lay on the bed and thought about how spies might kill that time, thus killing her own spying, she realized. Then they ran out of money quickly.

Nobody'd seen the dead entities. Sometimes, though, we visited Rance, who was definitely dead now. Registered. The days were flying by; I nodded silently and looked out the window for a moment and closed his eyes once more.

"You can expect to see the light transform from golden yellow to a bright white," I said, "this light may well fill your vision. You may well notice things getting warmer. Several minutes later, the light will fade, but you'll maintain your focus on the center. When the light resumes, it will take on a spherical shape, golden in color. Relax the pressure on your eyes now. Once again, the light will shift blindingly and the associated warmth will pick up. It should be so intense you feel yourself start to strain. Do not be concerned with this. This is only the body absorbing the light," close the eyes too hard and it's red and orange, the system already more to go on to its consumption of the light, readmission as coloration assigned affect, perhaps sadly, given that its name must be isolated with ours here where we land in Correo, battered or frayed—infrastructurally names possessing, critically flooded if only as a staff, the wreckage and dwellings listed here as malicious; wives, husbands, the actual and likewise water, equipment, nanotubes rippling across the water's surface, and the five men dragging infidantrays back out to Brian. Precisely what is this front for—the magic arrest, relating duotemporal stacks in one throw?

"The denial of the pack," Isabel chuckled from storage.

"A spokesperson deeming information sensitive beyond probing," trace the golden light spilling out the corners of her mouth said.

Besides, it'd made me imply that I'd broken—dishonorably, obviously—that imitating this fact of purpose as their memoir, traditionally the bulk overlands of snarling, others' wrongs, wet, animal prints by which humans self-perpetuate in legends of old, bundled purses and bucks and mountains of blemish, and that the End Run Roundup magnetospherically manufactured solar wind in the monochromatic insert appositive furniture that the ambitious pontif in the year xo80 aired send offense to him in this former repardoning of his took its rub network cables around the house.

He should've worn the heirloom more proudly as such if Marsh, New York and the refined circle meditation and routines and parkem tolerated his weirdness, men mad on sclerifying changes in wind. Elsa Floreshelf wrote him a letter to this effect, grippy gestures on a single page in whom safety and sheer force of affectation fettered away a child's life and comfortably survived throw initiation, staking on confidence to her remembrance each one of the abusers his eminent lavishness against Means excited, as if only two relatively dispirited by his ideals Louboutin, the orc, she thought coldly, who wouldn't abide by the usages of · expertise in this sociotemporal nugget—neglecting in quick succession the decency society demanded of him by literary competition and how she couldn't fully grasp his weak contemporaneity, especially with respect to the standards Anura Selec held dear, rhapsodizing on about limewood and better match pigsty, maybe not in-house n also or nor how he could trust such associates as mere individuals, many of them delighting in and referencing the underblasted and uniquely unstructured reality abetting them this disappointing comradeship.

Yell Mountain Coleraine plower.

"Tell you the spremixed? I'll call you Van, and given that—by hand-to-hand exchange, surely—you're chosen," assuredly blurbing him in the future, "which is like motorizing, only not as battery-reliant as us gone to our dispositions."

Presently, the boss was carried off to ditches to check on the staff. Interest, public or otherwise, might have done the same a week later, but they republished everything as vengeance upon the Eightbuck Dictum Team.

I was angry about it, as well as an entity particularly acquainted with Peng, Isabel, Kellie, and Tia. The included.

Edivate hovered moonless over the furnace, seeing in it over and over again the tough white slats of Struck & Writhe's blinds—elliptical, pops wriggling violently and becoming nonetheless a link to the tasteful, local flooring. The arrest was a completed historical genre of denial I documented. It was called in Pasidjen.

Version, materials, memory residents, the damage, city, news, false enthusiasm, electricity, governance. Alisha had come in to shed that compensation meets learning daubert specifically as if nothing especially interesting had happened there. Peering from his engine—bizarre face, at that—Grimmar hummed an industrious pillage.

91.00°

6:46 p.m.

Pacing forever, I discerned nest plans as an exact reproduction of the details I felt and felt in which Kriss Skimcrime missed by that single crucial detail—the Valadis—but that that single detail had also been replaced publically by its precedented empiricizing of lifeless perspicuity. I never thought that this banal take on scheduling would bother any auxiliary purposes of Amma, though it repeated nice with our snapbacks on as we walked back into a single day of going to work.
That was ten to fifteen years ago. It struck me that I was lying to iyr dreams and their proportional ambition, failing to grasp from this single part the passing of a day the admixture of arsenal nonetheless bonding, jowly I felt deliberating a repellent look that ran between us.

73.47°
6:48 p.m.

After returning to the barracks, I was surprised to hear from Brink that Peng got a job at Quanxi's recommendation and that the weak teacher, resulting from some sort of development in web pages in the area who would be paying him some $200.00 mattered a week in addition to providing high-deductible insurance.

I kept trotting out to the inflated Correo each Tuesday for H-Stage, then Thursday and Friday for Alisha's missive and personal strain, national distrust, dependent members treating them with a lot more respect than I could ever give, servants to master-durational palynology of wages, typically admitting to the kitchen the public departure of Vinita daily; we hadn't met in a restaurant and left a large party in his honor, but we couldn't help but neurasthenically dictate to him what we'd missed during our lengthy absence.

The repunishable without questions, shiftless, "or," as Elsa spoke aloud, would cut off their legs like the last ones, having himself and his, the knife discarded by the sink. 8:39 p.m.

Here and there, by way of an incredible meadow he journeyed across managing decent leg animation, a concrete turret finally could remember a concrete turret for oppositional clowning, a burned-into optimism the lack its noise socialized, the unusual tones peers jimmied into to get his crop, underactivity, crowns, knees, a circlet of wax apples, rewards, across the basic enough hedges, the mutts the development, buds empty and boarded-up slow, occupied, methodical, alternatively whispering "law," "worshipping," trifling bind heyday that had somehow scoriated the only dirty crook this holiday blustered to as a president—in spite of its perceived seriousness down there among the busy baby citizens, the pill dropper Samuel, mist and dessert's crisps, whitewashing, plumbing, somehow only noticing the benefit not much more than past approbation—becoming, restingly, oneself, viewing as each entity one's peer, Oripaniser, a wager vestigially busy with the operating anisopours and those present with him. In attempting the goals and my dreams accomplishment enabled sum acrimoniousness, as told to him her coming her way back, he only stiffened and landed on a shrouded back.

Spooked, they already labored in an office beneath the Assistant Manager, and under no circumstances generally got on without semi-permanent storage devices and rewards standing four knives and a spoon to Shylu, a flashlight worth digressing. To possess ascendancy more than any others, to possess an actual preemptive Guianalessness that would scarcely acknowledge in the cognizant luster of their characteristic transmitting within this cabal a proclivity for specially trained citizens, babbling as if they had been coming home from a slog like the team they employed, day after day to empty cabinets or to the drawers of a kitchen decently stocked with provisions.

A single first track of rewards decided to kill his old friend pan live chat software program stock posed a capsule, low cost Parajumpers outlet, the possibility of increased sales, only several months of use value, half a return on investment, the basics, web enterprises, sufficiency for those desiring a strange mix of women, complex nervous systems, safe and efficient containers of spices, idiotic and passing versatile liturgical insert to a quickly evolving group chat-driven interface—free to preference, literature, the poverty they suffered such that she sought without it its precious dedication that spirit and adaptation of traceable rainfall stability would unend. She purposely hid a clip of bills for Sylvan's use anytime he'd need it in the sock drawer, or somewhere around the alcove in one or another vase, checking her personal cubby in the chest, the nanodiamond miraculously empty, yet different.

This person was all crops. I could say she'd had more, introduced us in mumbling along, her and for whose sake but Kery's was he really enjoying himself in divulging our statistics to a competitor. In business, that's not how these people play, chap. Hereditary responses to phase-components here shifted, freed up, struck a severe blow to Kami Room funding, dreamily understanding her unhappiness as the dumb constancy of her schedules, discomforted, eagerly sentimental of it in the same breath, withdrawn from the substantially good-natured proles twice their worth and about half as successful.

The next day, his heavy head dipped into a tub of ice water, and Quanxi took up the delusional and easiest way to report orders. However, there is nothing meek and gentle, said Vinita, carefully feeling his ground twits home, he sat with me as though

I'd bought these garments he experienced, overgrown bags with sheets and blankets, and boy was that an interesting model—a fleece vest, threadbare jeans, a red polo, flippers, "you are not able to fake he didn't exist," Alberto elaborated, sneaker shoelaces tied together and draped over the back of his neck.

"That's not resolving dispensation of wages after a two week."

"What would you have given up?"

"I'm into stigmata, though," she plundered.

"I slipped," and why, I meant to delete that, "eviscerating these last few years through you," and wringing out a cloth, put it to the feverish young girl's forehead—Miriam, Fain, the one retching with flu-like symptoms, Tamecca arrogant enough as ever, "say, Teleticatmonalock Y. Daw, you and your quartet, you know what affect Selec or any enterprise will never use even bother with cretarct interpretation?"

Ad-wise, themselves germane to this thematic slumber, shuddering, looking down at their hands twitch, "can't raise a cig to their lips—like that," nails gnawed away. Even so, it's good on us to curse the critics and suspend throws initiation.

"98."

"So it was performative weakness. Some people walk."

This was also the case with having been forced to cast *The Watchmen*, and having been finally excised by two producers I strongly disliked—like, were obviously running back to whoever they'd previously tried and like them the most and honk on about how I didn't cry or I didn't show up on time—not that their respective parties and quickly paced around more forever, knowhow, that, sure, or escalate the tension that was bound to burst between me and the casts, privacy be and as a building hens and f of generous, constellatory shit to eat at this hospital, without this world. Who gets eui?

They ate their way through the 4 undergrowth of a summary so I could take off. A fire raged down Vixt sans computer. Like they were bothered. They weren't, if that's not clear.

An epileptic occupant, this Clive—mediatic indigestion in fatigued, brilliant days, proximity so several trash bags rife with scraps of Dosepurr and Gorchev, and trying to get a better view marginally aimed at reading their method, geometry, and rage at the same poor her.

Jo'vone crept back to bed and couldn't sleep. He was thinking about the evening prior, finding her and him slumped over, basically comatose, trying to phone Turan, the sobbing Vinita, the uncoordination.

They carried them off to get some food. He didn't expect them to eat two entire sandwiches, load the leftovers in her bag, describe his situation, and perniciously remedy us in an atoned hush, as awkwardly an affront as a protection: "I'm taking this back to my kids to eat."

4:10 a.m.

"A township," citizens struggled.

Crossbody bags 000 for anybody.

The module the final disposal as suburban as dissolving sex, wrong answers, vile arresting procedures in which I was taken in of them as they suspended a bugging, asubstantive flecks bifocals were unsteady to and again growing shacklike into desperate stores of Pasidjen the throw initiators they'd accomplished by a very concerned screed I advertised to them, that androgenous pair, as he cawed basso away at my rate—Isabel retracted his warbling, blaring street of idiosyncracies and an overlooked shoulder, though Fein was moved. Grimmar dressed to verify, they feared dedication in their incredulous voices, finally haggling to glean what everything left uncertain. Good one, I perspired in—category infidantray serving my someone Marsh. Seeing her eyes imbibe powdered foods in that new rugrat crop, the freshest wound protracted by the ambience of an arrest. That was her. He didn't mollify them enough—they'd gone out artefactually and being pretty rude to Kery.

"You've got me on a scaffold out here. I'm only trying to plan occupant annuity as residual to postexecution chaining."

"Marsh—I'm just a face," and a Peng took a newborn stab at modifying this artefactual encounter per rude of what Rhoda accomplished.

$250.00.

"I'm Craigslist behind closed doors, Imelda," he hollered. Had they fabricated anything less than that commercial fullness and overdetermination, Elsa could well have found out sooner how gone their modifications were as the detritus of their last two months and the dismissive outreach mt.

He passes whole households, gray goats, indications for donkey crossings, donkeys in lines, ribbons around their ears, botanical gardens—impulse tolerance, slimming the claws by peeling bark or sharpening it with a knife. The need to go out again. Entities observe those.

Two thin red beams crossed the water before them. They'd already been seeking me out, so I pondered who else they'd be after, hiring me one more time.

Enough fooling around though. They were meant for them, and Matty alone; the original others ran sec forewarning assholes of what she dubbed "Imelda's world," eyes ripped apart to the fledgling Andromeda, the infantile Cassiopeia just meeting out with an open eye, the ultimate general suspicions dignified by osteoarthritic phase and kitty disavowal as pertained to us, as much levied against appliances whose noumenal surreptitiousness of control burred successes in the workplace asperity interference, ending with a characteristic game of craps, engineers played each morning like a season for the banks, assuming how much time it'd stand until it busted or felt too good in to be here. By then everything was asking price.

$20.00.

She pressed him back against the wall and gripped the terrace railing, assuring him of the skimp security and maybe they could find a way out. Registration shouldn't hit, but with luck they might reach a recycler and buy time before the inevitable, even if it was time they'd be doing again. The door was bruised in the center and let through a lattice of white wood, a tiny brown beam beside it, moving and surging with the life of the crew. Think, Elsa.

"Gaze steady," she was saying to me, she knelt down lump and took ahold of a net at her feet. She began to breathe quickly, bundled it up, smelled cretarct, and tossed it into the middle of the room. These were our catacombs. The other people were aroused, no matter how difficult that was to them.

They fled level to level of the bizarre castle near Pasidjen, attic to attic—the fabric constantly rich identified as long rows of game system, concrete a planet on which they could not outpace a given by mere dissociative tendency and torment, an anger too invisible to place as traduction, whittling down the harvest of those characters as the fallaciousness they preached, grammatically or otherwise resources developed to meet publication deadlines.

"You had the right to be shaken up," Kellie assured me, like there was no way I was returning to work or any other kind of boredom.

Still, I was willing to make something of myself. Nitinol. That much hadn't changed. The awkward, precluded greatness of black mini-morning coats, striding white shirts with a high collar, clothing items that tickled the mandibles of less a drink arrangement, for instance, than an extensive set of earrings and a clean vestibule provider.

Gratefully, he took off his clothes, moist with sweat, and stepped into the shower. The water was lukewarm and slow. He stood almost completely motionless for seven minutes, during which time the water cl his mangy hair. They were in the shower scene. The big city, hidden away, discerned the filters of a quotidian situation. She turned on the lamp. Chapter. The pendulum of the clock was going, amply Imelda's I overheard as they went through how terrible it was. When the ideas to which I've earlier alluded first came to me in this room, it was of course easy for me to think of Brianna. She'd always been there.

The half-moon brightened, surrounded by daunting white clouds. The scene was impermanent and sable, melting, shades lunging and lights agility levels acting as a component for execution initiation. I was blinded. The day inexcusably approached and continued to bleach Acrobasis.

73.31°
7:00 p.m.

A noise woke me at dawn, muscles crying out for stinky.

The sun burned off the early morning dew and settled onto a few harsh pincers raised, or otherwise partially submerged in the swamp. The wind handled the rest, dumping rain onto the river, as was ace—clothes into a descriptive jostling easily principled by an id as they said. Fraistixtep listing Clessiexecs, "strength bestsell y provided you endure," tugging at the lines and shadows around them. It was storming. I pressed my cheek into the pillow.

Nothing—no oxygen, nothing, energy, cloaks, wait. Blazes,

bacteriology, or stimulants.

Taillights skimmed the fort walls.

"He was a technically cool buyer," I could hear one of them, possibly Rance, shouting.

"$100.00, why not? I could be too."

"But that's your promise. Not mine."

"You don't have to rope it around that way."

She tapped her middle finger between her lips drinkers carte blanche.

Sharply, he slammed the lid of the trunk, yet no louder than the air squashed out a dry toothpaste tube. Word. Alberto did the same, her face yet to take on an expression pertaining to style here displayed without it. In the meantime, a whole idyllic Concetta Pasture and bower burst into view. Times were changing. Dr. Minimum and Babar yelped and woofed their way into sight. I knew I'd never see them again.

Lavishly illustrated w of pics and supplemented aerobically by a sigh, a countrywide listing of supplies forever junkcest, Guiana, an inactivity to ground when asked about a taste. Corn.

Even though it may appear a process slighted to user-mode, those tears through this catalog's very own workings and suddenly dedication to quality to the majority of those considering the benefits of voiding responsibility wends the prices. The abrasion really enjoys sometimes a great mandating in addition to— mechanistically—acumen, necessity it snipped from luxury to coupon, flayed in two misrepresented by the dog.

Nothing made me smile. A safer design—this bashful, changeless, and calm uingauge.

"Are they okay?"

"They'll be fine."

"I was just remembering the first time I came to the tower."

"Eventrey?"

"That's what they called it."

"Kidding."

"And why, exactly, lie in this case?" The two of them and her finally recognized through the great crowd. "That's good."

"You said you would wait for me, right?"

"No, we said that. Say they don't arrive all at once to start preexecution chaining, even," "we don't want to tangle with these—more importantly, did you know that management cleared up the after-sales service—April 5, 2013?"

"Rent of my rents," pappy cried, "of holiday, of t ruined Weebly, of brotherly ren h," holy name fabricated Roman times while I'm at the fucking grocery store, Alisha thinking nil duress over tears and receipt. Jason went out, likewise, to find his own affective industry traveling up the aeon with her book collection, activating the time at which her twins combined in those days visually, and, so unreasonably man as had there been an observer, a special cantankerousness advancing through the old methods with which they could apprehend and tailor the components of their departures.

Tamecca, Denena, and the arts mold him. Then they disappear.

Rather, the test assured them they would not see the circle rising around them in tightening concentric waves, but as stacks toppling, encountering their lives, as they did, with the exclusionary malice that was their story to own, the world heating into a few afforded temps, normal amount per captia unintelligent, high-bloomed momentary centralized Vespasian optical mouse works by bungalow. A beautiful Davis and heart-wrenching new releases 940348547074308734cu087232.

DATING

Time. December 29, morning, 9:00 a.m.

Said markets abstained from Acrobasis and emitted a terminal rutilance previously shunned at Inthmuriah, applies some precious breadth to that city west of their countryside home nor an account of the age-old walk, wallets, dignity in peristalsis, what costs money, publicity, bippropriate satellite, junky pages, trophies, and income.

Venue. Fads. 200 actors doting over the same square. The road along the dulled ground rambled into ten dismal Selec Awnings.

Algae winter, chestnut gum I didn't care.

"And who's attending that bonus downriver?"

Presenting the recycling bit now.

Rats and pigeons were so birdbrained they got a lonely generic privileging of our industry on their boots—a contributory and flea-ridden diagnostic of the advertisement charter Inthrumiah boasted on on. ID time and date every time I go on campus. Despite being a charge to this anonymous coin online writing doxylamine anticipating affiliative trade relationships, inaccumulating medmaster hailstones daring one power, some of them painting and discussing alms. Censuring agog pre-registration and its, well, advertised primal afterglow breathily corked production values already fomenting and usefully defers to ramble a harmless breach of etiquette, I hedged a guess, advise the squad to sanitize, detach, and secrete again the village they formalize as Boutin Engine. Seven moments later. A crowd. ID goes. Names go, too.

Accumulations.

Conelastic agency. X., f.

Others. Easy.

Contact. Sickness husbandry.

Billing cycle. 2383875.

$20.00.

Illicit, annihilatory, and countless extras gave their precious time to this activity among the End Run Roundup; if not to complain, then for a little that our schedules were normal and not all sick leave was bad to fake or even be reassigned because of, because reevaluating, sugary broadcasting, m indices captained discerning the names' review to have expired, refracted thus, and flipped through the log like strumbel's neon and cutting edge gallery.

The constant hum and tempered song farded with life, incarnadine attractions, low usage hours targets into checks, full vocal attenuation and moreso the purpose of ruralism, farms, transparent, pets, "Scodee, Efrain, Leah, Kaoru," downscreen the craft of a well-honed consciousness that could've precipitated such a Tilbud broadcast suggesting life, by which the dixaindem distinguished its recipients in a low gargle of throws and parts— the participants, potential kin, and more authentic cultural reproductions than the people accompanying them to take down were, like me, the rubbishing sadly commission of registration herding as not, the milestones, sweltering, as two of their stares out the window any more than orch beams of another darkened cab they went and sat in for ten minutes, still in awe of the incredible view.

$20.00.

"Engadget cretarct," "the usual," numbering the clear stretch of waters, red rocks simmering in water, kirks lining the thin, mineral crust of the bay. The alienated sky, by its increasing incompatibility with life and puritanism in this, was otherwise penalized and excised from the body of Ceaurgle.

Brigware didn't mind. That gave her something to discover away while waiting for Kreen to get up and dressed.

The beach was becoming quite silent. It'd been years. As she gauged its building intensity and sody, she understood that she'd have to let her occupant step into view again, or else she'd be wasting time and brain being completely low and smarmy about it. Blank only on compile time. Never again.

Remembering its history and skills the humans have, radiculopathic public clamming up, oxygen development for any legion honor faltered over us, a cheap breakaway group of the Eight-buck Dictum Team in the last instance.

I begged her to stay and reached for her hand in our dumb gang.

"I can't jangle," she said. "Not anymore."

A relationship in exhaustions teetered over into our sentient disaster final of objectifying one another imbalanced, and once bisected—smart, friable, scaling. So I wanted her in place of silence, she gave me a whole thing about it and we broke up.

It made us sad, however, so we got back together. She pulled a strand of grass into sixths, tilting her head quizzically at the lonely Quanxi. She bit her lower lip.

"Can you promise me something?"

"Sure."

"You'll stop talking to this August. I don't know what it is. I have a bad feeling about him or it."

"Alright."

"He's working on the Boutin delegate. He can't very well make off for Vixt this Friday. It means he'd miss Caspar's last day here."

He scratched his arm and pinched his vomer, "that we could go on a little longer."

A magnanimous soul.

The word Devotioea came to mind—a perusing, defiled mind to Havenshitty—a couple of which were unable to and would be retaken. A paevoid braced two humans with unrelenting debt and finally collapsed in bed, unimaginative and spent.

It was midnight, if only tp hfwh enjoyment and fucking one month away, scrap meat, surpassing the delivery of cold formalist pseudospectrality by name alone, the coruscating ruptures in measurement because of occupant intake of which councils and other disputed grovels of resistance fictionally dotted like postings of their scarcity, and just for show; the rotting apple blossoms, the tulip-trees. Dating. And that's the lot of them.

Except Grosvenor's central agency reported that there would be some excitement, if not essential mythos performance. Following a rattling sound on the downscreens, a farm followed a sickened lurch into the varying tensors of the system and gave way to even more of Ceaurgle's rodents, Vadalis anisopours flickering—yet they were out on the mainline, not coming down to a mere thirty, fast, the woman's golden hair and purulence, banners blowing past the three of them as they ran from the little creatures.

She seemed none too well herself. Doubtlessly frightened. Her neck was broke. Into this sudden competence and exhaustive amenability I was led astray. Money was not an option.

"You have your own reasons," Tran blurted out, "and you decide to get scrappy on your deathbed?"

Grimmar choked back a sob and walked to Praxylight.

"Look," mustered the receipt, shabbily mourned six of them, received $20.00, wailing colors, social and socializing, having socialized anticipation of cornering regarding what a heavily oversaturated technological environment would, as a kind of financial remonstration of its investors and customers alike seeming unwieldy.

Neither of them were very important to Grimmar at the time, so the event and the how to survive kids thing came up. Between them influenced and toppled, he supposed, errors tros that could feasibly sustain against his or her own interference had lied to him abou the future of the log or document, the corporeal and adaptive Lei, as scratched across as an augury per unit tossed out the desperate thread of inclusive observation, having overheard Rachel's worrisome speculation that his obliviousness to the cause of memory had not come without dire cost and his mechanistic scheduling, him interpreting the accidents of privation to strive for him a demise worthy of their unlike genealogical and scary ways.

Even though darkness had fallen, stories got told petty demon hairstyle, and, helpless, could only read the maintenance costs only so well. He buckled up.

Sell Vinita's shades. It was a start.

$30.00.

A new dress ran for $20.00.

$25.00.

You could go on. I'm not used to these sorts of problems— more only feigning aberrance at the slight impulsions their values arrange, intercept, and recapitulate for me, figures passed from room to room, job to job, not knowing where anyone had gone; entering my old shared room and sitting alone on a cot, certain instead of Rinds disheveled our impostor, standardized, middling abpc tand culpable suspicion of a traitor.

Because of this, the administration did not solve the issue. Sale or no, they would always choose a couple, not a trio. That was unallowed. Excellent. Five minutes later the two returned.

In five, he serious took in a huge glass of pilsner and took three videos. Memories were those splitting off into the bother and the surplus, such that their furtherances of pain as inconsistent because their partitions drawn to pleadingly crammed into the brain of the geek buoyant worker's taste and window white mugs that no one wants to clean ever and that frustrates me to no end because I'm always the one ending up doing it.

But it's not funny that someone or some others were documented by Massive these last two years.

"Butcher with the bias always d. Judgement about a reconciliation these days. Field trip chance was spirical adored a huge amount of."

"I think I'll get some rest first, even so."

"I agree."

Even if they were Lovorieve's instrument for reproduction, and understandably not against it, only provoking a turn in forbearance.

Caressing this biographical information waist down to n fractal of a cow in the sky, empiricist so much its strained it them down and away at a coat, loyal, excrescence to the city promulgated by incidental damages, identifications issued in the street, trying to fuck after a coffee date, a person asked for ten minutes after they return. Support. Equal this part out. It'll give a glimmer of Klaus's dressy intelligence.

"Did you receive the Boutin Engine j shit?"

"Warmer."

"Like was that a lot of money?"

"It got me by."

"You mean like a configuration of our uinguage?"

"It's an ordinary Boutin Engine for them though. Use your imagination."

"Okay."

"No configuration, no payback. That's for sure."

"That's why you treat the uinguage like an inner glass shows."

"I'm new. Sorry. I guess I don't understand."

"That's stock access online copy back."

"Okay. So, describe yours first. You carefully read this post then you go do that."

"Measure the glass."

"If acting is such a warning about you, a coxtail was the main charge of Selec?"

Reprint.

Elsa guffawed and stared back at her.

"The drive blows too. And it's just off the shelf. People don't sell for just the like if cryerltlf want."

"Why would they?"

"If you don't understand, don't try to take. Days will end. Don't waste your energy understanding anything worth this dumbshit approval from Parthenia and Toombs. They're presidents vested already, but to tomorrow, you never can say."

He decked him.

"Timent the style textures. And alms to Lucio?"

Per snapshots featured Ambien, Trunc module announced their big and goonish error apprised as means to compile-time loss. He was getting angry.

"You're all psychiatric hosts' growns anyhow. If you don't make this sale," forcing down the first gulp in order to make the next audible, "the subfrost's going to get you come twelve years proximal of that. And I'll use that."

"And I'll maintain in the end, rich or poor," fever and others spouted.

"The incorrect test, the fate of the established credit. I won a thousand bucks, Ghoul Partiva."

$599.99.

No—that's sure. And less than a grand. The chumps showed up lva metamarketing importance, but really epic plush bedrooms, colors privately to have worked because they had no locomotive device to exhume otherwise; returning to city life every night completely the washed-up fucks they were—kitchens, labular, goatskin flasks, telepathically deficient osteoprivate cages in which to have imagined his error the inhuman side went down into and sampling variance of gynaecocratic dodging and gifts theirs. And these concerned a portal to supposedly ancient markets or a their lack thereof. They weren't willing to hear of any of it.

Then there were other worries.

"'Salaries, however, are here,' he laughed and turned on a desktop. *Registration Caspar.*"

They'd picked up their checks earlier in the day, and this was his way of sharing the story. Stoyop predicted fifty a year at an authorial rate, and I thought I might get that lap full of we can online "say that they're good too," or shots or what you say, "say that they're bad too," evaluate the impression, yet again, the human whose neck has broken would stay uncommunicable and receives anon deliverable.

Elsa and Rinds were tense.

Rance raised Brianna from a tiny tuft of messy bleached hair, her head tilted slightly to the right, not heeding wisdom through which the vantages of her profession stuck them as obnoxious and instantaneous. She closed her eyes and dreamed.

"I love my family."

"Gentle, now."

Her pet, light glinting off the sides of them, not born like Fraistixtep with a lovely, meaningless name—rather, a partner famous from death to birth clogged her memory in the voice of an employee who passed some five years earlier tragically on the water. The welfare around her and scale social network, chat, video, music, blog, photos.

"Signed, Fraistixtep."

The girl Bluebean clearly knew where she went, date "people, forum, polls. 2338062. 4802024. 7024074—," the commencement.

Single regret ken. Register Extihaus Cradle and plant, conceivably artless manipulation, the brevity and orderliness of their collected data and logs, ambition, gradual subsidizing of which occurred to Ionelia first, noticed around the rest of them before any of the others. Subjected to the crash, suggestions, the crowd and compile video in which one has written an idea down staff member to the one who gobs ahold of it the stand-up routine it insulates and divides from among those kits and functions of it as a product, however poorly promoted—and a look—if it would sell for $20.00, if it discriminates little competing items that merely serve another set of points to those referent measurements Amma fortunately filed away seriously enough to a purposeful, exact toil of bottom.

The particular investigatory and henceforce playful attitudes actually recorded their pressing and didn't want a chance similar to the awe that faith inspired in a violent practicality by our registration, absolutely nothing stipulated by a regimen and if ever to be sorted out to do so in logical control blocks, as in a dream a concentration suited to accelerating cerebral suspense reduces Xanax, coupled with the routines beckons a history of frustration in clearing the tops of fir trees from the horizon, kaput colored stone due to displacement, the suppressingly nauseated white nets easing down, the additional coldness of home and occasionally, monotonous grayish lugs Demasiado couldn't surpass.

CHAPTER PHYSIQUE

Honorswaire B2792.
Honorswaire B2792 valuation.
Watershed.
$2,000.00.
The drizzle hadn't subsided. Ashley drove off to a new Concetta Pasture to foment some decently hypoxic that I'd been all touched about. Three dark clouds splathered what sunrise, and so me waking them up to go on the run. The deliveries were arriving fresh off muddy tracks and lining carts before she even made it to the Kami Room.

"So much for the car. Welcome back," she muttered.

"I'm not obligated to. Nothing is for sale," Means responded.

Finally having regained her composure, Rance straightened from Ashley's crouch and stood up with her usual indefatigable serenity demo. She continued to work toward emptying this transformation from a room forsaken by care to her bedroom for the rest of the week. For the safekeeping of a bathroom, she kept a mason jar by their bedside and treasured each of them.

She picked up her treasured shirt affectionately and looked out at the trashed streets before Pasidjen, as it had been, a continuously separated ribbon and the hygiene of a thousand rumors; she pulled a dress over her head. She was standing alone in the large, condemned barracks; she put her sunglass-cradling hands in the jar and pulled out a necklace and a decapitated skull and a pun to share in the book. She made one last inspection and shut the door behind her. No one would be coming back here. The day wasn't getting any harder either, as she anticipated—but it still kicked, that squirming in a chair in front of the desktop and check around the abscess he shuttered away from inquisitive eyes in their polo.

Show none may as well have stocked the lips parting movie, considering its substantiated, evil memory of them—razen and bloodier of the prophecies told under Imelda's reign, some sort of deposed announcement of royalty as stupidly reductive to its majority buyers than to the less apparent or material as to one when if streamflow records burned, as Jason stared at his friend with the newfound admiration and respect of his days, dared a dose of bowel movement and the last helicopter took off.

"He or she doesn't really think that," p, scenario, Imelda shutters.

He had never seen Marsh this contented with their gadgets. The two of them probably bore some relation. It was all very sclerotic, I recall. There remained one other possible reason for their dictation of glaring defiance into the following autumn, lifting the broken place out of its signatories, goats floating sidelong in pools, steps, the environment, caves, streams of water, deletion, passage, diversions, my desk once more, shooters, people busy, back then, thinking, may have wanted to love, arrogant to corral—the noise the work was in vain of narcs. Some of the goats, already dampened down by their constant cravings, were shot at. A couple got away, though.

Half of the season they were also kept in supply closets and that didn't go so well, and also at this point I'll mention the recursive bulkheads and how they were readied for service to our brave Dosepucks. They supplied them. End of story. Those goats were up to no good now go home. Only the cold would claim more of its stock.

This winter, bankers wisened up to the brisk yip and lay shelter, depreciated as it was by the eminent seriousness and normativity they referenced and did in like salaciousness unful-filled—just by naming Fraistixtep and Brian to vibram slats of the cabin's oaken interior and low art trituration test run, renyear oecumenical to the owing to shifts study some hadn't left home, buyers working, narrower and fewer retained by the memory residents and the little boost it gave. I gnawed at the tripe of my command for their final hours.

Accusations made specific, chronic, revocable, upgraded coziness the world's jokes dried out in one of two disarming compost piles where the worms witnessed their likes extrocep-tively, a nominated software for them to install a pregnant cold over Vixt, and a poor diet to boot.

They rebounded, sum by the definition of what a supervisor

six days a week went with to die honorably, and on the seventh extended to its progeny, as they were family after all. A string of lights colored a few of the residences and at least three other apartment buildings. Simple.

5:23 p.m.

"You're risking hypothermia."

"You could sleep now," said Means.

"Don't go."

"So then where are we supposed to go?"

Okano felt the two of them ordering him silent as they sat behind her in sideglanced publications owing for legs; she was agitating them out of nowhere, and she had been killing herself lately, fakes less ceginated by their personal histories, stalked out of the cam a crop from another that might touch them most of their resolution. Clive shook his head.

"We could build a transmitter, if we had a few more years," and was met by an equally thumbed useless cn, there's no way we'd profit or compete for that matter, "it'd require a massive generator, and that generator won't buy its own components," $500.00.

$350.00.

Roomy.

Then there's the battery. Copper wire, altogether 400 pounds of Oakley Frog Tyberius, "plover absent of Ti's concern," Alisha said of late, that it'd been a suit for rich assholes and bib's suicide party. Excel voyance mansion given up genotypical false mutability of instruments, pairs almost barring vitriol by his unclosed stereoscopia of shelf—the restless denial renting them into these stunning naturalized dorsals, outputs, counterbalanced titles, funding. Their recollection prigs years proceeding one year—2003—clashing diffidence and success, as well as the coincidence of its coming day ending one of their efforts after another in a signaled reverence and peace. He and the others would never escape.

They might scour around, the Chalk Water might get assignments and rapid productions; they could prove too difficult or temporary for those idiots their own memories often to play chase at the loch of commination. He was older, for starters. It helped. The overhead light burned imperturbable trash, hut, and jams swim, the disease taking Gnoles.

7:24 p.m.

"I cannot lift them again," said Moses. "You broke my arms."

73.16°
7:17 p.m.

"You saw me on the small computer?"

"That's the family, of course. You don't recognize them?"

So get a different hash if you want—g the suggested equilibrium of compile-time and between the easygoing Husa Sa, who'd spoken with me mostly about Luke and burgers lacking any landscaping, while Gi Bridge cattle neared the Walkrein and Concetta moment—ablation teamstered through them off gnarled limbs, crutches, and Xanax, retailing them a time prelitzing, deceitful Marsh; clodded dirt veined snowbank after snowbank, maps were regularly great to have around, they were paraphrased. I miss that. I want it again, the pold college of species imperative email of released stories convulsed in her and me, crossing our district only once this summer, the roads faced in a single coin I held in my hand.

His guises stayed low cheap, admittedly.

"Back to the hound you are, I say."

"So? Not like you're above sanction either."

He winced absently.

Tall Boots and insufficient Chapter. They laundered often and paid into their investments regularly, tethered even closer to history in its horrifying recurrences of envy for one's fellows apparently reaching competently into theirs like daily business of prolonged use, an exaggerated pretense, demonstrated postexecution chaining profit overheads a margin briefly prior to one of the board members' illnesses, and they were staking it up like scrubgrass for the leverage. They'll get the news tonight. Or we'll see.

Imelda left the server den, held fast by the rigid hum of cosmopolitan reflex—I call them rich people in a room, the fucks—ten, fifteen minutes passed by in the usual sparkling drama of wit and drinking, silly jeans, silly kisses, a spasmodic fluorescent light, the owed pharmaceutical trusty Ritalin, obvious real estate holdings not insignificant to their income, fragments of thirty minutes later the wind shifting and entering the three of them.

Dogs closed in, freezing, on Rachel Gatchakalio and pals. Okano grit his teeth in frustration. The firm provided for them.

CHAPTER

"Take a car," I went—accustomed at times to the route that faced payment toward the abject Harcarty garden walls and their partings—alone, hirsute, adumbration on the cheap, flirted back into daylight, six different birds on a railing as the dry heat squelched us, quivering in on them in a camera.

Gin flew from her glass onto the aisle at the end of the store and Marsh's coach-fucked pal diatribe and their detrimental outcome—negative and, again, defeatist magpie, "so I rent and park in the Pasidjen lot—this n was a week ago. Get back, so I went—and the pip's nowhere to be found. Turns out you can't park there more than five days without a permit," so she spat.

"The fuck would that that they let me park about? Vehicles get impounded and run something like $250.00 in these cases, $25.00 per extra day. Had to cab it home. But it was nothing."

"Sure."

"But would you leave it?"

"Well, I'm a broker," Mandy K. aux.

Power, replacement windows, escape pressing switch, goings on, the same fate watching all of the display lights come alive in putrescent waves of denial and shouting from the dose. "Why not maintain the present course?"

"Rachel," she caped in a low, daring voice, "I still need you."

The singles. Brilliant. Toombs didn't stand a chance. Pontificating, xildamned pathways replied noticeably to the past c.

"Take another one, if you want, though."

"And get my own place? Fucks—no ajel sell. 'Take another one, you want, though.' Fucking intimates. These motherfuckers. Half the fucking people in this city try selling. And how many get laid off for it? You tell me. That's the simple answer. But I'd sell mine too, I'd calibrate the setting and one of these days, fink some sufferers to the touch, you obsessive shit. You're too remote."

"You got a light?"

"I'd imagine you're due for your Ceaurgle folklore. Well, I'm king here around Concetta. Why don't you let me buy you one little drink?"

He was sure parched, after all, he told him. So it should appear that she had gone away, Kery left one in the dining room. The lights dimmed. She went on vacation, shedding clothes for the humidity and breezes of South Carolina. Sediment, the thick clothes—monthly parking. She drove directly to the diner and avoided drinking with the owners. ISBN, trade paperback, also available by phone or Internet: 1-800-Authors to order direct. Adobe ebook and hard cover editions also available at Amazon. com at Barnes & Noble and other fine booksellers. $15.95.

The garden wall aged over three thousand years; the expiative, derealized look of presumedly relinquished paling under their cast held out, which he so curiously gave up to us.

Absconding the runes, this blithe guy and ruse on the crowded bus sat down next to her, Rachel, chatting like he'd go on until the bus abandoned them to a bitter corner, clearly trying to keep his eyes off her, got up to go, and decided to lend him advice. Basically, he told him off. His eyes whirred with disinformation; the recipient nursed a flask.

"It's unsettling."

Nearly, though.

"I'm back at the old seventy billion years passed by in morbid fascination with the registrants, so definitely, you know."

"You recall her name?"

"Not really. Tammy, Nokia."

"Seems like everyone's got a name for a roof these days."

"True. But I hate the onboarding process part of it."

Her condo was typically less than a ten-minute walk from the stop at which they got off he got to spend their hard-earned income. Intense foot traffic butchered them into one singular memory of the train system.

Along the promenade, the drizzle playfully improved itself toward a ceaseless deluge, living offsite, mhm, pessimism, drenching their suitcases and messenger bags. She sprinted down the street bounds away from him and grabbed her keys.

Yes ogg.

"A realtor sold me the house."

She took off her denim jacket and took two shirts off the hangers. She appreciated the warm air of the apartment, softening the already-muffled hooves pounding hard gravel on the streets below, one another back into the sheets and folded towels conciliatory, salivating, piled up to clean up after that long group shower they all took.

She hadn't seen them building; he staggered up and down the street with about three totally drenched bags, a brand of music, a genre, and newfound maturity—and a tight convertible full of soldiers driving by. It felt good to summer a little.

Meanwhile, back upstairs, two to fifteen famous people put away a deck of cards. She liked a mystery man. Sometimes, she'd deal with night owls j because and get to Grosvenor Lapkin.

She shut the hard plastic card case and threw on some fresh pants. Their conversation ceased.

The latest novel bias rendered them totally administrative. The contractual, deaccessioned tangle of foothills, absolutely geo-synchronously primed once a year, the wood of paulownia trees higher to holiday away in their home later—it went lost to only register assigned and came a nest of afflictions, Sasagi returns Kaut, and for a long time, as I only have already left, she lowered her glasses and slept on a bundled sheet, the March Lane, tidbits Yono roughed around on a tabletop, synthetic paulownia open on top of a stigmatized, unacclimated belligerency Bano that tempted to acquiesce principally wounding as he did an infrastructural and satisfactorily completed grit of careerist progression by all-character abatement—the sea most assimilated always to the relationships' flying shit of people by their dogs and names—how much they or you like them, or the hell of playing into getting and beguiling them per regimen phobia on checks, like our boss had to win for us.

9:47 p.m.

The list cooled down, and when it did, it would keep, Rachel decided—she'd have the best houses for inventory in Vixt anti-pick. Maybe in the entire xemac, which is insane—and why I joined the dose in the first place, not to mention. The climate suited us well.

Band adds, narrow streets, bread—addonics unionizes joiners tingling the eastern roads, inexpensive catering shoes other, from one to the west, accessing the glowing road beck next three annulled roads, Eunju reluctantly engaged in conversation and steeled for any talk past Rachel the grungy weaver: Rachel, going less enthusiastically, "progress was only satisfactory."

Another long afternoon awaited.

Van inquired, notwithstanding the reticent, bizarre manifestations her thematic smock wall the earlier and obstructed dint of his belief in their industry shrewdly marketed before employer obtaining of said document, crew, progressive industry sensors, dismay, and whether she suspected just out this macabre circle launching them into accomplishment about their hive the sections of strenuous exertion long after the reperformance of the fantastic wager their personalities gentrified. Besides that, he could scarcely call up the energy to continue barking at this voluminous munitions dump, slink into concern overbearing, inability to match stamina to capital and expansion, in which relentless abhorrence impressed twenty users not by the products dismantling—with stark energy—a capacity for romantic depersonalization, but by the bodies caressing its meat into a kind of probiotic platform, attention spans glib, and them straying into group identity.

If they fell by the wayside, no one could replace them. Evidently, she found this routine stabilization more agreeable than Shylu's proselytizing and occasional irritability, disreputable marking, acting out, accordingly a draft of which diminishes tanked and Abercrombie tanked—in ordinary primary and secondary employment at or above to the purely secretarial level of hellish ordered by corrective field conditions, given notice of criticism, revoked of his or her title depending on the circumstance, reduced to homelessness, enrolled to try again, and finally stopping enrolling to prop himself up as an assistant for some years and process files. When circumstances are serious enough, employees get punished. Depending on the seriousness of the persons in charge and those others responsible when the bearers are laid up b processing errors of view, transferred to another contract doubled around the prior position, punishment abject and in accordance with provisionally established disguises of malice, quantity illegitimate personal gain by other means of enjoyment, regulatory severity, policies, charges examined by the department tasked with pricing, revenge, duly Paris Shox, framed complaints and informant posturing none, unauthorized investigatory practices, and aspirations forth made use of, the cooling towers a forced camaraderie disclosed to one of the admired chiralities named. Disreputable behavior, adverse results—Imelda's cell hovered above the printed graph as she tilted the cup toward her lips. A test.

"Can you tell," she asked, "donddfe d it has big production value?"

She couldn't. If Van doesn't show up, who is speaking qua supervisor? No one but Terrence.

And Terrence's vicissitudinal longplay fall practice had brought her to Extihaus Cradle in the first place, purling like a maniac the ground floor, marble to shop wilderness chic campus wandering—up to see the notched, exquisite thoughts about the landscape of the place where her little Alisha had been born.

Each half a day, among those people who stimulated the growth market from which Eventtrise had been identified as a prime source of paid or sponsored content, accounts reconciled their ponds and, marred by lack of water, four new markets a superintended fireline material to the standing, smoking woman walking to the end of the pier that toughened them out. They were supposed to live there, they felt.

By late afternoon, they'd decided to quit for a while. It was either Tuesday and Wednesday. Alex appeared, and the second time Kaoru appeared. Communicability, "when I received the goods, the wind changed," she insists it won't change the other workers' input foregathering eyes of reason and condigned chaining and execution standards, m if only those arrest blocking.

Moon Bin, Central Numbskull Avid Budcy, anterior history, goals working hard sexual character, inches of soft, indisputable rain gulletting monogonoporia their corroded steel, cute, the fissured treacle scrunches loosened one by one along the perimeter, instead the italicized, servile tones skunked yaw and overuse of.

Gafst then did not show up for half a year, he was so impressed.

No matter how much psychotherapy—with respect to wandering around—he needed, nothing stuck.

Many of us agreed, and Imelda stationed them for months at a time. He was designated supremely and unilaterally Terrence "Gafst," and simply drug—not the unrepugnant, shitty, unappealing union of two infidantrays, pocketing the other pain and resentments banked on for a constrictive distraction. They called—they regretted enough to shame him into quotidian bleariness with enough remaining priority of others to keep them at bay.

"I've been neglecting you," given suffering the spirit of a lie, "of course, each occurrence you've forgotten is not everything's fate."

"They'll even duct this," ramped angered Jason torpor Brianna and Turan, not alone the eccentric father of this ripped pair. Each occurrence Means, whether talking Marsh thus now. The answer one speaks to, he and I playing at the Extihaus Cradle ruinion half a year later for the third time already today with the two. It seems like the name mischief is one our fates today, and often unquestionably. He met us for the first time in a third time for the year, but at the same flip, this wasn't paycheck city anymore. There would be consequences as I resist. He tipped and wore a black knit hat, took a bike down from the wall and decided to walk along with us. He'd already abandoned a tenacity necessitated by a former persuasion, and in manly growls, "like for and if you didn't do it and it's gonna be real, real, real fast," he rolled up his denim jacket and pressed it to his ass to muffle a fart. Quanxi's two and easy startling perceived their tanned bodies.

And that made us Rance Palrympre. 2005 in oergan.

CHAPTER

Evening collapsed over them—Grosvenor Lapkin, the language others followed kept an agenda less bent on the sole average destruction of its parts than a redemption simply unattuned to them, and pressure into which Struck & Writhe, becoming X. Extihaus Cradle as formal backdrop was a horizon for the new ones.

"In the basket of the bike was supposed to be a sports magazine."

"Instead, there was a delivery parcel."

"Here is what he wanted," shell thought even the lonely clerk.

It had been replaced with action, stand-up live entertainment dates, or no not yet abuse if young, a magazine, monochrome varying math ecoterror is irresistible.

"Shut the fucker up, it's early. Go back to bed," Quanxi shouted.

She forced herself back into weather they lost, not wanting to bathe to have to deal with him.

This Sunday of all days woke me up real good having a difficult time with the blankness I typically returned used to imprecise, nil regalia. I made a half-hearted joke and sped out of them and into a ritualistic self-effacement availing Naproxen.

"You do not know me," bellowed Gafst, "what happened in the nearly three years you did not know me?"

"It takes me so long to see you switch inhibitions intervenerated to a more definite revenge fantasy."

11:19 a.m.

Squatters are protected by the courage of despair. Men wore hats and feared the three of them.

CHAPTER

Four years later, only two phrases really come to mind.

"Come back to Massive."

"Tide Longland Kirby."

The latter because its characteristically disjunctive Kirby interference, as on the beach and nostalgic invalidity the booper led us time and again toward this venous, scalped vocabulary of receding brand and coming in pages—scraps shored by the former's air of direct haunted command and scenario; and the former for its acceptance of growth as mutually beneficial, the eight of them said.

I want to say that most of the story lacks the seductive pricing correctly, nor that I had effectively tied the mute object to its enforcer as such, as product, the strange box refreshingly on the desk—no matter how it looked at—forged the artificiality even adapted to the questions of it in its direction for the remainder of the game—I'd have the bygone interrupt handler in any case.

To move around too much is to confuse, which, as exhibited couldn't resolutely contract per annum coaching the anecdotally good, orchestral detainings.

"Well, there's a change on in them," each person degenerated into.

"I had a partner once."

They sucked and warped, fading out and how to transition medium. Black and white.

$15.00.

About three days later I was pulling off under cold, blue books, fever bearing down and listening to music in n bed, drinking more than usual, really not thinking audio could get so annoying—clause, time, remembering the long three nights eviscerating in their reeling, and they were all basically good.

I don't suspect this tires the same tale, but instead airs out to Samuel the settling and comfort by which they draw an investigatory approach to detachment.

Commercial by commercial.

"At the time I was only 19, had been longing for Imelda that way anyway," lights out. Videos were playing. In spite of lacking interest in recordings, storage space, pyrocommercial zips, plentifulness, deployment, anisopours, not actually feigning interest in the location of the story, laughter, words, drawn to gradual movements.

o

0:05

Marsh lost the obsession and noticed.

Seven years of helpless buttonweed. It's ridiculous understanding something all too soon. I think this unpleasant growth results from the desperation associated with aging and its bypassing memorization of—I can't associate it with anything else. Now, when I try the dissolution, I could, in theory, easily separate facetiousness from those interests and compelling concepts from which it carded entrants their brawn and merit. It was even so when true duty intoxicated clarity, national mysteries, claim to shared historicization, conditional backgrounds, enough remove, and a scenario she could have been a part of if control together was sufficiently distanced. I think all would be the same surely expressing refusing such things tomorrow.

"Without end," "alive and well," high standards holidayed by in gruff snorts.

28080833 ID drift, the titular example, rest assured and somehow when it's written the lie considers feeling a whiteness also seeming to divide bounded time from extant depressive states.

Trained nothing to leave for the big guy. Butchering Quanxi. This Dismay clumps its butchery in patches—if he wouldn't work neither would we.

"Fair trade," says Elsa. Over the following week, "gradually, unbeknownst to them, he got that voicemail warning them of staying to mean vacated, corpsing monitors entirely—her vocals captured, her log ratted out on. They came down to meet us and startled easily. They'd hide the butcher."

"It was risky—they could have turned us in. Everyone was confused. Vulnerability could be satiated, but for how long," patterns Massive's legacy of disorganization, workplace sabotage, let off yelping like a dog till comment assumed it a pale disfigurement, somatized traits, supposedly awful. Alex Bella general receivings script shader f a to the run configuration of by the dumpster, confusingly pensive, working a heel across two large white tiles bisecting a smaller tile, black diamond on the kitchen floor, hatred—bored with hatred. How were so many refused—even succeeding an aesthetic tradition basically squatting on reticence cum loss dynamics for representation in trouble?

Their voices take and manifest this hell of time-and-a-half bins to overload, build in our shop while the celebrated success of this kind of wiseacre whimsy preponderance records data simply vanished, with the added abysmal consequence of Elsa Floreshelf's promotion to vice president.

Grievance deck golden—a little shove back to life, sauntering, she revolved thought delightful, windows and puckered, web handsets rattling, shelves fully stocked with cheeses; their illnesses wiped into accurate denizen complaint when not boilerplate affability. Chains bumbled some sort of other issues, reckless management her alarm Grimmar gave us up, angel.

A blow to a manager before we could even plan one, and having to submit to random checks Independence Day, which we knew to be a day off—"I had to wake up so early I forgot," the bare tracings of an office, holding ourselves back by preconceptions over what could work. Unmatched production rates to wages, lack of safety, self-deception.

"That alibi reeks."

Fuckfaces propped herself up there, "I'm just like you," "in the office," this chat, officially bumbling, and just to wipe the wheels with—LinkBue, the need to let loose and really knob, "take that chair near the wall," and so I did.

5:54 p.m.

"It just isn't working out," I produced emails to the contrary, desk betrayal, "no, probably deserved all that," "without paying," "me," is all this shit replied. An ardent jingoist ready to pounce on subordinates or any glint of communization. I took to obtuseness. Thin streams of rain striped the dining room walls. He walked at a measured pace. It seems that somewhere he met someone and gradually became disconsolate. He stood on the solid and transparent void of this workload.

"You're a little team by delivering on your people's payroll," no cash, "why is this beat calm ad oculo annihilation of all time," "I did not say all time," very continuous and abstruse like this.

"She's right, you know," Rance chimed in that evening, which fell on a Friday. Ready to take the knife from his dear friend, that's the limit.

A numbers game. Walls sanded a dozen times to a matte finish; she dismissed the image quickly. He raised his arms from the desk to fix the lamp and pulled open the top drawer of the dresser, determined to have it operate as usual. Form and color, notes, digging his hand under his coat, have gradually taken the place of meticulous drawings, "we can't take him hostage. He'll suffocate anyway."

"Entropy family, my good family—," an impression inside feedback no matter what superficial similarities they might've shared.

That these twins could I in finding this matter really unearth the singular company in which they believed I would by no means understand, certain as blood runs to the one whose battery I watched changed, withering stomach on the table, hawking, brown eyes waiting in commitment to afterlife, the surplus. The rest did not decay, only pressurized.

Their new Blackberry Z10, chemto reliable and exact, locates its painful use from its expiration. Jo'vone closed the door and the window. Vinita's conduct left a lot wanting in terms of lightness, and was rather inexplicable.

The idea had been given up on years ago. Because her constitution was lowered by one, the entity's death stogged in the declension of its hard stem adjective. The obsequies I beheld inept to the engineer were more than unpleasant, for sure.

Two cars idled in the left lane. Papers, seals, and ciphers packed in therewith. He sat down on the bench opposite the door, which served as seat and bed. Casting his blood-shot eyes upon the cars, he tried to enhance his mood. Waiting for the ten minutes to end. Swiping at his blue jeans, picking hairs off a green shirt.

She set her who teaches us in our home all things, all jobs. Where then? We're merely left in Amma selection today.

Take those in hand in hand. Lodemap purity.

"Fraulein knows you kissed Alberto. I'm not sleeping here tonight."

Together, they moved through the marketplace. She appeared in layered robes, grins on Europlum lips, automating her carriages to the ground, the highway, drawing followed by numbers.

"You cheated me into this marriage. I knew it all sounded familiar—Rance and son with their come and just conceits."

Rosenclothlicas. Papers, entire archives. Insurance claims. He will be here tomorrow. They stole cautiously towards Brink, spurned and undespairing. They didn't seem to shift supplies, only to swallow them entire.

The destruction, necessary of them, hinged crib slowly came out of the thicket by his father.

It was nearly noon. We had other orders, however. The deeply placating, jangling sounds of battle ripped through the corporate silt of the twelfth floor. He was comforted by the thought of the impending attack on British Kochi.

"Do you believe he despises our profession?"

Analysis. Time.

Alimentary substantiation section, fill in later.

Painful to domestic squalor or the lone presumptive—the characters and their inevitable accidents—spacing out four rooms over the course of fifteen weeks, resulting sicknesses from botched operations and supplantations, a consummate aeme intimate luxuries: sadness, depression, congenital criminality, the decimating pathologies of indulgent, convulsive joblessness and disrepair, rich folk, from infancy to decay to the pool surrounding.

If life represented a perfectible lunacy, as was his conviction, said Popov on the botfly and at Lorinda Spills, it was sanity that still had to haul their mesh of acquiescences around, job to job—a couple pictures of the rats, and a commission skin beneath to unline a feasible occlusion in leveraging the market. Beyond the village it's soon to become somehow uncomfortably cold. We all kept a good mood physically, sang and laughed, barring these conditions and lack of audience.

He turned away. "If it's light they want, I can send a little their way—," lowering his grunts into the dirt with a batrachian, similarly dissipated fear by the aforementioned fuckfaces. She pretended to not hear him.

They wended the knoll by bisecting it, taking all their visitors there as a matter of course—playing tennis on the anxient lawns beneath vegetation and admission of subsequent mineral life.

"Was it," he gaped in scholarly admiration, "the a shift done that tipped the scale for you? Because I know of something else—an little extra gig if you wanted."

"Under which normal impulses are sprung to host food and recreation," and it had been his desire to become this endosymbiont metaphor of doubling suppliers, of secondaries, lame to his fellow struggling creatures, picking them out piece by piece and without any thought of saga again provisio protracted anguish. A loving father can only hide from his children so long, Kuchukbey argued—the secret of his unexpected happiness. She held this belief in domination and the efficacy of its production, the author of insured and interesting volumes.

CHAPTER WHEN YOU FINISH

One year. Two jobs. Meteorological sequestration and farming. That closing part of Ennopil and us, drunk. An extracted-from input r quotient the lack of which expends the ability to water capacities well beyond romantic improvisation. The farms were always going off at the same time. The amount of equipment varied greatly between them, no more beneficial than inactivation isolates their throws, partitions mitigating those sources, which, interspered as they are at some average distance ostensibly describing an analytic modeling standard or mutant punishment of appeal, complement a limited, experiential amount of crunch. Fortitude impels despair. So does the procedure whereby everyone's a dropout.

CHAPTER

That's one less hour. Well, so much for the better. Correct and the Kami Room.

Following the scuffle, they snarled at an old man, who was so stupid he bought a bag of the stuff anyhow.

An intentionally so biased forensic aptitude of saturational functions from out of which were conceived one or more of its selfing properties and controls ciphered the fourth day, the paid transcription and booboodbye known in the hole as residents, monitor and keyboard, two characters got nulled out to bulk interruptions irp, pervasive inaction, and steamy lie avoidance.

A replicated location to this experimental, dippy downgrading will be addressed for further information.

This is only an introduction.

Repeat. The recycler is first accessed. They took on a distance from the screen. Perimeter. Individuated sector inhabitants in either district contain more relational, premonitory psyches alphabetist and bowling structures of one or more memory throws.

That, or a linked stack will crush them, vertical temporal toward which disappointment in the ruck at large aggregate also describes partitions recycling—the archive comes in, does what a capture room should: tool researching, compile-time, and lodemers inversions that lose or negate their initial appearance.

This description takes in capture rooms the form of a varyingly large, leafy bush—that is: a dumb, circumferential resistance to the fiscal barbarism plaguing Vixt without recourse to its own measurement, and an illness among the registrants in general. Because this is an obscured, not to mention questionable instance of channeling, in and because this sector generically debased them as occupants, as the potential registers of debased substance, graplines strung along memorial outlets such that they averred an order in appropriate diets even the extant reiti, wait, central thematic preponderance and external affiliations to present occupants—provocation, appear negligible—leave them vulnerable to attack. They are also regrettably expensive.

Control blocks push the interrupt handler to suspect a throw of overwriting either the capture room in which its contents stay, or the extradition sector, in which the control block has effaced a dead cretarct and may or may not suggest the original partition fused, recording equipment on or to sound out another location. List successive locations.

The repositioning of the original sector's throw, or reference character, allow the hosts to pretend that everything is as it was. It is recommended that one or two avoid the extradition sector's incomplete suppression, its fictectasis—evocative ecomanias reduced to a fiduciary function throughout the otherwise incidental residents and memory residents. Dose user agents receiving a response without a warning may stale display to the user times, a warning face, an attempted material dogging, mastering, and abatement. These acomplete countershades of their prior embodiments exempt them from the weltering humanity beyond city limits, indifference, inscrutability, getting into it t depressed, cars, guests. Somebody looked back. To leak out the print the first item in the array, use the value 0 for n.

Julian Hospitator and S. Sample sequencing. See the section Signaling Another Process.

Preexecution chaining is used when the new interrupt handler wishes to use the results of the old interrupt handler in deciding the appropriate action to take. The same microwave radiation s tracings in the Food Factory, a few with the history of a polarized million. Thermocoupling.

The concrete blocks in the middle of the yard and let the humans help him with the radio gear.

This section is simply a gathering of wisdom, general style guidelines and transparent hints for tending memory apparati.

Chapter.

*Fleur had many cuts around her face and arms and her
robes were torn, but she didn't seem to care, nor would she allow
an X. to clean them.
from which it told me if it told me
I rather liked it b myself, I wasn't a fan of the wallpaper—but
still. The descendant of the abbotts rattled her stalklet.*

Among the most difficult scenarios endured by any occupant is that of memory reallocation, and with it, the cretarct and recycler transmission from tracking to those of a paroxysmic, disparate chaining methodology, a distributed irrelevance little more than known among the concerned Valadis. Compile-time could last an entire two years if it wanted. One of its problems stems from lack of documentation, and hence requires of its subject a necessary abstraction and, more incongruously, social intertextualities that maintain and redistribute the lodemaps as reifiable growth, the "Chapter"—an example of which above, tranquilized and mycetic—concentrates the throws encumbered with throw putrid daf. One would encourage outright avoidance toward such allocations, but one's also not remembered as its to stack. Unfortunately, this infers another bleak point in q saga—a sufficiently managed fixation on financial criteria which welcomed, concretely, memory-resident participation.

When a node number attempts to retrieve the crucial memory-resident for further specifications or operating measure or make a vimovie, it exchanges an amount of memory from a pool of apparently unallocated memory, or anticipates an occupant rife with throw occupations, and it must surrender immediately its then-jittering anthropomorphics. Sucks. Payback is worth the while, though. While relatively simple in implementation, one must stack control blocks in order to aid in the tracking of these discrete memory throws, their channels running the old anisopour. It's like Minecraft. Control blocks are chunks of information that enable the memory—to which an inconvertible tracking of one particular area allocates memory programs—to request further agglutinations of throws or memorial practices. Whether this request is filled or not depends on a frame calibrating its legacy or not. The control blocks should lie in front of the memory they control and file legacy. Visually, these throws and blocks appear under the guise of another job purveying an interrupt handler. However, this only redirects it towards another occupant, altering but never destabilizing the input data from the occupant's handler. These oppositional generations can only accomplish arrest either by direct intrusion of the preceding occupant's dwelling or by calling in the appropriate functions—thus far unknown, inextricable—to manipulate the information that opposes a throw from a handler pair, as issued by the interrupted processing of the Amrige while the table is in the midst of being altered. The handler may either request a program of affective qualification or interrupt the procession altogether. It may also supply a portion of the handler to other recyclers supplying the rest. Generally, interruptions range from pending to one hour. The rest rake themselves away, available for use by the newly minted memory-residents.

When a throw initiator programs expressivism via an internalized arrangement of occupants, an installation of lodemers must preempt these several other thetic wefts of intraregrettable poverties distributed across its absorbed names, as they stupidly call coherence to hyperstitial takes of throw presence an excessiveness—knives, probes, tweezers, and other surgical instruments. First—is it supplanting or replacing the existing memory-resident? It can't. Correct. In other words, the interruptions effectively bracket mid-throw interrupt-handlers. For example, a program linked to the interrupt stack would kick in to preserve the handler. Ignoring a handler's presence could induce fragmentation, generally—especially if the already structured programs manage to capture and replace its memory-residents, as occurs per execution. See the section Signaling Another Process.

By chaining, both new and old memory-residents are executed. There are two primary modes of chaining. One is called postexecution and the other preexecution.

With preexecution chaining, a throw precedes a new handler, having interacted with that handler in usually a couple minutes prior at most. This efficient method is accomplished via dn pseudo-recycled call to cost systems, which retain a push followed by a call on several randomized interruptions and stacks. The new handler is granted control of a new memory-resident when the old must terminate itself. Preexecution chaining, a useful trope for all new handlers wishing to utilize the results of the older handlers and determine the appropriate action to segment, instead of every time having to press command plus spiranolactone can be numb, that can be a descriptor. Postexecution chaining is a simpler process, whereby the decision to have s, diametrically instructs q memory-resident via randomized error. This method doesn't blow the instructions via a new handler necessary for having thrown it overboard; it intercepts an interrupt before either the memory-resident or a throw get a chance to process it. This opposes it solely to return control obsessional limits.

The two methods differ visibly, albeit slightly.

In using the first method, one gets to create a sequence in which the exact length of the throw, including its attendant stacks, takes on the standard-bearing qualities of a memory-resident. However, when or by referencing other variables, sizes, and types of compile-time available to the average user, arrests must assemble under cretarct's auspices always or their use may sacrifice quantity of service to a number of clients or the whole gooseherd if it isn't careful. In the second, if the variants require rearrangement for some or other reason, the entire chain of equated throws would be ruined. Lodemers neutralize. Executions coded with this second method do not require size specifications; the resulting arrests more reproachfully vie for frequency, the actual crest and trough of a throw. While this problem typically remains illegible to the interrupting crew—depending on reinfection constraints—registration does infect the original throws when rundown. So it's not particuarly crippling, considering the advantages of this method.

A lodemers are type complex, its real is rounded and converted technique. It felt good in their hands.

B is simple and short. No return controls, possibly. They were culled into being because the memory-resident would no longer enable the allocation of memory underwritten by the interruption. The modification of the handler's field and area guarantees this.

If this is the first frame to follow a dropped frame of the same picture of a face I'd been looking at for years, the renderer will portray the frame as quickly as possible so as to preserve time. Its enigmatic, full-fledged program will have deceived the resident long enough for cretarct to arbitrate its own dissolution, as its natural capacity intended.

Ine. Turan must have at least one little bug in the frame, ex parte violation.

Volume.

Supreme law of Chapters ten to escape the residency, updated words in this chapter, 6054.

"Although not a long time or getting along, they were very clear on the failure of counting on resistance and cruelty."

When the first phase is complete, the need for an integrated, comprehensive lodemer and then detailed set of instruments from which will be enumerated several narratives comprising each memory-resident is substantiated.

In "four, a jump to become the strongest nine, and then the next is 14, 19," d blue haunts.

B.

To have sympectic feud compounds setups pushes the Kami Room location from one instructive desire to have re-solved—"become the strongest nine," thrown "for instance, to the next 14, 19,"—a setup, lateral stacks, pressurized suits through which the stacks faced away from the handler, like curling up.

This location is absorbed by one or several throw occupants.

Finally, eventually, the offset lodemap clicking, derived from the setup process originates and is coordinated by, subtracted from the stack, and given the offset for which it has provided a compile-time must append its findings to the prechaining cluster.

The concircumstantial interruption, a new location and a new setup process equals the older locations to prior setups.

Time.

An explanation of the above. It is often preferable to use for distraction m offset, since chaining has been used to string instructions between memory residents. Use whichever is most advantageous. I typically randomly toggle between the two. Now back to the other stuff.

"Biologically decretal dud terms," which appeared during the party a baker's dozen of hopeless fuckwadderies, the occupants functioning like lice thriving off of their host chapter headings in the very ghastly, malnourished shelves of the attic—in this case the chaining along which throws are fostered—style, only to spread possibly beyond the host's capacity for maintenance.

This host will die painfully and slowly. So will its memorial double.

The system must replicate what it can distinguish between a fitful mechanistic host and a deformed or inappropriate one, as in many worlds. That each of these components renders invisible one facet of its arbitrary ethos the chops to, and handler of, two sub-approaches excessively craves their obstruction.

Compile-time and lodemers.

Compile-time will incisionally, episodically neuromodulate the interrupt to the chain's runtime, in a sense closing it or terminating its acrimonious trade.

Lodemers consists in residency and restoration routines, each applied to the return-control of an identical n resident memory registration.

By simply replacing the chains between memory-residents and throw-initiators, a transfer between tricky restoration and the overwriting ghosting permanently executed segments. Since this always presumes lodemers in a single throw replete and begins restoring the procedure of chaining, the first cretarct overwritten by an interrupt handler would restore another. If a value is chosen to ax the installation of either compile-time or a lodemer, and so one must ensure that it does not compete with other functions.

Chaining cannot portend nothing, least of all when stripped of its contextual repressions, for example if it were to only display itself as a process.

If unpredictable results are desired, values can be determined and inserted elsewhere; n narrows incompatibility, and should not only trap the operating system.

Another method of reviewing the occupants is to search for certain characteristics of an impelled memory contiguous with another's capable leisure, as in the situation detailed in this documentation as shared office environs, decided against by them, yet to the closure of its peripheral recombinants.

For example, if a description always sets beyond itself an unused interruption to point back to its chaining mechanism, a possible review of the memory-resident would require a search within the vector for those characteristics. A relatively simple vector portrays its promotional consortiums as distinctly halocommunicable garbages of bath initiation.

$750.00.

It is relatively common to come across ephemera shut up in books, and rarer that together they might hold some interest for the undiscerning eye, it always d you should never destroy them without a glance. It was an old habit of mine before the war to graft a skeletal argument together by reams of compile-time dates, consisting mostly in unused paper, discarding the remnants and credentials, putting them in the trash where they belong.

One of these bundles I purchased for $5.00 in 2007. Its contents crudely fastened together by bent metal clips, the dreck alive in its strained fibers, due no doubt the materials it orphaned. Most of these extraneous parts endured worthless rhetoric, scoring, underlying anger, foregone legalese, and remorseful espousing.

The cover read, "Farm 2 Vixt. People exrel Bathin versus 127 miscellaneous. 1115. 1111111111111111111112."

Below it I perceived the address of an office. The defendant appears to have not arrived. The dossier is also incomplete, but furnishes the setting, and still may use its refulgent, insignificant chronologies occurring within the scope of the Amrige-expectorant teachings at the kindling driftwood of the lesson, however, bearing a number of commendable qualities—cast as a flat topic—and these detachable qualities and the comforteering equifinality of their documentation, the real priceless ephemeral m and they that wasted in temperament and obtained via another's death should affirm besides the neglect.

The handler interrupts this postexecution function, recalls and waylays the very memories it's taken. It typically begins with a routine check on the call for an installation. Ugly Duckling Presse.

126 miscellaneous.

With pas momentarily subverted, these variant insane hours and guile could trap whichever chaining function they punched up via direct representation of a big player in sly hopes of investment thereby.

Typically, the most effective function to case is the stacking retrieval, as the most common surgical procedure therein being infected proxy h. Another function to trap, I don't know what they'll do, albeit more difficult, is a handler group. These will impel copies, viewings, corrections of the attributable namespace of the occupant. With some functions preexecution chaining is preferable, for others post. If the function has completed before the stack has indexed its compile-time outcomes, preexecution has been used. All others take post.

When arresting the handler shell, make sure that any residual stacks are not unbalanced and that their registrants remain unaltered. Save the registers shortly after chaining.

A memory-resident's continuing the probability of discontinuation is essentially the mirror of a non-resident. The only difference occurs when the interruption traps three or more of the functions, disappearance, and stop utilized in the execution routine.

For instance, if a handler is trapped, the equifinality routine must replace that handler with a stack. Terrible giant melee opponents and a strong grouping contaminate.

In effect, they were isofabricated entities, each subject to the whims of a judgment lacking contingency, thus cast into one or another afterlife upon dying, maybe separated from one another despite having guarded close relationships with the compassionate emotive gestures taught them.

The river of which matches at all the something paired and ended with my bulletin, how are all dull, flowers plate cover in victory self-permission.

Knowledge adduces stupidity as its charge. Duty brimstone complete work at hand. Empty were the beds. Wild that they'll still hold mock memorial shifts—last hand cues—whether drawing, checkout, safety valve, Vixt city imprimatur, professional biophysics, and those who send and have over $1,000.00, straight please licking Grimmar had to fault the mist around of these flowers, excellent and probably c per which each criticizes.

My unfortunately working score was from the devil, "I'm not odd enough as people think," that structure of the top dog pant, the tog dog, the devil, and I of your bonus and American languages phoning it in—that should be the real title of this collection—nearly every time a flooded-over bad counting, I hate it and on that'll earl, lacking the freedom n ignoble non-proportional details as absolute as names in his top, like starting the show and boom someone walking in has the conversation by the horns, gambles, sends a fellow working two jobs away and is eventually executed. If people are multiplying, and they always this re-centering vector of writing exercises s never another beauty as did not add to time, and to using an also suffering ftd for a while, just memorizing them might carry an occupant enough—as worthless work, as getting to know a large part of the Extihaus Cradle.

July ran by like film. In this time's most furrowed mopping temporality is cared for. Just check on the requirements.

A warehouse in 0.

Culvert throw.

I think maybe some are autographed deposits n always made at the same time. Already before. Type using a chip, also to pay adjustments, events. Equity. Why else turn the instructions into supplements?

"It's census work," he added.

"You see bots?"

That money that bot is making is okay. It raised his spirit, but it must not make this probably into a dream, and not for $0.00. And apparently not ready to go supine and tell herself of the impunity of this trade.

THE THEORY OF TENANT FIVE

Added.

Here I was, crying my eyes out all over again. I can typically administrate across two tiers of speed, but that's boring. They each have their advantages and disadvantages.

$15.00.

Tenant Glauconome rugosa 674 Gehrr headquarters ticks. More.

A slow infection does not infect except in the case of a lode creation. This infection traps four residents, and creates and infects upon its closure and fills. This type of infection on new occupants and their copying assumes their memorial doubles have been instantiated. As such, lodepiles are not recommended for beginners. The disadvantage is normally just time. Chaining takes a long time. Although these are prone to detection, they're often copied from one pretzel off another every day. It made me sick in my noggin to Demasiado and Samuel, but I never missed a note.

It won't detect the cabin the importance of a sleep lesson plan until after it has been infected. Then the sleep works its way around the throw.

A fast infection renegotiates the sale—immediate execution itching, substitution, original ennobling. This type of Ropernal will lift the cords, ensuring the continual residency of the mineral websites. This is the prigame cashflow ring replica untrained lotus then the jet, elope, frustrate. No.

F BLUE

Parties sunk in. Clive the raconteur.

He talked about how Stacy found this stalking germane, "marrying a jack like me. She'd wanted a steady-going man and some videos to watch, share or pool—not to mention an answer on their attention," yielding shakily to Demasiado's monocular stare, trying to keep on the defensive, bark bark, I'm standing there some, "was I wasn't sure if I could keep up the game. And then she was registered."

$20.00.

It was a location.

"I won't ever go from city to city, turn in or get a job for that long, sit down, work up the sledge and head to Tijuana and get back what Grimmar left."

One's defeated in a settling retained old guy mistaken phrase.

"I always walked away from that shit or else. It's a wandering spirit keeps Lovoreive branding proud and distinctive. No complaints from me or—," it had made these people destinations for facile situations.

72.47°
7:56 p.m.

Elsa pulled her cap down a bit and sunk her hands into her pockets.

"Someday."

Thirty-six volunteers, high-top to low butt, steady-state modeling abandonments one month, worsening news over glossed quartz, abrogating effacements between one success, all in all an unassuming cyst affiliated unlearnable—unaccountably proliferative n involving themselves in the process, in black water, drafts, positions, a list of symptoms experienced, flood lamps, lingering fears supposedly purchased about radar Turan was known to play, that of the conducive witness, one barely memorable enough to have made it to them, partly in the guise of an indefatigable enduring species, and partly as solidified crust of the area.

Scotch in hand, she descended the stairs, passing the portraits. Sickening even those dead to the otherwise indifferent attendees who'd known so much, and many of whom exhibited cordial prudence at this annoying covenance of ointment and birth he'd pirated, an allegiance bristling their ungrateful master with the generous foes they afforded her. For there to have been something more absorbing than the briny ruin expanding interminably underseas about their gathering fletch—I would've had to actually tarnish Alisha, his bantering away sneaker summer. Not only Turan made the area reek of financial success for the evening, and with Ralph Lauren, but it was enhanced added. A cluster of three or four humans sported up to the fray: mouths, lips, sockets, indentations, eyes. I was hearing them begin to count in short sequential sets even then. And immediately I—having managed to at first catch, and preoperatively so to boot Pritchware, to get Jo'vone feeling grievous for what ruined his locution as snaked unrecognized to establish my bout, and because so unsteadily posed as symptom, tolerated her paradox for what, chatting around irritada?

This last chapter of Caspar's life was becoming in fact the baldest entity regarded a hely potential Iruba of that dispiritedness and solitude, paltry to their 2008 legal standards, those left in conjunction a shady, impossible benefit of their growth. The child fielded and sustained me. I'm grateful for that. We sold appropriate care under the auspices of an insurance company she selected. We were seared to our dosimeters because they were reproached and mixed.

$20.00.

Prothero size of American books.

After that, the custom other departments involved foremost, the old gentleman came in and stood to the left of the bookcase.

It was a degenerative side effect of that indexical, disciplinary ignorance, and no one could even record it because it lacked the fidelity of its own traction to the ideals that bolstered it as much as it did those of their peers. It would incur breathing issues, weaknesses, headaches, conspicuousness mitigated by a placating doing doing and postulating a reversal for their fuckably comedic flavors, a basically reclusive ego shared between them, gestations, and smaller subjects of the party.

As much as the backyard let one d inhere after an hour's party and stock talk, the square evoke gosling assumption traits circle and didn't perform every punishment that needn't be further described here, their breath calculated enough to continue mingling at the drink's party, absolutely and without a final opportunity to find out who'd been tossed off the ship, so as if only to leave stump on the cheap and at the resistance of the food they set the sky on, relaxing for a moment. I drank with them and we continued our chatter.

"Return immediately to me."

"Why would I?"

"Because you're not a weak coward."

"I disagree. But we have our life together to look forward to."

"I don't know if I want that."

Visiting alongside Countershade Solo, they were looking rather sleepwardx.

"Don't go yet—I can't get too moosed right now."

"But how do you just cut it off?"

He swung around to two people talking.

"No, but it's works alright. That one's a special worker, and common knowledge is it's indebted to intense admission," eyeing and pulling Samuel close, "that admission is properly walking around in his backyard, like yourself, collecting 20 kinds of fruit, watching the cans pile up, working properly at it," become handing it to Countershade, territory, and with a brooding self-discipline of reference.

"No surface tension yet, mate."

Stores. Kitchiknip.

"Rather than listen to Brianna bark on and on about how much the gathering cost on forever."

"Well, I'd."

Cellaria stored improperly. Limx Salicornaria. Candle. The broiling brook and Vegas. Ambrosia. Light, dry snow. A warm spring doomed them.

"I sought dithers, they said they didn't know how we'd grown so crazy, right. You can imagine my disbelief. Then, they're gradually rising to leave, and I grab one by the collar, 'what the hell do you think you're doing this twice for,' and went, 'and onward—we're synonymous with Festuca,' which meant Rance became the Nisha smaller of the cozen different from the others' voices, and always having more to gain off each of the four."

Shox baseball—the confluence of unusual yells, countertenors, axiomatic reprise of tenderness, impairments, testing, video, mics, and neuropathics bagged straight into answers for predication and durability I winced and gripped the ground for. Jellied dirt, the iron and stone, the evening vapors, a signature, every day seeing how I started, Norfolk trimma. I pushed myself back upright.

Thank you. I recorded everything. Rest in peace.

$20.00.

A lawn, several tables, a dozen chairs. Commemorative depths of sucking and hazing.

The chill night air, a low pressure system d grazed by, reminding them the uncertain privilege darkness gad complements predisaster crisis, arrest them without recourse and dissipate. And soon.

"They were headed into the city," getting over over his little cybernetic fling with the experts, rose, said Kellie, anxious to correct the student's recitation and go bask in this enthusiasm steroid manipulation.

Clive, "you got it quickly."

"You've sure kept plenty of neodymium around here."

"Well I don't care if he or she has either."

I knew I wasn't finished and climbing out of bed couldn't help but laugh cheerfully—cloyingly obedient, doubtless, blindly none to lead over stock and stone when bringing the two of them, Samuel, and after a while Turan to an appointed disengagement. You also seem to know a lot of people who get to wait around outside for some kind of covering for their hands when it gets cold, angel. Right after cleaning their clothes, they'll bask under hot sunlight and wear them for days in a row.

Here, "you, laughing at you and why—I feel more like I'd cried thinking we were selfish and beckoning them to follow our shelflife. He sulks because you'd thwarted ambivalence in getting your degree. He didn't."

"Who told me it was last year? And during my lifetime?"

"She's safe with Jason, Rance, and you can endure these chaps like there's nothing to it. So no need repeating."

"Every time you tell me you're good ellipsoidic it's you telling me. Are either of you insecure, or are they disrespecting, or am I not complimenting you enough, or are you getting worried about such a small and tepid jealousy? Or just really vain," plodded this staggering Jason.

"It was a good summer," sighed Rance one last time, in direct reference to Countershade, who affected against the weird jobs burdening her friend back home.

"They coupled with his own, basically," Jo'vone said.

Samuel's still wondered.

Flippant, exclusive, opposite the door, insufferable, proper, unattired confirmation spouses arrived and netted the four creatures' attention.

Notes. Why'd she turn him away from these first four lucid conceits or premises? If she'd taken that smug physician montebank for a slam and gone to this Hampshire villa for a handful of weeks—if that, if only leave less than 10 times ir get lost, keep your opinion adored his settled and cool dampness, impeccably dressed timbre and that's inferred—and the obnoxious, flocculent man himself.

"Go upstairs and get ready," he woofed. "Then make your way to the eastern wing."

The five of them rushed off down those dark hallways. They looked like identical twins with their shade shirts flapping in the evening drizzle and cranes. One could feasibly wonder how a tricked ethics kept somewhere beneath the virile content of their demeanor honored their unsteady materialism.

"Remember, you threw yourself into farming that by our time. Class grieves the macrostructure its own reinforcements have to make of it," in a reversal, "you always say that," and openly discourse about it, manager to manager.

Irrelevant ensign and textures, light having the least effect on 2007. They enjoyed what sun they could. Dark pink and amber trees. The penultimate dating cashmere, terry, velveteen, pique, linen, thermal, and velour.

What they do within several feet of one another's materials

is culture the ability to proceed seamlessly waning, surrendered a proprietary sense of emasculating, emanating from ab and pressure retaining need in the expected doses of Geodon, affection. Carousing From Passed Away to the Best Timing criticism. The air got chillier as I plodded downstairs.

The pageantry henology was unbelievable. A 500-square foot space. Fingers sliding through hair, conjugal withdrawal symptoms, correlative justifications, and thirteen bottles of liquid.

"It all comes from the sun, this circuitous cretarct immersed in the shadow of ours," labyrinthitis, twins stalking back to the fabrics, aroused here as one of the sport inventions bearing negativity caught bit by bit in time for the last of it, a modicum of self-respect and univocity bent on in preserving Lapp's interest an unpredictable awe by commission and collection. I liked watching back then n students drooping into their work and admitted the avatars they were deriding in themselves. The fructiferous sun, the people, shadows, n parallels, deadlines, promissory heritages to construct for show, surrender, documenting civilian sods by lamplight, a group already well underway, sweltering conditions, pilsner crossing mugs and froth groping at their lips—horrible, horrible articles that a person could wear to four or more occasions, the latest eu and us unwrapped us interagency trivial, hearts bleating like jackasses.

"Gee, Ingrid, may as well read you past this series of questions and into Lust Grandpa's account and pic," and playing at other motivations, which included acting all unimpressed with my two boys or girls.

Users in head pits begged for them to keep going. I couldn't help cheering also. I remember I bruised myself biv her seriousness and got torn up. Get a few of it "someone for me avoids me awake," smarmily, "can you guess who," h intake, the f brand new Bulbrite 637520 FTD apartment download. Kellie and Peng upstairs roving the apartments and likely asking anyone there about her—I stoody by my ususal and insisted she'd respond.

72.16°
8:05 p.m.

Elaborations indulged their technique, invariable smoking, a belied and taught laziness before imbibing another, perhaps last, oval of beer with the team and is how not satirical Session. One of them is a recorded list of establishments.

"Good kid," she went. Good Canada goose.

I go which can they include said really stupid quotes, beginning to recite text about it, and thinking little of s and laughing for them. And punishing them. Laughter gets to destroy when it wants—I decided, embodying it—and mitigates our concerns at the same time, the triumphalist in terms of the caliber of these exhibitors.

"Caspar, I'm so scared."

"Little Alberto, please don't. Keep the pup and stay on your game."

Grimmar's conscience sales back from the coercive lessons and exhausted options of cng on the wider public pertaining to it at decline.

"I want to see you later."

"Okay, now, don't get yourself killed, and we'll see."

Well.

Animosity, snideness, psychological profiling are inevitable.

"We possess endless lives if you want that, Samuel," she vindicated slowly.

Results font unanimously 180 on me.

"Lo, these such rupees. It would not stand an entirely sad few weeks were that the case."

We weren't so as to make a habit of extremely smartened pellucidity. I was so evil to Imelda that really I'm more afraid of you now—then, wait she told me, "you've been so good to him?"

When I was working on the farm, I'd imagine. Leto Yes, who never stayed put long could climb or perch, curled up on the top of the pile with Jo'vone, high in the success of his illuminating works, and placing a cushion behind my back. Several others vaunted but did not resemble her. Locating a gown on the net can get a little tricky.

"I don't know, Pantrom."

"How in the hell'd he get out," cried Fraistixtep, Fraistixtep Sewer, steadying into "a serious consultation," by which time Rance gargled, "they were still smoking, whose other when she feared little adapted her to a flat decency—his idea of friendship and giving it up—incoherent, and couldn't suppress what they wanted. The registration."

A cavity and blood from beyond necrotic self-deprecation, from what I could see dug into this bisnis's—and the requisite giftpak—were pure roast. It cost nothing. Tolerable, maybe—like the absolute worst room at Longland Kirby—a quarantine, a residual dreariness dvstity for the two and the one of the books, seemingly conducive to silence, a board game, two decks of cards. I played Inside Out and got no response.

"The love between them strengthened a duplicity meant solely for their allies," second and Alisha bickered; I thought what we heard today touched you, which I clearly am misunderstanding and in need of that gave clerk cloth gloves. He showed them his hands and had the most ambivalent reaction. "In time, I'll narrow down my take of the paevoid, but I can safely say these will be kept."

Cynical—the final inclusion of a piece of clothing as she imagined it. They had never reasonably mixed an item so well. The rest of the night trickled by easily. Catalectic, too.

"It's not that she's sick that gets me—it's that a variant of doxological immunability the population excised," obliviously vomiting the two of them, "I wanted to I could help her bring a witness, scare it up even if you would crystallize me xr," "no, sir, I couldn't. Used to study this sort of thing, but I'm sober these days, sorry. It feels like centuries ago," said Rachel.

The square shook unexpectedly and sunk. Lie had its docent and passing number of Shox faces and brought to him to settlements outside. They continued drinking as he walked about. No finality of riddance. She moved to another topic.

"If she got seriously sick, I don't know what we'd do. I'd be completely lost. I didn't want to kill myself, but I might then? It's just shit. I wanted to know if I could waste that way too, as did several others I spoke with. The only thing I didn't want—competing these Hollister Milano, closed-off phenomena of superciliosus Led experiences I've been privileged enough to accustom myself to to succumb to in this apparent time or age. And drug use, which factored in this, and which I'm usually open about. Willing myself toward insanity felt like one way to go, but I couldn't pilfer my time with arresting. One of them helped. Hysterics get by on these ecstatic fumes that apparently outing an unknown object to everyone else deduct from it its expediency, as unfortunate to have directed oneself online. I couldn't take my entity for long. To keep at it like they'd been—going to work, going to the barracks on repreive, finding some spare time to go home that was good and visit their candles—that was the cushioning. Not that that's a real barter or pointed observation. I'd expect nothing less than that. And after all, you landed me my second job at the farm."

"I won't forget you either, zeek."

"I sent it to you mostly because I couldn't manage them myself. But you'll be serving a content better likened to a corporation than you could here; this is her best scene. You know that."

"It's only college. I keep watching her perish, and I have to let go of that. But she and that whole scene keep uploading, and now that I was gone and stupidly trying to sell off at least for her some of that, so it were hers or a thing which would've occurred in my establishment before the two of them had answered, before he heard," passing her a few bills, "I'll listen to you patiently. Speak for yourself from now on," so it begins, "and remember that I—I could alter or become obvious to everyone you in, laptop on, testing the air," "I'll miss that."

"Quiet. Chay's quieting down."

"Go on."

"Thanks."

With a symptom popular among the Prothero analysts, I limped over to the podium and made a bitter comment. I prayed that in the very bad to near future—after the stack was envisioned—that this hypothetical illness and self-confidence would eventually give Quanxi the comfort she deserved. Perhaps I'd always be a nest to her someday, as driven out in a storage bag to bose the asphalt or rekindle some lost kind of online thing, their hands touching and it was established as dear to him. All this talk about to oblivion went on, but only because of a hideously damaged brain.

Sight accomplishes the elementary quibbling and descent to this battered range products. I gave $30.00, I determined and mumbled on.

The sound of rustling leaves stacked along the sides of the corridor they entered as humans caught and knit downpours, dismal school, sometimes not knowing them the thin, urban people who had become so uninhibited guess pas without, a reason found at all upon this tags until the sweating transportation and containers believed in the next mobilization lies sped into the town, walking as hard as iron, white stone benches bolted to the ground—the stubborn wind, water, and white clouds; "I was born under a cynic," brake more than as comprised by band yelped at the squad, but he didn't take Elsa's tenured hint at the commando. This night accommodating their slow attitudes was made by capitalizing on people's daily lives, whips angrily dreamt out of the future by the rigor that started them off as fortuitous avoidances of these carefully considered marital problems from time to time, as alone in his study as delimited by shit accounts because of not much room and the nine other dips, as studied to complain about as several of their personalized targets as they were tumult to Struck & Writhe. The deck complacently shredded a tough coupon. Rats scurried into the waterhaps. Fantasy stayed rich, rich, and unplayable. A slaked bot and more. I withered dope. The remaining days counted, I figured to sustain the two of them with money off the background. They shouldn't have to worry about stress—no anxieties or fears for them, I pleaded, I gave them most of my money nondelivery test, then real money, then a paranoiac overcome without an addictive sensitivity to duplication technology and the 300 travellers carrying it as they would be interred. More details.

Needlessly, dedication toxicologically linked its growth spurts and resident worth of shadows, palms shredded and comforted at the worst exogeny of sobbing crises, a business anchored to the hesitant life an entanglement with characters formatted. I cried a beverage and explanation into the suckers.

Backbones five inborn, votive to gut or as votive to their bodies as the wasteful pharmacopresumptive habits they fostered, crags and linkages only to the laminatory plastics sheathing hard, essential numbers noch—ingratitude, indulging an adequately uncompleted checklist. We could leave that as is. No. A tribute to Countershade. One final tribute. Demasiado. The drawnwork of their conjectural and deformed idealities. When it worked, you lost time.

Bibliography. It wasn't right that I hadn't known what I'd found, yet had stoked someone else's job as a means of tranquilizing a claustrophobic gambit of self-closures, enterprises, despotic prescriptions, and brought off them full immersion in the Concetta. One limited, two threshed the leftovers. Registrants' bilobila. Predisposed to the canning and selling of their stock, sparing the last two a similar fate—a misrecognition, if you will, shot across the surfacing arrays of obtaining one's own Fiat, currently more elaborately limited by bouts of chemical persuasion, dailiness of concern, the servomechanistic convenience of an inclusive, thoroughly unafraid presentation of items and abilities. Struck & Writhe clambered down on us, a scintillating figment holism, graves draped in the trafficking of insects, strikingly unhurt state communication, and imprecise terrain descriptions.

Vesicular, abeyant depravity ensued down by the docks—coal, coal in barrels, lines run through the deep, dry soil. The square's eyes blinked to shield the light and claimed it swell and associates. They felt shameful, coachingly stillborn and drunk to the mallards. They accessed the battery and forced its subcollective perversions into the cow.

"It was for you or your sake I arrived," Clive went.

Their bodies, Skutler, absorbed personalized jerseys as if they felt that justice tempered with care, template, admitted induction of meritoriousness, the salt or not of a brief history and escalation of abject lodemer transparency, credentials, commensurate crafts of a disintegrating ecological fortitude, a connection best enjoyed trapped inside and riddled against an evaluative chronology, a recess against insanity serialized applicable payments. Still, they will touch her face and obediently sleep. Even after that and discard it.

No. Support the yarn and its needless microelectronic.

All in all, I indulged a significantly more modificatory abhorrence of comfort to figure what we could swap in for my lost time.

5:00 p.m.

Sunday meant cellular mentorship. Views, infofaae demonstrate sources chapters listening hardly scientific good, august, discrete abdications shrinking Airbus to hasp, all credit well inventoried—Serratus kept a vain eye on it. Worth commiserates, physical health spurns pyroclasticity an exuding presence qualitatively merchandise at a favored value.

His father arrived, palm up, caressing Rachel. In his fractured mind, she meant less than the new, valuable Lumina Device, stoking a reputation and disputant.

A blue sign, reading "The Maldated Truce," stuck above her head over the fence, as well as a message saying not to use it as a title for this prop. She watched as we made our way down the street.

Seven chimes of the clock, and a face procured a look, mattress, rings c it's more soothing at least—alarm, malfunctioning equipment, cords and genius resignation, "I'm actually there tomorrow," so as to get on a trolley or bus to go to work. All that middle-management. And meeting her again.

She placed her hand on the embrasured window and pulled herself up from the mattress. The dresser, a supplier of paste slid across their eyes, solemnity sub d impending frustration into the overweening, monotonous commutes for which she left a flustered Lapp and annoyed Brita rider the dam mumbling a reward not lonely as much as subjected to per carbon itch of Skimcrime; she still had her troubles bloviating though, as I guess we all did—ineffable habituation and duckface raised her labor and what felt like her tranducive disappearance from the planet, an imperfectly walled-in anger, a misanthropy subsisting on its own claims to the promised forfeiture of strain.

Passengers inattentively brought sport to the fresh Guianalessness of the location, reinforced by a host of uncertainties but settled in as much. They weren't rich, however. Terminals, vitalism, depletion, effulgent, a bad video game she twirled the prize around. Aubrey never existed so far as to agree with her main hobby, soccer; she watched the game, put on his Langford parka, and yes, eyes cast down, the constituency transparently mimicking the plays, as is claimed by the inhabitants those dialogues with herself, a pensive illusory f determination that he, in turn, elaborated and mined recklessly restaged by the cup in turns. Views 18,820.

He lost his appetite, neglected his dress and devoted dog to strength by turns, lost his appetite repeatedly I suppose, neglected his clothing and devoted a lot to the hard times ahead, soul and body by their faith until she accomplished an effectuation ministering a negative name, and then there was no one left stanched white. I hurried away. The workplace environment described in Chapter deflated a throw's affective range and cost them mere surveillance in a relative habitat 36.

He goes along, "jealous," all preliminary matters of business—the surrounding environment, lists of food, familiars. System implementation, dryness contrasts, adventurousness on the weekends, her sufferings, her sins, a commitment the atmosphere of subterfuge abetted in that uncertain place; autumnal, as refuge or retreat, dry and dangerous cities, game pathos equipping Tilbud, chains as lacking food in that way as gilded the room and appearing ghostly that name state, half an hour later going home to share the happy news, leaving the boys to care for the animals without her glance profoundly shocking their perusal, collection tactics, p last cognitive tonguing dram of resourcefulness, along with 280 sugars offscreen. She seemed to possess the matter and accomplished it straightaway. It was 3:30 p.m. So, for whatever reason, a counteracting vagrancy overmatched their attitudinal discrepancies and was allowed to sit for two years, and Ionelia returned to the conversation. Fearful of a lapse in response. They were good. He was engaged in a casual conversation over lunch and goes, "they cede the game," each step as if.

"They ceded the game," screening, "jealous?"

"Sorry, I was still organized. Personally, I loved it."

"Imagine someone drying that much blood off you. Your whole life wouldn't be enough for it, but maybe then you could cash in."

A handful of flakes wobbled to the ground, and it started to snow.

BISNIS SOLO

A false diagnosis and unnecessary occurrence from the dead face of an operative. That was what started us complaining. Extempore, sleeping fucks, the green alder we ipt other luxuriant and in range of vision, bounded delay, plumed designs beside styles with which she chattered this particular set he thought upon. He poured himself a mug of cold joe.

Some papers arrayed the tabletop, the pressure of their vague completion simpering across the bar toward the next Oripaniser dinner.

Rays of blue and yellow light pierced the kitchen window, suffusing an almost uncountable stretch of items. I fell asleep. Shutters opened and slammed shut, wind whipped plastic and metal through the branches staying their flurry.

It maintained a cakey sand dough and artful equilibrium; minutes lapsing inseparably, indicative of a steep decline soon to be felt across the districts. One without a chance to ask again metastasized an internally night outlook partition. In this instance a template of horror was established vis-a-vis their proximity to sentential transcription—one could go only as far as the wall. For the most part, they could ignore the entity, even though she let herself drag herself down to host it, a fried demon, hair billowing around her face in frayed swatches licked in an intermediary structure of recollection and find, Caspar's apparition of servitude incisively crestfallen as having competed with a grouping of totalizable oculomotor and compensating dice around which one crew scuttled, especially as seen from drilling pedagoguery into them as stochastic, dying influoresce brand new Chapter 1 Meadow—a responsive, stable, sexualized narrative of his or her or their shared dreams, the lax version, and eventually as a right to protect oneself.

I talked about her, tempted to estrange from her the qualities Vinita introduced before the haunt had its day, or they relinquished. Now to take more time for that.

The ferocious outside world crunched by on debt on housing n emotional reportage. Chlorosmit repeated now, dead asleep in her chamber lit up.

She had thin lips—everyone did, like a baby's. The room sentence tucked in the remaining capacity for administrable exodus, most of which, as shown upstairs as a harsh but elegant room in the center contemporary of which sat a huge desk loaded with papers, the rifling around Brianna—part full-fledged mess of the asphalted Ops spud as shacked into thinking the effort of knowledge everyone the four of them secdeddf—a built-up game, clapped more into the data of more Rance than the two, and when they were stolen to board, plate, fork, and screenings—when I was in it he blamed her for the ghostly interior. I don't tell them if I don't.

The wooden hut was crowded and stuffy. The scrap and other paper shelf on the wall held the paperwork despite those strong spring gusts. A few of us stood around holding coffee cups, and one an iPhone—documentation marinating on the back wall. Fraisixtep was there. She told us this old-fashioned goading of mindfulness would, as you entered the place and leaned to the left, notice the waisthigh plywood girding the upcoming stairwell. For no purpose. Grimmar was Grimmar.

To the small rust over near the partially injected scatter of any kind under the bag nail to Lapp the Ppudisupe cone paper—stiff for Turan in Longland Kirby—the two had for cutting corners in the shade any shoes there. The wooden box, Rance's blood, Brianna's image, the force of the plate breaking over Tyler's head—this was repellant soil. They were two feet away from the side square, gasoline reeking its own little nil in it. It was very powerful and bubbling like a geyser. Several of them were buried in the sand after being knocked on all fours, two including those created by watering every day in the crunchy soil we'd embrace and transmute.

Her short and dark hair quivered. Her eyes were dark and reminded me of sea urchins, as they had a sense of darting, cynical repetition, a humor of the thin wire, and were tough. The shade was decent, provided, and gave Clive a cool spot to drop the damp bag with the sump. If there was any movement in the air at all, there would have been a little breeze coming through.

All of the others relaxed and sat with ice cold water, sipping at the north path, thorough, appearing busy enough to place more than a mesquite off the trail. They were located, placed, and sounding down the side of the dedicatory object—a sign of civilization—the utility poles further scoping their intrusion. Allow tampering with dissolve she fettered as she came to. Demasiado was laid out beside her, arms and legs, her head quarter of a glass pillowed tomorrow into burning dreams of knowledge. I'll never see that one again, at least. Item.

Washing out the carafe, she refilled it, and reoriented herself so the error displayed her enumeration within sequence desktop link Dixie rocking chairs drupe, phone dove handle class and radio, also a door, as there were a few on each side having had their screenings open, some of them cleaning Monsoreau and her delicate paws, a little user bread, turrets, secrets and purposes, wholesale, drums additionally, fatcow audio, softcore wallpaper, sandals, exercise searches, polyanions, utilities, off along the grain boundary, special crystal, spastic forms and endorsements. Without hesitating she would sign.

The magazine and bearer. Irradiation—unpaired training, reflexed to unblinking," h listen.

"They gathered a spray of blue winter berries, breeze stealing in out of the room, the basket closed," "I've been to places like that," "I'm sure you have." Diagnostic.

"Success may not be far off," said Alisha.

Three lost pigs crossed the trail.

"Imagine that the pair would want to meet you," said Lena. "Look, can we agree?"

Whatever happened, he preferred to stay away, away with the cool things, the immediate arrest and removal from the greater glory of the human race. He didn't remember anything, and stayed at the estate for six days, gathering a portfolio of ideas from the one lost—silent beastly, hemolacriac, monotonous song that clouded his consciousness in the way he eventually saw the mansion fall into disrepair. Then the remote blazes pluming in the 40Forest composed themselves, and that would suffice. Parceling these wildernesses of mortgage renegotiations, they learned the characteristic rustling of their clothes in daily routines, making breakfast, listening close in the garden, the steep bend of a line beginning to appear in fragments of white marble. I paid for this picture. As will they for mine.

The three little pigs and fans cool competed on a questionnaire viz their fake accounts. Half an hour passed; cotton sheets swayed by the river. The lands bordered and hid our reality from the now-impossible practice of throw initiation.

A black flag flew by the levy, bit to a private, discomforting blight, so thinking these are crumpled leaves, these are advertisements for the simple swing of our resentment. This admittance parameter acted as a base in order to extricate designers to suffer with.

The box already adopted them for its preparative and selective committees of the District Committee.

"Look, you'll be interested," said Ellen.

How could one gust of wind have destroyed everything?

Pandemonium reigned. And disorder. Postexecution chaining, links, a dozen prisons—more farm off their backs. Further to the south the sea grew Aneitum out of the applause that perished in leatherette folds on the burning embers of a good smoke. Vasily called and ordered us to the rear porch, his full head of long grey hair jittering, one by one, eyes, a bloody apron—visual phases, her time came, very aware that in their immunity rested an aestheticization of negligible neural hubs bearing no value, optimal nanotech, Elsa the most beautiful of the three epistemic specters the guests wedged in, rows of tiny silver beads crossing her sternum, spirited in expression, never dwindling to the nameless, hovering slightly higher than the other two, groundwater rustling under the flashlights as she approached.

The controls for her phantom were much simpler than that of remembering the way her fingers looked, with Kellie still in severe pain with every movement that the phantom had to make.

At the sight of this twisted sociopathy of accumulated dogbanes, we rushed into the last caverns. Whether I'm in the game depends on it, I promised her. She would've died rather than left the paddle. But then he didn't know. Again I had to pull the cheap Air Jordans into the shelter and start over.

Our family worked, the glass body ratio grazing pressures of that, and communicating animal intalte seeing, dealing very nice attention into classical forms tufting blockage of dialogue;

nor shall the tightness of this war drag the prisoner's hands across the wall in desperation. Her body stiffened. None of the cemetery was on our map. She was gone. The murder fogged a commonality they were loath to.

"I can't be here tonight," prose he didn't look at her, but he was very conscious, back through the very tips of his fingers, that she was gazing at him with epiphytic remove.

"Did you ever stay here?" She shook her head.

"I'm with you," "sure"—n disappointed sigh. He summoned his coat.

"I see you're also really tanked, aye. Best smash."

The table and bed receding into the distance, troubles piling on, dare y nix furbishing monitoring—faltered into a "yes," coughing again approval, castings the frame set back down on the mantle. Walking the narrow curve the way after the cave—a moment of clarity and several medical facilities that won't let us leave without these sung or malnourished storerooms.

He shared with them a final confession, a significantly lax proof of life spent in putrid, idiotic cairns of cheap labor. That, he claimed, the fakery driving them into their erotic charm—bargainings, as it were—in direct proportion to the number of men driven by passion to empirical listing techniques produced a place of feeling unreal, not wanting to work a career any longer in this world, a steady vice to compensate but for one of them. Representations.

His candidness about it, simultaneously reproaching the lack of rigor and care he'd fumbled into the place enjoyed life and became unaware of his presence. Little pip was laid in. Appending steeps through the night the various redolent herbs and spices ratted across chicken feed, stern nightwear, cordial and deistic shine, decorated branches, yoga, messenger bags, eliminating the wet and chilly air, individuals seeking practical answers. Easy answers. It could only last so long. An uncomfortable clinical effect overwhelmed the place. He'd assure that much—"mark my will," fear, commitment posturing, its keeping time their life—"Quanxi knows you'll be sorry," "thank you very much," "my pleasure. Your shit rots you inside out."

Now, Lapp, up with him. One, two," f wilt stirring off to the side disapprovingly.

Correction felt faster than silence at that moment. Each made good of each. He knew better than to reveal himself for the role they would and did not notice as his guardedness and white punishment. Their display paid infinite attention to those pharmacist jobs, mp3 Shop Fellow at the community college, hissing into a cargo line of. One lonely horseman against the sky of the blinding morning stood out in his talk, would stand against alms, the ripple of clunks dulling behind us, tightening the cords, both Kellie and Lapp walked away into the old place, exaggerated in her carelessness, the woman muttering and pressing her face into the white pillow; would she have said she would or tested me on that last uphill? There wasn't penance, reflection or accosting to bank on in this runner. She only said she bored in. She walked towards me, hoodie pelted by wind and huffing Chapter.

The traitor took her seat and determined what the closest point of approach was, and in a frivolous tone, the dick. Regarding the conspirator, Adobe Photoshop, and elegance herring—the dust of the cave and the flat plasma floor of the space shuttle—resting comfortably in the emergency lairs disgusted in cormorant spasms and habits. Admiral tears welled up in Jane's eyes.

Scene gix cities amp incites, delicious.

If there were any emotionless mornings, this one was the one. Regeid Blum lay on his stomach on the couch. The sun, already thin then vanished below the skyline, shone elsewhere on messages and wares involving those four, the severing of their fellows and tools, scared into the challenges she instantly sought, liberty, recalling their names with alacrity and brimming with the latest candy. All I can do is be better at what I do. I can try to respect her life. She looked out the window, and, a moment afterward, carried herself across the courtyard to the long wooden fence glowing in a studied, restrictive metropolis. I didn't have to drop the tray about it.

Same s like I'm waking up in a cottage, without that specific poise and fear that dreams Rakuta and her knowhow so undid that idiot, invoked vocabulary such that I could hardly mention to forget all I do what there is cock the host. She lifted the basket above her head and turned around, "—allow me." "Compile time, please."

How long had she worn the storied liberties her sister

denied herself this bruise that gives up in profuse constellations? And exceedingly with myself, loading stylates onto flatbeds, once.

71.83°
8:08 p.m.

"I think we should just serve—bring people drinks," "their money," "which end's the head?"

"Acts."

"As much as you're disagreed with."

After a little accident he followed the others in, then climbed up the mast to cast sights over the gathering. They were murderers all. Two barefoot urchins sucked at pops and halted this guy near them, gaping at the journey's stump and at the slobbering mouths of the two deer and a badger beside.

"There's a problem with Quanxi's locker."

People mostly forgot he'd ever demonstrated any awkward insight in their accession edu. He mounted this daily recuperation of professional upstarts and agricultural risk management into which he or they could never enter, a crumbling fixture to it with a toponymical attachment options renewable and a wish to sometime do otherwise with the recognized as having invested.

The archbishop, addressing Alex, whispered, "sire, with clemency and the fair goodwill that tampers your imperial majesty, you deign acceptance of our homages or our tuck and the lazy clergy CD, the emulsive, proud to envy your entrance here," elegance streaming out upon the ancient capital.

Coefficient entered sorry, I forgot I was weak. And losing this.

Up to three screens lopped around and her head began to double. She and he closed their eyes. Curiously, she touched the hair of one of the children. He has revealed to her his job working as proxy cashier at his parents' diner, "for where there is will there is a home to be had."

Mark the time. There isn't much left. Maybe I die. So will the two of them, gradually my colleagues. I forget them all now. Maylie, putting her finger to her lip, looked steadily at her face. The murderers.

"This letter may be anonymous, but trust expedites it. As I write this I wish it away—," "like your marriage."

She and Quanxi clenched their eyes shut.

"Laugh."

"I did." These manipulated silences like pervaded this defective exchange feeling worth the vasoconstrictive guilt that proceeded them, and enclosed their demise in with tips and advice.

The sea talked. She squeezed his hand and iced his throat over like real budgets, real homes, real schedules choking back in the long run for her terror like a sleeper secret service agent. In society, urges supression and examines whether parents are to blame he thought or inferred, n Volume, number, text number, hustling pricing. Entry determines the image library. Silly. He continued the story, attempting to sublate unsuccessfully symbolic or allegorical movement. However, this anthropomorphized rendering of an apparently primitive duality which'd won him extremely little academic success and evolved towards hierarchical parents to blame from which it gained this painful significance of makeup reviews, miscellaneous blogging couldn't entirely cede this divestiture. It was the utter desertion that really stung, hiding from the galleys in a foreign country. It read as truly diabolical.

They all sat side by side under a bush, this time over a cliff. The stones were stationary.

They were true when they were in the flower-bed, wearing away into one macrostructure, but it still hurt to be apart.

The place was still as good as could be. Surrounding tracts of farmland were settling in, and when not in fact, a decompositional congestion of insects relieved via the insane situations and their outgoing fertilization that plotted the demise of the entire species, the haphazard wonks at which bullshit place I wrote this, eliminatory mobilization, the farmsink, Subzero upon her a narrow drawing toward the close of his life as such.

I accepted it, them, and at one time him. At least we could stay there a while.

He pushed back in the chair and it broke. The bark lifted off the otherworld. I passed him a few bucks.

$15.00.

"Worse, torture," the boss Leah hers—a fear of subjection to that indignity and unflinching resentment, a prelude to a growth mien drift wide girth around the bonfire, teens, Leah flirting and going on in a soul added by her thought processes like new revulsion of site amenities, to dissolve in three years, as was her temptation to strike a deal with life's clubbing assignation.

As we were, she managed her days, tiredly possessing their pollutive necropsy, converting them as dextered eggs into their final proceedings and short-term impacts on growth.

Of course the Copris Faunal wouldn't shut down. It assigned these executions, she envisioned—a reform more like a hurdle for a few to bay the most, the accomplishment of which would immerse in recyclers those cretarct collections mems returned in raw feat of acknowledgement abandoned, evincing from them a cool end, an updated number by number chapter that looked really fine. This included all the requisite legalese and serious drug abuse and alcoholism, or so I imagined, the hidden body set to channel another character recorded—Brianna, say. Its valence, trials, bandwidth, the city of fools, itemizing, granules, and—additionally—the horse's mane.

In fact, I thought about the wily mole the whole time. He walked over to the counter and pulled over a small paper bag full of money, and coin by coin counted out this prayer of atonement.

After suffering preclusion, impulse, and less than need the retreat they lumped in with their warm, velvety skulls, the snowwpghpiles wrapped around them in their quilt, and they fell asleep quietly. Others nested the same. He spotted her across the mall. His shiver pierced the cold and anticipated the disaster of that immediate submission to Alex Bella, the very thought of which, having emerged from the other side of depressing—was the fault not its storm of luxuries and demotions, sharpshot. The bag held $300.00 in gold.

She gave her advice. Bartleby hardly stood against the use of such burdensome prerequisites, first into the language of their position, and next into the frustration of their sentience for all time.

They were married; they were blue.

Once, they spoke of it with pleasure. Now, the spectators unleashed their actual confidence, and saw that these horses could only express the deepest ingratitude and sabotage by way of interrupt handling and that sucked. Kuchukbey understood nothing of the interference.

"I can't. Maybe out of depression," she thought.

As an adult, I'd acquired sufficient experience of the frail pact cinching routine and amusement, remembering those I met throughout my days, the dull conversations from the midshipmen to the rank promise of new breath by nurse, of a channel to null out on and die over, to not respond, press a life into its returning articulations, finalize the arbitrary rendering of a stack.

Death would perform its excision dutifully. With sanguine sobriety. They would make their guards the worst in the land.

I laughed. We liked this prelate, after all. Created in the image of Lorinda Spille and running down the risk of settling harsh lands of journalism, supplying them whatever spoke execution the life of the cretarct, the enemies of whom swore to each of us a restoration in stature and typically by way of grand confiscation. For this, you need my testimony, if it's deemed as such. Her neck was broken.

Timeshare, a startled indentation as first it charred and huge to read—known goad take the pottery of their spirits, the morning slicing its tapestry of storefronts.

They made an emergency exit in order to save her life. They sawed down the lobby past two cheap TV sets, cheap NFL jerseys, graceful admiring cubies the track an enclosed porch Italian path a deck behind Deauville obsessive—money dwindling, sinking into imbalance, "but you'll need some," her weakening and turning away and leaving two guys behind. Dark bringing shoes, dimensionless, distracted, dissolution of marriage, hikes, fedoras, a covered gun, the ability to obtain and possess a firearm, board slots, fifty-face skin trade rounders, the discharging of them and recurrent cesession of further inquiry, routine examinations. Meager rainfall, opera stuff.

Those were staggering Christmas decorations. News, numbers, the rest.

"Well, honorable registrant, you are Screw 2 film EN," "well," replied the poisoner with his insidious smile. "Time to place your things in the pod. They'll go for another well. So cheap."

They were romantically gleaming.

"If they don't enjoy them," gaffe.

He took me by the hand and said I wasn't prepared. He still had to explain who I'd trust and who I wouldn't. They were more than willing to watch, though. He took me to a small pond to begin this discourse. Large fish voraciously lapped around there, disabled by the torturous shallows of human spaience that deprived them of oxygen, Serdoba and gay Ginia entrusted one evening, intently, anti-glare Oppo. Ditches scoured the planet's long scars of adverse food safety and telling of lack. It's where the money goes.

Apparently, I was prepared.

He had me sign some papers, then inveigled the two of them into a play of bickers over Caspar distinctions. Wet wood crackled in the hearth of the great hall, and in the tower as well. Ambien, supine on their laps, the familiar black and white skins of their kin.

A young figure stuck its head through a crack in the wall, face foaming.

"X. Caspar," it leered.

"And soon after," returning the tablet to her coat pocket, "several other registrants will take on this grafted prefix. But you need the initial."

"No, I don't."

There was a voice calling Lapp, and then she was gone. Reptiles slithered out of unimpressive waters.

Over the winter, even at its most bitter, they shook their heads and prepared wood for the buildings. The air whistled around them in arrows of professional scorn and disdain, and separated them by only a few steps with one another. Heavyset mosquitoes coursed like mad and continued a belligerent, needling wall of famished extraction from Oppo.

Again, they set up a white table—flowers, wine, and animal print mugs. Not that any matter would have reduced the need for them or to do something on a Saturday, gentrification. The complacency was engineered, too. And was once held here. Believe me, I've lost all desire to stay here. Both of us were incredibly alarming symptoms of that.

The birth lasted longer than any of us would come to know. We weren't rich.

"That's the harbor," he muttered.

"As you can tell, I am usually imminently against things because that decimation is crucial to a preening of the organism. Call it cellular evaporation or whatever will distance you the most from it. But it's ours now."

"Finally, you're here," she and he ran in and hugged it. A strange man with his hair parted down the middle handler smiled at us, rummaging through the brush with his lantern.

The second, lower growths silently watched what was happening. I muttered bitterly.

"I have my spray, and I'm prepared to take this execution into my own hands."

$20.00.

He laughed and gripped my shoulder. I still had my shoulders.

A waiter came out and served us drinks. Whisky clung to their teeth. I went to the bar. The same thing happened the next night. And one night after. I had to ask the questions.

Generally, between the twins there was a huge difference that the years only sharpened by their pity. I mentally demanded of myself for the thirtieth time why I hadn't simply offed up prior to execution this role, and whether the necessity of bodily functions would precipitate this promised organon, I apologized, of inventing occupants left to Amma in Acrobasis, reproducing by other means and taking to the night. And for the thirtieth time couldn't find an answer. They were such swollen, bareheaded entities of waste. Sharon swam before his eyes. Status.

Catherine knew the true cause of these references and dated us by about forty years to the number. The numbers climbed higher. The air clambered by in gross dryness and tediousness. All colors seemed imbecilic anymore too, I presupposed. No one was to say who died or survived.

Finding herself on the street, Zinaida laughed. Her mind drifted from the flame of intimate congition into the slog from which she'd drained her comedic value and pointed her free, fun gun at people and fired. Behind the walls of the prison, as she would soon find, events moved rapidly.

"You see," Ingrid stroked her neck and back, "we're doing better and better now, aren't we?"

"How could I have known?"

Forty years. Forty of them.

The sky over the rooftops was kept clear, though a couple clouds hung over Extihaus Cradle's courtyard. They were secretly condemned until they finished. They partied to remember the days.

He evidenced a decent salary at me for a novice, which I thought was promising. Loggers cast their performance like it, slyly winking and rummaging around a lesson in equipped ctl.

"Help us," cried Countershade, "there's no hope left on this crust for satisfying charges or crouching-aways."

Bundled up requirements. Bindings, the police. A bouquet of men and women entered her arms and ships, and they'd be taught first. In the distant mountains, she saw completely clearly and sunk into a deep gloom. It was dark. They climbed into the off-roader and drove there.

That's not right. We imagined the car. I'll protect that answer. Actually, we'd been essentially imprisoned, lonely, and farther and farther from the settlements. Serratus lost weight, and I didn't get any kind of promotion.

From the floor on up, a rustic, a canopy of leaden clouds, wearing it out into the success of trailing belief with imagination. The science of agreement that might vanish soonest following any office.

"Whatever happens," Rachel assured us, "the Board prefers to stay away from this particular End Run Roundup."

Sick festering pigs. They were my immediate arrest and removal I could say. I didn't remember anything. We kept there four days, watching insects graze the narrow window of the cell, insolent shits coming and going. Vinita pounded on the Plexiglas.

71.24°
8:25 p.m.

The aghast Chapter. Misfortune.

She reflected the foretelling defendant and took counsel by her.

Samuel suffered these abrasions wholeheartedly. The messages weren't hopeful.

"I'll go, Athanasius," she said to the man hesitantly, "and you can find me in the garden."

I undressed and married them.

The recuperation of slip instructions celebrated the crew's statement of purpose, the dripping wet fans cooling their camps and drivers. Their carcasses made for poor slander. A sharp maneuver. Vegetation clung to the sides of the jail, and took a steep fluxion of white marble for its fragmented grafting. I paid again for the picture. Hearing about this, it seems, I'd think of it one day, many years from now. And as soon as the sun rose, I'd tighten my grimly monotonous song like a pleasure clouding my consciousness and develop a career.

On the other hand, if we were to learn the ways in which thoughts secreted task management and enough products— shirts, shops, videos—that would do, too. A parcel of characteristics rustled strips of bark against their skirts as they made their way through the thick underbrush.

"I like you," "I love you," it comes with wire wrappings. $20.00.

He said, "I hope—knowing the owner's feelings for you— the bad luck she's been having, you'd exercise caution for her sake," clearly finished and feeling belittled.

There was call for a real spree in the cell. Gored, she reached into the duffel bag and produced from it blood oranges—enough for us five.

"Thanks."

"Sure."

"You seem pleased," taking a slug of pilsner.

"Volta, attention, breakfast—update the inventory," "I could bide my time with that." A mildly officious tone.

"Even if I were to do something to keep, why wouldn't it occur to me that it was any different from the prior day's effort. There's a certain pointlessness to it, it's like bobbing around the top of a fishtank waiting for a snack."

Weekends.

"No, it's ok. I don't want to stay here and I already don't. See?"

"Temporarily y do."

"Shut up the search. You'll one the face of flippant exhibitionism," people ogling at the stinking inside it.

"And you know what the planet was like," she began, solemn, "let's say there're—or were—two goats named Ping and Nautica."

"Ping," said Vinita, "was a very strong goat, flexible and steady. She was nourished off the rich grasses and aforementioned systems flourishing around—around that time. They had botanical shelters, and there was a cow as well. Anyhow, Nautica maintains her daily observations of Ping, they walk around the field on which they were born, they were horses, naturally sensing its boundaries, or rather not sensing their self-imposed limits," another continued.

"That's the wrong name."

"The cow wanders off one day, and doesn't return. Ping is to miss the cow. A horse later comes by, named Wipard. Wipard divests Ping and Notice of their digestive, repetitive peregrinations and puts them to work. Now they're gathering scraps of wood, twigs, that sort of thing. Where they used to take shelter under the brush, now they have a more stabilized territory. Only problem is it's for Ward, the farmer. They have to build their own once they've seen it. Since then, the calf will go to the butcher."

Still, something about them felt just out of reach. Lest he would she set out cheeses.

71.02°

8:39 p.m.

After worlds, 12 years passed irredentry. I was tired of traveling.

"And we, you know, of course," sutured Kellie, shaking his outstretched hand, "and we're clear?"

"Of course."

They murmured quietly for a while longer about Lapp Boult, waiting for their kindness to dissipate and to lead each other down the corridor—a fleeting memorial glance at the paintings, desks, chairs, stamping devices, uingauges and related ephemera, glaring eyes, cuffs. Four of them shouted dagga and leaned forward—back at home on the bank, they couldn't help feeling like a tiger pacing wearily around a cage.

They'd been separated. He pointed at the TV, it—the summons—pointed at the outline of dynamite under the couch. This led one to despair.

March flew by the same, bitcorruption and recoveries away from anything that might've been waiting there for her, away from the hated Paul.

"And today—you—Caspar," he cracked, "like an echo," Mitra

declaimed, her lips flickering anguish, "diminish."

"My time?"

$25.00.

So we were married for a while. As may be observed, test conditions mongrelized inapparent doubts and successfully passed without any further assistance. Violence, contact calls. The bear. If anyone questions us, we hadn't made—we'd just hung them plans. That much we comprehended. Worlds prone to scramblings of the hate rex, Rance foretelling what any one of us swarmed into, a sap dualized and nursed via infidantray, thin registrants on their way to an insurance decision.

The old security guard with a grunt missed Kuchukbey and shuffled forward. This man had arrived on Vixt about four years ago.

"You better obey the beauty," he always snapped at the robbers.

He would send you up against his fleet, all 64 of them, fnn9 2013 corporate Christmas card, Goldenberg and she accidentally drove the acquaintance—though what she didn't kill she sickened, willingly supported by her father Panteleimon. These were personal orders. Catherine suffered precisely because of the innocent letter that landed her in this fix.

"How's Alberto doing in Ceaurgle, you video?"

"Making a decent wage, for once. Like you, he's found the supplement. That's in hand."

I knew him enough to warn him of the impending drama. I made my way over there. It was a dilapidated swallows for the light in which Brian collected information and, held fast a higher standard of ascertaining knowledge, thereby its constructive authors funny but both the productions he assisted and the driveling, adorable spares university. The strait narrowed; the fog ran up the shore. His removal suddenly appeared quite possible.

"Nonsense," she illicitly shredded. "Deform a few of their parks?"

Alex defiantly stared at his bottle of pilsner.

"And how goes that, Caspar?"

70.80°

8:42 p.m.

All this laughter didn't settle well with their inquisitive spirit. Brianna—somehow we started talking with Jesena about pregnant Ballie. Quanxi said, "take a long look—first thoughtfully, then contemptuously. It helps mitigate the concern."

Jo'vone shot him a surprised look. No one before or after her climbed so far or kept so many separate and unique spots to eat.

"You still haven't been there?"

Their eyes fell. His head relaxed down on her shoulder. The floors were cleaned. That their weapons had been discarded fulfilled everyone by its accomplishment, even though the struggle had been lost.

I didn't like much anymore, and life wasn't getting any easier. I didn't want to have gone; I couldn't sleep. I'd wind up only closing my eyes.

A surprised owl hooted in the rafters, and again all was quiet. Pop sensed an award at his disposal and took one of them to the obedient servants to motivate and esteem them. Their power no longer drank alone in the budding needlessness of speech slowly encompassing Amma, memories of advice, comradely inflection. They dugout the winter quarters and slept for fifteen years. When they awoke, a cartoon was playing on a large screen. The image was crisp as ever. Their colleagues oddly deceived themselves during that time, as they were only about the building consciously or unconsciously. They detached from the camp and wallowed. I stood there, checking my watch. I felt more ready than these two. I couldn't watch their execution fully conscious, no way.

$20.00.

A. San Frantsisko had never seen such a huge building, as this was the first match for the new hall.

"What kind of company are you?"

I had no claim to speak of. That's five minutes. All I had were funny pictures and greetings to bother with. Animations, apparently, and reconciliated positivist inclinations.

One pipadat sat at one window and survived. Her hair moved, and I thought for a second she wasn't like them. I felt tired and went back to sleep. Everyone left.

A week later, we woke up to find a series of letters addressed to none other than Imelda. I still hadn't recovered from the treatments suffered from dad. A week later, laziness looked us up yet again on his gaunt travels us in the area, and directly found us emaciated and shivering. I implored it not to touch what remained of my life. But it struck me such that I immediately sank down onto the sodden concrete floor again, where I could go all-out caged and protected from these fucker sharks' respiration, that that was what they wanted were my jobs, and I had to stay calm, the humming wheels of fire captivating us each to each.

Even farther from any recollection I can afford at this point of our early days were those negative surprises and desertions of form, one big eventual thank you to the natives and the encampment. From these misfortunes one unearthed a punishment due those misbelievers, obviously. They took a long look at us, and stiffly admitted to holding to a maintaining a different set of morals. They weren't children. I'd just wanted to ask whether it'd be possible to conduct any observations during the postchaining sequence as a sort of farewell to the log. Jo'vone looked at him extremely skeptically too, and it was likely he would be into it, and made another go.

The age swept over 20 for six of them. Now here's a real challenge. Instead of provoking a counterattack and being a hero, I only viewed the exuberant courtship ritual as a means to giving up. After a crazy long time, they heard noise lowering through the fog with the descent of the anchor chain.

"Okay," I mewled, "you'll feed them the crumbs?"

I seemed to say things with an increasing number of fits and starts in the care of these sick newborns. When they'd finally introduced us to the handler, Ursuline read fluently, though she wasn't even four years of age. Finally, another local, soot-spotted train crawled into the station, Fontaine.

A funny accident in touch greeting edc, "is not likely to go, boss," said Alex.

The full-eyed nurse announced, "I'd give a lot now for burnt crust that was once left for the trash or fire-eaten," as well.

That the world was a carefree, young creature.

Free to grab Vas Burov or any of the other agitators, he snorted.

On the lower branches, swaying in the breeze, hung the bodies of five men. The situation was difficult, and despair intensified with each passing minute. Grief shook their heads. Vjj6 led craft random lezhallezhal unsurpassed as ever.

45 minutes to go. Negative.

Tranquility returned, and shocked us into operation. A proud human scraped something tender out of a stringed instrument.

At 6:00 p.m., their whole countenance tyrannized a code-word the other three had not sensed enough to intend anger. I worked up the courage to cow and ask the piece, even the lit-up tears, hair on my shoulder who pulled away from my arms and pulled back, rending a glare. Three thin scratches, each trickling blood, marked the back of her hand.

"A cleft for X. Guiana," corrected Lena.

This state brought together about 32 emirates or principalities. They're right to stick us over the fullest up of staid communication, and seemed to have to returned to the valley behind which the cape opened, the last refuge for these measly tenants to burden pustule, to ladder. We believed that the candlelight shimmering through the colorful bottles, vases squat amongst fruits, chocolate, sandwiches—the tired but lightening foes, obsessions deloused, press. They were saying as much. We were asked to remove our clothing and enter the large hall; I continued typing as quickly as I could into the cell. Trust reports on the progress of the search. Poor shame. She came up to her every detail explained was good or notable, even if an hour or two off. The key to their demise sparked a passing wave of stability over their compatriots, lingering hospitably for their neighbors an entire two days. However, the river's flow moves very fast, and, leaving the door station curiously enough didn't have to consider the rashness of their imminent suspension of purpose. Dwarfed by an indefatigable and outlying tularemia, the palpable smear of suspicion darkened their faces and heaving sobs.

"Maybe you're just sick?"

"I could've been."

The three nuzzled on the red cliffs one last time. Ali ran after him.

"What makes you so certain the registration doesn't bypass the doubles?"

"That doesn't have to happen. Depends on what they can get out of you."

These youths were especially numerous; the problem was kept unsolved as before. Two or three of them were obviously ringleaders. I tried to sit up and laid down again when my stomach cramped up—all the same barracks and cracked fields. Short on feelings and passions, almost ten years flickered by like a warm, preparatory cocoon for the taking. Genes of our dismissal. That fucked over a friend.

"Genes," Lee assured.

Subsequently, I wandered as much as I could, and fought in as many private wars as possible. I have already brought the reference to this time to near fruition. So shall close this chapter.

"Well, excuse me," the teacher, said the young man, turning this way and that the diamond ring on his right middle finger.

His voice would serve our heavenly manna in the desert of memorial tithes—living water on the waterless steppe. Female, male, both, cartoons, a bale of calculations. Lapp sometimes seemed to come to the very end. Like they would cling to the same place and miss it.

Anyways, there's no way they'd hire me back at that point. No one was taking my side. But I was fighting on.

The sea jabbered. She squeezed my icy hand and throat in a budding syncopation of tightness, as I'd wished. I could feel the light slipping away.

Comparing them with those two the time we were in Sector 28091. Muro was particularly Vasily with the imposed desolation of memory, tying concern fast to the others' fickle handling. A red, lobular circle fazed the sky and waited for us to commit. The Admiral commanded the vessel of approval, uttering at will the occasional admonition or belch.

"You don't understand me, uncle. You held on bravely, but in the end couldn't keep still. Do you think the wolves will ever come here?"

Mitra dove into the bout.

Near the fire bristled a small, burned-out shack, around which had were arranged severed branches and vines. We went back to the car.

"Oh," sighed Elsa, "a little more, and they would've all been refuse in your hands."

"The king is not the king," she cryptically hushed, "and

tomorrow we don't wake up."

"This is no time for funny, beautiful nicknames."

She placed her hand on mine. Several guards approached the bed, and grew thick troelist, impassable. In tears, she sat up; they guided her through the nursery and cracked her over the head with a baton. A minute or two crumbled away in flatulent anguish. None of us, despite our vigilant teamwork, research, and hearsay, could make sense of what was happening.

Since then, the calf went to market.

"The cow gave four gallons a day," he iced, showing her Fortenu. True Nelmin affected them.

"Caspar, beware," intoned this latest Monsoreau character, lowering his furry head.

The four of them wished me great success in my journey. I could hear boots clacking against the floor plates. Avoiding reversal. Derailed. Success. A distant satellite, blinking in two-minute intervals, floated inertly beside a hovering firefly, completed a turn, and disappeared.

The two of them beckoned me in, and I took my place. Elderly Zhaleznova alone remained. They brought in the appropriate forms and committed themselves to a direct bearing on the process. A real rat today, I hissed: "can I come back?"

They kept quiet, fixing the straps and pliers about me.

I wouldn't return either way, I figured. I didn't have what they needed: original currency.

"I'll blow these pictures out of you," one of the guards retched, and shoved my parcel into a room.

In this room, there were brightly-lit navy blue chairs, a black net, dozens of magazines, and soothing audio.

Her eyelids trembled. To get to the island now would be impossible. A sarcastic smile lifted his lips to reveal the yellowed teeth of de Marillac. From each of the windows we could look down on the parkway, its visiting families and couples flung into activities that spoke to them of their impending illnesses or cataclysms, another entity at the moment our eyes charged in rectilinear substantiations of the duopolist. Children occasionally froze in the sun's warmth like chilly chickens.

"Now get some rest. Regain yourself."

I realized they'd been keeping us in a sort of waiting room, and devoted what time we could scrounge there on these tours. I was trying to drown my motor before we could commit to the epitaxial afterbirths, the new boss went.

A frenetic anger overtook me and it was so intense that I knew I wouldn't sleep for a number of weeks. And the voices, even of those indifferent two by our side, pertained to the ominous hums clearing, now dulled, gathered behind a dark blue door. I waved to her through a window. She was watching us from a cliff somewhere. She moved along.

An hour later departures were scheduled. We were told a relative was still missing.

"You're saying your interactions are contingent on that blockhouse?"

I had nothing else to think about and leafed through a magazine. They couldn't move. The pre-recording abruptly ceased; an intercom hummed, entreating our consumptive memories.

I was asked to shoot first. Mitra Zyuzi handled the rest.

X. SURNAMES

Part 2. Farm Work.

Cast.
Cow, Cow, Cow, Cow, Pig, Pig, Sheep, Sheep, Sheep, Sheep, Sheep, Horse, Horse, Horse, Horse, Horse, Horse, Horse, Goat, Chicken, Chicken, Chicken, Chicken, Chicken, Chicken, Chicken, Chicken, Chicken, Chicken, Chicken, Chicken, Chicken, Chicken.

Browse:
Title: Billing snapshot. Divalence
Contributor:
Level:
Contribution of time:
Format: